Highland Hunger

Books by Hannah Howell

ONLY FOR YOU * MY VALIANT KNIGHT
UNCONQUERED * WILD ROSES
A TASTE OF FIRE * HIGHLAND DESTINY
HIGHLAND HONOR * HIGHLAND PROMISE
A STOCKINGFUL OF JOY * HIGHLAND VOW
HIGHLAND KNIGHT * HIGHLAND HEARTS
HIGHLAND BRIDE * HIGHLAND ANGEL
HIGHLAND GROOM * HIGHLAND WARRIOR
RECKLESS * HIGHLAND CONQUEROR
HIGHLAND CHAMPION * HIGHLAND LOVER
HIGHLAND VAMPIRE * THE ETERNAL HIGHLANDER
MY IMMORTAL HIGHLANDER * CONQUEROR'S KISS
HIGHLAND BARBARIAN * BEAUTY AND THE BEAST
HIGHLAND SAVAGE * HIGHLAND THIRST
HIGHLAND WEDDING * HIGHLAND WOLF
SILVER FLAME * HIGHLAND FIRE
NATURE OF THE BEAST * HIGHLAND CAPTIVE
HIGHLAND SINNER * MY LADY CAPTOR
IF HE'S WICKED * WILD CONQUEST
IF HE'S SINFUL * KENTUCKY BRIDE * IF HE'S WILD
YOURS FOR ETERNITY * COMPROMISED HEARTS
HIGHLAND PROTECTOR * STOLEN ECSTACY
IF HE'S DANGEROUS * HIGHLAND HERO
HIGHLAND HUNGER

Books by Jackie Ivie

HEAT OF THE KNIGHT * A KNIGHT WELL SPENT
ONCE UPON A KNIGHT * A KNIGHT AND WHITE SATIN
KNIGHT EVERLASTING

Books by Michele Sinclair

THE HIGHLANDER'S BRIDE * TO WED A
HIGHLANDER
DESIRING THE HIGHLANDER * THE CHIRSTMAS
KNIGHT
TEMPTING THE HIGHLANDER

Publishing by Kensington Publishing Corporation

Highland Hunger

HANNAH HOWELL
JACKIE IVIE
MICHELE SINCLAIR

KENSINGTON BOOKS
www.kensingtonbooks.com

KENSINGTON BOOKS are published by

Kensington Publishing Corp.
119 West 40th Street
New York, NY 10018

All Kensington titles, imprints, and distributed lines are available at special quantity discounts for bulk purchases for sales promotion, premiums, fund-raising, educational, or institutional use.

Special book excerpts or customized printings can also be created to fit specific needs. For details, write or phone the office of the Kensington Special Sales Manager: Kensington Publishing Corp., 119 West 40th Street, New York, NY 10018. Attn. Special Sales Department. Phone: 1-800-221-2647.

ISBN-13: 978-0-7582-6152-6
ISBN-10: 0-7582-6152-7

First Kensington Trade Paperback Printing: September 2011
10 9 8 7 6 5 4 3 2 1

Printed in the United States of America

CONTENTS

DARK EMBRACE

Hannah Howell

Chapter One

"Bleeding bitch! That witch is cursing us!"

Raibeart frowned at the words cutting through the predawn quiet. He had already paused in his ride to the caves because of the noise of people thrashing their way through the woods. Whoever the fools were, they were stumbling their way all over the path he had chosen to get to his shelter. That could cause a delay, and time was not something he had much of. He moved his horse deeper into the shadows of a small stand of trees fighting each other for space.

"There she is!"

Just as he wondered if he could slip around the men, Raibeart caught sight of their prey. Her pale hair was a beacon for her enemies. Even men without the keen sight of a MacNachton could see that hair in the dim gray of approaching dawn. Slender, her skirts hiked up high to make running easier and revealing strong slim legs that swiftly stirred his interest, she did not look much like the women men usually decried as witches. She was young and buxom. The slender form he grew more interested in by the moment suddenly stilled. He watched as she caught sight of her pursuers and then she bolted.

"Wheesht, Tor, the lass can run," he muttered to his horse as he watched the woman race through the trees, leaping over every obstacle with nimble grace. "Shame she is doing naught but running in circles."

Despite their clumsiness, the five men chasing her managed to herd her into the center of the small clearing and soon encircled her. Raibeart studied the way the woman crouched slightly, moving with care to keep each man in her sight. There was something about the way she moved, the way she so skillfully evaded each lunge of a man, and the way the men approached her as if she were some dangerous animal that sharpened his interest in her beyond mere physical appreciation of her beauty. Her hands were curved in a way that resembled claws as she slashed out at the men, and he could hear her growl softly. If not for the waves of fair hair hanging to her slender hips, he would think she carried MacNachton blood.

He looked up at the sky. A rapidly approaching dawn had already lightened the dark of night into a paler gray. The sun would begin to climb into the sky soon. The safety of the caves beckoned but he shrugged. He had time to rescue a fair-haired woman. Raibeart secured the reins around his left hand, studied the ground, and touched the sword sheathed on the saddle.

"Ready, Tor? I am thinking we have a few moments to be gallant, aye?" He began to walk his horse closer toward his target, wanting to be just a little nearer to the woman before he charged. "A little fun before taking our rest. Mayhap our journey will then be less of an utter failure."

Una struggled to catch her breath. She was not as strong or as fast as she needed to be to fight these men. Blood loss and months locked in a cage had sapped her strength. The thought that she was failing the ones who depended upon her to help them only added to her growing weakness, stirring a weariness that went to her soul. She had such hope in her heart when she had first fled Dunmorton, but that hope was rapidly turning to ashes at her feet.

"Ye are more trouble than ye are worth," said Donald, the one Una considered the meanest, ugliest, and most slack-witted of the laird's venal minions. "I dinnae ken why the laird wants ye back."

She suddenly recalled that not all of the laird's men knew why the laird held her and the others captive, except to give the old man a ready supply of young women to force to his bed. That did not explain the two youths or the two children, but the men of Dunmorton were not known for their deep thoughts. She wondered if telling them the truth would turn them against the man. These men were already jealous of their laird and his favorites, angered that they did not share the women they kept caged. That jealousy could be turned to rage if they discovered what else the old man was not sharing.

Then she met Donald's narrowed eyes and cast aside the thought of stirring dissent in the ranks. It would probably work but would be of no help to her. Donald would do his best to kill her before he raced back to the keep to demand his fair share of the laird's bounty. Una did not think the knowledge that Donald and the lackwits with him would be swiftly killed would offer her much joy, for she would be dead. And, she thought, if these men learned the truth, the people she had hoped to save would soon die as well.

"I dinnae believe the laird would appreciate his lackeys questioning him," she said.

"And he doesnae appreciate his game escaping its cage, either."

"Tsk, it seems disappointment must be the madmon's lot this day, aye?" She turned her head to hiss at the man trying to creep up on her side. "Back away, ye wee bastard, or I will rip ye open and strangle ye with your own innards."

She could tell by the way Red Rob narrowed his eyes that her reference to his short stature would cost her. From the moment she had been dragged to Dunmorton and he had realized that she was several inches taller than him, he had loathed her, taking what few chances he got to add to her misery. If these men caught her, Red Rob would make sure that she suffered every step of the way back to captivity.

If? Una almost laughed aloud. There was no uncertainty about her fate. She could not stop the men from capturing her. The only thing in question at the moment was how much damage she could inflict upon them before they brought her down. Una prayed it would be a lot.

Failure was a bitter taste on the back of her tongue. She had tried so hard, planned so carefully, that it struck her as monstrously unfair that she should fail. Even worse, Una knew she would never find a chance to try again, nor would any of the others. They would all spend what remained of their pitiful lives locked in cages, the women dragged to the laird's bedchamber whenever he demanded it, and all of them bled repeatedly to make the laird and his chosen men strong. The thought of the youngest of the laird's captives suffering such a fate made her want to scream out in rage.

Una was just thinking that she would put an end to the game by going on the attack when the sound of hooves thundering over the ground made her and her enemies tense. The way her attackers' eyes widened and they all stepped back, scurrying away until she had no one at her back, caused Una to glance in the direction of the approaching sound. If whatever came their way frightened her enemy, it could only be good for her.

Her glance turned into an open-mouthed stare. A huge black horse was galloping their way, but it was the man seated on the impressive beast that fully grasped her attention and held it. He was big, big enough that he needed a horse that size just to carry his weight. Long black hair, broad shoulders, and a wide grin on his handsome face—a wide grin that revealed a glimpse of what looked like fangs.

She did not flinch when he leaned down, holding out a hand as he drew near yet barely reining in his mount. Una weighed her choices in that heartbeat of time it took for him to reach her. Five men to battle or one big one. The choice was clear. She grabbed his wrist and leapt up, noting his strength as he easily drew her up behind him.

The men who had encircled her scattered before the charging horse. She wrapped her arms around the man's waist as he rode around the clearing twice, driving her enemy farther away. When he then kicked his mount back into a full charging gallop, riding away from the laird's men, she hung on tightly and tried to decide what she should do next.

Una frowned when the first thought to enter her head was that the man smelled good. His thick black hair brushed against her face as they rode, and she liked the feel of it touching her skin. Cursing softly, she forced such strange thoughts from her mind. Men had proved to be nothing but a threat to her from an early age, and she refused to allow such womanly thoughts to distract her from the most important thing—escape.

Leaping from the back of a galloping horse was not a good idea, she decided as she looked down at the ground, which passed by beneath the animal's hooves at an alarming speed. If she did not break her neck, she would certainly break something else, making escape impossible. She glanced up at the brightening sky and knew it would be a clear, sunny day. By the time the sun was at its zenith, she would have to find shelter or be too weak to get away from anyone. It appeared that her only chance to escape would come when her rescuer slowed down enough for her to leap off the horse and run, but he showed little inclination to do that.

She frowned even more as he headed straight toward the hills. There would be shelter there but only if she stayed with or near this man. Una was not sure why he would take her into the hills, but she doubted that his reasons were ones she would like. She inwardly cursed, knowing that she would soon have to make yet another quick decision, whether to run or stay and take the chance that this man was truly intent upon saving her. He could be, but she knew how quickly that could change if he discovered what she truly was.

Life had not treated her fairly, she thought, allowing herself to wallow in the mire of self-pity for a moment. She had lost her family to a fever that had never touched her. That had only added to the villagers' suspicions that there was something different about her. As if being blond, blue-eyed, and taller than most women, even some men, was not enough. Still grieving for her family, she had been driven away from the village, forced to survive on her own for years. Then she had found herself caged and bled to fulfill the dreams of a madman who wanted a long life. That made all she had already suffered to stay alive pale into insignificance.

Una shook aside her maudlin thoughts. She was still alive and, at the moment, still free. That was all that mattered now. She still had a chance to help her fellow prisoners.

Idly studying the wide shoulders and strong back of the man she rode behind, and ruthlessly smothering the spark of interest such a sight stirred within her, Una tried to decide if she could trust him. Even more importantly, could she take him down if he proved to be untrustworthy? She was strong, she was fast, and she had very sharp teeth. All had kept her alive and freed her from many a man's attempt to take what she did not wish to give. None of those men, however, had been as big and strong as this one.

She briefly considered immediately ending whatever threat the man who had pulled her out of the trap she had been imposed. It would be easy to wrap her hands around his neck, strangle him or simply snap his neck. The mere thought of doing so, or of using her teeth to inflict a mortal wound, turned her stomach. He had rescued her from certain capture, from a return to the cage the laird had waiting for her, whatever his reasons might be for such an act. It would also be cold-blooded murder, and she had never stooped to that. Una quickly smothered a sigh. She would have to wait to see what he would do next before she acted.

The woman pressed against his back was thinking so hard Raibeart was surprised he could not hear her. From the way her tempting body had tensed, slumped, tensed again, and then straightened, he suspected she was trying to decide if he was friend or foe. Obviously rescuing her from those men had not been enough to win her trust. Considering she had just been chased down by five men acting like hounds on the scent of a hare, he was not surprised.

"What is your name?" he asked as his mount made its careful way up the rocky slope of the first hill, toward the cave that would shelter him from the sun's killing light.

"Una Dunn," she replied after a brief hesitation.

"I am Raibeart MacNachton, Sir Raibeart MacNachton."

"Weel met, sir."

"Truly? Ye dinnae appear certain of that."

Una scowled at the back of his head. She struggled to ignore how his long thick black hair tempted her with the urge to touch. There was no way the man could know all the doubts she was suffering from. She had learned to hide what she felt very well over the years.

"I have no doubt that I needed to be rescued," she said.

"Just about the rescuer."

"I dinnae ken who ye are, sir. I would be a fool not to be wary about a mon I dinnae ken, have ne'er met, nor have heard even the smallest rumor about."

"True. Ye can come to ken who I am as we rest."

"Rest? But the day has only just begun. The sun isnae even fully risen yet."

"And I have been riding through the night so I must rest for a wee while. I suspect ye didnae get much rest, either."

Una was not sure why, but she suspected he was not telling

her the whole truth, that he was hiding something. But, then, she was holding fast to a few secrets herself. She would welcome a rest after her ordeal as well as shelter from the rising sun, but she would not openly admit to that. Sheltering from the sun for a large part of the day had been one habit that had marked her, and her family, as different, stirring whispers of witchery and Satan. Not everyone had swallowed the lie that it was because the women of her family were so fair; the sun easily burned them. Una doubted this man would believe it.

The man reined in his mount and Una looked around. It took her a moment to see the opening in the rocky hillside. Her rescuer planned for them to seek their rest within a cave. Her mind sought fruitlessly for a decision about what step to take next. Go with the man into the cave or try to flee. The laird's men were nowhere in sight, but she needed rest and shelter. It was not a need she could ignore for much longer, not if she was going to have the strength needed to go on. She struggled to make up her mind as he dismounted, and idly noticed that he kept the reins clasped tightly in his hand.

Then she looked into his dark brown eyes and all clarity of thought fled. Thickly lashed, set beneath straight dark brows, they were the most beautiful eyes she had ever seen on a man. There were faint specks of amber decorating that dark brown that fascinated her. The way he looked at her with both amusement and understanding touched something deep inside her, something soft and womanly. Una abruptly realized that she had a lot more to worry about than whether or not this man was truly her rescuer.

Chapter Two

Raibeart needed only one look at her beautiful face to know that Una was ready to bolt. He was not sure what he could do to calm her fears, to win at least enough of her trust that she would come into the cave with him. A quick glance at the sky told him that he did not have long to accomplish that before he had to seek shelter from the sun, with or without her.

He knew horses not women. Unlike many of his brethren, he had little experience with women. He was renowned throughout his clan for his skill with horses, however, and being able to make almost any horse accept and trust him despite the scent of the predator he knew he carried. Raibeart was proud of that, but at the moment, he heartily wished he had learned more about women. He doubted that a few pats on Una's flank, soft words, and a handful of oats would calm the wary-eyed woman still seated on Tor.

"Come, we need to rest and this place will be safe and easily defended," he said.

"I do not need to rest," she said, knowing it was a lie, for her entire body ached for rest. The way he cocked one dark brow told her that he knew it was, too. "It would be best if I just continued on."

"To where?"

Una silently cursed, wishing he had not asked that question. She had no idea where she would go. All she knew was that she needed help, an ally who would assist her in freeing the others held hostage by the laird. Instinct told her that she could trust this man, that he could prove to be the very ally she had been looking for, but Una had tasted the bitterness of betrayal too often to trust in her own instincts.

"I can find a place when I need to," she said. "I am nay helpless."

"Ah, nay, ye certainly are nay helpless." He smiled. "Took five men and a long hard run to corner you."

The approval in his deep rough voice stroked her vanity in a pleasant way, but she tried to ignore that. "Which proves that I can take care of myself."

"Lass, I have no doubt ye can, but against five men? I could see that they were verra determined to catch you and didnae plan to be gentle in the doing of it. I heard them decry ye as a witch and ken weel the threat behind such accusations. I can see the bruises on your wee face and arms, see the hunger and weakness ye suffer. I also think ye have the wit to ken that those men willnae cease to hunt ye down, aye?"

"Aye," she agreed and wondered why she did because it told him far too much about her situation.

"Then trust me, if only for a wee while. I swear that I mean ye no harm." He held out his hand. "Share my poor shelter and mayhap ye will tell me why ye are being so avidly hunted."

"I could be a murderer," she said even as she clasped his hand and allowed him to help her dismount.

"Nay, I think not, and I will trust my instincts in that."

It occurred to Una that Raibeart had as little reason to trust in her as she did in him. Less, actually. His instincts could be wrong as easily as hers could. She could be a murderer, one who used her smaller size as an excuse to creep up on a man at his weakest and cut his throat. She knew she would not hesitate to do so to that mad laird who had kept her prisoner and still held the others caged, not if she knew it would free them all. Sir Raibeart MacNachton might be big and strong, but he was also taking a very large risk. Not as great a one as she was, but still a risk. That realization eased some of her wariness.

Una was deep inside the cave before she realized she was looking around as if she could see easily in the dark, which she could, and she tensed with alarm. It was something she had always taken the utmost care to hide. A quick peek at Raibeart revealed him settling his mount in at the rear of the cave, moving about as if he, too, had no difficulty in seeing in the dark. Nor did he reveal, by look or action, that he had noticed her ease of movement.

The way he walked right to the hollowed-out, shallow pit in the middle of the cave, gathering wood from a pile in the back, made Una frown. His every step was sure and steady. Not only could he see well in the dark, this cave was very familiar to him, an obviously well-used shelter. She sat down opposite him as he worked to light a fire. She knew without asking that he was not doing so because he needed the light but because he wished some warmth or because he thought she needed the light.

Her heart began to pound with a rush of fear and excitement. Then she recalled that she had thought she had glimpsed fangs in his mouth when he had ridden to her rescue. Could he be one of the cursed, akin to her and the ones she hoped to save? Una rubbed her suddenly sweaty palms against her skirt as she frantically tried to decide what step she should take next. Ask him bluntly if he was one of the cursed or wait to see if there were more clues to be even more certain? She could not allow her desperate need for an ally make her act with a dangerous haste.

"Did ye bring your whole larder with ye?" she asked after watching him chop a rabbit carcass into pieces, toss the pieces into a pot of water set over the fire, and then begin to chop up some leeks.

Raibeart grinned. "Nay, but I ne'er miss a chance to gather food as I travel."

A smile so fleeting he would have missed it if he had not been staring at her mouth like some lovesick fool crossed her face, but the shadows quickly returned to her eyes. Raibeart had the oddest urge to tell her that he did not really need the meal he was making, that what he needed to survive flowed through that vein he could see pulsing faintly at the side of her long, graceful neck. He never felt such an urge. Every MacNachton learned the value of holding fast to such stark truths in the cradle. Something about Una Dunn made him reluctant to hide behind the lies that came so easily to him and all the others in his clan, the lies that meant survival.

"So, lass, why were those men trying to capture ye?" he asked as he searched through his pack for a few more things to add to his stew. The food might not provide him with what he needed to survive, but he had always had a liking for the taste of a hearty stew, for a lot of the foods Outsiders ate, in fact. "Nay because ye committed some crime. I cannae believe that."

"Nay, I committed no crime." She took a deep breath and considered what she could say that would help her decide if he was the ally she so desperately needed. "I am but different and their laird collects people who are different."

He tensed as he tossed a few wild mushrooms into the pot, sensing a tension behind each of her words, as if she sought something from him even as she told him what he wanted to know. Raibeart thought back over the first few moments after they had entered the cave, the very dark cave, and a deep darkness he had sought to alleviate for her by making a fire. She had shown no hesitation in moving around in that thick dark, had not even revealed a hint of the fear most Outsiders had of such darkness. Then he recalled the feral noises she had made when she had been cornered by the men trying to chase her down, her grace and speed while running through the woods in the near dark of approaching dawn, and even the way she had curled her hands until her fingers were curved like the claws of an animal. He had dismissed the fleeting thought that she had MacNachton blood because she was so fair, but he now wondered if he had been wrong to do so.

"How are you different?" he asked in what he prayed was a gentle yet coaxing voice, a voice that would prompt her to be completely honest.

"Weel, I can see verra weel in the dark." When he just nodded, his expression one of calm and interest, she gathered her courage and continued. "I am verra strong and fast for a lass, stronger and faster than many a mon even. I also heal very quickly if I am wounded, and I rarely get sick, even when all around me are felled by some fever."

"And?" he pressed when she fell silent and just stared at him, her brilliant blue eyes glowing in the fire's light, her unease so strong he could almost smell it on her skin.

"Is that nay enough? Why do ye think there is more?"

"I sense it. I could almost hear the *and* in your voice even though ye then ceased to speak. So, what else makes ye different?"

"I have verra sharp teeth."

Raibeart studied her for a full moment, adding up all that made her different, and then asked, "Sharp like these?" He smiled wide enough to reveal his fangs, which, although not lengthened by the scent of blood, were still very noticeable, and readied himself to catch her if she grew too afraid and tried to flee.

Una bit back a gasp. He did have fangs. She had not imagined seeing them. They were not as long as some beasts', but much more sharp and deadly than any man's. When he closed his mouth, she looked into his eyes and saw no fear of her. He looked intensely curious and as if he ached to ask many more questions of her but hesitated, just as she did. There was only one thing left to reveal, one thing that could easily turn him against her or prove, beyond any further doubt, that she had stumbled upon someone burdened with the same curse she had been born with.

"Do ye like your meat barely seared?" she asked, unable to keep all of her rising fear, and hope, out of her voice.

"I do. And, because of these differences, ye think ye are what? Cursed? A witch as those men called you?"

"Nay, no witch, but, aye, I am cursed, as was my mother and her mother. Grandmother was the first of the women in our family to be burdened with this curse."

"Ye are nay cursed, lass. S'truth, I think our families may have joined together at some time in the past. Do ye ken who sired your grandmother?" He frowned when she blushed.

"Nay. My grandmother was a bastard child. She told my mother that she was born of darkness and violence, that her sire appeared out of the night, took her mother by force, and then disappeared. He ne'er returned."

"So, nay even a name for her mother to curse at."

"Nay, but Grandmother said that her mother was terrified of the night from that time on and that, when she realized the child born of that night was cursed, she wept. I gather from Grandmother's tales that the woman wept a lot. But she eventually wed a good mon and Grandmother did as weel. The curse has waned some."

" 'Tis nay a curse." Raibeart sighed when he caught the glint of fear in her eyes, for he knew he had nearly snarled the words at her. "What did your grandmother eat and could she bear the light of day?" He could see her fear in her eyes, and it was even a light scent upon the air, but he did not know how to ease it. "Nay, dinnae fear. I willnae condemn ye for the truth. 'Tis verra important to me that ye tell me the full truth."

"Blood," she whispered. "Grandmother drank the blood of any slaughtered animal, and she couldnae step outside once the sun rose, but spent the day in the darkest part of the cottage."

"She was of my clan then. She carried MacNachton blood."

"Are ye saying that your whole clan is cursed?"

" 'Tis. Nay. A. Curse."

Una lightly bit her bottom lip to suppress the sudden urge to smile. The way he bit out those four words and scowled at her should have frightened her, but it did not. Not even a little.

"Then what do ye call it?" she asked. "I cannae think it some wondrous gift or blessing, nay when it stirs others into a dangerous fear, causing them to decry one as a witch."

Raibeart sighed and dragged a hand through his hair. "Nay, although it should be seen as a gift. There has to be some good reason for the MacNachtons to be what they are."

"But ye dinnae ken what that good reason is yet, do ye?"

"Nay, but that doesnae matter now. What matters is that ye are of our blood, our kin, a MacNachton. Our laird has been sending us out to hunt for ones like you. Our ancestors were a brutal lot, arrogant in their strength and power. For a long time they harried all the nearest villages, taking what they needed or wanted. There are still whispers about them, tales of the Nightriders used to keep the bairns close to home at night. It was recently that we were shown that they had left behind more than pain, destruction, and dark tales. We found ones of our blood, ones bred of that dark time, and now we search for more of them. We call them the Lost Ones."

"How could ye nay ken that bairns could have been born of such raids, of the taking of the women?"

"Because MacNachtons breed few children. Our laird believes that is because we have been too much alone, breeding only amongst our own kind. That begins to change."

He looked at her, studying her expression closely but seeing only curiosity and just a hint of disbelief. The latter was no surprise. The truth about his people was difficult for most Outsiders to believe, and she had been raised as an Outsider.

"But that is of no importance now," he continued. "What matters now is what ye were running away from and whether that trouble has aught to do with the MacNachtons." He handed her his wineskin. "Drink this. It will make ye grow stronger."

It took but one taste for Una to know that the wine was enriched with blood. She almost tossed it aside, her fear of revealing her dark hunger to anyone deep and old. Her body demanded the sustenance, however. She drank deeply, her injured body welcoming the needed nourishment, and then handed the wineskin back to him.

"And now tell me your tale so that we may ken the best way to free ye of the trouble dogging your heels," he said.

"I escaped in the hope of helping the others who are still held prisoner at Dunmorton," she said. "My plan was to find someone to help me free the others, but something went wrong, for I was not gone from the place for very long before the laird's men were fast on my heels."

"Mayhap one of the other prisoners told them."

"Nay. They all ken that they are trapped until they die unless someone helps them. And they all ken that nothing they do will gain them any ease from their torment or mercy."

"Why?"

"The laird began merely hunting ones like us for sport, killing us, or sending us to another who undoubtedly killed us. He caught poor Allana and decided he would rape her first. They fought, for Allana is no meek lass, but she lost that battle. In the fight, however, the laird swallowed some of her blood. It healed the wounds she had given him and made him feel stronger, younger even than his fifty years."

She frowned. "Considering how he looked when I first set eyes on him, he must have had a hard life or lives hard and unwisely, for he looked far older than that." She shrugged. "I think Allana was saved from execution at first simply because he wished to abuse her a few more times, but he quickly saw that she might have more use than as a reluctant leman. He did not need much time to discover that he was right, that Allana's blood healed him, made him stronger, and he began to make potions of it to share with the five men closest to him." She nodded toward his wineskin. "Much like ye have in there. Then he sent his men out to find more of us. He now has eight, aside from myself, and he keeps us caged, attempting to abuse the women and bleeding all of us for his potions so often that we are all weakened by it."

"He raped all of the women? He raped you?" Raibeart had a fierce need to get his hands around the man's neck.

"Nay, only Allana, Nan, and Mora, and, although he still attempts it from time to time, he no longer can do it. Allana told us not to fight him, that he needs a woman to show fear, to fight, before he can become man enough to take her. Nan and Mora still fought but quickly learned not to. Madeleine is able to swoon at will so was ne'er even taken away."

"And you?"

"I dinnae ken why, but he fears me. I am but beaten now and then. And he may share his potion with his men but nay the women."

The man needed to die, Raibeart thought as he fought against a surge of mind-searing rage. "That makes five. You said there were eight aside from yourself. The other four?"

"Two youths, Bartram and Colla, and two children. Two wee lasses. Joan who is six and Alma who is five."

"He takes the blood of children?"

"Aye. Do ye see why I must find an ally?"

"Ye have found one."

Una's relief was so fierce it made her head spin. "Thank ye. We can leave for Dunmorton as soon as the sun sets."

"Nay."

Chapter Three

Una wondered if one's heart could stop when assaulted by such a rapid, fierce change in emotion. She had been so relieved, almost elated, when he had declared himself her ally only to be struck by a crushing grief and disappointment when he said nay to going after the others. Her mind, filled with plans to save her fellow prisoners, was now empty. She was unable to gather the thread of a single thought.

Raibeart watched all color leave the woman's face and cursed himself for not softening that nay. "You misunderstand me. I *am* your ally, lass, but we cannae save the others on our own. Two people cannae storm the laird's wee castle and take away eight people who are undoubtedly weakened by what they have suffered, nor protect them as we flee the place."

She took a deep breath and let it out slowly. For a moment, as she regained some calm, she thought over all he had said. He was right. Two people could not rescue the others alone. Even if they could get inside the keep, defeat the guards without an alarum sent out, and free the prisoners, getting that many people out safely, including two small children, would be impossible. Una knew that would be true even if all the prisoners were in good health, and they were not.

"I ken how to slip in and out of the keep," she said, reluctant to leave the others at Dunmorton for any reason, even one as sensible as getting more help.

"And do ye nay think they now ken that?"

"I am nay sure they do. There is more than one way to get in and out unseen. The one I used was old, verra old, and I dinnae think it has been used by this laird. Mayhap his father or his grandfather, but nay him."

"How did ye find it?"

"I wasnae a verra weel-behaved prisoner." She gave him a brief, narrow-eyed glare when he grinned at her, even as her heart gave an odd little skip at the way the smile illuminated his handsome face. "Thrashing me didnae change that." She nodded when his grin abruptly disappeared into a scowl. "I was made to scrub the filth from the walls and floors of the dungeon, clean the cages, scrub the ragged clothes and blankets we were allowed, empty the slops, and all of that."

"All the filthiest work."

"Aye, for I had revealed a need to remain as clean as I could despite the rough conditions of my imprisonment. So, one of the times I was scrubbing away I found the opening to a tunnel."

He served her a bowl of stew. "Were ye nay guarded as ye worked?"

"Oh, aye, but nay closely. The men guarded the ways out. At least the ones they kenned about."

"Ah, and they were nay guarding that particular opening."

Una took one bite of stew and realized how hungry she was. It was not going to be easy to retain the good manners her mother had taught her, not while filling her empty belly and trying to tell Sir Raibeart all she knew of Dunmorton. The amusement revealed in his midnight eyes told her that he recognized her dilemma. Una decided she would just ignore that and do her best. She was too hungry and too eager to tell him everything to be concerned about embarrassing herself.

"Nay, they ne'er came near it though I lurked round it many times," she said between bites of stew. "I decided that they didnae ken it was there and, if they didnae, then neither did the laird."

Raibeart nodded as he filled his mouth with stew. It was not the tastiest stew he had ever made, but it would serve to fill her stomach and help her regain her strength. Una probably needed such food since she was not a Pureblood. Most of the Lost Ones they had found revealed a need for both Outsider food and blood, their need of the latter much less than a Pureblood's but still there.

"How could ye be certain it was a tunnel that would lead ye out of the dungeon?" he asked.

"I couldnae be certain but couldnae think of what else it might be. It was verra weel hidden behind old ale kegs and one of the cages, so I kenned that I just needed one wee chance to explore it, one short time where I could slip in and out of it unseen by the guards. It took a fortnight before the guards ceased to watch me all the time. Allana was in the cage next to mine, and when we were left alone at night, she and I tried to think of ways to make certain the guards were thoroughly distracted, and for long enough, to allow me to make certain it was a tunnel I could use."

"What did ye decide on?"

"Allana and Madeleine decided they would fight. They are in cages next to each other. The laird had the cages built just to hold us, and only the bairns are caged together. He doesnae want any of the rest of us together." She realized she had finished her stew and was just thinking of asking for more when he took her bowl and refilled it.

"Nay, I can understand that. He kens your strengths," he said as he handed her back the bowl. "Two of ye could cause him and his men a great deal of trouble. It would be a lot more dangerous for his men to e'en open the cage door."

"I thought that was the way of it, too," she said between bites. "Wee Alma took a piece out of his leg when he stepped into the bairns' cage to take their blood. He sends two men in there now."

Raibeart waited until she had nearly finished the second bowl of stew before asking, "So Allana and Madeleine held the attention of the guards?"

"They did. They started arguing, hurling insults that had the guards all laughing and urging them on. Then the guards yanked Allana from her cage and threw her into Madeleine's. They wanted to watch the women really battle each other. Allana had said they would, but I was still surprised to see that she was right."

"Two lasses tussling, skirts flying up, legs bared, mayhap a bodice ripped away? Aye, men would watch." He grinned when she gave him a look rife with feminine disgust. "So was there a tunnel you could use?"

"There was, which is why I am here now. It was easy to see that it had not been used for many years, but it was still passable and it led to a place near the edge of the burn that runs along the south side of the keep. I moved as fast as I could, getting in and out quickly, but it was still a very close run race. The guards were already dragging a cursing Allana back to her cage."

"Why did ye nay just flee when ye had the chance? Why risk them seeing ye coming back into the dungeon?"

"I couldnae leave the others. I needed to talk with Allana and the rest before I did try to leave them. There might have been some way for all of us to flee, even though I hadnae seen one. Nay when there are always four guards and only I was let free of the cage." She set her empty bowl down and sighed. "I hated to leave them. I am certain they will suffer for it."

"Ye were their only hope of getting help. Are ye certain none of them are the reason those men found ye so quickly?"

"Verra certain. I am also certain they didnae find the way I got out, either. I should have had enough time to get clear of the area, for the women were going to distract the guards again and, as I said, they didnae watch me all that closely, for they were guarding the only ways out as far as they kenned. The fools probably think I made some spell. Either my absence was discovered far too soon or someone caught sight of me as I slipped out of the bolt-hole near the burn. There was a cleared area I needed to cross. And there is always the chance that the laird or some of his men chose that time to come down for more blood and realized I was gone when they began to dismiss the guards. They ne'er let the guards stay when they come for blood."

"And ye are certain 'tis only the laird and his five closest men who ken about the blood?"

She nodded and idly rubbed her cheek. "The laird doesnae trust anyone. I am nay sure he even fully trusts those five men. And once he discovered our blood could heal him, strengthen him, I believe he even ceased to trust the one he used to send our kind to. He must believe that that mon had already learned the secret and wasnae sharing it with any of the others who hunt our kind down."

" 'Tis likely he is right to think that. What of the other people of Dunmorton?"

"Some bad, some good, just as it is in most places. There are nay so verra many of them for the land is poor and the laird rules with a harsh hand. Many have left to try to find a better life elsewhere, even his two sons. The laird liked to boast on how he would probably still be hale and strong when his ungrateful whelps died of old age."

"So, there may only be six men we will need to kill."

Una stared at him in surprise. The cold, firm tone of his voice told her he meant every word he said. In the flickering light of the fire, he looked predatory, all the soft amiability gone from his features. It should frighten her to see him like that, but Una realized she was comforted. After being alone and frightened for so long, she had finally found a strong ally. He would do whatever was necessary to protect her and help her friends.

"Are ye certain they must be killed?" she asked although she believed the laird and his men deserved whatever fate Raibeart dealt them. "We could just steal the prisoners and slip away."

"I fear the men ken too much. We have only just discovered that our blood can heal Outsiders ourselves. This is a secret that cannae be allowed to be told."

"Outsiders?"

"Those who are nay of MacNachton blood. Our laird decided that we were dying, no bairns born to the clan for many, many years. Not amongst the Purebloods. He was born of an Outsider and a Pureblood. He also realized it isnae so easy for us to stay hidden at Cambrun anymore, that the world outside its walls is growing, secrecy becoming more difficult to maintain. For our own survival as a people, we had to begin to look outside the clan for wives. He found one and both his sons can tolerate a lot of sun. He thought we could breed out most of what makes us so different and feared, but the Lost Ones are showing us that it may ne'er all go away."

"Nay. And it can come back a wee bit now and then. 'Tis stronger in me than it was in my mother." A fresh pang of grief struck her when she thought of her family's deaths. "I wish I had kenned that my blood could heal. I might have been able to save my family."

"How did they die?"

"A fever."

"It may have helped, but ye cannae be certain, and we who have lived with what we are for hundreds of years didnae ken what our blood could do for others until recently. Ye couldnae have helped them when ye didnae ken how."

Una nodded. "I ken that. It just hurt for a wee moment. What do we do now?"

"We rest and then we go to Cambrun," Raibeart replied as he moved to lie out his bedding.

"How far away is Cambrun?"

"Three nights' ride if all goes weel."

"Then, at the verra least, it will be over a sennight before I can rescue the others."

"At least. It willnae take us long to plan our attack for, since finding the first of the Lost Ones, we are always at the ready to ride out. The only thing that slows us down is that most of us still need to shelter from the sun. That is a weakness I will be verra pleased to see bred out."

"Ye cannae abide any sun, can ye?" Una was weary but could see that he had only enough bedding for one, and she was not looking forward to sleeping on the hard rock floor of the cave.

"Verra little. We all have heavy cloaks so that we may ride or go out in the early morning or at the end of the day, but I am a Pureblood and the sun is poison to me. 'Tis as if it slowly draws the life right out of me."

"I have felt the same when caught out in the middle of the day." She frowned as she thought of the ones still trapped at Dunmorton. "I think some of the other prisoners may have a stronger dose of MacNachton blood than I do. The bairns say they cannae abide the sun much past the dawn. So the weakness your laird tries to breed out appears determined to linger in the blood."

"Or they are the get of one of our men who went awandering and ne'er returned. Some go looking for a mate but find only death, too often betrayed by the verra woman they thought was their mate."

Una wanted to question that word *mate* but yawned instead. With her belly full for the first time in far too long and the blood-rich wine she had drunk healing and strengthening her, her body now demanded rest from the ordeal she had suffered. She knew she needed sleep to continue to regain the strength she would need to help the others, but she wished she had had the chance before fleeing Dunmorton to grab a few supplies, especially a blanket. The hard rock floor was sure to leave her with a few new aches in her battered body.

"Ye can share my bedding," said Raibeart as he set aside his boots, placed his weapons close at hand, and stretched out on the bedding. "There is room."

Even though there was the fire between them, Raibeart watched her tense and lean away from him. She may not have suffered rape at the laird's hands, but she had no trust in men. Her beauty guaranteed that she had been the victim of unwanted attentions, especially if she had been alone and unprotected for any length of time. There were too many men out there who had no respect for women and little care, thinking it their right to take what they wanted even if the woman did not want to give it. Una Dunn was going to be a difficult woman to woo, he mused, and he now had every intention of wooing her.

It would amuse his friends and family to know how hard and fast he had fallen. Her grace and beauty had caught his eye first, but that was no surprise. Una was a woman made to catch a man's eye. It was what he had learned of her as they had talked that had grabbed hold of his heart and would not let go. Her loyalty to her fellow prisoners, her need to free them at any cost to herself, her clever escape, and her courage all drew him to her. He could only hope she would see something worthy in him in time.

"I willnae touch ye, lass," he said and then smiled. "Wheesht, in a wee bit I will be as near to dead as any mon can be anyway, at least until the sun begins to set."

"Ye sleep that deeply?" she asked, wrestling with the urge to take that next step in trusting him and sharing that much more comfortable sleeping space.

"Near to. Come, ye will be safe with me. I swear it on my life."

Una cautiously approached him. She remained tense and wary as she sat down to remove her boots. It was frightening to be so close to such a big man even though she was inclined to believe in his promises. She was still a maid, but she had fought hard, too many times, to stay that way. Nor had she ever found a man she trusted enough to allow him to know her secrets. Raibeart knew what she was for he was the same. It was enough for her to trust him in some things, but not all. She kept her body tense, ready for flight, as she settled down on the bedding, keeping as much space between their bodies as possible. When he tucked the blanket over her, she stared at him in surprise, for the way he did it was gentle, almost tender.

"Ye are akin to one of the horses I train to accept MacNachtons," he said as he turned onto his side to watch her. "Skittish, wary, wanting to trust all while ye want to run."

She blinked, uncertain as to whether she was amused or insulted to be compared to his horses. "Ye are comparing me to a horse?"

"I ken horses. Dinnae ken people as weel, especially women. But, I mean to teach ye that ye can trust me, trust my clan. I mean to calm your fears, to show ye that the beast ye scent in me will ne'er hurt you."

"Why?"

"Because I mean to woo you." He kissed her on the cheek and then turned so that his back was to her.

Woo me? Una touched her cheek. The spot his lips had touched burned and that warmth seeped through her body. She may have found herself an ally, but Una began to think that she had also stumbled into a lot of trouble.

Chapter Four

I mean to woo you.

Una glared at Raibeart's broad back as they rode through the forest. He had kissed her cheek again to wake her up. As before, he had quickly moved away from her after kissing her, this time to prepare some food before they began the journey to Cambrun. By the time she recovered from the shock of being kissed, he was well out of reach and acting as if he had done nothing unusual.

She knew that part of her anger was born of how that innocent touch of his lips on her skin made her feel. Warm. Safe. Womanly. He was trying to calm her just like one of his cursed horses, she thought. Instead of a pat on the flank, he gave her a kiss on the cheek. Instead of an apple or handful of oats, he fed her stew and porridge sweetened with honey.

What truly annoyed her was that it was working, and quickly. Una could not believe she could be so easily *wooed*, but she was. The proof that Raibeart obviously did not know the first thing about truly wooing a woman only worked in his favor. No man who was trying to trick her, or seduce her, would be so inept at it. She could actually feel a softening inside her when she looked at him, a warmth that had little to do with the fact that he was big, strong, and handsome.

It was going to be difficult to resist him, she realized. Even now, with her arms around his waist, he occasionally patted her hands where they were clasped over his taut stomach. Soothing her again, she thought, just as he did Tor with an occasional pat on the animal's strong neck, and almost grinned. Most women would be outraged to be treated by a man in the same way he treated his horses, but Una had to admit that she was finding it strangely endearing.

I mean to woo you.

And what was so wrong with that, she wondered. The voice of common sense quickly answered. She did not really know the man aside from the fact that he was like her and that he was ready to help her save the others held at Dunmorton. They had known each other for only a day and that had been spent mostly in sleep. It was ridiculous to think of him in any way save as an ally, a man who was going to help her save her friends. She could not allow her innocent girlish dreams of a lover—a husband, a home, and children—make her act recklessly. She certainly should not contemplate giving away her innocence just because a man kissed her on the cheek, not after fighting so hard to hold fast to it for years.

Raibeart suddenly tensed, pulling her out of her thoughts. "What is it?" she asked in a whisper.

"Hunters," he replied in an equally soft voice.

"The ones who are after me?" She waited as he sniffed the air, not surprised that he would have a keen sense of smell.

"Aye, and they are mounted now."

"Stand and fight?" She touched the hilt of the knife he had given her, which was now sheathed at her side, yet another of his gestures that warmed her heart in a dangerous way.

"Nay, not unless we have no choice." He cocked his head and listened carefully. "Six men. The laird must ken our weakness, for 'tis unusual for Outsiders to go on a hunt at night."

"He trains men to do so."

"So do the others who hunt us."

She glanced up at the moon glinting through the trees. "A clear sky and a fat moon dinnae help us much, either. So we hide?"

"Aye, we hide."

Una hung on tightly as he wound his way through the trees, using as much speed as he dared. She had not planned much beyond finding an ally and cursed herself for a fool. She should have considered the fact that she would be hunted, that she would put anyone who helped her into danger. Raibeart was big and strong, with speed and natural weapons, but he was still one man against six. The men after them also knew the strengths of the ones they hunted and would not be easily caught off guard.

"I have put ye in danger," she said, guilt a hard knot in her belly.

Raibeart grunted softly. "MacNachtons have always been in danger. E'en more so since these hunters have caught wind of us. I dare nay think on how many Lost Ones were murdered ere we learned of them or I would weep like a bairn. All ye have asked of me is to help ye save eight people with MacNachton blood, and I ne'er thought it would be a simple matter of rapping at the door of that mad laird's keep and asking for the prisoners to be released."

The man could put a nice bite behind his words, she thought, and smiled. Her good humor fled quickly, however. If the laird's men had found their trail already, it could be a long, harrowing ride to Cambrun. A long ride with a lot of chances for a dangerous confrontation.

He reined in at a place deep in the shadows of a thick cluster of trees. "We will wait here to see if they still follow us."

"But they could pass by us and then be in front of us. Would that nay be worse?" she asked.

"Nay. If they have followed us, then I have just succeeded in leading them away from the path we need to take to get to Cambrun. We will but slip back round them and ride hard for a wee while."

Una pressed her cheek against his back. She liked clinging to him far too much for her own peace of mind, but that was not enough to get her to stop doing it. It felt good to be pressed so close to him, good in a way that was both exciting and a little frightening. He even smelled good, she thought, and then rolled her eyes at her own foolishness. She began to think that no woman was safe from the risk of growing foolish over a man.

Raibeart was peering out into the dark. Una did the same but suspected his vision was far more acute than hers. She had no doubt that at least a few deaths would mark their trail before they reached Cambrun. All she could do was pray that neither Raibeart nor she were one of them.

She tensed when the hunting party rode into view. The five men who had been chasing her when Raibeart had rescued her were there, but it was the sixth man who made her blood run cold. It was Angus, a man called Death by the other men at Dun-morton, although never to his face. He was big, strong, and lethal. Even more dangerous than that, he was an excellent tracker, deadly with a blade, and cunning. He was not a man it would be easy to lose.

It felt like hours before the hunters rode away, even though she knew it was only minutes. Una had kept expecting Angus's cold gray eyes to fix upon them, for a knife to bury itself in Raibeart's heart. Angus was one of the laird's best hunters and knew how to bring down ones with MacNachton blood. She did not feel all that relieved when they left their hiding place to ride around the hunters and head for Cambrun. Una could swear she felt Angus's cold gaze on her back, the spot between her shoulder blades itching in warning.

"Why are ye so afraid?" Raibeart asked. "Ye were trembling. Still are a wee bit."

"Angus was there. He was the sixth mon. He is an expert hunter."

"The big red-haired mon with the cold eyes?"

"Aye. He willnae lose our trail for long. He led the men who caught every one of us, the ones the laird sent away and the ones he still holds. He isnae one of the laird's five favored men, but he is close. Verra close."

"Do ye think he kens the secret about our blood?"

"I couldnae say. 'Tis possible. He spends a lot of time with the laird and his chosen men." She pressed her forehead against his back. "What Angus is, is a coldhearted killer. He kens enough about us to ken ways to hurt or kill us without risking himself much. I swear, if he didnae have the kiss of the sun so clear to see on his face, I would think him one of us. He is that good at hunting us."

"Dinnae fret, lass." He patted her clenched hands. "A Mac-Nachton is nay so easy to bring down, and I suspicion that mon has ne'er faced a Pureblood."

"I think I heard a touch of arrogance behind those words," she murmured. "Ye are stronger, aye?"

"Stronger, faster, and more lethal. And, more importantly, verra hard to kill. Ye heal fast, aye?" He felt her nod against his back. "I heal faster. Ye will soon ken exactly what breed ye descend from, so trust me when I tell ye that I can rip the throat out of one mon and be doing the same to another ere the first one hits the ground." He waited tensely for her reaction to that hard truth.

Una was shocked, even more so when she realized that those words did not frighten her. In fact, her first clear thought was that, if she and the others had had the skills of the Purebloods they were descended from, they would never have been caught and caged. She slowly became aware of how tense Raibeart was and realized he was braced for her disgust or rejection. Despite all her efforts to remain sensible about the man, her heart softened and she lightly hugged him.

"I think there is a lot I need to learn about what I am," she said and smiled against his back when his chest moved with a sigh of relief.

Twice more they had to elude the hunters, and Una was bone weary by the time they sought shelter from the rising sun. This time Raibeart took her to a small shepherd's shelter, well hidden behind trees and shrubs. He secured his horse, fed and watered the animal, and led her through a trapdoor in the floor to a shelter below the hut.

"Now I understand why a poor shieling had a wooden floor beneath the dirt," she murmured. "Does your clan have such places scattered everywhere across the land?"

"In as many places as we can," he answered. "Each time one of our men weds a lass with lands, we add even more. This is a poor place and we cannae have a fire, so I fear 'tis naught but wine, oatcakes, and cheese for ye this time."

"Ye keep feeding me," she said as she sat down on the blanket he spread out and accepted the food.

"I suspicion food has been scarce for ye for quite a while."

"Certainly since I was captured. The laird wants us kept weak but nay so weak he cannae take our blood when he pleases." She tensed briefly when he sat down beside her and draped his arm across her shoulders.

"Each thing ye tell me about that madmon only adds to my need to kill him," said Raibeart, the cold promise of death clear to hear in his deep, rough voice. "The worst of his sins being that he treats bairns with such cruelty."

Una nodded as she ate, deciding she would just try to ignore what was almost an embrace. The way the laird and his men fed off the poor children like greedy leeches made her stomach churn.

She lived in constant dread that the men would kill the little girls, weaken the children so much that they could not recover. The men took far too much blood and gave them far too little food and water to help them recover from the loss. The suffering of the children was one thing that had made all the others agree that she needed to risk escape from the dungeon.

"Aye, he should die for that alone." She looked at him. "For a wee while I was sickened by the thought that I was like him, for did I nay need the blood of another from time to time just to survive?"

"Nay, ye . . ." he began, but stuttered to a halt when she held up her hand.

"I decided I was wrong to think that way, began to look hard at the differences. He and his men dinnae need that blood to survive; they just want it to make themselves more powerful. I then learned that the others were shamed, too, thinking much the same as I did. I spent a lot of time convincing them that they were nothing like those leeches, and, in doing so, convinced myself." More or less, she thought, but shook the lingering hint of doubt aside. "I dinnae ken how ye, who are purer of blood, do it, but I, and the others, take mostly animal blood and only now and then. We would ne'er keep people like cattle, feeding off them and nay even trying to be certain that they had what was needed to survive. He isnae worried that he is slowly killing us. He will just hunt down more, aye? That is why he must die, that greed for power and that callousness toward the very people he is stealing it from."

"Purebloods dinnae kill to feed the hunger. In truth, many of us also use animal blood," he said. "It suffices most of the time. I cannae say we were so noble in the past, but it has been a verra long time since we killed for blood, long enough that the tales of those darker times are but whispered tales told to bairns to keep them from roaming outside at night or to cause the timid to shudder."

He reluctantly pulled away from her to spread out the pallet for sleeping. It was enough that she had not pushed him away when he had put his arm around her. Raibeart quickly pushed aside all thought of how perfect she had felt tucked up against his side. It stirred his hunger for her, one that grew fiercer with every moment he spent in her company. That would be difficult to hide once they were bedded down together, and it could easily bring back all her wariness around him.

"It is going to be a long, dangerous ride to Cambrun, isnae it?" Una said once she and Raibeart were tucked under the blanket.

"Ye dinnae think they will give up and go back to Dunmorton?" He turned on his side to look at her.

"Angus doesnae give up, and the others are too afraid of him to do so if he demands they keep on hunting us."

"Then, aye, the journey to Cambrun could be a troublesome one, but we will get there. Others have done so with hunters hard on their heels. It was the hunters who died, nay the MacNachtons or the Lost Ones they were saving."

"Such arrogance," she murmured but smiled, for his confidence actually calmed her fears.

"Aye, the MacNachtons are an arrogant lot." He lightly stroked her thick braid draped over the shoulder closest to him. "A mon needs to ken his strengths weel or he isnae at his best in a fight. We may have this weakness that causes us to have to hide from the sun, but we also have many strengths and we learn young how to use them. Ye have some, but, I think, ye have always done your best to hide them away and never learned how best to use them against your enemy."

Una frowned and then nodded. He was right. She had used her strengths in times of danger, but in a wild, panicked way, not with any true skill. Nor had any of her fellow prisoners who were still held captive. They lashed out wildly, as she did, and such an unskilled attack was probably easy to plan against.

"Ye could teach me how to use those strengths," she said, seeing the way he stroked her braid when she turned her head to look at him, but finding she was unable to protest the touch, as she knew she should.

"I can and I will." He could feel the need to sleep creeping over him and knew the chance to take the next step in his wooing would soon be lost. "And I will. We can start as soon as the sun sets," he promised and then kissed her.

Although he did not rush at her like some untried youth, Raibeart moved quickly enough that she had no time to protest. Her small hands slapped against his chest, but she did not push him away, and he did not try to press his body any closer to hers.

Her mouth was soft and sweet, the taste of her one he already craved, but he tightly leashed his hunger for more than the innocent closed-mouth kiss he gave her. When he lifted his head, he winked at her before lying back down and turning his back to her. This time it was not just to avoid any recriminations or arguments but also to hide his arousal. For once he was glad of the way he could not easily deny the need to sleep as the sun rose.

Una stared at Raibeart's back and touched her mouth with trembling fingers. She could still feel the heat of his mouth against hers and her heart was pounding, but not with fear. It occurred to her that she might have misjudged Raibeart. The man might well know a thing or two about wooing after all.

Chapter Five

"This is a crypt."

Raibeart looked at Una and almost grinned at the way she scowled at the effigy of a knight that topped a large stone coffin. She did not appear afraid, but she was definitely not pleased by his choice of shelters. After two nights of hiding from and eluding hunters and sleeping in shelters that were little more than holes in the ground, he was pleased to be in a large place with stone walls and a floor. He suspected she would grow less dismayed when he showed her the place where she could actually take a bath. It was one reason he always sought this shelter when traveling this particular path to and from Cambrun.

"Aye," he said. "There isnae much left of the wee stone chapel that used to cover it, though."

"I noticed." She realized she had seen no house, no keep or peel tower. "Whose is it?"

"A wee part of the Chisholm clan used it. The family who built this and tended the lands here died long ago. Plague took them all, and the few shepherds or villagers who survived went elsewhere. I suspicion many fled once the first person fell ill with the plague. Naught left here but these old bones and ruins." He walked up to her and lightly tugged on her braid when she frowned. "And, nay, ye willnae catch the plague by staying here."

Una grimaced at her own foolish fears, more so at the fact that Raibeart had guessed them. "I ken it. 'Tis mostly that even the word plague is enough to make one tremble."

"Weel, I ken of something that will please ye enough to take the fear away." He took her by the hand and started to lead her toward the rubble-strewn rear of the crypt. "Trust me. Ye will like this."

She was not quite sure what there could be to like in a house of the dead, but she did not resist his tug on her hand. It made her uncomfortable to be inside the crypt, but she did prefer it to where they had slept for the last two days. Those places had been enough to leave her with a fear of being buried alive.

The sound of water drew her attention just as Raibeart led her around a corner and into a smaller chamber. She gaped at what she saw. There was a deep hollow in the rock floor and water trickled down the stone wall to fill it. It was obvious there was some way for the water to escape the stone basin or the crypt would have been flooded long ago despite how slowly the water ran into the pool. A light cloud of mist hung over the pool. She tugged her hand free of Raibeart's grasp, knelt beside the pool, and dipped her fingers into the water.

" 'Tis warm," she whispered in astonishment. "How can it be warm?"

"There are springs that can run warm, e'en hot, here and there." Raibeart moved to the corner of the room where there were several bundles stacked on a rough wooden shelf. "We keep some supplies here." He opened a bundle and held out a length of linen. "My clan stops here whenever they can and, I think, 'tis mostly because of the pool."

"I can bathe in it?" Even as she asked, she stuck her arm down into the water, uncaring of how she soaked the sleeves of her gown, touching the stone at the bottom just as she reached her armpit. "It has an odd smell," she murmured, taking a deep breath. "Nay bad, just a little odd."

"We have decided that, whatever it is, 'tis verra soothing. Takes away the aches of a long ride."

Una took the drying cloth from his hands, eager to bathe away the dust of their journey, but suddenly realizing she had a problem. "I dinnae have anything clean to put on after I bathe."

"Between a drying cloth and one of these shirts someone left, ye could cover yourself decently enough. Then ye can wash out what ye wear now."

Raibeart found himself pushed out of the room before he could say another word. He laughed softly and went to make a fire. It would be best if he kept busy or he would think too much on how close Una was, naked and in the warm water of the pool. He stopped and closed his eyes, shuddering at the thought of how close he was to all he craved to hold. It was going to be a very long day.

Una tossed aside her clothes and slid into the water, a sigh of pleasure escaping her. She sank in up to her chin, rested her head against the edge of the pool, and closed her eyes. Raibeart was right. The water might have an odd smell, but it soaked away every ache in her body.

The moment Raibeart came to mind, she thought of him sharing this pool with her, his fine, strong body as naked as her own. Una opened her eyes so quickly and widely they stung. Her heart was pounding and parts of her itched, ached even, at the mere thought of Raibeart naked. She could almost feel his skin against hers, feel him kissing her, touching her, and her body grew warm.

Just as it had when he had kissed her on the mouth the third day they rested, she thought. He had nipped at her bottom lip, causing her to part her lips, and had slipped his tongue into her mouth. The way he had stroked the inside of her mouth as he had pulled her body close to his had made her ache, in her breasts and between her legs. She had clung to him not only because she liked to touch him, but because her knees had actually grown too weak to hold her upright. It had been the same when he had kissed her when they had wakened. It was the same now and all she had done was think about it.

This was lust, she realized, and sat up, the sudden knowledge clearing the fog of fear and confusion from her mind. Una grabbed the small bowl of soap Raibeart had left her and the scrap of linen to wash with, and began to scrub herself clean as she thought over what she now knew. She had never lusted before and was not sure what to do about it. A maid did not just trot off to find someone to soothe that itch, not like a man would. And, Una knew only one man would do for her anyway. A man who was close at hand and was attempting to woo her.

"Curse it, just what does he mean by that?" she muttered. "Woo to his bed or woo to be his wife?"

Setting aside the cloth and putting a little soap in her hands, Una began to wash her hair. The way her body was so quickly enflamed by Raibeart's kiss told her that her lust for him was a powerful thing. It would not take much more of his wooing before she found herself no longer a maid. What she needed to do was decide if she wished to allow that or if she should step away from him now, make it very clear to him that he could do no more wooing. She would stay a maid.

Why? whispered a voice in her head and she had no answer. Why indeed? She was three and twenty and had been on her own, without home or family, for seven years. In all those years she could count the number of times she had felt safe or happy on the fingers of one hand. Raibeart made her feel both. There was also little chance that she would wed because of her differences so whom was she saving her maidenhead for? Should it not go to the one man in her whole life that made her feel safe, happy, and even beautiful?

Una grinned as she stepped out of the pool and dried herself, wrapping the damp cloth around her wet hair and then donning the shirt he had left for her. She wanted Raibeart and she could take what she wanted for once in her life. As she rinsed out her clothes and spread them out to dry on some of the rubble cluttering the room, she wondered exactly how she could do that. When she stood up to return to the large chamber, she suffered the pinch of uncertainty but shook it aside. Raibeart had shown that he wanted her, even said he intended to woo her. Whether he meant seduction or marriage no longer mattered. He was about to be claimed. She unwrapped her hair and used the cloth to rub it dry as she went hunting her prey.

Raibeart looked up as Una entered the chamber and he nearly choked. She was slowly rubbing her hair dry as she walked toward him. The shirt she wore hung to her knees, but he knew she wore nothing beneath it. Each time she raised her arms a little to rub her hair, the shirt slipped up to her thighs. His hands itched to touch all that smooth skin she was showing him. Instead he nodded and hurried out of the room to take his own bath. He just wished the water were cold.

The sight of her clothing draped over the scattered rocks did nothing to help him regain his calm. It reminded him all too clearly of the fact that all that stood between him and her beautiful skin was one thin shirt. He had always considered desire something a man could easily control, but he had no control around Una, his body demanding that he claim her every time he looked at her.

Raibeart shook his head as he shed his clothes and entered the pool. He was going to have to try harder. His wooing appeared to be working but, after all Una had suffered, he doubted she was ready for a man half blind with hunger for her.

By the time he was bathed and dressed in clean clothing, he was again in control of his desires. Then he stepped up to the small fire she sat near and she smiled at him. His body clenched tightly with the wanting he had just thought he had conquered. Gritting his teeth, he sat down beside her on the blanket she had spread out. Despite all his attempts to keep his gaze fixed on the flames, he was soon staring at her long, slim legs and clenching his fists to stop himself from touching them.

Una picked up Raibeart's wineskin, turned to offer it to him, and grew very still. Raibeart was staring at her legs much as a starving man stared at any scrap of food. She wondered if there was something alarming about the MacNachtons he had not told her, and then told herself not to be so slack-witted.

She recognized that look on his face. The tightening of the lines of his face, the hint of color riding his high cheekbones. It was desire. She had seen it on a man's face before. It was a look that had always preceded a flare of violence and then her running for her life. It was a look she had learned to read as a warning of danger. Now, seeing that look on Raibeart's handsome face, everything within her read it as an invitation. Una was just not certain how she could answer it in a way that was not too brazen.

Still holding the wineskin, she shifted until she was kneeling, facing him. Her breath caught in her throat when his gaze met hers. His dark eyes had gone feral, lightening until they were more a dark amber than a brown so dark it was almost black. It did not frighten her, however. Instead, it stirred to life a hunger that rose rapidly to equal the one she could read in those beautiful predator's eyes.

"Do ye wish a drink?" she asked, a little surprised at how low and husky her voice was.

"Aye." Raibeart took the wineskin from her hand and set it on the floor, never once taking his gaze from her face. "I do. A deep one."

He kissed her, and Una shivered, heat flooding through her body the moment his lips touched hers. She wrapped her arms around his neck, threaded her fingers through his hair, and held him close. The hunger she had seen in his eyes was revealed in his kiss. This was no gentle wooing. This was a man telling her that he wanted her, a man demanding that she give him what he needed.

It should have frightened her. Men had demanded before, had expected to be able to take what they wanted from her. It was why she had never settled anywhere since being driven from her family's home. Each time she had tried, some man had thought she was free for the taking and tried to do just that despite her refusals. Una did not fear Raibeart. His demand did not make her want to fight him and run; it made her want to give, to share. She returned his kiss with a demand of her own.

Raibeart was close to shaking with the force of his need by the time he pushed Una down onto the blanket. He was not surprised to see the fine tremor in his hand as he began to unlace the shirt she wore, kissing each newly exposed patch of skin, inhaling the scent of her, and becoming drunk on the taste of her. The voice of reason in his mind tried to warn him to go slow, to be certain that Una was ready to make love, but it took several minutes before he grasped enough control to heed it.

"Una," he said as he gently tugged the shirt aside to expose her softly rounded shoulder, "ye have but a heartbeat or two to tell me nay, to stop me."

"If I was going to say nay, I would have done so ere ye got me on my back," she whispered and nipped his chin.

He laughed but it was rough sound, more of a growl than anything else. "There will be nay going back." Raibeart knew she would think he referred to her innocence, but he did not have the strength or the wit to explain what he really meant now.

"I ken that."

Una placed her hands on his cheeks and tugged his mouth down to hers. She did not want to talk. Her mind was settled. She would have Raibeart, hold him close for as long as he allowed, and deal with the consequences of the heedlessness later.

When he tugged off the shirt she wore and tossed it aside, she could feel the heat of a blush sting her cheeks, neck, and chest. No man had ever seen her completely naked. Raibeart raised himself to his knees to tear off his clothing, and Una lost all concern over her own nudity. He was beautiful, all hard muscle and dark golden skin. She caught a quick look at his manhood, rising hard and long from a thatch of black curls, before he returned to her arms, but she pushed the image from her mind. That part of a man had represented a threat to her for far too long; she did not want the sight of it to chill the fire his touch had set blazing inside her.

The way he caressed her body with his large, calloused hands burned away the lingering uncertainty still lodged in her heart and mind. This was what she needed, what she wanted. When he followed the path of his hands with his mouth, she lost all ability to think at all, fierce desire grasping full control. Soft cries of delight escaped her as he kissed her breasts, whispered praises against them, suckled her like a child, and slowly slipped his hand between her legs. Each caress brought her such pleasure she feared she would lose herself in it but could not bring herself to care.

A touch of unease nudged her mind when she felt him begin to join their bodies. "Raibeart?"

"I dinnae wish to hurt you," he said.

The growl of the beast echoing in his words was but another spark added to the fire consuming her, and she wrapped her limbs around him. "Nature and God say ye must, so be quick about it."

She had barely finished speaking when he thrust deep inside her, ending her innocence in little more than a heartbeat of time. A sharp pain tore through her insides, but she swallowed her cry. The pain was gone almost as quickly as it had arrived. Una held Raibeart close, smoothing her hands over his broad back, his forehead resting against hers, and his gaze fixed upon her body as he caressed her, soothed her. She was filled with him, surrounded by the scent and the warmth of his strong body. Never had she felt so safe, so alive.

Raibeart kissed her and began to move, thrusting in and out of her with a steady, gentle rhythm that brought tears to her eyes. A tight knot of hot need formed low in her belly, and she began to match his strokes. The need grew more demanding, the pleasure carrying a hint of pain, and then something inside her broke. She called out his name as she tumbled into a torrent of intense pleasure so sweet, so beautiful she never wished it to end. His voice caressed her ears as he thrust into her several times, so fiercely that her body shifted along the floor, and he growled out her name in a voice that was barely human. A sharp pain on her neck turned into a searing delight, desire's heat rushing through her body so strongly that she plunged into desire's abyss for a second time. His strong body bucked against her, shuddering as a warmth bathed her womb, and then he collapsed on top of her, their heavy, panting breaths as perfect a match as their bodies.

It was a long time before Raibeart found the strength, and will, to move. He wanted to stay deep and warm inside Una's body. It had been a struggle not to turn the bite he had given her into the mating bite, her blood so sweet and intoxicating he had nearly lost control. It was too soon and she deserved to choose him of her own free will. Raibeart finally eased their bodies apart and lifted his head from her full soft breasts to look at her.

"Are ye weel?" he asked.

"Ye bit me." Una was unsettled over how much she had liked it.

"Aye. Mayhap I should have asked first, but I wasnae thinking verra clearly."

That was very flattering, Una thought. She decided she had liked the bite too much to deny it, too. "I was just a wee bit surprised is all."

"Ah, weel, then, I can tell ye that I mean to surprise ye a lot."

Una grinned. "Do ye now?"

"I do, but 'tis best if ye get some rest now."

Although painfully embarrassed when he cleaned them both off, she settled comfortably in his arms when he returned to their rough bed. Sleep tugged at her so firmly that she rested her cheek against the warmth of his chest and closed her eyes. She was just tumbling into the blackness of exhaustion when she thought she heard Raibeart say *mine* but could not rouse herself enough to ask him what he meant.

Raibeart looked at the woman curled up against him, her long dark lashes a soft crescent against her pale skin, and sighed. He was sated and content, but there was a tiny worm of unease in his heart. Una was his, but she had uttered no words of love, as he would have expected of an innocent who had just allowed a man to make love to her. Then again she had willingly given him that innocence. That had to mean something important. Instinct told him, however, that she was not fully his. Not yet. He had a fight ahead of him. Raibeart could only hope that it was not a long one. Now that he had shared such a fierce passion with Una, he had no intention of letting her go.

Chapter Six

"Try it again."

Una opened one eye to look up at Raibeart. He stood over her, grinning widely, and she wished she had the strength left to kick him. Asking him to teach her how to use her MacNachton strengths to fight with some skill might not have been the best idea she had ever had, she decided.

"Nay," she said. "I think I best save what little strength I have left for the ride ahead of us."

Raibeart laughed, bent down to grasp her by her wrist, and pulled her to her feet. "And we should be riding from here soon." He tugged her into his arms. "Ye did weel. Verra weel. I think ye have a lot of MacNachton strengths but a lot of what our laird was hoping for as weel. Ye can mix with the Outsiders because ye can endure time in the sun and ye eat their food. A fine and helpful mix."

"Ye eat their food, e'en cook it weel. S'truth, I think ye may cook with more skill than I do."

He kissed the tip of her nose, loving the little freckles that marched across the bridge of that small straight nose. "I like the tastes but none of it will keep me alive. If I dinnae get blood, I slowly weaken and die. There is no escaping that dark hunger."

"Ye could have some of mine," she said, shocking herself with the offer. After being bled by that mad laird for so long, she was surprised she was able to offer even Raibeart her blood.

"Nay, lass. I am fine." He brushed a kiss over her mouth. "And I had a wee sip this morning, aye?" He laughed when she blushed. "The wine is enough for me and I can get what I need when we get to Cambrun."

"We should have been there by now, aye?"

"Aye, but it may weel be another two nights now because we have had to travel in such a winding path, trying to shake those cursed hunters from our heels."

He could see her disappointment reflected in her eyes and he kissed her. Raibeart decided that kissing her was a craving he had no wish to control. The way she tasted, the way her passion rose so quickly to meet his and warm him, was not something any man could resist. When he ended the kiss, he looked into her eyes and the shadows were gone again. What had replaced them, however, was a wanting so strong and so hot, he nearly pushed her right back down on the ground so that he could bury himself deep inside her.

Taking a deep breath and letting it out slowly in a vain attempt to cool the searing need he had for her, Raibeart said, "We will free the others, Una. Aye, it would be verra fine if we could do so in the sennight we had first thought, but I swear to you, there will be no delay once we reach Cambrun and tell them what we need. I dinnae think we will e'en linger to make a plan, for we can do that as we ride for Dunmorton. Whatever happens, someone will see them freed and cared for. E'en if we dinnae reach Cambrun, I have left messages for my kinsmen at every shelter we have been in so that the next traveler from my clan will ken what needs to be done."

"I ken it. 'Tis just that, now and then, I fear for what they must be suffering. It tears at my heart to think they are being punished while I am free. Ye dinnae think he will kill them because I escaped, do ye?"

"Nay. He wants what only they can give him. Trust me, what he is getting from his vile potions he makes from their blood is nay something he will easily give up."

She nodded. "That is what I keep telling myself. I also tell myself that I *had* to escape, that it was all that could offer us any chance to survive."

"And ye are right. Ye found me, my clan, and the MacNachtons will get your friends out of those cages and kill their captors," he said even as he mounted Tor and pulled her up into the saddle behind him. "Now, we really must ride. Staying in the open like this isnae safe, nay when I havenae completely shaken those cursed hunters off our trail."

Una clung to him as he rode using a cautious speed, for his

mount was invaluable to their escape from the hunters. She knew Raibeart cared deeply for the animal as well. That could be seen in how he cared for the beast, the way he spoke to the animal, and even in the way he petted it.

He petted her a lot, too, she thought, and grinned. Raibeart was a man who liked to touch and she was heartily glad of it. Una wished they were not in a race to escape their enemies, a race to get to Cambrun to get help for her friends. She would like to spend more time with Raibeart, more time to savor and explore the passion that raged between them. She would also like some time to talk to him about exactly what he meant when he spoke of wooing, if she could ever gather the courage to do so.

Numerous times since they had made love she had started to ask him what he had meant, only to choke on the words. That cowardice surprised her. She had never suffered from an inability to say what she thought or demand answers to any questions she had. All she could think of concerning her sudden hesitancy was that she feared the answers he would give her. She did not want to ask Raibeart about wooing for she was terrified he would speak only of passion, need, or want, and not say a word about love or some future together.

Una pushed those thoughts aside. She had decided not to trouble herself with recriminations, regrets, or doubts and needed to hold fast to that decision. If she allowed such doubts and worries into her mind, it could taint what she shared with Raibeart, and that was the very last thing she wished to do. Despite the danger they could not seem to shake free of and the pressing need to save her friends, she was actually happy. Una could see no harm in allowing herself to revel in that for just a little while.

Raibeart frowned toward the woods Una had disappeared into. Even with his keen vision, he could not see any sign of her and he suspected she had made sure that he would not. Although he understood her need for a few moments of privacy now and then, he did not like her to be completely out of his sight. He had managed to elude the hunters, but that was not the same as escaping them. They were still out there, still trailing along behind.

He cursed softly. His attempt to find any Lost Ones had been an utter failure. There had been the hope of only one, a hope held briefly and shattered when he discovered the lass had been murdered by her own husband. The way the man had wept and moaned about demons had given Raibeart a good idea of how the lass had died, and it had taken all his will not to just snap the fool's neck. Now that he had found a Lost One, and one he had every intention of keeping for himself, he could not seem to get her free of the men hunting her. It was obvious that, in the future, he should just stay with training horses, he thought morosely.

Just as he was shaking free of his self-castigation and wondering exactly how angry Una might get if he went looking for them, he heard a sound that did not belong in the forest. A soft grunt and then a low, mean laugh. The sounds sent an icy chill down his spine. He moved Tor deeper into the shelter of the trees, drew his sword, and slipped into the woods, becoming part of the shadows as he moved silently toward the sounds.

The sight that met his eyes when he found Una caused his fangs to lengthen and the beast to roar to life within him. Two of the hunters had grabbed her. It was obvious from the thin trail of blood on her face that they had not been gentle in the capturing of her. They had also gagged her and were mauling her while she struggled. Their plan to rape her was clear, the scent of their lust tainting the air.

Raibeart could almost taste their blood, his fury making him eager to rip out their throats. It took a moment for him to regain enough sanity to plan his approach. The men would die, but he did not want Una hurt any more than she already had been. He needed a cold, clear mind to accomplish that, but he promised the beast inside him that it would be fed as soon as she was safe.

Una heard a twig snap as she busied herself brushing off her skirts. She spun around and found herself facing a grinning Red Rob and Donald. A quick glance around showed no horses, although their mounts could be just beyond her vision, secured in the dark shadows of the trees. More importantly, she saw none of the other hunters. That meant she had only two men to fight off. Not easy, but not impossible.

"I was right," said Donald. "I was sure they were circling us, but that arse Angus wouldnae listen to me."

"Nay, he isnae a mon to doubt himself," said Red Rob.

"Ye will come with us now, lass."

Una looked at Donald as if he was a complete fool. "I dinnae think so. I have no wish to return to that madmon ye call a laird."

"Ye would leave the others to suffer for your freedom?"

That stung, but she told herself not to let Donald pluck at her own sense of guilt and her fear for the others. "The others cannae suffer any more than they already do."

"Nay, mayhap they cannae. But they can die."

"The laird willnae kill them. So, I suggest ye just run along back to him and tell him ye couldnae find me."

"Or what? Ye will call that brute who took ye away from us?"

She blinked in surprise. She had not even thought of calling for help. It had been so long since she had had anyone to aid her that she had simply fallen into the habit of caring for herself, not thinking of how useful Raibeart would be right now. Una opened her mouth to call for him only to find herself slammed to the ground by a charging Donald.

All the breath left her body and she could not have cried out for Raibeart even if she had been able to breathe before Red Rob gagged her with a filthy strip of cloth. She glared at the man but then saw a look in his eye she had become all too familiar with, and it made her heart clench with fear. Red Rob meant to sate his lusts on her, and the glance he sent Donald who sat on her back told her that he had no doubt that man would join him in the assault.

Panic gave her strength and she fought, thrashing around until she bucked Donald off her back, but her freedom was short-lived. Both men wrestled with her, struggling to pin her arms and legs to the ground. Una managed to strike several good blows and even gouged Red Rob's arm with her nails, but they still managed to get her pinned to the ground. Terror washed over her, threatening to drag her into darkness, but she refused to faint and make it all so much easier for them.

"Bitch," Donald growled as he wiped at the blood pouring from his nose with his filthy sleeve. "Ye will pay for that."

Red Rob glared at her after he looked at the deep scratches on his arm. "I will make ye verra sorry for this, too."

So many angry words crowded into her mouth she nearly choked on them. They were angry because she fought against their plan to abuse her? Una was just thinking that the world would be a much better place if such vermin were eradicated when Donald was suddenly lifted from her and tossed up against a tree.

"Move, love."

Raibeart's voice was so rough, so like the growl of an enraged animal, that Una barely understood him. She could see a white-faced Red Rob trying to get to his feet so frantically that he kept stumbling and getting nowhere. It did not surprise her that the vicious little man looked terrified. Raibeart was a huge, strong, fanged predator. Even as she scrambled to get out of the way of what she suspected would be a very short battle, she now realized why Raibeart spoke of the *beast* inside of him. He was looking very feral and very dangerous.

She moved. Knowing her legs would be unsteady because of the terror that was only just leaving her, she scrambled backward, using her hands and feet until she came up against a tree. Una tore off her gag and watched as Raibeart stalked toward a trembling Red Rob. These men may have hunted ones like her, caught them, killed them, or imprisoned them, but they had obviously never met one of the clan she and the other had descended from.

Then, whether from sheer instinct to survive or from sudden surge of courage, Red Rob leapt to his feet and pulled his sword. Una nearly cried out a warning but knew it could distract Raibeart and clapped a hand over her mouth. A moment later she knew she did not need to fear for him. He exchanged a few sword thrusts with Red Rob before easily knocking the sword from the man's hand.

"What are ye?" squeaked Red Rob.

"Your death."

Una winced when Raibeart grabbed Red Rob, slammed him against a tree, and then sank his fangs into the man's neck. She wanted to look away but could not. This was what she was, the blood thinned through marriage, but still MacNachton. Red Rob was still alive when Raibeart raised his head, idly wiped his mouth on his sleeve, and then snapped the man's neck.

She looked at Donald at the same time Raibeart did. Donald was on his feet, his sword in his hand, but the look on his face told her that he knew he was about to die. Una did not flinch when Raibeart treated him the same way he had Red Rob. When Raibeart started to walk toward her, the feral look on his face slowly changing to one of uncertainty, she struggled to her feet.

The way he had killed the men had been shocking, but she was not disgusted or afraid. Those men had killed a lot of her kind, had hunted them like animals, and had intended to rape her. She would have killed them herself if she had possessed Raibeart's strength.

Raibeart cautiously reached to touch her cheek. When she did not flinch from his touch, he was almost weakened by the strength of the relief that swept through him. It was not until he had looked at the two dead men that his fury had eased enough for him to realize what he had done in front of her. He had let her see the beast that lived inside every MacNachton Pureblood, but she showed no fear of it. Unable to help himself, he pulled her into his arms and kissed her. He smiled with pleasure when, as he released her, she stumbled a little and it took a moment for the clouds of passion to clear from her eyes.

"Can ye ride?" he asked when she started to brush off her skirts and revealed no sign of any serious injury.

"I have been riding with ye for several days," she said, a little confused by his question.

"Nay, can ye ride on your own? Their horses are just inside the woods. We can take them and then ye will have your own mount to ride."

"Will that make us able to move more quickly and help ye to fight if the need arises?"

"Aye. Tor is a strong beast, but he is carrying two people, isnae he? One would be better, for I could get a wee bit more speed out of him without fear of tiring him too quickly."

"Then let us get their horses." She glanced at the two dead men. "Do we leave them for the carrion?"

"I think we have to as the others cannae be too far away."

"So be it."

In moments, Una found herself seated on a horse of her own. She looked down at Raibeart and smiled. "I have done little riding in my life so I hope ye will be patient with me."

He patted her leg. "Ye will do fine."

She watched him mount Tor, securing the reins of the third horse to the saddle, and grinned. He had just patted her. Shaking her head, she nudged her mount closer to his as they began to ride through the trees. She was going to miss being close to him as they rode together, holding him near and enjoying his warmth, but he was right. There would be a lot of advantages to their each being mounted.

The sky was already growing lighter by the time he led them to a small stone house. Una winced as she dismounted, her muscles aching. It required a lot more strength and attention to handle her own mount. She suspected the fight with Red Rob and Donald had added a few aches as well.

She was still sore after they ate, and Raibeart laid out their bedding while she washed up. Despite her best efforts not to, she let out a soft sound of pain as she settled down beside him. Una really wanted to taste the passion they could share again but suspected her body would make that impossible.

"Turn onto your belly, love," Raibeart said, "and I will rub away some of those aches ye arenae hiding as weel as ye think ye are."

She laughed as she turned onto her stomach. "As we are both naked, I was rather hoping we might be doing something else."

"So was I, but ye have had a hard day. Ye need to rest and let the battering ye took heal a wee bit."

The soft sounds she made as he rubbed her back and shoulders made him hard with need for her, but Raibeart did his best to hide it from her. She needed rest. The tension of pain began to leave her body beneath his hands and he was not surprised when she soon fell asleep. Raibeart settled down next to her and pulled her into his arms, smiling when she cuddled up against his chest without waking. He would get no loving today but there was always the night.

Chapter Seven

Una woke to a fire raging through her body, the heat of Raibeart's mouth upon her breast surging through her veins. She opened her eyes just enough to see his head against her skin and tangle her fingers in his hair. Then she gave herself over to the desire he stirred within her with every caress, every kiss. She did her best to touch him, to caress his warm skin, but he began to slide out of her reach, kissing her belly, and then her legs.

"Raibeart," she called, clutching at his shoulders and trying to pull him back into her arms. I need . . ." She stuttered to a halt as she vainly searched for an appropriate word in her passion-clouded mind.

"So do I, love."

He did not think he would ever get enough of the taste of her and the feel of her soft skin. Raibeart had wakened with a naked Una curled up in his arms and a need so fierce and demanding he had groaned. He knew they should be getting up, collecting their things, and riding hard and fast for Cambrun, but he could not resist the temptation to make love to her again. They would have little time for such pleasure in the next few days, not with eight other Lost Ones waiting to be saved.

Beneath his hands he felt her body tense with shock when he kissed the neat vee of blond curls between her strong slender thighs. Raibeart ignored her gasped protest and proceeded to make love to her with his mouth. She quickly went wild in his arms, her soft cries of pleasure sweet music to his ears. Una made him feel as if he was the greatest of lovers. When she cried out his name, demanding he join their bodies with all the haughty command of a queen, he laughed even as he obeyed her.

He thrust inside and paused, lightly pressing his forehead

against hers. She was so tight and hot he wanted to stay there pinned on the knife's edge of desire for hours. Then she wrapped her legs around him and he lost that last weak grip he had on his control, taking her with all the fierce, greedy hunger that had built up inside him, and sending them both tumbling into release.

Una barely twitched when Raibeart gently cleaned her off. She did not think she would be able to move again for hours. A small part of her mind tried to make her feel shamed, or at least a little embarrassed, over all she had allowed him to do, but she silenced it. He had driven her mad with need and she really hoped he planned to do it again. If that made her shameless or wanton, she was prepared to accept that. She smiled weakly when he returned to her arms and kissed her.

"This wee stone cottage is verra nice," she said, idly stroking his strong back. "As dark and dry as the crypt but no dead sharing it with us."

"And, sadly, no bath, either." He kissed her cheek. "Ye can have a bath as soon as we reach Cambrun."

"Tonight?"

He nodded. "That is my plan. We may have to race for the gates, however, but that has been done before. Some of our men have brought Lost Ones home with hunters hard on their heels."

"I am bringing danger to your home."

"It has come before and, nay doubt, it will come again."

"And ye are certain your clan will help us save the others caged at Dunmorton?"

"They will be aching to ride out the moment the sun begins to set." He slapped her lightly on her thigh and then stood up to stretch. "And that is what we should have done but"—he winked at her over his shoulder—"I woke to a temptation too great to resist."

Una slipped out from beneath the blanket the moment his back was to her so that she could dress. It was impossible to take her gaze off him, however. He was so big and strong, his shoulders broad and his muscles taut. His skin was dark, as if he had spent a lot of time basking naked in the sun, something she knew he could never do. When she caught herself reaching out with the urge to touch his taut backside, she shook the haze from her mind and hastily finished dressing. Raibeart was certain that they would soon have all the help they needed from his friends. It was time to cease thinking of smooth broad backs, lovemaking, and wooing.

Una took a deep drink of the enriched wine Raibeart apparently had an unending supply of and watched him as he studied the shadowed areas all around them. They still had not shaken the hunters even though there were now only four of them. She was surprised the hunters had not given up yet, especially if they had found the bodies of Red Rob and Donald. When Raibeart turned to look at her, she held the wineskin out to him.

It had bothered her in the beginning that drinking the blood-enriched wine could make her stronger. That need for blood had always troubled her, and she had been glad that the dark hunger had risen only rarely. Now she was stronger and healthier than she had been in years and, at some time during the journey, she had accepted that part of her. What preyed on her mind now was that she had the urge to bite Raibeart when they made love, just as he bit her. She was not bothered by his need to *take a wee sip*, as he called it, but she was not sure she liked the fact that she was rapidly wanting to do the same.

"No need to frown so, love," he said and reached out to lightly rub away the lines on her brow. "We will be at Cambrun soon."

" 'Tis that close?" She had no intention of telling him what was really making her frown.

"Two, three miles. Ye see that wee mountain just ahead?"

"I see some of it and then it disappears into a misty cloud."

"Aye, there is always some mist sheltering us from view. I think 'tis one of the reasons our ancestors chose this place. That and the caves beneath the keep."

"Ah. But, if ye live in caves, why trouble building a keep?"

"The keep is kept dark, too, and our laird stays in it. And the caves arenae like the one we stayed in. The Purebloods have made themselves a fine place down there." He decided not to tell her that he, too, had a place down there, that such news was best held back until she decided to stay with him.

"And if the hunters follow us right to the gates?"

"They will die there. There is no mercy for the ones who hunt us."

"Nay, I wouldnae expect there to be any. I dinnae care to

think on how many poor souls have died at the hands of men like the laird, and I suspicion nay all of them were truly of Mac-Nachton blood."

"True, but too many nonetheless. All MacNachtons carry the weight of those deaths. We should have kenned the chance that bairns were bred outside the clan. It has happened at Cambrun, so we kenned it wasnae impossible."

"That was the responsibility of the men who bred those children, nay you. They didnae tell ye that had bedded a woman here and there, so how were ye to ken that there was any chance of a child?"

"We all ken how a child is begotten, so when a mon would boast of what pleasure he had found, or taken, for himself, someone should have considered the possibility that there would be a child. Now no mon leaves Cambrun without being recalled to that responsibility." He suddenly inhaled deeply and then cursed.

"What is it?"

"The hunters draw near, love. I can smell their sweat and their horses. We are going to have to ride hard and fast now. Will ye be able to do that?"

Una nodded and gripped the reins of her mount a little tighter. "Will the horses be able to follow the trail at such speed?"

"Easily enough for a while as the moon is bright and, once we are on the path that winds up the hill, our enemies will have to slow as much as we will. Ready?" he asked even as he freed the third horse he had secured to his mount, knowing it would follow them now.

"Aye."

The moment Raibeart kicked his mount into a gallop, Una did the same. She did not look at the land they rode through, knowing she would be unsettled by the sight of all the trees, obstacles that could prove a real danger to an unskilled rider such as she was. Instead she kept her gaze fixed on Raibeart, knowing he would lead her in the right direction.

Raibeart could hear the hunters riding hard behind them. It was going to be a close-run race. If it were only himself he had to worry about, he would stop and face the four men squarely. In truth, he would have stopped running and stalked them, a silent killer slipping in and out of the shadows. But, he had to think of Una's safety first and not just because she was a woman.

She was *his* woman. Leaving her on her own so that he could hunt down the men hunting them had never been a choice.

Once he started on the winding rocky path up the mountain, he signaled Una to slow down. He knew that, from below, it would soon appear as if they had just disappeared into the mists, but he doubted that would stop the hunters. They had come too far and lost two men. The laird of Dunmorton could also have promised punishments so dire that failure was more frightening than facing a MacNachton. At least until he met them face-to-face, he thought with a touch of satisfaction. Soon the men following them would discover why his clan was still feared despite the fact that all that was left of their vicious past were tales whispered in the dark.

Una stared at the keep before them, barely noting that the path they followed had grown a great deal wider. It had appeared out of the mists with little warning and was a formidable building. It looked as if it had grown straight up out of the rock it was set on. She wondered if the ones who had built it had made it look so threatening on purpose. From what little Raibeart had told her of his ancestors, she suspected they had.

She was about to ask Raibeart a few questions about his overpowering home when he suddenly turned to look behind them. Una turned back as well and cursed. The hunters had caught up with them. She had the fleeting thought that it was odd for Angus to be riding behind the others, for he was a man who led, not followed, and then Raibeart appeared at her side.

"Tell my kin there are hunters on our lands," he said and gave her mount a slap on its rump.

Her horse jumped forward and began to run toward the keep, the spare horse right beside it. From what little she could see while attempting to rein the animal in, Cambrun was set in a rocky valley between two mountains. Daring a look back at Raibeart, she saw him draw his sword and face Dunmorton's hunters. When it looked as if the still mounted Angus was actually backing away, leaving the other three men to face Raibeart, Una decided being on the back of a running horse was making her vision play tricks on her. Angus was one of the laird's coldest, cruelest killers and not one to back away from a fight.

Then four men came running toward her and she knew immediately that they were Raibeart's kinsmen. They were all tall, strong, and too darkly handsome for any woman's peace of mind. "Raibeart is facing hunters just behind me," she said quickly as she finally managed to slow her mount down a little.

"Keep riding to the gates, lass. We will take care of those fools if Raibeart doesnae," said a lean man with cold amber eyes.

Una had not ridden far when screams rent the air and were quickly silenced. She suspected any armed strangers coming into Cambrun lands would have met a similar fate. When everyone found out what Dunmorton's men were also guilty of, any unease they might feel over the swift execution of four men would fast disappear. The fact that Raibeart had ordered her to say there were hunters told her that such men were already considered enemies to be killed without mercy.

A tall slim man with thick black hair, golden eyes, and softly pale skin caught hold of the bridle of her horse and forced it to a halt. "Who are ye?" he demanded.

"Una Dunn," she replied. "I came with Raibeart."

She glanced behind her to see Raibeart and the other men approaching. Raibeart nudged Tor to a trot when he saw the man holding her horse. He looked down at the man as he reined in next to Una and, to her surprise, patted her thigh right in front of the man. Since she was neither hurt nor showing signs of being upset, she wondered what game he played. The way the other man grinned made her wonder if some strange message understood by only men had just been sent out.

"Cousin Einar," Raibeart said and nodded in greeting, "I thank ye for sending help so quickly."

"Weel, I ken that ye could take down three hunters with ease, but the lads were bored," drawled Einar.

"Three?" Una frowned at Raibeart. "There were four."

"Aye," Raibeart said, "but Angus was gone but a moment after I sent ye on your way. We thought on chasing him, but he had good start ere we cleared the path and 'tis too close to dawn to go ahunting."

"He will hie himself right back to Dunmorton."

"He has no knowledge that will change anything, love. He but kens that ye escaped with me, and, mayhap, that ye are now with others of your kind."

"Ye dinnae think that will cause trouble for the others?"

"Nay more than they already have."

"So ye found yourself a Lost One?" asked Einar, frowning a little as he looked Una over. "The blood tie is an old one, aye?"

"Aye, her grandmother's mother. One of the cursed Night-riders, I suspect." Raibeart dismounted and then reached up to pluck Una out of her saddle.

"But enough of one to already be drawing the hunters to her."

"Aye, and from what she tells me, the mon leading this pack has a lot of MacNachton blood on his hands."

"Best come in then. First ye can bathe the dust away and then come and join us in the great hall. I ken ye must be weary, but, if the tale ye have to tell is of great importance, the quicker ye join us in the hall the better. There isnae much time left ere many of us will have to seek our rest."

The moment she stepped inside the keep, two plump, cheerful maids took Una away. She was thoroughly bathed, her hair washed and rubbed dry, and then she was dressed in a lovely blue gown. It surprised her that the gown was not too short. Perhaps the women of Cambrun were as tall and braw as their men, she mused, and briefly smiled at her own foolishness.

Once readied to face the others in the MacNachton clan, Una stepped out of the room only to find Raibeart waiting for her. "Ye didnae have to wait. The maid Jenna told me how to find the hall."

Raibeart took her by the arm and led her down the stairs. "I will escort ye to your chair."

"I was wondering why Angus fled as I didnae think he kenned that there were any of us who were stronger, had purer blood," she said. "He couldnae ken that ye were stronger and more dangerous than any he had met before."

"Mayhap he did. He could have heard a few tales. Was he born at Dunmorton?"

"Aye, and he has been a hunter for the laird for a verra long time. The laird is a follower, nay a leader, but he has been doing this for a long time under the orders of another, so 'tis verra possible Angus has heard some tales of your clan."

She stopped walking when they reached the big heavy doors to the great hall. There were a lot of strangers awaiting her inside the hall, people who did not know her but were tied to her by blood. Una was suddenly terrified that she would do something that would make them all wish she had remained lost. Then

Raibeart pulled her into his arms and kissed her, making all her fears burn away before the rush of desire his kisses always caused.

"Ye will be fine, love," he said, pulling back and returning her arm to its place, locked with his. "We need ones like you. Our blood is thin and old. We need fresh blood to survive. Now, take a deep breath, let it out slowly, and come and meet your kinsmen."

Chapter Eight

"Eight?"

Una looked at the laird, Cathal MacNachton, wondering how a man could put such fury behind one small word. He was a very handsome man who looked to be in his thirties, his much smaller blond wife a few years younger. Bridget was obviously the laird's Outsider bride. As Efrica was Jankyn's, she thought, casting a quick glance toward the couple who were both so gracefully beautiful they made her feel like a cow.

"Aye," replied Raibeart. "There are eight Lost Ones at Dunmorton. Four women, two youths, and two bairns."

"Bairns? He is holding bairns prisoner?" Cathal hissed.

"Two wee lassies named Joan and Alma. He keeps them in cages in his dungeon."

Raibeart nearly grinned when every MacNachton in the great hall growled in fury. He glanced at Una and had to swallow a laugh. She was not afraid but she was certainly surprised. He had wanted her to see that anger, to see that proof that the MacNachtons would truly rescue her friends. Raibeart knew she had not fully cast aside her doubts about their readiness to help her. This show of MacNachton rage should be enough to show her that his clan was not only ready, but also eager. He had eked out the tale of their meeting and what she needed in a way guaranteed to feed that anger.

"Why?" asked Bridget. "It saddens me to even say it, but usually these men just kill the Lost Ones, or any MacNachton they get their hands on. Why has he caged these?"

"It appears this laird is mad, milady," Raibeart answered. "And, by a stroke of luck, a bad one for us, the mon swallowed the blood of a woman named Allana when he fought with her, trying to force her into his bed. The wounds she had dealt him healed quickly and it gave him an idea." He nodded when both Bridget and Efrica paled. "It didnae take many potions made from her blood for him to see that he was right, that the blood made him healthier and stronger. So he captured more Lost Ones for their blood. He now shares his potions with five chosen men, his personal guard."

"E'en the bairns?" Bridget whispered.

"Aye, milady," Una replied, "and 'tis the wee ones I am most afraid for."

"And I thought the one who held my son for such a thing was but an aberration."

"This has happened before?"

"Once. It was by men who hadnae planned on taking a prisoner for his blood. They were but testing our strengths and weaknesses."

"This madmon doesnae care about that. He used to hand the ones he caught over to some other laird, but he wanted Allana first. He and his men are nay very careful in what they take, either. I told the fool he would kill us if he wasnae more careful, that he could nay keep us starving and bleed us for long before we started dying. He just said there were more of us."

"We will leave as soon as the sun sets," said Cathal. "That madmon and his guard must be silenced and our kin released."

The cheer from the others in the room was so loud Una nearly covered her ears. She noticed that the other women looked inclined to do so as well. Nevertheless, it warmed her heart. These people wanted her and the others, wanted to save them and give them a home. She quickly took a drink of cider to quell the urge to cry. When Raibeart slipped his hand over hers, she clung to it.

"And, now, Una Dunn," the laird said and fixed his golden brown stare on her, "we need ye to tell us every little thing ye ken about Dunmorton and its people. This laird not only harms our kinsmen and women, he now kens a secret about our blood that must never reach the ears of others."

Una nodded. "I ken it. When I realized what he was doing, I kenned it could mean doom for anyone who was like the others and me. The superstitious and the hunters are danger enough but can be fought and watched for. If people thought our blood could heal all ills or make them more powerful, every mon who heard of it would be hunting us down. They would fight each other for the chance."

"Exactly. Are ye certain Dunmorton's laird isnae the head of this snake?"

"I am certain. He speaks of the other one, has sent others he has captured straight to the mon. Now he doesnae trust him and doesnae send him anyone. He thinks the laird who has been ordering him about has been keeping the secret of the blood all to himself."

Cathal nodded. "That is quite possible. 'Tis disappointing that we have yet to find the one who leads these fools. The few we have e'er spoken to ere they died had only kenned the mon who leads them as The Laird. Nay verra helpful. With the escape of this mon Angus, there is a chance the laird will be warned of our coming."

"Mayhap, but I dinnae truly think so."

"Why not?"

"Because he kens we are all orphaned or unwanted. He will think that, because ye didnae take us in years ago, ye certainly are nay going to come rushing into a battle to save us."

"Ye dinnae think Angus will tell him about Raibeart saving you?"

"Och, aye, he will, but that was mere chance and Angus ne'er saw Raibeart, um, acting like a Pureblood." She looked at Raibeart. "Ye said he was gone by the time ye started to fight with his men, aye?"

Raibeart nodded. "He fled the moment he realized I was at a place where I could call for help and get it. At best, he may think I am like you. Howbeit, that may be something he rushes to tell his laird, so I think he will need silencing as weel. If he paused in his retreat for e'en a moment, he would have seen the others come to my aid." Raibeart shrugged. "He is the leader of that pack of hunters, though."

"Reason enough to kill him," said Jankyn.

"Ye are going, arenae ye?" said Efrica, looking from her husband to the laird and back again.

"Aye," Jankyn and Cathal said together.

Bridget sighed and stood up, revealing a well-rounded belly. "Come along, Effie. We shall need to leave word concerning the supplies they will need for the journey ere we seek our beds."

Cathal stood and kissed Bridget's cheek. "Dinnae stay awake for too long, love. Ye need your rest."

Una watched the two women leave, Efrica's shape revealing that she, too, was carrying a child. Her womb clenched in a spasm of jealousy, but she shook it aside. It was foolish and now was not the time to think on her own future. Eight people were suffering. She turned her attention back to the rescue plan, ready to answer all the questions the MacNachtons might have. Una also grabbed the chance to make it clear that she was going with them. Reminding the men that none of the prisoners knew them finally won her that argument.

She was trying to fight a yawn only an hour later, and Raibeart gently urged her to go to bed. Una politely excused herself and retreated to the room she had been given. A maid appeared to help her, and within a very short time, she was in a fine linen night shift, washed, her hair braided, and curled up beneath warm blankets on a fine feather-stuffed mattress. Her last clear thought was to wonder if Raibeart would be joining her in this bed or if, now that he was back with his family, he would step away from her. She was so tired that even the hurt that thought caused was not enough to keep her awake.

Raibeart took a drink of wine, knowing both Jankyn and Cathal were watching him closely. He sighed, put his goblet down, and answered the question he could read on their faces. "Aye, she is mine."

"I didnae see the mark on her," said Cathal.

"Watching how the rest of ye struggled with your women, ones nay born to this life, I decided to wait and talk to her first. It wasnae easy, for the beast in me is demanding I mark her mine, but kenning that she is a lass who needs to choose, I have held back."

Cathal nodded. "Aye, she has suffered and nay only at the hands of that madmon who kept her in a cage. He treated the women as his own wee clutch of lemans, didnae he?"

"He did, but he didnae get to her. She said she feared her. I suspicion she could look him in the eye, and even though she is three steps away from being a Pureblood, the MacNachton blood runs strong in her. I would have recognized her as a Lost One the moment I saw her except for that fair hair. She fought like one." He looked at Cathal. "She isnae the Outsider bride ye were wanting for me, though."

"Wheesht, it doesnae matter. She is still new blood. She is also more proof that it might be impossible to breed out all that makes us MacNachtons. I accepted that long ago. She doesnae ken all the secrets of our blood though, does she?"

"Nay, although I am thinking that mad laird does." He told Cathal what the man had said about outliving his sons.

"Have ye told her how old ye are?"

"Nay. 'Tis another thing I thought I had best be cautious about."

Jankyn grinned. "Aye, old mon. Best step carefully around that hard truth."

Raibeart looked at Jankyn. "Ye are nay so much younger than I, but I think, after a wee shock, she will accept it. After all, we now ken that she can stay young, too, and she has no reluctance about her small need for blood."

"I wish ye luck," said Cathal. "Ye are already lucky in that she was nay raped and she is accepting of what ye, what all of us, are. I meant to ask ye if all the other lasses were treated as harshly."

"Aye, but nay too often. Allana, the first he grabbed, learned that the mon needs a lass to be afraid and to fight to make him a mon. Two of the others didnae or couldnae heed her advice to not fight the bastard and did suffer some. Another, called Madeleine, can swoon whene'er she wants, so she has escaped that cruelty. None of them can escape the cages, the lack of food and water, or being bleed, though."

"We will free them. Get some rest, Raibeart."

As he climbed the narrow stone steps, Raibeart knew he should leave Una alone and retire to his own bedchamber down in the caves. He did not have the willpower to be so discreet, however. In his mind and heart, in his very soul, she was already his. What he needed was for her to accept him in the same way. Despite the fact that she had gifted him with her innocence, he could not be certain she cared for him as he needed her to.

It was a bad time for this, he decided as he slipped into the bedchamber she had been given. There was no time to woo her gently, no time for slowly telling her the full truth about the Mac-Nachtons. One had to ease into such revelations and be prepared to stand firm through the storm that could result. Instead, they would both be riding toward Dunmorton as soon as the sun set.

When he climbed into bed beside her, she softly murmured his name and curled up in his arms. Raibeart did not want her to go back to Dunmorton. The journey and the freeing of the prisoners would be dangerous. She had lived with enough danger in her life. Yet she had argued the need for her presence with reasons that could not be denied. She knew the way in, knew where to look for the guards, and knew where the laird was within the keep itself. Easy things to tell him, but better if showed by the knowledgeable one when they actually got to Dunmorton.

It was her reminder that they were after rescuing eight people, four women, two youths, and two bairns, all whom had been gravely abused by their captors, captors who were all men, that had really won her place in the rescue, however. The quickest way to calm the prisoners and herd them out was to have a person they trusted do it. He would just have to make certain that she was well protected every step of the way.

"Raibeart?"

He kissed her on the forehead. "Aye. Who did ye think it was?"

"I wasnae sure if they had put me in your bedchamber or nay," Una said as she stroked his chest, enjoying the feel of all that taut, warm skin beneath her hand.

" 'Tis nay my bedchamber, but I was told where they had put ye."

"How presumptuous of the maid."

"Actually it was the laird." He grinned when she laughed, her warm breath caressing his chest.

"I should be humiliated." She decided she was too tired to care what others thought. "Does he think I am your leman?"

"Nay, he just kenned that we were lovers."

"There is a difference?"

"Aye, of course there is, but dinnae expect me to explain it now or my tongue will get so tied up in knots I willnae be able to kiss you."

She lifted her head to smile at him. "Is that what ye plan to do? Kiss me?"

"That and mayhap a wee bit more."

"Och, nay, 'tis ne'er a wee bit."

Raibeart was still laughing when he kissed her.

* * *

"Raibeart?" Una called as she began to recover from the passion they had just shared.

Sated and weary, Raibeart managed to mutter, "Aye?"

"There is something more about the blood than I ken, isnae there?"

"Now why would ye think that?" He was suddenly wide awake, wondering if he should be proud of her for being so sharp-witted or heartily curse a clever woman as other men did.

"I could hear it in the laird's voice, see it in the wariness in your kinsmen's eyes whenever it was mentioned. If I had kenned it all, no one would have had to look so wary, as if weighing every word spoken on the matter."

It annoyed him that he would have to tell her the truth so soon, but he could not try to talk her away from the truth. She would soon guess what he had done and see it as lying. He had won her trust and it was precious to him. He would not destroy it because he was too great a coward to face her reaction to the truth.

"There *is* something else our blood can do for people," he said, watching her very carefully. "What it does for us is to help us live for a verra long time. The laird's wife is the one who realized that it could help our mates live as long as we do. Something ye told me the laird said makes me think he suspects it, too."

For a moment she just stared at him, and then Una slowly sat up, clutching the blanket to her chest. "Live a long time? I suspicion that since it makes ye healthier and stronger than most that it would make ye live longer, but that isnae really what ye mean, is it?"

"Nay. How long do ye think the laird and his wife have been wed?"

"I dinnae ken. A few years. Five?"

"Eight and thirty."

She blinked. "Dinnae be ridiculous. She is my age, mayhap a wee bit older, and she is carrying a bairn."

"Eight and thirty years. We live a verra, verra long time, Una."

"But, if they have been married for so long, she should be past the age where she can carry a bairn."

"Una." He grasped her by her upper arms and gave her a little shake. "Ne'er mind that."

"How old are you?"

Raibeart winced, wishing she had not asked that question but, now that he had begun this, he had to finish it. "One hundred and five."

"Ye tease me," she whispered, but something in his eyes told her that he was telling her the truth. "Nay. Ye would be long dead and buried."

"Nay, Una, I wouldnae. To some of the Purebloods in the great hall tonight I am nay but a bairn."

"So anyone who makes a potion of your blood could live, weel, forever?"

"We are nay sure how long we can live. 'Tis a verra long time, but if a mate is lost or a time comes when one of us feels the long years like a weight upon his shoulders, he will do whate'er is necessary to die without committing the sin of dying by his own hand. Aye, 'tis a miraculous gift but it can also be a curse."

She thought about that for a moment as she battled her fear and could see the truth of it so clearly. Long, unending years of life, especially if there was no one to share it with, could be a torture. The last of her fear faded as she began to realize that Raibeart would be around for a very long time. Her happiness over that died abruptly as she thought on what else such a strange gift meant. If anyone discovered that secret, the MacNachtons would become a besieged people, everyone eager to bleed them dry. It was a chilling thought and she flung her arms around him.

"That madmon has guessed the truth," she said.

"I think he suspects, aye." He stroked her back, wondering if it was the fact that MacNachtons could live so long or that Dunmorton may have guessed the truth that was making her tremble. "That is why he and the ones he keeps close have to die."

"Aye, but are ye sure a mon as ancient as ye can do it?"

Raibeart stared at the top of her head for a moment in shock and then laughed, both with humor and a heady relief, as he pushed her onto her back. "Wretch. Ancient, am I?"

" 'Tis naught to fret over, Raibeart. Ye do weel enough for one of your great age."

"Weel enough? I intend to show ye that I can do a great deal better than just *weel enough*."

And he did.

Chapter Nine

"'Tis such an ordinary place," murmured Raibeart as he looked at Dunmorton. "Looking at it, ye would ne'er think that some madmon is holding eight innocent people in cages set in the dungeon and is taking their blood to make potions."

Una looked at him and then returned her gaze to the keep. It chilled her to even look at the place. She was outside, lying on the ground beside Raibeart, with a dozen armed MacNachtons but a few feet away, and yet she was still suffering the bitter taste of fear. It was going to take a long time to recover from what had been done to her at Dunmorton, and she had not suffered as badly as some of the others.

"My friends are going to need a long time to heal from this," she whispered and reached out to clasp Raibeart's hand.

"They will have it," he promised. "They will be kept safe. Ready?"

"Aye." She studied the walls for another moment. "If Angus has returned already, then the laird didnae consider anything the mon said worthy of changing his guard in any way. 'Tis just as it was when I left here."

"Cathal and Jankyn will already ken the pace of the watch so that we can cross the open space unseen," Raibeart said as they both wriggled backward until they could stand up without being seen by the guards on the walls. "We dinnae want to spill too much blood. 'Tis just the ones who . . ." He frowned when she pressed her fingers against his lips.

"Ye dinnae need to explain, Raibeart. 'Tis a matter of survival. Nay more, nay less."

He wanted to kiss her and almost pulled her into his arms when they stood up. She understood what needed to be done, and it was a great weight off his heart. He doubted a day went by that there was not a battle somewhere, man against man, army against army. This fight would not be with only fists or swords but with stealth, teeth, and claws, as well. Speed and silence were important if they were to keep to the plan of killing only those who had committed crimes against his clan or knew the secrets of MacNachton blood. If all went as planned, it would be no battle such as the troubadours sung of but predators taking down a threat to their pack with swift savagery, and he had feared that she would be appalled. Instead there was a look on Una's face that told she not only understood; she would join them if necessary.

"Ye are here only to soothe and free the prisoners," he said as they rejoined the others.

Una smiled with such sweet innocence Raibeart was immediately suspicious. He had no time to repeat his command or get her to promise to stay far away from the fighting, however. Jankyn asked her about the guards, and moments later, everyone but the two youngest left to watch the horses was headed toward the tunnel entrance near the burn.

Raibeart, Una, and two MacNachtons were the first to cross the open land, slip down the rocky bank of the burn, and enter the tunnel. They had not gone far when he heard others behind them and knew they would have enough men to take down the guards. By the time they reached the opening into the dungeon, Raibeart had decided that he hated tunnels, especially ones so cluttered with debris he had been expecting the roof of the tunnel to collapse on top of them the whole way along.

"They have increased the guard down here," Una whispered so softly only a MacNachton could hear her. "The side of one of the cages will hide ye as ye step out of here. Stay close to the wall to the left and the old ale barrels will then hide you. There are also abundant shadows in the dungeon."

One by one, the men crept out of the tunnel while Raibeart stayed next to her. "Ye stay here until I call for you."

The moment the last of the other men slipped away, Una gave him a quick hard kiss. "Thank ye for wishing me to be safe, but that willnae work. Remember, two of the prisoners are wee lassies that can make a lot of noise if they are frightened. So, too, are there women who may think they are about to be stolen away and taken to an even worse fate. I will be careful and stay near the cages, but I must let them see me so that they dinnae set up a cry that brings others rushing down here. Toss the keys to me when ye get them."

He cursed softly, having no good argument to weaken the truth of her words, so he followed the other men. When Cathal and Jankyn looked to him for the signal to proceed, he held up his hand. When he saw Una glide through the shadows and reach the children's cage, he signaled the attack with one sharp movement of his hand.

The MacNachtons attacked the guards, and Una hastily stepped out of the shadows. She noticed no one was surprised to see her, their ability to see in the dark as keen as hers. Little Joan and Alma huddled at the back of their cage closest to her.

"Dinnae fear," she said, loud enough for the prisoners to hear her but not so loud that it would attract the attention of one of the guards. "These men are here to free you."

"And from what I can see, that will happen verra soon," said Allana as she watched Jankyn hurl a guard against the wall, picking the man up and throwing him as if he weighed nothing. "*Jesu*, they are like us," she whispered in shock a heartbeat later as she watched Cathal sink his fangs into another guard's throat.

"Aye," said Una. "There is so much I need to tell you."

"Una," Raibeart called as he took a ring of keys off a dead guard's body. "Catch."

She easily caught the keys tossed her way. It was not until she turned to start unlocking the cages that she realized one was empty. Una feared she had returned too late to save all of them.

"Where is Madeleine?" she asked as she opened Allana's cage and moved on to the next one.

"The laird's fools took her away," replied Nan as she darted out of her cage as if she feared she could lose the chance to escape if she moved too slowly. "She swooned as she always does, but I heard one of them say it didnae matter this time, that Angus would enjoy his reward whether she was awake or nay. They believed that would be a fine entertainment."

"He is giving Madeleine to Angus? But, he ne'er shares the women."

"I dinnae think he sees it as such a great gift he is giving Angus."

Una let the little girls out last and they both rushed to wrap their arms around her legs and bury their faces in her skirts. The three women stood together, watching the MacNachtons closely. The two youths, Bartram and Colla, flanked the women. They looked prepared to protect the women, but the faint tremor in their hands revealed their fear. Una did not blame them for being afraid, for the MacNachtons had quickly and savagely killed all eight guards, and she did not see that a single MacNachton had been harmed in the doing of it.

"These are the allies we needed," Una said. "They are the MacNachtons and 'tis their blood in us that makes us what we are. They are going to take us to Cambrun where we will be safe among our own."

Allana studied her for a moment. "Ye certainly look much healthier than ye did when ye left here."

Raibeart stepped up to Una. "There are only three women. Are we too late to save them all then?"

"Nay, they have taken Madeleine to the laird's chambers," replied Una. "It appears that Angus has returned, and whatever he told the laird pleased the madmon enough to reward him. Angus gets to have Madeleine, awake or no." She nodded in approval when all the men's faces hardened with fury and then told them how to get to the laird's rooms.

"Einar, I want you, Skelli, Erik, Ranald, and Filib to get these people out and to the horses," Cathal ordered and then he looked at the cages, his rage at the sight of them easy to see. "Put the guards' bodies in the cages. Let them rot there. The rest of ye come with me." He strode away, Raibeart and the others close at his heels.

Una handed Einar the keys before standing back with her friends as the MacNachtons tossed the bodies of the guards into the cages and locked them. She pushed aside the pang of guilt that tried to settle into her heart. The guards had not been terribly cruel, but they had not been kind, either. They had allied with the laird in imprisoning innocents and ignoring the abuses heaped upon them. She suspected they had not been entirely ignorant of what the laird was doing to the women and children he held. When she saw Einar pocket the keys, she knew the man intended to see that his laird got exactly what he wanted. The guards would rot where they were.

As Einar and the other men helped her get her friends out through the tunnel, Una fought the urge to run back to be with Raibeart. She knew, if only from watching the MacNachtons take down the guards, that the men were all capable of taking care of themselves. It did not stop her from worrying about Raibeart, however. She silently prayed that he would return to her unharmed.

Raibeart was surprised at the lack of a guard as they made their way to the laird's rooms. Even though they were approaching through the man's escape route, there should have been someone on guard. The ease with which they were advancing on their prey made him wary. When he stood by Cathal outside the door that would take them into the laird's rooms, he pushed aside that unease and fixed his mind on the battle to come.

"There is a spy hole," said Cathal in the low whisper that only his men could hear. "Looks to be a tapestry over the door with the hole cut through it as weel. Why would he put one into his own chambers?"

"Una said this room used to be his wife's bedchamber," Raibeart reminded him.

"Ah, of course." Cathal made use of the spy hole. "The woman is on the bed and all the men are looking at her or that red-headed fool, but none are right at the bedside. Seven men so that bastard Angus is there. They are all armed but their backs are to us." He moved back a little and began to cautiously open the door. "Let us pray no one sees the tapestry move outward. Slip in if ye can but attack immediately if someone sees you."

Sword in hand, Raibeart was eager to cut these men down and not just because of the helpless woman on the bed, one who had MacNachton blood in her veins. When he had seen the cages Una and the others had been held in, seen the two frightened children huddled inside one, rage had nearly blinded him. The killing of the guards had not been enough. He wanted to kill the man who had put those innocents in a cage and fed off them.

The men in the room were so intent upon the woman, eagerly awaiting her rape, they never saw the MacNachtons slip through the door and into the shadows. Raibeart looked at Angus as he moved toward the man. Angus's hard face was flushed with lust, but he was obviously hesitant to take the woman in front of six leering men. It would not be long, however, before the crude taunts of the others pushed the man to act, and Raibeart tensed, ready to stop him if he put one hand on the woman.

Then Angus tensed and looked around. Raibeart silently cursed. Una had said that the man was a skilled hunter. Raibeart should have anticipated that Angus could scent the death that was encircling them all. He moved quickly and grabbed the man. A sharp pain in his side told Raibeart that Angus had already prepared for an attack and had armed himself. Ignoring the pain and the damp warmth of blood soaking his shirt, he smiled at Angus. The way the man paled, his eyes widening, gave Raibeart pleasure. This man was responsible for hunting down Lost Ones and sending them to their death or a living hell. Raibeart let Angus see his beast in its full feral glory and then sank his fangs into the man's neck.

Once he had drunk his fill, Raibeart snapped Angus's neck and tossed the man's body aside. A quick glance around told him that only the laird still lived with his throat caught tight in Cathal's grasp. The ones that knew the secret of MacNachton blood were all dead save for the laird, and Cathal would soon end that man's miserable life. Others at Dunmorton had undoubtedly aided in sending Lost Ones to the leader of the hunter, but although slaughtering them all had a certain appeal, Raibeart believed that the real threat of Dunmorton would die with its laird.

"To whom and to where did ye send the others ye captured?" Cathal demanded of the terrified man he held captive.

Thomas MacKay, laird of Dunmorton, no longer looked like the brutal man he had been. He was sweating, shaking, and had soiled himself. Raibeart shook his head. It was hard to believe that such a coward had done so much harm.

"I dinnae ken!" The man's voice was high and tremulous. "Ne'er met him and wasnae told anything about him."

"Then how did ye send him the ones ye captured?"

"Took the prisoners north to a wee cottage and his men came and took them away."

MacKay told Cathal every step taken, from holding the prisoners while a message was placed in that cottage to meeting the laird's men and the coin he was paid for each prisoner. The laird who had turned the hunters from a few groups of superstitious men into a true threat was very careful to keep his name and his whereabouts a deep secret. The only thing MacKay said about the man that might prove useful was the fact that every message and every prisoner was sent north of Dunmorton. Raibeart leaned against the wall, pressed his hand over his wound, and tried not to be too disappointed at the lack of information as he watched Cathal sink his fangs into the man's throat, drink his fill, and then snap MacKay's neck.

He watched the laird toss the body aside and then joined the others in looking at the unconscious woman on the bed. Raibeart hoped they decided what to do with the woman soon for his legs were trembling with a growing weakness. Although he had fed on Angus and the wound the man had inflicted before dying had ceased to bleed, Raibeart decided he had lost more blood than he had realized. Either that or Angus's blade had done more than pierce his skin, injuring something inside him that could require more blood and more time to heal. It pinched at his pride that he appeared to be the only one who had suffered a serious wound, but he told himself not to be an idiot. They had saved the Lost Ones and killed the ones who knew the secret of MacNachton blood. His wound and even his pride was a small price to pay.

Cathal moved to the side of the bed and said, "Your enemies are dead. Ye are safe now. Una and Allana sent us to get you."

Raibeart nearly laughed when the woman opened her eyes, sat up, and looked around. "Una said ye could swoon beautifully whene'er ye wanted, but I hadnae realized how verra skilled ye were at it," Raibeart said and smiled when the woman looked at him, a sharp intelligence clear to see in her light green eyes.

"Some of it was real," she said in a low, husky voice that immediately drew the interest of several of his clan. "The fool bled me and I always swoon when he does that. Cannae abide seeing my own blood." She looked him over. "Ye appear to have lost some blood yourself and so can see that observing the bleeding of others doesnae trouble me much at all."

Raibeart held up his hand when Cathal started to move toward him. "The bleeding has stopped. Lost a lot of blood, however, and I may be wounded inside. I shouldnae be feeling as weak in the knees as I do," he admitted reluctantly. "But I can get to the horses unaided."

"Ye *will* accept some help," said Cathal, and then he looked back at Madeleine. "We are here to free you and take ye to Cambrun. Ye are one of us, a MacNachton by blood. 'Tis time to meet your people."

And this one had the look of a MacNachton, Raibeart thought as they all left the bedchamber, pausing only so that Madeleine could spit on the laird's body. She was a little taller than most women, beautiful, and had long, thick black hair. He accepted a supporting hand from Jankyn as they made their way out of Dunmorton, listening to Madeleine's whispered tales of her mother's lovers. The description of the man her mother had believed was her father certainly sounded like one of his kinsmen. There was a good chance that Madeleine would find some close family at Cambrun.

His heart skipped in his chest like some untried lad's when they reached the horses and Una rushed to greet him, her worry over his wound clear to read on her face. Raibeart began to believe that she cared for him, but now was not the time to try to make certain of that. He exchanged a grin with Jankyn over her head as she helped him with Tor, and then gave himself into her care. It was nice to be fussed over by a woman now and then, he decided.

Una quickly pushed aside her fear for Raibeart as they traveled back to Cambrun. He had looked so pale and weak, his clothes soaked in blood, when she had first seen him return from Dunmorton keep that her heart had clenched in fear. Each time they stopped to shelter from the sun, however, one or more of the MacNachtons would offer him blood, and she could see him grow stronger. She stayed close by his side, uncaring that she shared his blanket in front of everyone, and the last of her fear for him faded away. He had told her that he was hard to kill and she began to believe it.

She also began to believe that her friends would find a home at Cambrun. The women were treated with a courtesy she had rarely seen. The men readily accepted the boys, and she could see Bartram and Colla growing stronger and less wary by the hour. Little Joan and Alma were in serious danger of being heartily spoiled before they even reached Cambrun, the men revealing their love for children in their every word and gesture. Her friends were safe and would be cared for. Una knew she could cease to worry about them now.

Her concern over her own place at Cambrun grew, however,

no matter how hard she tried to smother it. She was Raibeart's lover, but she ached to be so much more. Nothing he said or did gave her the confidence to think that she was or ever would be.

As they rode through the gates of Cambrun an hour before sunrise to be lavishly greeted by the rest of the clan, Una decided it was pride that held her back from reaching for that commitment she craved. She was going to have to swallow that pride and conquer her fear of being rejected. The moment everyone was settled, she was going to confront Raibeart. She loved the man and could no longer continue on as just his lover, waiting in terror for the moment he would set her aside. By the time the sun rose for a second time, she would know if she had a place in his heart, if she even had a small chance of finding one, or she would be preparing to live away from Raibeart. She could not endure the torment of uncertainty any longer.

Chapter Ten

"Those two bairns are going to be spoiled."

Raibeart grinned at Bridget. He had not seen her since they had arrived just before dawn and gone straight to their beds. He idly wondered how she could look so much more pregnant than she had when they had left. It had been less than a week.

"Aye, but I think they deserve some spoiling," he said.

"Verra true." She shivered and idly rubbed her arms. "It sickens me to think that a mon could treat two bairns as MacKay treated them. Him and his men. They didnae see two wee lassies. They saw animals, beasts they could feed on. They were no better than your wild, arrogant ancestors."

"Aye, and yet they think us evil and strive to kill us all."

"Weel, that threat is gone and we have one more small piece in the puzzle that is the leader of the hunters."

"I had hoped for more, much more. 'Tis verra clear that this leader doesnae even trust his most ardent followers."

"We will find him." She looked around, nodding slightly each time she saw one of the rescued women. "I think those women have cast aside most of their fears. They willnae remain unwed for long. Our men are nay ones to blame them for the abuse they suffered, and, once they see that, they will find themselves claimed. And our men will have the sense to be gentle with them."

" 'Tis nay what the laird wanted. They are nay Outsiders."

"Wheesht, he doesnae care. They have the mix in the blood, some more than others, so 'tis still new blood for the clan. Cathal just wants his men content. After seeing how the cat still lingers in my Callan blood, despite the many years we have diligently tried to breed it out, he kens now that it will be impossible to rid the clan of all that makes it different and feared. He even admits that he is happy about that. Enough will fade so that many of us will be able to fool the superstitious into thinking we are just like them. So, ye dinnae need to fear that he will disapprove of ye mating with Una."

"So he said and I havenae mated with her yet." Raibeart knew that was not exactly true, that he had claimed her in his heart and mind, and accepted Bridget's look of feminine disgust as well earned. "Everyone kens she is mine."

"Do they? No mark, no claim."

Raibeart frowned when Bridget pointed toward Una and he saw Einar was working his charm on her and Madeleine. He told himself that dark stirring of jealousy was unwarranted, that Einar was flirting with Madeleine not Una. Then Una laughed and lightly patted Einar's arm. He heard Bridget laugh when he growled, but he ignored her and strode toward his woman, intending to tell her quite firmly that touching other men was not allowed.

"Ye are a wee bit slow, Raibeart," said Jankyn as Raibeart started to pass by him. "No mark, no claim."

"I mean to change that soon," he said and then cursed when he saw Una walk away to go to talk to Allana.

"We are a clan without enough women for our men and it isnae easy for one of us to find a mate. Going outside of Cambrun is a risk, a deadly one. If she is yours, make it clearer than just sharing her bed. If not, stand back."

"Oh, she is mine. I have stepped carefully because she was so intent upon rescuing her friends. Once I heard why she sought aid, it was something I was also intent upon. I have told her a lot of things about the clan, but nay about the mating bite. I told her I was wooing her." He shrugged when Jankyn gave him a pitying look and shook his head. "I held myself back from giving her the bite because I also thought that she, more than many another woman, needed to choose, to be asked."

"Ah, aye, ye were right in that, but I think ye failed in letting her ken just how much ye want her to choose you."

Raibeart grimaced. "And take the chance that she doesnae wish to choose me? Nay an easy thing for a mon to do." He held up a hand when Jankyn started to speak. "I will grasp my waning courage in both hands and do it verra soon."

"I am thinking ye dinnae need as much courage as ye think." Laughing softly, Jankyn slapped Raibeart on the back and walked away.

Was Jankyn right? Raibeart wondered as he watched Una talk with Allana. It did not matter if the man was, he decided. Until he heard Una tell him that she was his, the doubts would remain. Since she did not appear inclined to speak from her heart, then he would have to take the first step. She had not shied away from any of the truth about what the MacNachtons were. She shared a hot, wild passion with him. She had fussed over him when he had been wounded. Raibeart took comfort in those signs of caring as he planned the best way to get her alone.

"Your mon is looking at ye again."

Una frowned at Allana and then peeked over her shoulder. Raibeart was talking with the laird. It had troubled her a bit that he had not stayed at her side, but she had busied herself with making certain all of her friends were content.

"He isnae," she said. "He is talking to his laird."

"Our laird now."

There was a steely conviction in Allana's voice. "Ye have decided that ye will stay here, become part of the clan?"

"Aye, and I am a part now. Have the blood, dinnae I? But, it isnae just that. I feel safe, as safe as one of us probably can ever feel. I have spent my whole life being in fear, being different enough to draw the dangerous attention of the superstitious and the so verra righteous. I am tired of it. I belong here, with these people. I dinnae have to come up with some tale for why I shy away from the noonday sun or hide that dark hunger that comes o'er me now and then." She suddenly grinned. "And there are some verra handsome men here."

Una smiled back but then asked quietly, "And ye think ye could be with a mon?"

"Och, aye. Nan, Mora, and I all talked it over, and we think we can get over what was done. It wasnae done for long, was it? Once that fool failed in the bedding of one of us, he didnae want to see us in his bed again. Our good fortune was that he was a greedy bastard and didnae want to share us, either. And it was just a way to beat us, wasnae it? To shame us and make us cower.

The best way to see that that bastard failed in that is to get on with our lives."

"True, 'tis just that it is such a deeply personal wound."

" 'Tis, but it isnae mortal. Ye planning on getting on with your life, too, or are ye just going to leave that bonnie big mon of yours wondering?"

"He is bonnie, but he isnae really mine." She frowned when Allana made a soft sound of disgust. "Weel, he isnae. He hasnae said he is."

"Una, men dinnae always say what they feel. 'Tisnae monly, is it? He hasnae e'en looked at the rest of us. He watches ye as if he is afraid ye will disappear. And, if that isnae enough to make ye ken what ye could have, ye didnae see his face when ye were laughing with that bonnie Einar. Someone always has to take the first step and, when it comes to matters of the heart, that someone is usually the woman." Allana patted Una's arm. "Ye love him. Let that be the source of the courage ye need."

Una was still thinking over what Allana had said as she undressed for bed. All her friends were free and obviously settling in at Cambrun. The women were already being courted. The little girls had found an aunt who wept with joy. Both the boys had found relatives as well. No one was certain yet who she might be related to, but Jankyn had promised that he was looking before slyly assuring her that he knew for certain she was not related to Raibeart.

"And I dinnae think I want to ken why he had searched out that fact so quickly," she muttered as she crawled into bed.

On her back with her arms crossed beneath her head, Una wondered if Raibeart would come to her. He had crawled into bed with her when they had sought their rest after rescuing the others, but she was not certain if that was just habit born of their time together, or because he really wanted to be with her, even if all they did was go to sleep. She blushed as she suddenly recalled how very wide awake he had been when the sun had set.

Passion was not love. Innocent though she had been before she had met Raibeart, even she knew that. He had saved her and helped her save her friends, but he was a knight and that was what they were supposed to do. She and her friends were also of his clan, carrying MacNachton blood in their veins. He was always touching her, but that, too, could have its roots in fickle passion. The only thing she had to cling to as a hope that she might be more to him than a lover was that he had said he was wooing her.

Una was just deciding that she would give herself an aching head if she kept trying to understand his every gesture and word when Raibeart walked into the room. She watched as he moved around the bedchamber as if it was his when she knew it was not. He washed up, shed his clothes, and climbed into bed with her as if he had every right. Since they were not married, he did not, not even if he had been her lover.

"Is something wrong, Una?" Raibeart asked as he propped himself up on his elbow and looked down at her frowning face.

Raibeart decided that Una did not look like a woman ready to be made love to. Nor a woman who was in the mood to accept his fumbling declarations of love. She looked like she wanted to hit him.

"I am thinking that ye act as if ye belong here when I ken that ye have your chambers down in the caves," she said.

"I belong here because ye are here."

That quiet statement, Raibeart's rough voice full of emotion as he spoke, made her anger flee. It was no declaration of how he felt, but it was enough to touch her heart. He did belong at her side. What she needed to know was just how long he intended to stay there. Una did not want to push him to say things he did not feel but began to think she had a right to know what plans he had for her.

"I cannae be a leman, Raibeart," she said. "I cannae bear to shame myself like that before my friends."

He placed his hand on the side of her cheek and brushed a kiss over her mouth. "Ye are far more than that, lass, and there is no shame in our being together."

She was about to argue that when he kissed her. For a moment, she tried to hold back the desire that his kiss always stirred within her. They needed to talk. She was ready to take the chance to speak of what was between them, to try and grasp for more than passion from him despite knowing how it would tear her heart out if he proved to feel no more than desire and liking for her. Then he unlaced her night shift and slid his big warm hand over her bared breast. Una wrapped her arms around his neck and decided they could talk afterward.

The way he stroked her body, touching her as if she were some precious piece of glass, made Una's passion run even hotter. She caressed his back as he kissed his way to her breasts, and arched in delight when the heat of his mouth encircled the aching tip of one while his skilled fingers teased the other until she burned. This time, when he kissed his way down her stomach and began to make love to her with his mouth, she did not flinch, but immediately opened herself to his intimate caresses. Una wanted to try to make him see what was within her heart by completely surrendering herself to the passion they shared.

Lost in the wildness of what he could make her feel, it took Una a minute to realize that, although he had joined their bodies, he was not moving. She looked up at his face, reaching up to stroke the high color on his cheekbones with her fingertips. He looked so fierce and determined, she thought as she slowly wrapped her legs around his waist and, using her heels against his buttocks, tried to make him move.

"Una, I said I was wooing ye," he began.

"Ye wish to talk about this now?"

"I but wish ye to ken that I wooed ye so that ye would have a choice, me or freedom to go and find another."

Beginning to guess what he was working himself up to say, Una nearly grinned at the way he growled out those last six words. Raibeart did not want to let her go and find another. In fact, if she did try, that *another* could be in real danger. The possessiveness beneath his words thrilled her.

"I dinnae want another, Raibeart."

"Good, because tonight I mean to mark ye as mine."

"Mark me?"

"Aye. I am going to give ye what we call the mating bite. It doesnae fade away like the others I have given ye. We dinnae ken why, but once given, it stays and is a sign all MacNachtons can read."

"One that says *mine?*" Una wondered if she ought to tell him he was sweating rather a lot and then just smiled at him. "How intriguing."

"I want to give ye the chance to say aye or nay," he said between gritted teeth, his body screaming for him to move, to give it the release it needed.

"How sweet. Aye."

"Una . . ." He choked when he felt her inner muscles squeeze him like a hot fist. "Jesu, woman," he gasped. "Ye cannae do that when I am trying to talk, to tell ye that I need ye to agree because . . ."

"I just agreed," she snapped and, grabbing him by the hair, pulled his face down to hers. "Aye. Hear that? Aye." She kissed him with all the love and heated passion she felt for him.

Raibeart gave up even trying to talk and lost himself in the heat of her. Just as he felt her body tighten around his, the throb of that impending release echoing in his own body, he pushed her hair back from her neck. He was fighting to find the wit to ask one more time when his delicate woman placed a hand on the back of his neck and pushed his face against her neck. If he was not burning alive with desire, his fangs aching for a taste of her, Raibeart suspected he would have laughed.

Even as Una felt her body shudder with release, there was a sharp pain in her neck. As before, that sent her passion soaring to new heights yet; this time, it was even fiercer, even more blinding. She was so lost in her own pleasure that she only faintly heard Raibeart call out her name in a feral roar followed by the word *mine*. Una held him close to her even as the searing delight she had felt tear through her began to fade away. Nipping his ear, she whispered of her love for him.

It was not easy, but Raibeart finally found the strength to move, pleased to note that he had retained enough wit to collapse just to the side of Una and not flat on top of her. He touched his ear, the one she had whispered into, and eyed her warily. Usually the sight of her sprawled on her back, her lovely breasts rising and falling as her heavy breathing slowly eased, made him proud of himself, for it was proof that he had pleasured her well. Now he wanted her with her wits all intact so that he could ask if she had really whispered that she loved him.

He touched a kiss to her mouth, pleased when she opened her eyes and smiled at him. "Ye are mine now, Una. This mark will ne'er fade."

Una lazily lifted one hand to comb her fingers through his thick hair. "I ken it."

"Ye whispered in my ear whilst we were in paradise."

She bit back a grin for he looked very much like a small boy trying to find a way to get a special treat without bluntly demanding it. "I ken it. Wasnae sure ye would hear me with all that bellowing ye were doing, though."

He blinked and then shifted so that he was on top of her, most of his weight resting on his forearms. She was teasing him. "Say it. Say it whilst looking me in the eye and whilst I am not so lost in passion that I probably wouldnae recognize my own name."

"I love ye."

Raibeart could hear the hint of uncertainty in her voice and pulled her into his arms before rolling onto his back. In his eyes, Una was beautiful, strong, clever, and all else a perfect mate should be, but he realized she was still a little uncertain of him. She needed to know what rested in his heart as badly as he had needed to know what rested in hers.

"I love ye, too." He tensed when he saw the glint of tears in her eyes. "Nay, no crying. 'Tis what ye wanted, aye? I cannae take it back. I can ne'er take it back. Ye are mine."

"Hush, 'tis but the shine of happiness, Raibeart." She laughed softly when his body heaved from the strength of his sigh of relief.

"We are mated now, but ye can have a proper wedding, a blessing by a priest and all that."

"Ye have a priest?"

"Aye, a cousin. Do ye want me to fetch him?"

"Raibeart, this"—she touched the mark on her neck—"is enough for me, but I would like a priest's blessing. Nay for me but for the others saved from Dunmorton. A wedding between us, with a wee celebration, will be perfect for giving them that last feeling of being home, I think."

"Aye, ye are right and it will be done." He reached up to stroke her cheek, idly wondering what he had done right to deserve such a gift. "Are ye sure, Una? Are ye verra sure?"

"Verra sure."

"I think I loved ye from the moment I saw ye. It would have been wiser to find a way around the trouble I saw that night, but I couldnae. Told myself it would be a good thing to do before I had my rest, but I could never have ridden away from you. I accepted that ye would be mine in the cave and ne'er wavered."

"I think I loved ye from that day as weel. I didnae run away, did I?"

He thought of all she had suffered and suddenly realized that she was right. She should have tried to escape him, especially since she had just come from being chased down by five men. He had been a stranger until they had realized they were alike, a stranger she had the wit to know could have snapped her neck in a heartbeat, but she had stayed.

"It was fate," he murmured.

"I believe it was." She kissed him. "I stayed and never thought to do anything else."

"And now ye are mine."

"As ye are mine."

"Forever?"

"And a day." He kissed her when she laughed, thinking that he was a very lucky man to have claimed that music for his own.

A Knight Beyond Black

Black

Jackie Ivie

Chapter One

She felt him before she saw him. As if the ballroom suddenly went off-kilter without warning. Tira stumbled, feeling oddly light-headed.

"Forgive my step, Miss Coombs. I over-rotate at times."

Her partner's words had a slight edge to them. Everything Sir Robert Graves said displayed a distaste of the eldest Coxton-Coombs sister. He preferred Ophelia. Most men did, for no visible reason. The elder sister was renowned for her beauty, although she'd never have Ophelia's blond curls and blue eyes. Perhaps it was the russet shade in her warm brown locks they didn't find attractive. It might be the glint of amusement in her green-tinged eyes. Perhaps it was the hint of lines about those eyes further evidencing her age; maybe a perceived lack of grace.

She was flirting with spinsterhood, but tonight she was determined not to think of it. But flirting wasn't even accurate. She was so close she was standing at the precipice and looking right over it. Speaking of looking over . . .

Tira looked across and down at Sir Robert Graves and felt the slide of curls along her shoulder with the move. He didn't meet her eyes, but he rarely did. It drew attention to his lack of stature, showing the balding pate, weak chin, colorless eyes. That was before the thin shoulders, white, limp hands, and smallish . . . Tira stopped. There wasn't much about Sir Graves to eulogize. But she guessed he probably most disliked her because his mother favored an heiress and made no secret of how few would accept his suit, should he offer it. Tira shook off the dreary thought again. Time enough for that later.

After this incredibly horrid ball.

"Could we . . . sit now, Sir Graves?"

He didn't finish the rotation before turning, unaware of Tira's quick glance toward the entry doors where she'd felt something or someone. She'd actually hoped it might be the man portended by Christa; a man of such presence he'd alter her entire world. It was against all reason and advice to listen to her maid, and now it felt foolish as well. Christa claimed to be fey. Tira swallowed disappointment at the empty portal designed by Robert Adams.

Tira tightened her lips, looked back, and froze. Everywhere. Even her toes in the too-tight slippers designed more for elegance than comfort.

"I've come for our dance."

It was a man: large, well bulked, and Scot. Even without the brogue attached to his speech, she'd have known. He was full Highlander and not averse to showing it. Dressed in attire that looked barbaric and harsh: a knee-grazing kilt, tasseled socks, a plaid sash scoring what looked to be a massive chest, a black velvet jacket, lace-touched jabot, silver canteen hanging at his hip, while what could only be a sword hilt could be glimpsed over his shoulder.

A sword? In Coombs Court ballroom?

Tira cracked open her fan and started fluttering with it. They'd never allow a weapon at this ball. But she instantly knew no one would stop it. The newcomer defied argument. He looked readied for trouble and sure of victory. She'd never seen anyone so completely sure of himself. Masculine. Immense. Brawny. Impressive.

Exactly as Christa foretold.

Reaction was happening as musicians and dancers limped to a halt, stared, and whispered. Tira sensed it. She didn't hear it. Her heart was giving her issue with how it moved to clog her throat and then fill her ears. If her jaw hadn't loosed, opening her lips, she'd have had trouble breathing.

There was more. And it was worse. This man was handsome, easily eclipsing those she'd seen or imagined. His features went right into the realm of beautiful; enough to cause swooning. Lengthy dark hair was pulled back, highlighting a face made for sculpting. She'd never seen such a man. Her knees trembled, pings of sensation sent moisture to her hairline, and her lips opened even more. And he knew it. All of it. It was in the coal dark eyes meeting hers over the top of everyone's head. That was another thing about him. The newcomer dwarfed her. He did the same to everyone, including the trio of clansmen at both sides of him.

"I—"

Her voice ended. She sounded breathless. Anticipatory. She should argue. Demure. Tira fluttered the fan faster, lifting wisps of hair from her forehead. She hadn't many names on her dance card, but for certain his wasn't one of them.

" 'Tis time we met. This night."

"To-to-tonight?"

"Are you na' a score and one on the morrow?"

Tira's lips snapped shut with the same motion she used on the fan, releasing it to dangle from the cord about her wrist. Of course she was twenty-one tomorrow. Everyone in the household worried over it with the possible exception of her father. And he'd just announced it to her lone suitor, Robert Graves.

"Sir Graves." The Highlander nodded toward Robert, as if reading her thoughts.

"Your Grace."

Sir Robert released her hand and left. Tira didn't see it. She couldn't move her eyes as the newcomer put out an arm, tipped his chin, and favored her with a pulse-stopping look. That's exactly what happened, too. Her heart dove right to the pit of her belly to pound from there, sending a flush to every single portion of her.

"You're . . . a duke?"

"It matters?"

He stepped closer, taking up space, teasing her nose with male scent before he took the hand Sir Robert released. It must be cold outside for the temperature of his skin chilled. But that was ridiculous. She was nearly overcome with heat.

"No," she replied, since he seemed immobile, awaiting it.

"Verra good. Come. We'll dance."

There wasn't any music, but that changed as if by magic. The moment he moved with her, strains filled the room: lilting, haunting, and sweet.

They played a waltz. Tira got pulled effortlessly but stopped before connecting with him. It didn't matter. Her breasts sensed him and reacted, both nipples tightened from a rivulet of shivers she couldn't stop. All of it totally foreign.

His thumb outlined her knuckles, running along ridges of the hand he'd captured. That sensation was heightened by the texture of his velvet jacket on her other digits. She barely touched him and it still overwhelmed her. He rotated easily and gracefully while her knees weakened. She stumbled. The arm at her back tightened, pulling her right into him, where an immediate loss of air collided with a total impression of flesh-covered iron. She really did risk swooning. Her knees sagged. Her vision dimmed. This was much worse than Christa warned.

And much better.

"I'm told you're christened Tira?"

His rumble of voice went through her. Tira blinked once. Again. And as many times as it took to get the man's shirt back into focus and her limbs from their disembodied state.

"Pardon?"

" 'Tis Gaelic. And proper."

"Oh no. None of this is proper." Tira glanced up, touching her chin to the white lace at his throat. It was insane. They hadn't even been introduced.

"Iain."

"Iain?"

"Iain Duncan Evan James Alexander MacAvee. The fourth."

He was reading her mind again. Tira stiffened and spoke her next words to his upper chest. "This won't do. Not at all, and I'll thank you to—"

He interrupted her with more rumble of voice, completely ignoring her protest. And that wasn't at all normal. Or acceptable.

"There's more that I've nae desire to state. Unless you require it."

"I don't require a thing."

"I've titles to add. The newest being Duke of MacAvee. Afore that, Earl of Glencairn and Blannock, chieftain of Clans Avee, MacGruder, and two other clans. I doona' wish to bore you with them at present. Mayhap later. After another dance."

Another? Oh no. And another no. And a third and fourth one as well. It would create gossip and speculation, and those Tira couldn't afford. Not with imminent spinsterhood facing her. She moved her gaze, met his, and everything on her reacted with a jerk into the band of arm behind her. She stumbled again, and this time she got lifted. And then held. Close. She couldn't gain breath . . . not with his cheeks narrowed, putting a kissable shape to his lips, and she didn't even know what that would look like. Her body had the weight of a feather, the consistency of a cloud, and the stamina of a puff of air.

"You dance verra strange, lass."

The voice rumbled through her again. She couldn't miss it, not with her breasts crushed against him. If anyone noted how closely he held her, Tira would hide in embarrassment. What was she thinking? Of course they noticed! It wasn't possible not to.

"You . . . need to set me . . . down. Now."

As an order, her whisper didn't have much impact. As inducement, it seemed to work perfectly. Tira's eyes widened as he simply raised her farther, bringing her eyes level with his chin. Then his cheek. His entire frame vibrated against hers with the most alluring hum, while a heady sensation bubbled through her, increasing her heartbeats. And that just seemed to elevate his.

"Do I?"

"This . . . is creating . . . comment." And then, to her absolute horror, she giggled.

His trembling increased, apace with the tightening of everywhere she touched, while a nerve throbbed at the side of his jaw. Tira watched it as he focused somewhere into the throng of dancers about them. And then he complied. Tira found her feet back on the floor during a spin and then held until the floor ceased swaying. His arm loosened, releasing her. Tira couldn't face him. She watched the silver of his brooch for a bit to gather her wits. Tira Mirabelle Coxton-Coombs was known for her intelligence, her conversation, her sense of propriety, etiquette. This sort of reaction was irresponsible. Incredible. Unseemly. And entirely thrilling.

Patience.

Iain ran the word through his mind until it worked. It took all his concentration and strength to ignore how every beat of her heart tugged his into ragged rhythm with it. But it was difficult!

He finally had her, right in his arms. His mate. Near-forgotten needs and urges flickered into being, pumping desire and lust where he'd long ago tamped. Hardening. Stiffening. Elongating.

Soon, Iain. Soon.

The lass had no idea how close she was to getting lifted over his shoulder, taken from the trappings and frippery of this ballroom, and then ravished within a scream of her life. He never wanted her to know. It was enough that he did. The vestige of civility had slipped, but he'd caught it. That should make him proud, rather than locking his jaw in an agony of frustration and want, while all of him ached and trembled. And lusted.

He'd waited for her to reach the proper age. He could wait another night. He forced the urges away, blinked, and looked back down at the woman.

Chapter Two

Tira smiled slightly and ducked her head to hide any reaction. It wasn't possible, but just about everywhere she went this incredibly dark, dreary, and rain-filled morn, she'd glimpsed something that reminded her of him: that Scot. Massive. Incredibly handsome. Iain Duncan . . . James. And more names she couldn't recollect . . . MacAvee.

She hugged her shawl closer to her as she led first Ophelia, dressed in a yellow day gown that seemed to wilt with every step, then Ophelia's maid with Christa, and behind them came two Coxton-Coombs footmen, whose duties were carrying any purchases the sisters made. They made quite a retinue as Tira chose which shops to patronize and which to pass. This expedition was her birthday present to herself, but the inclusion of Ophelia and her maid were a decided curse. Especially given the girl's acidic remarks on Tira's lack of decorum last eve. As if she could have prevented the duke from dancing two times with her.

Two times? More like five . . . in succession. Tira puffed her cheeks out and then blew the sigh. Dancing before an introduction was decidedly improper. And then doing little more than watching as he'd bowed over her hand and exited? Without one word to anyone else? All of it was beyond bad form. It was enough to get her ostracized.

Tira forced her shoulders back. She was grateful to live in this enlightened age. Why, a generation earlier, she'd have hidden in shame at such behavior. Now, although it was a chore to force a bright smile to match the tinkling bell as she entered a dress shop, it was still done. But then she had to keep her expression as Lady Higginswale met her glance. The woman must still hold out hope that stays could be manufactured to cinch in her bountiful shape. Nothing could be done about her gossipy tongue, however.

"Lady Higginswale." Tira greeted her and waited. The woman made it a long wait, too.

"Mistress Coombs. You look lovely this morn."

"Love-ly?" Tira's voice reflected surprise, despite being prepared.

"Your ball was a great success. I vow, I've not been so entertained in weeks. I do hope you'll soon have another. Thank you, Mistress Elsie. I'll be back for a fitting on the morrow. Good day, ladies."

"We'll see you at the recital this eve?" Ophelia spoke up as Lady Higginswale passed her.

"This eve? Of course, Miss Ophelia. I look forward to it."

Ophelia's expression did more than show disbelief. It was comical. She'd expected outright social censorship. Especially after spending a good part of the morning pointing out how improper Tira had acted with *that* Scotsman. Tira watched her sister's gushing conversation with Lady Higginswale as she walked with her to the door, passed out onto the walkway, nodded to passersby. Nothing made sense.

Tira fully expecting and deserved to be gossiped over and then sent home to the country with her cheeks burning. She didn't know how Ophelia would manage, but Tira hadn't worried. Much. Four seasons without an offer for her hand was good training on surviving social gossip. It always passed on as something more interesting and scandalous happened. But to emerge unscathed from her outrageous behavior of last eve was unsettling and odd.

A bolt of seafoam-shaded silk caught her eye. Tira grazed her fingertips along it. There was something sensual about the material. She blushed at the idea of such a fabric touching her in an intimate manner and what might happen if a certain Scot gentleman was there to see it . . . and then she looked up at Iain MacAvee's chest—right across the table of fabrics from her. Without one bit of warning. Not even from the little bell atop the door.

He hadn't shrunk since last eve. If anything, he'd increased in size and presence and impact. He was clad in the same pattern and shade of Highland plaid, although it looked a bit more casually tossed on, he had the black mass of hair pulled back in a queue again, and he still had a sword hilt peeking over his shoulder, as well. In a ladies' dress shop. As if he belonged there.

And actually looking like he did.

Tira faced the rawhide lacing of his shirt for the count of eleven heartbeats, holding her hands to her bosom and wondering not only where her wits had gone, but why Ophelia hadn't even noticed and reacted.

"You take forever to select, lass."

"I . . . beg your pardon?"

Her words came with an exhalation of breath. He matched it. His chest filled with air, exhaled, moved the rawhide lacings apart with the move. Tira's lips parted.

"You. Flitting about from shop to shop. Looking over wares, yet selecting naught."

"I have not been flitting." Tira thinned her lips as a sign of reprimand. It didn't seem to work.

"You fancy this?"

He reached forward, across the table of fabrics, to place his fingers where hers had just been. She didn't dare look up.

"I believe I also hanker."

He could be reading her mind. Again. And what she'd been envisioning sent a rush of mortification all the way through her, rooting her in place.

"You needn't flush so, lass. I'm well acquainted with the vagaries of a woman's desires."

Tira gasped. Sputtered. "Of . . . all the licentious—Bold. Unbelievably crude—"

He interrupted her as much with his words as how he reached for her hands still held close to her bosom. It wasn't possible to not be shocked.

"So young. Untried. Naïve."

"Naïve? You continue to bring up my age, Your Grace. Very well. I admit it. I'll have you know I may not be in the first flush, but I'm well versed in social proprieties. And you are offending all them."

"Who wants that?"

"Everyone wants proper behavior."

"Na' that, lass. This first-flush thing. Only an untried youth values such."

Tira's jaw gapped. She lost her words and her breath. She almost lost her balance.

"And I'm well past that."

"H-how did you get here?"

"Back door."

"Why is no one else noting it?"

"All establishments have back doors."

"Not that. Why isn't anyone noting you?"

"Should they?"

"Of course. You're a man. A-a-a Scotsman. And you're very large. Immensely so. Impossible to overlook. Especially in a ladies' dress shop surrounded by females."

"You wish others noting us? Listening?"

Heaven forbid. "No. I just wonder at how anyone could miss such a thing."

"It's fain easy."

"Really?"

She was whispering. He wasn't. As if he wanted everyone to not only notice that she was meeting with him, but overhear what they said as well.

"All I needed was to locate you."

"How did you do that?"

"Your sister has a large voice."

True. Ophelia did have a loud way of speaking. And had said a lot of words. As did he. None of them her answer.

"The better question is more the *why* of my locating you."

"All right. I forfeit. Why were you . . . locating me?"

Tira lifted her head and damned the solid pump of her heart as her eyes connected with the obsidian of his. Silently. She couldn't do a thing about alien lurch of her frame. Nor could she prevent his sure knowledge of it as his lips quirked and then went to a grin, showing a glint of teeth. It highlighted his handsomeness. Totally unnecessarily.

"Did your da na' tell you?"

"Who?"

"Your da. Father."

"Father was to tell me something? What?"

"That's for his lips to speak, lass. He should have done so well afore last eve. Was he there?"

"He's bedridden."

"Truly?"

"Has been for years."

"Good."

"G-g-good?" Tira gasped and her eyes went wide. Her tongue wasn't working, either. She'd worry about her pronounced stammer later, when she wasn't being assailed with the view and smell and impact of this particular man.

"Forgive me. That sounded . . ."

"Brutish?"

"Nae, lass. Honest."

He smiled, but it didn't have the same effect.

"I-I think you'd best leave. N-n-now."

"I meant nae disrespect to His Lordship. 'Tis well and good he has reason for his lack of guardianship. Leaving you open to interlopers such as Graves. When he kens the consequences of laxness. Fully."

And like that, his joviality vanished, replaced by such intensity Tira stepped back a step. And then another. But one blink of her eyes had him right before her, as if there hadn't been a solid structure between them loaded with bolts of fabric.

"I dinna' mean to frighten you."

"I'm not . . . frightened." It was a lie. She was disturbed. Angered. Shocked. And frightened.

"You'll forgive me?"

Tira tipped her head.

"Please?"

"I—"

Tira's voice stopped. She found her hand plucked from her bodice and held in one of his, gently, as if it was the most fragile thing. He was cold. Again. Still. Chill sent trembling through her and she knew he felt it. He had to. His head bent forward and he pulled her closer at the same time—on feet that moved despite any order of the contrary. It was pure insanity to be drawn to a man in such a short time. Especially one of mercurial temperament. That didn't stop it. It was too intriguing.

Tira's lips parted, allowing each gasp passageway. The pulse was loud in her ears, overwhelming everything else, while every breath of his touched minutely on her, gaining volume and cadence with each one, matching her. Breathing as one.

"Iain!"

A sharp whisper stopped him, and the next moment, she was in a folded semi-crouch, held to a wall of flesh-covered iron with one arm and facing a kilt-clad man. The duke's other hand already held his sword, blade out, while the sound of steel sliding against the scabbard echoed about them, loud and harsh and foreign sounding.

"Come."

The man gestured and Iain stood, sheathing his weapon without looking while maintaining his grip on her. She had no choice but to feel the muscle-covered bulk of him moving against her, but she really should've held back the sigh.

"I must go now, lass."

She nodded.

"Tell your father I'll be there this eve."

She'd been released to face the fabric table that looked stable and solid and real. Tira gripped it until her legs belonged to her again and her knees ceased wavering. Such a reaction wasn't due to anything attached to His Grace, the Duke of MacAvee. She only hoped he didn't think so.

"He . . . does not take vi-visitors."

"He'll take me."

"I . . . truly don't think—"

The slightest sound of feminine chatter started filtering through the air, surrounding them with the sense of women. Lots of women. She blinked rapidly and continually, recognizing first Ophelia, since she was the loudest, and then her maid. And then she heard his whisper.

"Prepare yourself, my sweet."

Tira whipped about and faced nothing more than the maw of shadow that was the dress shop's hall leading to the back door. It was empty.

"Are you going to mull that purchase all morn?"

"Wh . . . at?" Tira turned back to face Ophelia, flanked by both maids.

"That silk. If you want to purchase it, say so. Don't just stand there, running your hands on it, while you daydream."

"Day . . . dream?"

"What else would you call it? We've been here nigh on a quarter hour, while I've had three dresses drawn up for me, and you've done little more than moon over that bolt. I'd say just buy it so we can leave. I'm parched."

"The duke . . ." It was whispered.

"MacAvee?"

Tira shook her head. She was confused and it would sound worse. But it felt too real for a daydream.

"Well, don't act as if he's going to miraculously appear. There hasn't been anything resembling a man near this shop all morn. Unless you count Sir Graves."

"Who?"

"Who? Your beau. Sir Robert Graves. Are you feeling ill?"

"Sir Graves . . . is here?"

"Oddly enough, yes. He's right outside, waiting our appearance. But I wouldn't call him a man anymore. Not after the example we got last night."

The ladies twittered amusement of Ophelia's comment while Tira watched. Like an outsider. And then she moved, ignoring the silk. If the fabric could bring about such a vivid experience, she wanted nothing to do with it. She didn't give it another backward look.

Chapter Three

He hated sailors. Especially the drunken ones.

Iain lifted his head, pulling back his teeth at the same time and grimacing on the cheap gin odor that filled his nostrils, dimming any enjoyment. It was the same with every sailor they brought him. Sotted. With cheap gin. Or cheaper whiskey. Nothing a Scot would allow past their lips. And here Iain was, destined to consume it.

The man at his feet shook slightly and groaned. His eyelashes quivered.

"We need leave, Your Grace."

"Aye. Now."

The warnings were unnecessary but always given. By these Honor Guardsmen, and their fathers, and their fathers before them. Exactly as it had been for decades. With exactly the same effect: none. Iain wouldn't leave until his prey woke. He didn't care. He'd made the promise after the first time he'd tasted blood and felt the effect it had on his senses—acutely. And then he'd had to suffer what happened. He'd never take a human life again. Not for anything as mundane as sustenance.

"Now!"

The word was hissed and Iain moved, leaping from a crouch at the back of the alley into a second-floor window opening with little effort and less sound. It was the six guardsmen shadowing him that made noise, moving in differing directions down uncountable alleys, while the seaman sputtered and then shouted. And then stumbled to his feet to yell some more.

Iain had needed this last one. Not for sustenance . . . more for endurance. For what he got to do this very evening with the woman fated as his mate, destined, birthed into this world just for him. Forever. She was his. He'd known it twenty-one years ago and he knew it now. With every moment that passed. He little cared that she'd been born into a Sassenach family with only a hint of Scot roots and even less claim of honor. She was his mate and he knew it. The moment she'd existed he'd felt it. Every leaf in his orchard and every animal in his stables had reacted. Or Iain's senses had been reborn again, with even more height and breadth and scope.

Three hundred lonely years he'd waited and now she was here, within reach. As succulent as a ripe peach, as deep as a windswept moor, and as beautiful as every moonrise he'd watched. More so. This Tira was all woman, every bit of her. Finely built. Curved in all the proper places. Tall. And she was his. Or soon would be. Fully. Iain wiped his hands on his kilt band, wondering at the damp feel of his palms.

The man in the alley stumbled, growling and cursing and then staggering into a wall. Iain watched it unfold exactly as the last one they'd brought, not a half hour earlier. Both men would wake with a headache and a sore neck, and bruises they couldn't explain from a fight they couldn't remember. Suffering a hangover from a drunk they couldn't recall. And then they'd brush themselves off, enter the nearest tavern, and start all over again.

Hell. He hated seagoing men.

Tira wasn't allowed in to see Lord Coombs until late, after pretending a headache and watching Ophelia and Aunt Adelaide leave for the recital. The day was already interminable. What with Ophelia fussing which dress was eye-catching in the event the mysterious Duke McAvee attended, Tira's emotions rarely felt so stretched. Taut. Elevated.

Excited.

She was on her third visit to her father's chamber before his manservant, Timms, allowed her in, for a few moments only, if she spoke softly and didn't upset the earl.

"Father?"

He looked to have shrunk more since yestermorn when she'd visited. Legs, long useless and withered, made little impression in the coverlet, while his face had never looked so drawn and pale. And old.

"Father?"

"You've come about MacAvee."

"Y-yes."

"Come. Sit."

"What does he want, Father?"

"He didn't say?"

"He told me to hear it from your lips."

Her father took a heavy breath that didn't make much change in his covering, and then made a rattling deep in his chest as he exhaled.

"Of course. And it should."

This wasn't good. The earl's reply meant the visit in the dress salon hadn't been dreamed. And it hadn't been imagined. And that meant it was impossible.

"I met MacAvee almost twenty-one years ago. No. That's wrong. I met his father, the late duke."

"Twenty-one years?"

Her father nodded. "He arrived at Coombs Castle with a retinue of servants and outriders to make a man's jaw drop. All of it in exchange for what I had."

"And that was . . . ?"

"You."

"Me?" Tira launched into the room outside the reach of the candles. It hid the instant reaction and her inability to curb it.

"As wife for his son and heir."

"You went behind Mother's back?"

Her father coughed hard enough to bring Timms to his side, a glass of brandy in one hand and a cloth to catch blood specks in the other. Tira watched them from her position at a bureau, resting her head on the wood for the support and to mute the sounds of labored breathing. Then the liquor started to work, granting her father time to talk and the strength to do so.

The earl was always this way before the brandy worked, and just before he'd get morose and depressed over the carriage accident that took his wife's life and made him an invalid. It hadn't been his fault, but that didn't change it. His wife was still dead and he was still half a man . . . or less.

She'd be asked to leave before the next stage. But that was counterproductive to why she'd forced this meeting. Tira straightened her back, bringing her head level with the furniture piece, and waited.

"Your mother . . . was in full agreement. Her signature is on the document."

"There's a document? In this day and age?"

"His Grace insisted upon it."

"But why, Father? Why?"

She didn't feel anger, resentment, or resignation. And it definitely wasn't repulsion. It wasn't even shock. It was something worse and with much more power, something akin to excitement.

"I don't understand the issue. MacAvee chieftains are well known for power, and presence, and vast holdings . . . and other things that women whisper of."

"I don't care what he owns and what his titles are."

"What of the man? You care little for that, as well?"

"I . . . hadn't noticed." And she was terrible at lying about it. Timms barely caught a chuckle, while her father moved something on his upper body as if to join in.

"I've heard he . . . favors his sire. Even my sister, Adelaide, spoke of it."

"She knows?"

"No. She visited me this morn. Asking that I proffer an invite to MacAvee . . . for her sake. And Ophelia."

"Aunt Adelaide? Ophelia?" Tira wasn't jealous. She told herself the instant flash wasn't jealousy. It was better labeled anger.

"You need to come closer, Miss Tira. He can't shout."

Timms gestured her to the chair set at her father's bedside for any visitors he might entertain. Everyone knew only Tira sat there. Tira settled onto the brocade and wound a ribbon tie from her gown about her index finger.

"According to your aunt, marriage to this MacAvee would be a pleasant thing."

"She said that?"

"And more."

Tira didn't answer. Her tongue felt swollen, her throat tight, and her cheeks burned. She found the thought of her marriage to MacAvee very pleasant . . . especially the idea of intimacy and what that might mean. But that wasn't the issue. She spoke the next to her ribbon-wrapped hand.

"You still should've told me, Father. Or at least warned me."

The earl sputtered, Timms dabbed at his lip, and then both men turned toward her. "That was your mother's duty. Along with . . .

all the other things a mother tells her daughter on the . . . day of marriage."

"The . . . day?" Tira's eyes widened. She hadn't expected that.

He nodded. "Your twenty-first birthday. Today."

Tira sucked in a breath. "Even if I agree to this outlandish arrangement, I can't possibly be expected to wed with so little time. Notice needs to be given to the papers, invitations need to be organized and sent out, and I don't even have a gown."

Her father snorted. The cloth in Timms's hands caught the smattering of blood spots. He held it there as the earl shuddered through another coughing spell. It didn't sound like his usual, however. If she didn't know better, she'd swear he was laughing. Then he calmed, gulped another swig of brandy, and looked back at her.

"You've little . . . choice, Tira. And little reason. He favors his sire. To the minute. In everything. And that includes . . . his impatience."

"I can say no, Father. This is not the Dark Ages where daughters were treated as chattel and wed accordingly. I run your estates. I'm well versed in it. I don't have to wed at all. At least give me some time."

He sighed. "Twenty-one years is a powerful amount of time, Tira. It feels like an eternity when you're just starting out. Some days it felt like forever."

"Is that why you agreed?"

He rolled his head back and forth on the pillow. "I never expected my brother to pass on, and as the sixth Earl of Coxton-Combs, I've responsibilities. It takes gold . . . to maintain. Lots of it. I didn't know where to turn. I had a worm-eaten estate and little more than debt. The east wing was roofless. The Norman wall collapsed. There were accounts to settle, pensions to pay out, and farmland to either work or lay fallow, letting everyone starve. And no one could overlook your grandfather's debts of honor."

"How much did he pay?"

"It was your hand or debtor's prison. For the lot of us."

"How much, Father?"

"Everything. The man set up a fund to cover everything. All we have was paid with MacAvee gold. Your clothing, the food and wines we consume, the horses we ride. All for your hand."

"I can't wed a man I've just met!"

"It shouldn't be too great . . . a hardship. Just look about you. He's wealthy, powerful, and according to Adelaide . . . very manly."

"It takes more than that for me, Father." The blush was back, and with it a flurry of shiver.

"How much more, lass?"

Tira stumbled to her feet, upsetting the chair onto its back while the earl started such a coughing fit, Timms looked overwhelmed. All of it because a man stood at the edge of the light, allowing glints to flicker on the silver of his outfit and the six men always shadowing him. Tira dropped her gaze to the floor between them.

"Your Grace."

Little things helped with the absolute horror of reviewing what she'd just said. Etiquette. Propriety. Tira consciously followed it. Greet. Curtsy. Continue breathing. She didn't move her eyes the entire time. It was easier.

"You dinna' answer my question."

"How did you get in here?"

"We were announced. You failed to hear it."

Tira couldn't look anywhere near him. Not until she had the embarrassment fully hidden. She'd cringe over it later. "You eavesdropped on private words."

"He told you, then?"

"Private words," Tira repeated.

"Had I na' arrived as I did, I'd na' ken you found me . . . lacking."

There wasn't a hole in the floor between them, regardless of how she kept looking for that very thing. He was waiting for an answer. The entire room felt like it was. Tira swallowed.

"Lack . . . ing?"

The word got split in two, the last half making little sound since he moved so quickly and silently; within a blink he was right before her, breathing whiffs of air all over her exposed neck and shoulders. She should've changed into a high-necked woolen dress for this visit. Worn a heavy shawl. A cloak. Or stayed in her room and hidden.

"It does na' help if you frighten her, Iain."

One of his men spoke, denting stillness that held only her father's attempts to breathe and the hard pulse of her heart. The man before her pulled to his full height, sending light between their shadows on the floor. He put his hands on his hips next and inhaled, deep, heavily, and loud. "You heard her. She finds me lacking."

It sounded worse every time he said it. And she didn't find him lacking. It was the circumstances. She opened her mouth to somehow put that into words but got forestalled by them speaking to each other in a foreign language of some kind.

Chapter Four

"She finds me lacking. You heard her. Grant, decipher this."

He spoke in Gaelic and was answered in kind. The man on his right stood straighter before turning his head to lock gazes. "I doona' believe that is what she meant."

"You heard her. We all heard it. She finds me lacking. Me. Iain Duncan Evan James Alexander MacAvee. The fourth. Duke of MacAvee. Chieftain and laird. Me."

"She dinna' truly say—"

"How am I lacking? In what way? With what facet? There is nae equal throughout the land. And if there is, he'll also fall once met. 'Tis my bane and what I've been cursed to."

"All true."

" 'Tis also true that I'm the most landed Scot? My properties encompass a goodly portion of the Highlands. Am I na' the largest? Strongest? Most lauded with medals and honors?"

"Aye."

"And doona' the women find me pleasing to look upon?"

"You need ask a woman, Your Grace," Grant replied.

"You've heard complaint?"

Iain had both hands on skean handles. The man on his left answered.

"He means . . . as your Honor Guard . . . uh. Well. We all ken you're the most pleasing to women. 'Tis na' something we speak of, but we'd fight any who doubt and slander it. That is what my twin seeks to say but canna' get his tongue to assist."

"Then what could the lass find lacking, Lenn? Somebody tell me."

"Perhaps she speaks due to ignorance. She's na' been around

Highlanders afore. We're forthright. Honest. Our ways are na' as
prettified and tactful as a Sassenach."

"This is your fault, Grant."

"Mine?"

" 'Twas your advice to wait. Stay from her. Allow her time to
reach full womanhood afore claiming her. And look at the result!"

Iain gestured to Tira and watched her start. Without reason.
He clenched his teeth further, gaining a prick in the cavern of
each inner lip. That made him grimace. And that had the lass
stepping back into the wreckage of her chair.

All of it unwarranted.

"She pulls back from me. *Me.*"

"My laird."

The man went to a knee, his sword held out by the hilt and
his head bowed, offering his neck for his punishment, in a Sassenach lord's bedchamber. As if that were normal and accepted in
this country and this time. Iain swallowed and reached out a hand.

"Rise, Grant. She already thinks us barbaric and crude. Taking your life for such a thing is centuries overdue your forbear.
Trust me. Now, cease this foolishness and assist me with this. All
of you."

"Perhaps the woman is simply startled?"

Iain turned to Grant's twin. "Of what?"

"You. Us. Our appearance. So bold. Swift. Without warning."

Iain swore, and then howled words to the ornately plastered
ceiling above his head. "Then help me with this! She near faints
with the fright at me."

"Reacting so is na' assisting."

"What should I do then?"

"Na' what you wish to."

Iain speared his smallest man, Rory, with a glare. "And that
is . . . ?"

The man pulled his sword, planted it into the parquet floor
beneath him, his actions causing a gasp of sound from the English, obliterating any other sound. Rory winked.

"Haul her over your shoulder and take her. There'd be little
fight, and should there be, we'd engage it."

Iain took a step in her direction, coiled his fingers into fists at
his sides, and then staunched the emotion. Not more than a century ago and with any other woman, he wouldn't hesitate. But

not now. Not this one. Tira was special. She was fated to be his. Forever.

He sucked in unneeded breath, watched as Tira's eyes widened, watching him, and then he eased the air out slowly, deflating his chest back to normal width, while she watched, unblinkingly.

"Rory is na' helpful, Iain. The lass needs civility."

"Civili . . . what?"

"Civility. She's na' used to our ways. She needs words spoken to her. Na' more show of power and threat of harm. Words."

"Words?"

Grant gained his feet and sheathed his sword before finishing. "Aye, words. Softly spoken. With loverlike tones."

"Softly spoken?"

"With loverlike tones."

"And what, pray heaven, does that sound like?"

"You wish a demonstration?" Grant's tone deepened, filling the chamber with baritone. Iain shoved an arm out to stop the man's advance on Tira, should that be his next move.

"Tira is mine, Grant. Mine."

"Then go. Speak to her. Use their ways to sway and then claim her."

"I canna' do this."

"Try."

Iain sucked in both cheeks, lowered his head, and regarded his second-in-command. "This is what happens when I trust a Sassenach, putting my fate in their hands. Regardless of the gold placed in those same hands, nothing is gained save betrayal and deceit."

"None betray you, my laird."

"My own tongue is about to," he replied.

He approached where Tira stood, her hands clenched so tightly her fingers looked white. She had beautiful green-shaded eyes, the color of Loch Nyven's deepest pools. He'd been drawn into them from the moment of meeting. Right now they looked the same shade of black as his. Beside her, the near corpse of her father watched, his mouth opening and closing like a salmon fresh-pulled from a burn, and at the other side of the bed, the manservant stood, the shaking shadow he cast giving him away.

"You've naught to fear from me, *leannan*."

She shook her head and moved back another step, making the tipped chair slide with it and losing a bit of the candle's light on her features.

"You ken?"

"I . . . don't understand," she whispered.

At least, that's what he thought she said. It was difficult to hear over the sound of her increased pulse toying at his ear, the perfect smell of her nearness filling his nostrils, and the essence of her surrounding him like a lover's embrace.

Iain gulped. "I'd never harm you, *leannan*. Uh . . . sweet. Ever." He reached for her hand, but she flinched and stopped him in place.

"English, Your Grace."

Iain straightened back up and looked over his shoulder at his men. "What?"

"I doona' believe the lass kens our Gaelic."

"Was naught done correct and to my order?"

The lass backed farther, stopped when a wall met her back, and then looked to cling there. Iain moved his gaze from her face to the floor and then to his outstretched palms, glimmering with dampness he was forced to swipe on his kilt. *Damp palms?* At his age? He tried again, softening his tone.

"I said you fear without reason, lass. I'll na' harm you. Ever."

"I don't fear you."

She looked to be ready to faint of it. Iain straightened and regarded her. She didn't move her eyes from the area of his chin.

"Truly?"

She nodded.

"Good. Then give me your reason. Please."

"For what?"

"You find me lacking. I wish to ken how."

"That . . . was not for your ears to hear."

She was going a rosy shade, suffusing her cheeks with darker tone. Or the candlelight lied. Iain regarded her for long moments, willing a meeting of gazes until it finally happened. And then, if he still claimed a full heart, that was what thumped, startling him with the violence of it. He watched her eyes go full wide before she dropped them to the area of his chest.

"But . . . ? You said . . ." Iain voice's dried up. In three centuries, he'd never had this issue. Yet now, facing this slip of a girl, he felt the start of his own flush, flustering and annoying and embarrassing him.

"I said . . . nothing of the kind."

"You'll wed with me now?"

"No."

"Nae?"

The word was ejaculated without regard to anything other than his Highland roots. Honest and forthright. And angered. She might have reacted, but it didn't sound in her voice.

"That should teach you to eavesdrop on private conversations. Your Grace."

She added his title as an afterthought, as if making certain he felt and heard the disdain. That just wasn't right or correct. And it surely wasn't happening to him. Iain pulled back slightly.

"Grant?"

"My laird?"

The man materialized just behind Iain. On his right. Iain watched her assimilate it without one show of fear.

"Help me with this."

"Miss Tira?"

She tipped her chin up and easily met his man's gaze, without one bit of fright or anything else. That started a wash of emotion right through Iain. Like the harshest Highland wind and just as chilling. As if he could still feel such a thing.

"The duke—"

"Can speak for himself. And if he wishes to continue speaking with me, he'd best start."

"Your Grace."

Grant bowed in defeat and deserted him. Iain watched it before pulling in a breath for something to do besides facing her and wondering over the prickle of gooseflesh that roamed his limbs, raising bumps and startling him. He could feel such? Now? With her? Realization and joy had to be the sensations making him light-headed and weak feeling. Like a youth with his first lass. Iain could swear his knees even trembled.

His knees trembled?

He swallowed, but it was more a gulp, loud in his ears. He hadn't felt so alive and unfettered in more years than he wished to remember. It was thrill and joy and absolute bliss. And it was his. Or would be . . . once he solved this problem. He grunted and heard the rustle of weaponry from his men as they reacted to it.

"Well?" she asked his chest.

Loverlike words. Iain searched his mind for the right ones and got them on the first try. "Forgive me, lass."

"For what, this time?"

"Eavesdropping. Startling you. Arriving without warning. And especially for my appearance."

"I never said anything about . . . that."

Iain blinked. Staunched what felt like champagne bubbles erupting in his chest. Spoke again. "Which, lass?"

"Your appearance."

"You find me pleasing?"

"I never said *that*, either."

"You dinna'?"

"It's this betrothal you claim. That is the issue."

Iain grinned. She hadn't answered his query and that sounded like an answer, especially as she'd touched her glance minutely to him, before shying back to the vicinity of his chest. He knew when a woman found him pleasing, and this one did. She couldn't hide it. Which meant something else caused her to demure. He tried again.

"The MacAvee chieftain is considered a great matrimonial prize, lass. Fathers from all over the region requested a union with me. Their visits were in vain. I was already promised. By dint of a betrothal contract, signed twenty-some-odd years ago. For you. As my bride."

"Why . . . me?"

Iain couldn't explain. He didn't even know. "And so I have come. To claim her—you. To claim you. As was agreed. And I find my bride verra pleasing in face and form. . . . Verra. Yet she has a decided aversion to me. And I canna' ken why."

"I wouldn't call it *aversion*."

"Then what is so displeasing?" Iain lowered his head to make certain he heard the reply but was stopped as the door to the chamber opened behind him somewhere, letting in light and sound and interruption. A slight blond wench and an older woman entered the chamber, followed by manservants and fuss just when he'd been about to hear what he needed to. Iain barely caught the snarl as he whirled about.

"They tell me we've visitors! At this time of night. And in your bedchamber? Father? What is the meaning of this?"

"Your Grace."

Both ladies said it in unison as they reached him, curtsying and filling his nose with sneeze-inducing lilac scent. Iain folded his arms and regarded them. The earl saved him in a weak, quavering, ill voice that sounded loud as a trumpeter.

"The duke . . . has come to finalize . . . a betrothal, Ophelia. Adelaide."

"He wishes a union? Oh, Father."

The blond clasped her hands to her bosom and smiled up at Iain. He watched the vein pulsing in her throat with interest and then, from behind him, he heard his answer, coming clear and sweet from his Tira's lips. Exactly as he wanted and without having to mouth one more loverlike word to her.

"The duke is offering for me, Ophelia."

"You? But—"

"We're betrothed. Isn't that right, Iain?"

The lass actually said his name with pride. It enveloped him with a heady sensation. He had no choice but to hide it, along with everything else.

"Ul . . . rich?" The name came out louder than Iain wanted with a higher octave on the first of it.

"My laird?" The requested clansman was before him, ready.

"You may begin."

"Exactly what do you think you're doing, Iain James MacAvee?"

His soon-to-be wife didn't sound elated. Her voice had a disciplinarian edge Iain hadn't heard in more years than he could remember. He cleared his throat.

"Wedding with you," he replied. "Exactly as you specified. Just now."

"I said betrothed. There's a lot to do before wedding. Invitations must be sent, an announcement to the papers. A-a-and . . . we need to get better acquainted."

"Acquainted?" His eyebrow rose. If he still claimed feelings, he'd swear his breath caught at the little stutter she'd made.

"We've yet . . . to even be . . . seen together."

"You'll see more, lass. Just get the words said and I'll show all to you. 'Twill na' be of issue."

Her eyes went wide, showing their green color. Iain swallowed to squelch instant need and want and absolute, pure lust.

"That is not what I meant. We should . . . ride in the park. You could call on me. Perhaps attend to a ball or fest together. In the proper attire."

"Proper attire?"

"Without weapons and battle gear. You know . . . proper."

"How long?"

It was harshly said. Both women at his side reacted. His Tira merely looked up at him with an unreadable expression on her face.

"A month."

"Nae." His voice was rising. Despite the hold he put on it.

"A fortnight then."

"I will na' give you even a sennight, *leannan*."

Her eyes regarded him for long moments. And then she tipped her head to one side, blinked. "Five days," she replied.

She bargained? With him? Iain pulled a deep breath again, not for need but to expand his chest. He watched her gaze drop there before returning.

"Four."

A smile touched her lips, making them look fuller. Ripe. Made for his kisses. Needful of them . . .

"Done," she replied.

Chapter Five

"Another bouquet. How odd."

Tira looked over at Ophelia, fussing at the enormous flower arrangement that was Iain's excuse for not attending to anything he'd agreed. Her sister's sarcasm wasn't disguised. And it hurt. Somewhere beneath the bodice of her high-necked day gown, where Tira would never admit.

"Well . . . he is a lot of man. Almost more than a woman should be required to handle."

"Is there a note with them?" Tira ignored Aunt Adelaide's pointed words. Nothing could be gained by defending the duke. And she didn't want yet another discourse on his manly attributes. Especially not from a woman old enough to be his mother.

"You expect one?"

"Just checking," Tira replied without one inflection that could be labeled hope. She given it up and would be mortified if it still showed. Unlike the first three days when every arrival at the front door had started her heart to thumping and her palms to going damp.

"More gifts and messages for Miss Tira."

"Nothing else?"

It was Ophelia speaking for her. The footman shook his head as he entered, bearing another huge bouquet. He was followed by two more men laden with more presents and congratulatory notes, and invitations she wouldn't accept. Not without the duke at her side. The news had engendered the exact scrutiny she'd worried over, and worse. Every woman who called had a veiled remark or two about her dowry and how much the Scot duke must need it. Tira didn't answer any of their barbs. She just listened and hoped. She still didn't know why he'd wanted her. And why, once gaining her, he'd disappeared.

"He should at least send explanation. That way I wouldn't be at a loss when everyone asks where he is," Ophelia said.

"You needn't answer," Aunt Adelaide answered.

"What? And appear rude? The next thing you'll offer is that I stay home, avoiding anything to do with society. Like Tira."

"Tira isn't avoiding. She's busy."

Aunt Adelaide was wrong. Tira was definitely avoiding. She accepted the batch of envelopes from the salver with grace and practiced the same skill on the other Coxton-Coombs ladies.

"She's leaving me with all the unpleasantness. And doubt. Over the authenticity of the announcement. Why if I hadn't witnessed it, I'd be questioning it as well. . . ."

There were more spite-filled and jealous-laden words. Tira shut them out. One of the envelopes had large bold writing on it. With ink-laden swirls showing a heavy hand with a quill. She knew it immediately. Her heart stuttered into a faster rhythm as she tore the seal and then gasped.

"What is it? Is it the duke?"

Tira nodded.

"What does it say?"

"He'll be here. Promptly at nine. As escort. To the Devonshire ball." She didn't tell them of the last line. It was enough it burned her eyes.

"Oh my. What shall I wear?" Ophelia's voice warmed. "Everyone will be looking. It will be so exciting."

"They won't be looking at you, my dear," Aunt Adelaide answered in a tight voice.

"Look to your own laurels, dear aunt. And allow me mine."

"It's rumored he has a large appetite for the ladies. It's a family trait. At least that's what I've been told."

"I hope Tira knows what she's getting into with that man."

"You only wish it was you."

"Of course I do. And it should be me. What man wants an old spinster?" Ophelia smiled sweetly.

"MacAvee. Obviously. Or he'd have asked for a little girl," Aunt Adelaide parried with her own smile.

"The next thing you'll aver is that he's fond of old widows."

Tira stood, settled her skirts about her, and left them. She didn't care what caustic taunts they tossed. As if the duke was a prize to be fought over and available for such a thing. Tira held the note to her bodice as she climbed the stairs. He wasn't available to any other woman. She didn't care what the rumors were. He was hers. And soon would be. His last line promised it.

"I should replace the lot of you. The moment we reach Loch Nyven's shore."

"We're your Honor Guard, Iain. Sworn to it."

"And subject to replacement. At my whim. Without recourse."

"There's none to best us, Your Grace. We won every challenge."

"In contests of strength. Endurance. Loyalty. But na' one of you has the cunning to see me fitted correctly. Just look."

"Get the duke another neckcloth."

"'Tis na' the cravat thing concerning me, Grant." Iain pulled at the crotch of his superfine wool trousers, concerned as it pulled where it shouldn't.

"You should don pantaloons first. As specified."

"There's na' enough room. Look at me. What lass wishes to see this?"

"All of them, most like."

Iain speared Grant's twin with a glare that usually got results. But something had changed since meeting the lass, Tira. His men acted differently around him: easier, relaxed, high-spirited.

Odd . . .

"You've been tupping the wrong wenches again, Lenn."

The man's grin widened at Grant's teasing. *They were teasing? Around him?* Then, Ulrich spoke up.

"'Tis correct attire, Your Grace. Truly."

"Encasing a man's legs? Outlining things? Nae wonder we wear the kilt. I doona' even have my sporran."

"There's none to match you, my laird. And after this appearance, there'll be nae one questioning it, either."

"He's right. We'll have more issue keeping the lasses from you. But we'll try. And I've first call."

That was Rory. Snickering. As if he had the right. Iain regarded him for long moments. The glee didn't fade, and the man still grinned. Like a fool.

"If this is a Sassenach's proper attire, they've changed. Markedly," Iain remarked finally.

" 'Tis na' that bad."

"Only if he stands in one spot and doesna' move."

" 'Tis exact to specification. Even Brummell would approve it."

"Who?"

"Beau Brummell. Arbiter of men's fashions. As followed by the Prince Regent. During my grandsire's time. At least this is what I've read."

"Someone should keep Ulrich from the history tomes."

"And me from appearing near naked," Iain added. He couldn't even believe it. He *was* teasing. For a moment nothing came in the room except stunned silence. And then some chuckles.

"Your Grace has us there. I've nae doubt you'll send lasses into a faint and gents to their dueling swords."

"They doona' allow dueling swords in their ballrooms, Lenn. Take it back or His Grace will be for strapping on his blade, Empirical."

"And just how would he use it? The slightest move might create scandal."

"Perhaps we can cancel?"

"Word's been sent! She has a promise of escort. This eve."

Iain listened to their banter, coming in rapid fashion, without thought to retribution. Consequences. As if he were normal and such a thing as a man's prowess could be joshed over among men. He shook his head to stop the thoughts plaguing him. And Grant spoke up with an apologetic tone.

"Your Grace?"

Iain sucked on both cheeks, earning a prick on them. Then he released the expression. "You're dense louts. The lot of you. And na' one of you has a grasp of measure. This is the best you offer? After four trips to three differing tailors?"

"We dinna' have full measure, Your Grace."

"Light excuse."

"You could've warned us."

"Or accompanied us."

"Daylight drains me. I canna' rise unless 'tis dark or rain filled. You all ken this."

"His Grace is right. We've had naught save sun. For three days."

"You still should've warned us of your . . . uh . . . size."

Iain looked them over, one at a time. His men were attired in burgundy-shaded cutaway coats, MacAvee plaid vests, gray trousers, and each one sported an intricately tied cravat at his neck. They looked gentlemanly. Stylish. Proper. Exactly as he was to have appeared.

It was too late to change. Too late to regret the nights spent assuaging craving, trying to kill frustration that came from waiting, wanting, lusting, hungering. He'd been feeding when he should've been fitted. Tailors could be bribed. Then he wouldn't have to worry. One stretch of his arms would split a seam somewhere. He already knew. They'd heard the rip. His shirt was the lone thing sewn large through the middle. As if a man of his dimensions sported a belly to accompany it. And his trousers fit without one bit of room to accommodate him. It was enough to make him pitch the entire ensemble into the fireplace, don his *feile-breacan*, and disclaim all knowledge of the niceties of English society. Except he'd promised her.

"It is na' that bad, Iain. Truly. Look for yourself."

Grant gestured to a mirror and then his arm fell. They all looked uncomfortable. Iain waited, watching. He'd never worried over a reflection until now. Because it had never mattered.

"Call the coach, Rory."

"And bring along some smelling salts. For the ladies."

"Lennox Geoffrey MacGorrick."

The man grinned at Iain's tone. "In the event you forget and move too quickly. Or something of a like nature."

He was late. That didn't mean he wasn't coming, but it didn't portend he was, either. Tira sat on the edge of a damask-covered settee in the salon and practiced at ignoring every tick from the clock and how her sister and aunt preened, argued, paced, checked ceaselessly in the large, ornately framed mirror. Paced again. As if they were the woman the Duke of MacAvee had betrothed and promised to escort.

They'd taken care with their appearance. Few would miss their appearance at the ball. Not with the scarlet gown Aunt Adelaide had donned, the color contrasting vividly with her ash-blond hair. It was theatrical and meant to be. Ophelia wasn't going unnoticed, even in a gown of ecru-shaded silk that proclaimed her debutante status. She'd had the neckline lowered and wore a peacock blue sash just beneath her breasts, the entire effect making certain none could miss her décolletage. She probably shouldn't have crimped her blond locks into little ringlets all about her head. It might be the style, but it didn't suit her.

Or so Tira thought. She'd ignored the hairstylist's advice tonight and foresworn crimping and curling, opting for one long braid wrapped about the crown of her head and falling down her back. She'd had her best gown pressed and fingered the rose-on-rose–colored embroidery on the skirt. She probably wouldn't show well against the other Coxton-Coombs ladies, but she didn't have to. It was obvious they were in competition, and just as obvious for what prize.

"His Grace, the Duke of MacAvee, and—"

There was more said, and at the same tone, but Tira didn't hear it. On the heels of the door opening was Iain, looking a perfect gentleman. And more. He looked a perfect, stunning, jaw-dropping gentleman. And that's exactly what happened to hers.

Chapter Six

Time stalled, encased in candlelit wonder. Tira didn't hear his approach. She only knew one moment she was standing while he entered, and the next he was right before her, his eyes holding hers, while every heightened gasp she made seemed to reverberate through him. He had his head tipped down, lashes shadowing the curve of his cheek, and then he smiled, revealing a flash of pearl white.

Tira's body pulsed, lunging into the space between them in a barely perceptible move that startled her. And then it looked to move through him, even as he reached for a numb hand and took it to his lips.

"*Leannan.*"

Candles from the chandelier glinted on shiny black strands of hair he'd pulled into a neat queue that looped over the white material about his neck. Now that she saw him dressed as fashion dictated, she realized the truth. He wasn't handsome in the accepted way. He was more. He was absolute masculine beauty, framed incorrectly. MacAvee's brawn and strength wasn't encased in velvet and muslin and satin; it was barely restrained. He should be free of encumbrance, attired as his nature hinted, in a kilt, sleeveless shirt, doublet, sporran, a plaid.

And then she heard a rip.

Iain lifted his head, sending a whispered curse into the air before he swiveled, looking himself over for damage. Tira barely kept the amusement from sounding. That was the expression on her face when he stopped, moved his gaze back, and sent a solid thump of a heartbeat all the way through her.

"What does that mean? That name you call me? *Leannan?*"

She didn't think he'd answer for a spell as his cheeks pulled in and he avoided meeting her eyes. And then he looked to have decided something, for his chest enlarged and he sent the sigh of air into the space between them. He met her look again, and that sent a whoosh of sound so strong through her ears that she had to guess at his words.

" 'Tis Gaelic."

"And the . . . meaning?"

" 'Tis an endearment. Of sorts."

"Sorts?"

"Pester me with this after our wedding, lass. And the consummation that will follow. Immediately thereafter."

Tira swallowed, controlled her eye width with force of will, and regarded him. "You don't know me well enough for such a comment."

"I doona' need to."

"Well, I certainly do. This is what the acquaintance time was to remedy. The acquaintance time you failed to provide."

"Forgive me, lass. I could na' attend to you as required. Because of what else you required."

"You make little sense, Your Grace."

"Iain. Always. Iain. We'll be wed within hours, lass."

"I have another day."

"Oh nae. You have three hours. And na' one moment more. Exactly as you bargained."

"But you failed your part."

"I'm here. Escorting you. In Sassenach frippery."

"Three days overdue."

" 'Twas na' possible sooner. There's a dearth of tailors in this town that can fit a man proper."

"You look proper enough." And more. *Stunning.* She finished it in her thoughts.

"After three days of trying. You little ken what dragons were slain in order to accede your wishes."

"Dragons?"

" 'Tis a metaphor. For the curse of trousers. And the poor lads forced to wear them."

Tira glanced down. Her thoughts stalled. Her eyes went wide, then her mouth. And then she blushed. Severely. She moved her view to the wallpaper-covered wall over his left shoulder.

"And this is the best fit. English tailors are an untalented lot, or a Sassenach is nae match for a Scotsman. You tell me."

"You could have worn your kilt thing."

He sighed. She felt it. "I'm here now, lass. And you've three hours. 'Twould be a powerful shame to spend the time with words of dissent."

"That would be a cheat, Iain MacAvee."

He didn't answer for so long she had to look at why. He was regarding her with a set jaw and an aura of danger about him that frightened and yet thrilled, causing goose bumps to ripple over her arms.

"Were you a man, I'd have your throat."

Tira gulped. "I need . . . another day."

"Give me one fair reason."

"We could have vast differences. Our union could be doomed from the start."

"You're the woman fated for me."

"I don't believe in fate."

"You doona' believe in destiny?"

"The only thing I believe is the ability to reason. That and solve problems. This is what I believe. The future is not fated. It's open. Changeable. Adaptable."

"I swear it to you, lass. We've been fated. From birth. Perhaps farther back than that. You're my mate. Soul to soul and flesh to flesh. Or we verra soon will be. Did you na' read my note?"

He was trying to shock her. Tira moved her attention to the room behind him for several heart-calming moments, watching Ophelia and Aunt Adelaide and his men . . . then the three manservants posed in Coombs family uniforms, ready to serve refreshments. They were in the act of chatting. Smiling. All of it in the same room, yet nothing penetrating through to where the duke stood, taking her focus into some fantasy realm. She shook her head and met his gaze without blinking.

"How are you doing that?" she asked.

"What, lass?"

He smiled, his lips gapping slightly to allow tips of teeth to show: wicked-looking, sharp teeth. Tira moved her glance from there to his eyes and kept them there. She couldn't control anything.

"It feels like we're alone. Encased. While surrounded by others."

"How do you ken 'tis me?"

"The same thing happened at the dress shop, didn't it?"

"Pester me with this as well. Once we've wed. And have consummated our union."

He wasn't answering her questions. None of them. Tira tried another tack. "How old are you, Iain?"

His smile disappeared. He drew straight. "Auld. Verra."

"Give me a number. In years."

He moved his eyes from hers, brought them back. Looked away again. "Twenty-five at last count," he finally told the wall behind her.

"That is not very old."

"To some." He shrugged, there was another ripping sound, and he did another check of his clothing before returning his attention back to her.

"Why do you want . . . me?" Tira pulled in a breath and asked it.

"Ah, *leannan*. I doona' fully ken why. All I ken is the fates have delivered on a promise. When I least expected it. Within this small hand lies my happiness."

He encased her hand in both of his as he spoke, rubbing his thumbs along her skin without thought. Or if he gave it thought it didn't show, although the vibration he put in play should be entirely noticeable, perceived, detected.

"Can you na' feel it as well?"

She was feeling plenty. Starting with a shiver of emotion making him blur and ending with a deep thump of pulse from where her heart felt like it had fallen. Surprisingly, she still stood. Her legs hadn't one halfpence of strength, but they still held her, upright and spellbound.

"I . . . need more time."

"Why?"

"I don't even know where you live. Where we'll live."

Tira pulled her hand free and he let her. He didn't react as she stepped back a step and then another, until she sensed the wall. He just watched her with an unfathomable look, and then he answered.

"In a castle."

"Truly?"

"Aye. MacAvee Hall. Or Castle Strathmore. Or there's Blannock, Avendale. Glencairn. You have your choice. 'Tis all the same to me. As long as we wed."

"That many?"

"As long as we wed."

"Which do you prefer?"

Murmurs of voices were starting to resonate in the air about her, giving the impression of a crowd, speech, the tinkling of goblets.

"You stall and I will na' allow it. We wed tonight. Midnight."

"Can we not simply travel to one of these castles . . . and then wed?"

"Nae!"

His eyes flared. The candles all about the room seemed to have the same affliction, sending light that blinded for a moment before it subsided.

"How did you do that?" she asked.

"I'm done with words, lass. I warn you."

He had his head down, his shoulders forward, and was breathing so harshly she felt each of them launched across the gap, sending wisps of hair flittering about her forehead. It was far different for Tira. She couldn't breathe. She didn't dare blink.

"Oh, there he is! And looking fairly discomfited at conversation with my niece. Your Grace."

Aunt Adelaide split the space, separating him from Tira with her curtsy. She was joined the next moment by Ophelia, granting Tira a reprieve from him and the intent evident all over him.

Discomfited?

The woman had no grasp of men. Iain gripped both hands into fists, lifting his chest with breaths that had a ripping sound accompanying each one, and struggled with an emotion that had nothing discomfited about it. It was elemental, feral, immediate. And vast. Such full-vein rage belonged to his past, when once he'd walked the earth filled with the same lusts other men enjoyed. He was experiencing rage? Him? Iain MacAvee? And all because one woman told him nae?

It was incomprehensible. He didn't know why the fates meant this one woman for him. And he didn't know why every moment with her kindled long-dead emotions. All he knew was it happened and it was difficult to control. Iain shook in place with it, glaring over the other women at *her*.

"Your Grace?"

It was Grant at his right side, his twin on the other. Iain ignored both of them.

"We're fair certain it meets with your betrothed's approval. Miss Tira?"

"Wh-wh-what?"

She stammered when she spoke. Iain narrowed his eyes. She appeared to tremble, too, her eyes wide and dark while her lips parted to gasp in air. As if he'd harm her. The sight sent the oddest cooling sensation through him, tamping the burn. And that pulled him from the challenging stance he'd assumed without any awareness of it.

"The journey," Grant continued, speaking for him.

"Journey?" the older woman asked.

"His Grace dinna' tell you ladies?"

"Tell us what?"

His Tira shook her head. She didn't take her eyes from his. The women separating them might as well be nonexistent, despite their chatter. Like little twittering birds.

"His Grace is needed at his estates. The journey takes four days."

"That's ridiculous. No coach travels that quickly."

"And we've nothing packed."

The women were answering again and Grant continued speaking for him. Tira didn't move. She just stood there regarding him with that deep green gaze of hers, unblinkingly, sucking all of the anger away.

"His Grace's yacht stands readied."

"How extraordinary. We're to travel by sea?"

"I've never been at sea. I hope I'm not the seasick type."

Iain shook his head.

"We're not going by sea?"

"You're na' going." He forced his attention to the other ladies with an act of will before he lost all scope of reality and found his existence riddled with cloying, twittering women.

"You can't possibly expect my niece to travel with you unescorted."

"And without me," Miss Ophelia added.

"Tira has nae need an escort. Or companion. Or a maid. She'll have me. All of me. On the morrow."

He didn't look to see what reaction Tira gave. It was enough the ladies before him gasped in unison.

"Tomorrow?"

That was the older one speaking. The younger hadn't managed to shut her mouth enough to form words.

"Once the sun sets, we'll wed. As bargained and now agreed. Tira?"

"Y-y-yes?"

She was still stammering, sending a tingle through the area where a heart had once been. Iain concentrated and set it to memory for enjoyment later. He'd never felt such a thing. Or if he had, he'd forgotten it. Another first . . . because of her.

"You have one more day. For readying."

She looked at him for long moments before smiling with such a sweet expression, the instant stab of joy nearly unseated his head. Iain couldn't contain it and forgot everything, until the smile faltered and disappeared. That's when he realized he'd been grinning like a fool, displaying his fangs. He slammed his jaw shut with a motion that opened two slits in his lower lip, and he couldn't meet her eyes. It was too soon. She was too skittish and he'd nearly forgotten centuries of training in hiding, protecting, lying.

Grant cleared his throat. "Now that everything's settled, and everyone's readied, we'll be seeing to that escort. Ladies?"

Grant held out an arm for the older woman, leaving his twin with the one named Ophelia. Iain caught the swift glance of disgust before Lenn turned toward the door, guarded by Rory and the others, looking gentlemanly and civilized as they waited for Iain to escort his betrothed. Despite her fear and what she'd just seen.

There was nothing for it. Iain lifted his gaze to hers and held out his arm.

Chapter Seven

She'd fantasized of something like this. It had dimmed since her debut, but the experience of arriving at the Devonshire home on the Duke of MacAvee's arm almost exactly matched that fantasy. Or it would . . . if she could banish the image of Iain's teeth. Long, and tipped like fangs . . . belonging to a wild animal.

Tira shivered in the foyer, five steps above the Devon family grand ballroom, holding her cool satin skirts with an even colder hand and watching the reaction below them as heads turned and conversation stopped. Iain was at her right, her hand resting atop his bent forearm. The Earl of Devonshire had a major domo who possessed a large projecting voice. Iain and her names and titles were perfectly modulated, and with the silence descending below them, easily understood. It seemed everyone listened and watched as Tira Coombs, the spinster daughter of Earl Coxton-Coombs, made her entrance with her fiancé, Iain MacAvee, Duke of MacAvee, Earl of Glencairn and Blannock, chieftain of four clans, and owner of seven castles along with all surrounding lochs and glens.

Seven? Good heavens! What man needed so many? And for what reason? There were taxes to be paid on every building and land cultivated. The amount of funds and manpower needed to maintain a castle and surrounding lands was enormous. It had to be and she only had Coxton-Coombs Hall for comparison. And he owned seven? How was such a thing possible in these times?

"Centuries of conquest, lass . . . along with grand bargaining skills and a patience to match."

She stumbled. Iain caught her perfectly with a tightening of his arm against his chest, holding her upright without even looking. Having her mind read and then being clumsy wasn't part of her fantasy. She felt him move something beneath his sleeve, the knot of muscle teasing her fingertips, and then he turned to her. This time he caught the stumble exactly as she made it, since the steps ended before her descent.

"Doona' fail me now, *leannan*."

"Fail . . . you?" She was going to do worse if he breathed much more on her exposed neck, sending trills all the way to the soles of her feet with his whisper. She was going to lose her ability to stand, and then she might even swoon.

"With this purgatory you've set me to."

"Purg . . . atory?"

"I've a room full of Sassenach and na' one weapon on me."

"We're not at war."

"A Scotsman is ever at war. And ever ready for one."

"Truly?"

"Aye."

"With the English?"

"They started it," he replied.

"I'm English, Iain. Mostly."

She got another breath touching her flesh and a resultant tremble in her knees. She tightened her grip on his arm and that just seemed to make the flesh she touched harder.

"Aye. But soon you'll be MacAvee clan."

"What . . . will that make our . . . offspring?" And where were her wits? Tira felt the blush rising and worked at controlling it before anyone else spotted it. She couldn't believe she was speaking of children! In a roomful of observers?

"Bairns?"

He drew back as if surprised. And then he looked stunned. And then his lips fought another smile. As if having children was an abnormal part of wedlock.

"You don't want children? Heirs to all those castles?"

"Heirs?"

He said the word as if it were foreign.

"See? This is what our time together was to bring out. Our differences and the insurmountableness of them."

"What differences?"

"Your aversion to children is a fairly large one, Iain."

"I've nae issue with bairns."

"Then why . . . ?"

Her voice trailed slightly as the setting started intruding, as if each blink dissipated a fog about them, allowing sensation and experience back in, until the ballroom and its occupants were clear and vivid.

She caught a glimpse in a mirror set to her right, her gown shimmering with rose-shaded highlights the candlelight picked out, while the coronet of braid about the crown of her head gleamed with russet tones. It was how she wanted to look . . . and if she could just get a peek at her escort . . .

Tira craned her neck to catch a glimpse of burgundy-shaded coat and then missed her opportunity as their hosts approached. Iain turned her toward them. The slight stab of disappointment was replaced at the jealousy in her hostess's look, before the woman turned a completely different expression upward to Iain. The countess spoke first, sounding effusive, gushing, and slightly out of breath. Tira watched the woman tip her head in order to display her creamy rounded bosom. It was obvious the countess was proud of her figure, even without the frame of ecru lace and the sapphire necklace to draw the eye exactly there.

The experience was disconcerting and exhilarating at the same time. Tira recognized the emotions exactly as she experienced them. She'd never been the object of anyone's jealousy. And then the gossipy Lady Higginswale appeared, her plump form encased in plum-shaded silk. Tira watched the Countess of Devonshire glance askance at that display while her husband bowed and then left them. It was rather like observing a play that no one else was watching.

"Your Grace."

"My Lady . . . ?"

"Higginswale," Tira informed him.

Iain put out his free hand and bowed slightly. For a moment Tira thought Lady Higginswale would pop right out of her bodice, and she caught her breath. But the dress held, and the woman was back upright. She didn't even glance over to Tira. That was dismissive and meant to be.

"It's lovely to see you out and about. Finally." Lady Higgensale simpered it.

"And at my ball," the countess inserted.

"Escorting the Coxton-Coombs ladies. Pardon us."

Ophelia pulled into view on Iain's far right, her hand on Grant's arm. Or it could be Lenn. Tira couldn't tell the twins apart and didn't waste worry over it.

"And looking so presentable."

"Yes," Lady Higginswale added. "I don't think I've ever seen a Scot looking so . . ."

"Refined?" the countess asked.

"Masculine," came the instant reply. And then the woman looked directly at where Iain's trousers weren't disguising much of him, if anything.

Tira stiffened. In her fantasies, she'd been envied for the man at her side. She'd *wanted* a man that other woman coveted. She'd never thought through the consequences. And Iain was oblivious or something. Not so the guardsmen about them. They were clearing throats and shuffling feet and grinning. As if having women fawn over Iain was normal. Tira narrowed her eyes and tightened her fingers and immediately felt the hard knot of muscle rotating beneath her digits.

"My thanks, ladies." Iain's reply came in a low tone that gave her shivers. She only hoped the other ladies didn't have the same sensation.

"I'm having a gathering at tea on the morrow, Your Grace. You'll be receiving an invitation," Lady Higginswale said.

"No. Please. You must visit me for tea." If their host had stayed at his wife's side, he might've been able to prevent the low, evocative tone the countess used to proffer her own invite.

"His Grace has yet to finalize plans with me, ladies. I believe he'll be unable to attend to anything save that," Aunt Adelaide moved in, inserting right between Higginswale and Iain.

"I thank you for the invites, ladies. Truly. But I only take tea with one woman. My Tira."

With that, Iain turned toward her, lifted her hand to his lips, and stole her ability to breathe, think, and do anything other than fall.

His Tira needed to do something other than look up at him with liquid pools of green that dominated his world anymore. Everything on him reacted, in full view of a good section of high Sassenach society . . . and in these accursed trousers. Not that he cared. Society changed; morals and strictures adapted to each wearer of the crown; but he knew his Tira cared, and that meant he did.

Iain groaned and pulled her toward him more for concealment than the loverlike embrace it appeared. He noted only absently how she came as if she collapsed into him.

The slight blush that bloomed up her cheeks matched her gown and sent torment atop nuisance, and suffering atop that. She was such a beauty. Lush. Womanly. His loins weren't the only thing craving her. His teeth were elongating at the glimpse of pulse beating in her neck. The perfectly formed skin shaded with an infusion of fluid.

"Perhaps . . . we'd be better served . . . dancing." Her lips moved, drawing his eyes, but his ears let the words slide right through until she walked two steps from him toward where couples were rotating.

Dancing? Was the lass insane? He couldn't dance. He couldn't even walk. Iain held back, unmoving until she was forced to stop and turn back.

"Aren't you escorting me?"

He watched her lips make those words as well, but couldn't hear them over the rush of sound in his head. He shook his head. She frowned and that he didn't want.

"I canna' dance, lass," he told her.

"Don't be ridiculous. I've seen you. You dance divinely—I mean very well. You've danced with me. Five days ago."

"What the duke means is he canna' dance right now."

It was Rory speaking for him. Grant and Lenn were busy keeping a tight rein on Tira's female relatives, exactly as he'd tasked them. But Rory? The man known as a practical jokester? Iain swallowed, worked at tamping the near consuming desire and craving his body was experiencing, and wondering why, if fate had to give him these emotions back and the woman to cause them, why couldn't the same fate send the ballroom into oblivion, the crowd into the same, and gift him with one bit of privacy and a bed? Or even one of the shadowed benches they'd placed along the wall.

Iain's eyes went wide and his nostrils flared as he glimpsed one of the benches the moment he thought of it. It wasn't possible but the plague of lust got even wilder. He held the air and concentrated, sending power to alter time, mute the surroundings, and encase him, allowing him to move without awareness. It was futile. Nothing worked. All he could do was tremble in place, locking every muscle as he fought feral and primitive need no maid should face, displayed with probable accuracy in the damn English trousers if the fabric's tight grip on him was any indicator.

"Whyever not?"

Rory cleared his throat before replying. "Modesty, Miss Tira."

"Wh-wh-what?"

She'd turned her attention to Rory, but that little stutter of hers tied Iain's tongue worse. He moved his right hand to encase the one she had atop his left arm, and then worked at making certain his grip wasn't enough to break bone. He pulled her closer to him, needing her skirts for concealment even if it came with torment over just a hint of her scent.

"When a man . . . uh . . . desires a woman, he . . . uh."

There wasn't a way to explain to her what tortures Iain was suffering, but it was almost amusing to hear Rory try.

"We—we have to do something aside from standing here waiting for more women to act . . . I mean, react. Is it always this way?"

"What way?" Iain had a voice but it was croaked. Harsh. She looked toward him, sent a blaze of fire right through his chest, and turned back to Rory.

"More times than na'," Rory answered for him again. The snipe.

"Truly? You're saying everywhere he goes women react like this?"

"Well . . . most times 'tis na' an issue."

"Most times?"

"His Grace does na' stay about to endure the attention."

"You *are* saying women react like this?"

"And some gents."

"Rory." Iain's threatening tone needed work as the upward wink his man gave him clearly showed.

"Is that why he's been absent?"

Iain struggled with the intoxicating sensation of her nearness, enduring a mingling of scents from the braid at the crown of her head just below his chin, the cool weave of her satin dress, the unmistakable aroma of woman; and where she'd tipped her head, he could see the heightened pulse in her neck . . . thickening, going a bluish shade with life fluid.

"Nae. The weather is to blame for that."

"How so? It's been beautifully sunny and warm. Unseasonably so, actually."

"Exactly."

Every word she uttered damned him further. Each inflection of her voice, every nuance of her face, the minute brush of her breath across where the cravat thing should be enough protection. Everything about this woman called to him and made him ache for her, increasing the desire and lust until the Sassenach-designed trousers grew to a painful level.

"Exactly . . . how?"

The swift glance from Rory should've alerted him if Iain had control over his body anymore. Or could gain it. Or find one bone in his body that wasn't hungering.

"His Grace has an aversion to sunlight."

"He does?"

"He canna' abide its rays. 'Tis a family trait. Passed down. Sunlight brings on a massive rash, like near to death."

"He has a-a-a weakness?"

Weakness? Only to her. In any other context, he'd take a man's head for saying such. Anger filtered through the fog surrounding Iain, sending control where he hadn't any. If he thought long enough, he'd be thanking Rory, rather than the opposite. Iain lifted his head from contemplation of the lass in his arms, focused on a large fireplace, and worked at finding a voice to stop his Honor Guardsman from saying more. Only these men knew Iain's secret and the curse that followed him. As had their sires before them. They all took it to the grave.

"Never!" Rory's voice sounded scandalized.

"I spoke wrong, then. I shouldn't have called it that. I meant . . . he has a flaw."

Flaw. Was that better?

"His Grace has nae flaws!" Rory was getting loud. Iain noted others starting to move closer in order to hear.

"Are all Scots this bristly? Quick to take offense? I merely mean . . . he isn't perfect."

"His Grace is more! He's—"

"You'd best cease defending me, Rory, while you still have limbs."

"Your Grace." The man tipped his head in a nod.

"See to Grant and Lenn. They need to be relieved and the women still require escort and entertainment."

"Both of them?" Rory made a face clearly showing his disgust of the assignment.

"Take Ulrich. Send the twins to the punch bowl. As diversion."

The lass waited for him to move his attention to her. She had her lips pursed into a sweet shape resembling a kiss. Iain moved his glance the moment he saw it.

"Diversion?" she asked.

"My Honor Guardsmen are special chosen. From all other clansmen."

"What would you have them do?"

"Stand about. Flirt with the ladies. Escort a few onto the dance floor. Engender interest and speculation."

"Not start a fight?"

"What would give you that idea?"

"The more I'm around you, Iain MacAvee, the more I wonder."

"About what?"

"You . . . and civility."

There was that word again. Grant had been right. The lass craved civility. But being attired in English-tailored clothing and squiring her to a ball wasn't it?

"It takes more than cloth to make a gentleman," Tira told him.

She read his mind. Iain's eyes went wide as he stared down at her. His heart thumped once and then stopped. And then started up again with a harder thump. He was afraid she'd notice it.

"Ah, lass. The more I'm around you, the more I thank the saints, the Father, the gods, and any and every other being responsible for the fate that brought you to me."

"You just threatened your man with losing his limbs."

" 'Twas an empty one. Na' in use since afore the last wars. He kens it."

"What of this family . . . trait you suffer. Is that why you don't want children?"

"I never said I dinna' wish bairns. 'Twas your assumption."

"You do want children, then?"

"Should the fates grant such."

"Are you saying you can't have children? Is this another family trait?"

He dipped his chin, clenched his teeth, and looked away. "I doona' ken."

"Oh . . . Iain."

And with those two words, spoken with a hint of tears, she took his heart completely.

Chapter Eight

She'd invited him. He went early.

Lady Higginswale had a house resembling her: plump, with no sense of balance or structure. She even had material adorning her walls that was padded between the tacks that fastened it. Iain brushed a finger along the fabric of her bedchamber. The striped silk gave a hushed sound like a whisper. It made him yearn for thick stout castle walls built of stone and, where they'd divided the rooms, hard wood. Those walls had lines and permanency and structure. They weren't padded with fabric. They were draped with tapestries woven by skilled hands over the centuries: stout, impregnable, harsh.

He approached the bed to look down at the white perfection of Higginswale's neck and upper bosom, just glimpsed over the top of her lace-bedecked nightwear. Her veins called to him, exuding thick fluid with every beat of her heart. He could sense it, already taste it in his mouth . . . healthy, untainted by cheap gin and cheaper ales. Blood this thick and nourishing would be a welcome change from the sot-soaked vermin of the docks. Iain went to a knee and slid an arm beneath her shoulders, lifting her toward him, ignoring the snores that touched his forehead and nose. His lips opened, allowing space for his canines to lengthen, tipped with a sharpness that wouldn't even wake her. Or if they did, she'd find it ecstasy.

Exactly as he'd been invited to provide.

Iain held her limp body in position, the veins pulsing and dark against the skin of her throat, calling him, begging him . . . taunting him. It was ever the same with women, regardless of their station in life, their nationality, or their age. Every woman held a perfection of taste to her blood. When he'd first changed and noted the difference, he'd been a slave to it. That's all he wanted and it made him harsher than necessary with the male providers, leaving more than one at death's door. And then even that got old.

Iain spent his second century wandering the land and waxing philosophical. Women were a bane as much as his immortality was. They were put here to torment a man. Make him hard and lustful and in a state of pure longing even in the afterlife. So they could deny. It wasn't until a ship wrecked on his coastline, bringing a slate full of men and women into his care that he got the opportunity for study. And tasting. And experimenting. That's when he ascertained the true reason behind it.

Women held a touch of immortality in their very core. They were the bringers of life ... and he was wasting time. He had Lady Higginswale in position, limp and prepared and ready, her skin touched with the slightest rash of gooseflesh where he watched.

Iain licked the center of his top lip, between his two spikes, and lowered his head, felt the reaction through his entire frame as everything male on him responded, his rod growing large, heavy, taut. As if in preparation for its own feast. His loins throbbed beneath his kilt, craving its own rapture from a woman. . . .

And then something changed.

Iain stopped at the moment of piercing, his teeth scraping flesh and his entire body feeling primed and angered at the denial. The total recollection and then sensation of Tira flashed before him and then went right into him, making his arms tremble with the jolt of reaction. The intensity of it stunned him, lighting the interior of Lady Higginswale's bedchamber like it was full daylight and not the hour before dawn. Iain settled the woman back onto her sheets before he dropped her and stood, backed from her, put both hands to his temples, and panted with the all-consuming vibration of need, want, and desire. For Tira . . . and her alone. It was overwhelming. A new curse. Everything about her assaulted him: her beauty, her scent, her warmth, her wits; her lifeblood.

Iain bolted for the chamber window, sailed the two-story drop to the cobblestones with a bound, before starting a run that churned his legs and ate up streets. Back to the docks and far from any other woman, the entire time realizing the extent of his Tira's power. She'd ruined him for any other woman. Ever.

And he was ecstatic.

No day had ever loomed as lengthy nor passed as slowly. The morning fog wasn't even on her side, sliding away into a weak watery daylight that dissolved any rain to a mist-laden consistency. Tira watched it from her chamber window between watching the hands on her clock and waiting. Her three trunks had been packed and picked up already by MacAvee Honor Guardsmen. She hadn't recognized all of them, although Rory was easy with his quick wit and winks. Even Christa blushed. She knew it wouldn't be Grant or Lenn assisting with the transport of her belongings to the duke's yacht. It appeared they'd been given the dubious pleasure of entertaining her aunt and sister. Tira smiled. Iain was thorough. She had to give him that, even if he was leaving her alone.

At least she knew why now and sent another glance at the streets outside. The day wasn't dark enough. It had to be the same reason his father chose a woman from an impoverished English family as Iain's bride. The MacAvee family had a secret flaw, a weakness . . . an infirmity. Iain had no idea how it endeared him to her! No wonder he was so odd and secretive. From what she'd been taught of Scotland and its people, they lived in a harsh clime ruled by harsh decrees with deadly consequences. Weakness and frailty weren't tolerated. It had to be immeasurably worse in their chieftain. He'd have to hide it behind eccentric behavior. Furtive movements. Excuses. And here she'd been a termagant over his absences.

Her afternoon tea tray sat undisturbed on the table, the dress she'd chosen for the ceremony hanging beside it. Christa was below in the kitchen overseeing the heating and transporting of water for Tira's bath. The hip bath was already in place before her fireplace. They'd even lit a small blaze in the event the rain-filled day chilled her. All of it in preparation for her wedding in the Earl of Coombs chambers. Tonight. Tira glanced at the clock again and frowned. The hands didn't appear to have even moved.

Would evening never get here?

She should sleep. Iain probably kept night hours. If she wanted to be at his side, she'd have to keep the same. But her bed already looked rumpled and tossed about from her last effort at it. Lying prone with her eyes closed started the most delicious shivers; and those just led to urges and tortuous cravings she didn't understand. And that just ended with her tossing about until she gave up.

It was exactly the same as when she'd first gone to bed, three hours past midnight, once Iain brought her home and aroused all of the sensations with the lightest brush of his lips on her wrist. She could've sworn he'd touched her with his tongue! There was the slightest hint of a scratch on her skin where he'd touched, and the area continually throbbed without reason. It was quite possible he'd known what would happen and done it on purpose as punishment for making him wait another night.

Foolish. That's how she felt. What else had he called her? *Young? Naïve? Untried?* All of them true. Which made this waiting her fault. And that got her to wondering if he suffered anything like this.

"Look what's been brought, miss! From that dress shop on Turpin Street. We visited it the other day. You recollect? Oh my . . ."

Tira turned her head at the door opening to see Christa, her arms held high to keep a shrouded garment from touching the floor. Behind her were three footmen, all burdened with buckets. Without a word, they tipped their burdens and left, the hot water sending a warm, steamy aroma into the room. That's when Christa hung her garment right beside the other, unwrapped it, and gasped.

It was the seafoam green silk, fashioned into a dress like nothing she'd ever seen. Where the empire waist was in fashion topped with a square neckline and cap sleeves, this design was cut completely different. There was a long crossed bodice, creating a well of draping to frame the bosom. Long sleeves tapered from gathered shoulders to an elbow length, while the skirt had been cut in the bias, looking like a swirl of foam-flecked water rose from the hem.

And everywhere it sparkled with diamante, catching what light the fireplace sent.

"Oh my . . ." Tira breathed it.

"You ever see the like?" Christa asked.

Tira shook her head and approached, mentally inventorying what undergarments she hadn't already sent, and discarding them, one after the other. Her chemise had too much stitching on it. Guessing at the close fit of this gown, ridges of stitchery would show. Her crinoline would never fit beneath that skirt and would spoil the design of it. It was a losing exercise and she barely kept the disappointment from showing.

"Those ladies will be eating away inside with jealousy over this. You mark my words."

"I can't wear it."

"What? After that man went to the expense and genius of having such a thing crafted? You'll be ready for him promptly at sunset, or I'll resign my position."

"I've no undergarments." Tira blushed. Set aside the instant thought of wearing none, and then she reached the dress, lightly brushing the silk just as she had at the shop.

"Not to fear, miss. He had that seen to as well."

"He didn't!"

She should be scandalized as Christa went back to the door. She wasn't. There wasn't room for anything other than pleasure. And warmth she insisted came from a steam-imbued room and not from any blush.

"I should wear the tam. Grant?"

"We'll be indoors, Your Grace. Nae man needs a hat."

"She wishes this civility you speak of. She even told me so."

"Tie your hair back. That'll suffice. Gives a better view of your face as well. She'll like that."

"How do you ken?"

Iain glanced over at Rory, who was cracking nutshells with his hand ax, making more than a few of them inedible bits from the hit.

"She's well aware of your handsome face, my laird. Fain wanted to scratch a few eyes out last night, she did."

"How do you ken that as well?"

"I saw it."

"You watched her?"

Iain had Empirical pulled from the scabbard in the same movement he swiveled. Rory stopped in the motion of hitting a nut.

"I never said I watched her. I said I *saw* her."

"This is not civil behavior, Iain."

Grant again. Iain supposed only his second-in-command had the courage. Iain twisted the hilt until the chain design embossed onto it felt melded into his palm. He sheathed his blade and regarded them one at a time before ending at Rory.

"Verra well. You may explain."

"The lass finds you handsome. Virile. Verra pleasing to the eye."

"And how can you see all that?"

" 'Twas obvious to the others about you. And obvious to me."

"I asked you to explain, na' quibble." Iain toyed with the skeans along his belt next, flattening two that had rolled with the quick way he'd moved. He used the time to temper the instant emotion he wasn't labeling rage but had no other definition that fit.

"The lass canna' take her eyes from you. The lone time she does is when another woman eyes you. And then you should see the looks your Tira gives them. Fair hot enough to scorch."

"She does?"

"Help me out here, lads," Rory said.

"What the whelp says is true."

"You've been watching, too, Sean? You?"

"You'll na' take my head for saying it, will you?" the leanest clansman asked, crossing his arms and moving a step closer to where Grant stood.

Iain regarded him for long moments before returning to fussing with his apparel. He was clad in MacAvee chieftain raiment: a *feile-breacan*, finely woven muslin shirt worn without sleeves, a lace placket buttoned onto the front holding a diamond stud, silver armbands at both wrists, and the same metal glinting off the hilts of his skeans and the sporran at his hip.

"Nae," he finally replied.

"Good thing. I've only watched the lass because I was tasked to it. Her safety. Her protection. Her well-being. As you required."

Iain nodded.

"Then trust this. She finds you verra pleasing to look upon. 'Tis nae surprise. All women find you thus."

"They do?"

" 'Tis a full-time occupation, keeping them from you. According to my learning, it always was."

"Truly?"

"Your turn, Lenn." Sean motioned to the man at Iain's left.

"Sean is na' saying anything false, Your Grace."

"What times, Lenn?"

"Well . . . there was that ship that foundered a decade ago. You remember? 'Twas filled with captives all bound for sale in some eastern port. Probably destined for a potentate's harem. They were all begging for rescue until spying you."

"I dinna' touch a one of them. Much," Iain countered. He hadn't, either . . . other than a slight bit of life fluid while they slept.

"You dinna' have to. All a woman has to do is get a look at you and they're smitten. I doona' ken why, either."

"You dinna' pay much attention to His Grace in trousers then, Rory."

"Verra funny."

"You do recollect our difficulty with getting those lasses back on a ship bound for London?"

"They were a mite forward, weren't they?" Ulrich spoke up.

"A mite?" Rory inserted. "I have scars from the nail raking one of them gave me as I hauled her off."

"Perhaps you should speak sweeter words."

"And what of the French comtesse who arrived, seeking an escape from the guillotine? According to my grandfather, she was still screaming when he drove off with her, tied into the carriage for good measure."

"So that's where she went," Iain mused.

"And you recollect the shipwreck in '82?"

"Barely," Iain replied.

"According to the tale, every lass aboard went from weeping survivor to lovelorn wretch. In a matter of days. Just from your appearance."

"*My* appearance?" Iain put a hand over his shoulder and grabbed the hilt of Empirical again. Lenn backed a step as it happened.

"My brother misspeaks, my laird. 'Tis actually said how your great-great-grandsire set their hearts aflutter. 'Tis a family trait, this . . . handsomeness. Passed down from son to son, as normal."

Iain looked from Grant to his twin, released the sword, and felt powerfully sheepish. "Oh."

" 'Tis also said they had to be physically forced to leave Castle Blannock. En masse. Not one would leave without the others."

"Ancient history, lads. Ancient."

"And then, there's that Spanish contessa."

"Which one?" Grant asked for him.

"The one haunting the east tower at Glencairn."

"That explains the weeping sound. Great story there. All about unrequited love."

"Aye. 'Tis said she perished of a broken heart."

"She took a fine time of it, then. She was nigh a century old."

Iain did his best to ignore them and squelch the reactions: remorse, guilt. He couldn't remember the last time he'd felt those. It didn't help that he'd asked for this listing, either.

" 'Tis also rumored the MacAvee chieftain has a fondness for wenches with reddish-shaded hair. Exactly like Miss Tira. Mothers with daughters of that ilk make certain to cover them. In the event the duke is out and happens to see."

"I've heard 'tis far worse if the aforementioned lasses happen to spot the duke. Then the mothers really have their hands full."

Iain knew he flushed. He didn't need to see it. He could feel sweat at his hairline. He disguised it with a move to bind his hair back into a queue. "Enough lads. Perhaps you could tell me something helpful."

"Well . . . you did start it."

Rory pointed it out. Iain regarded him for long moments before deciding to ignore it. He pulled to his full height and looked them all over in turn. They made an impressive sight, all attired in MacAvee plaid, all looking like perfect Scot gentlemen.

"Why is it this particular lass above all others?" he asked.

"We doona' ken why, we're only grateful."

Iain pulled back at Grant's answer. "For what?"

"Being there to assist with keeping the other lasses away. Have you na' been listening?"

"Oh. Should I wear the English trousers, then?"

"Nae!"

Several voices said it together. Iain winked.

"You should actually be shrouded with a full sett . . . only that would simply show your size."

"Why is that an issue?"

"The more you're out and seen, the worse the attention gets and the more we lose sleep."

"Lenn's right, my laird. Trying to keep the lasses from you is akin to damming a burn with a bit of piss and peat."

"Why . . . much more time in London and we'll have a riot, and then we'll have you in their Tower, and then we'll have prices on our heads for taking their stone rampart apart to rescue you."

Iain looked at his second-in-command and sobered. "I guess I'll leave the trousers for another time."

"We sail with the tide?"

"We'll board ship the moment we wed. You keep the path open."

"And grant me the aunt this time. That Ophelia has the mind of a bog fly."

"Unfair. And as the eldest, I call escort rights," Grant replied.

"By half a minute, you weasel. Half."

"Wrestle for it."

Iain ignored where the twins tussled, deciding the issue with strength while he worked at gathering it. He had to be strong enough to tell his Tira about his curse and await her decision. He wanted her with need that hampered each step, but he wanted her freely, with full knowledge, and of her own free will.

"Hold!"

The twins smashed into a chair, then another. Iain watched Sean sidestep them. He only wished there was someone capable of putting a hold on him.

Chapter Nine

Every candle had been lit in the earl's chamber, sending light onto every available surface: her father's wasted body beneath the cover, the servant's worried expression, three MacAvee Honor Guardsmen attended as witnesses . . . and her. Ulrich was presiding over the wedding, looking and acting official, and much older than his thirty years. The twins were missing, their bruises telling why Lenn was escorting the sister. They had orders to keep those ladies occupied or lock them into their rooms. Either way, there wasn't to be any disturbance that might upset his Tira.

And that included him.

But then she appeared, the silk skimming her frame as he'd known it would when he'd purchased it and ordered the design. All the while knowing it was self-destructive, but he hadn't changed it. The torment was ceaseless in nature and ever increasing as well. Iain realized it as the barely leashed beast within him stirred, striving to release all the pent passion, power, and lust. The combination went to a threatening degree as he approached and took her hands within his, the contact adding to his ordeal and heightening its effect, as if the creature within him laughed at any effort of control and was determined to undermine it.

Tira had her neck craned, meeting his gaze with eyes as clear and bottomless as Loch Nyven, looking lit from some glow within and not simple candlelight. Iain's suffering worsened the longer he delved into her eyes, his heart quickening, his loins thickening, and his frame trembling, and yet he was powerless to change it. It was impossible to keep hold of her and equally impossible to let go. Everything on her seemed to vibrate, as if calling to him, and no one seemed to notice as Ulrich started the ceremony.

The chieftain *feile-breacan* was woven of thin, barely tensile strands of wool to a drape that shouldn't be a problem, and yet as Tira's unblinking regard continued, the plaid grew hot, cloying, and thick . . . as restrictive as those Sassenach trousers. Words swarmed about his head, barely denting the incessant buzz sound in his head, and he watched Tira open her mouth to answer.

"I do. I take Iain, uh Evan? James. And did you say Duncan as well? Yes?"

Her words carried laughter, and Iain pulsed in place although nothing on him moved. He worked at control, holding every muscle to a painful degree to keep the hunger for her at bay. Her laugh threatened all of it. He'd warn her if he dared as she continued adding to his distress by more words exchanged with Ulrich.

"Alexander, too? The fourth? Very well. All of those names. Him. I do take this man with all those names as my husband. Forsaking all others until death. Yes. Definitely. I do."

Iain forced his gaze to where Ulrich stood, smiling broadly at both of them. Then came his names in order, all of them; a listing of his titles, all of them; and then his clansman listed all the responsibilities and honors and properties that came with his hand, although Iain didn't hear much, if any, of it.

"I do."

He choked on the vow. He was in a new hell. Or he'd been granted heaven. Or they'd joined the two. Iain wasn't thinking as he pulled at her hands, stepping close in order to take their conjoined hands to his lips. He felt her gasp as he grazed teeth along her knuckles, bumping along the ridges and sending flickers all through him. In over two centuries he'd had little issue with the harassment caused by lusting for women, yet everything altered when he met her. Iain shifted forward, got the heavy solidity of his sporran against his loins, and hoped no one else noticed how it moved, flashing silver glint off the embossed edges.

He was drunk and hadn't touched a drop of whiskey, dizzy like excessive battle once caused, confused as if he'd taken a blow, and this lass was at the center of it. He was certain of it. It was obvious with the way she clung to his hand, as if she needed it for balance and stability. *Balance and stability?* The thought was laughable. The lass rocked his world off-kilter so much he shook. And then he realized why, as want and need and absolute desire worked away at his control, clouding the scene. Iain tightened every muscle in search of control. More . . . Harder . . .

He heard words through the fog that seemed to envelope her, highlighting and showcasing her perfect features and lush woman curves. It was a fog of his creation, imbued with her scent as it surrounded and then impaired. Iain swallowed hard, heard the words pronouncing them joined: husband and wife. Then he heard something about how he should cease standing there like a Druid stone and kiss his bride.

Kiss her? Had Ulrich gone mad? Iain didn't dare kiss her. He was barely keeping his powers at bay. He didn't know what might happen if they got released. He was terrified to find out. Him. Iain MacAvee. Creature of doom. Afraid.

He felt and heard her pulse increase, gaining cadence and volume until it dragged his into rhythm with it. She lifted her lips, sweetly pursed and holding every form of rapture. Iain groaned as the beast flexed against its leash. He pulled her right up to his chest and lowered his head to brush his lips with the lightest touch against hers.

And then she moaned.

Iain latched on to skin, feeling his teeth elongate despite everything he used to stay it. There was just this perfection of moment, encased and defined . . . for them. Her palms were flat against his chest for a buffer. It didn't work. Iain could feel and sense every bit of her heart as it raced. Time ceased to function. The room ceased to exist. Nothing mattered save her breath as it touched on his cheek . . . his nose . . . his upper lip, her touch moist as soft skin got bruised beneath his; and then he tasted the absolute nirvana of her blood as it flicked against the cage of muscle and will he had about the beast with a temptation no man should ever have to endure and survive.

Nae!

Tira's eyes flew open as Iain pulled his head back to roar a guttural word toward the ceiling just as both casement windows burst open, sending gusts of rain-filled air into the chamber. Candles extinguished, plunging the room into darkness. Tira heard her father's garbled exclamation and a thud as his servant dropped to the floor, and from far into the depths of the house, what sounded like screams of rage and anger from Aunt Adelaide and

Ophelia. Then she was fully in Iain's arms, moving out the door and into the hall as if every sconce held a torch and it wasn't complete blackness. If she had any experience with the absolute wonder of what had happened to her with his kiss, she'd have done more than cling with her arms about his neck and her face pressed tightly to his shoulder.

"Sean, fetch Grant and Lenn! Rory, see us to my ship and doona' waste another moment. And Ulrich? If you *ever* do anything so stupid again, I vow—"

She barely felt his lunge into a carriage before speaking the punishment Ulrich might earn, then she experienced the rapid sway of a vehicle in high motion combined with the harsh rhythm of breaths Iain huffed continually and with absolute precision all over where the bodice left her skin exposed. His ship was impossible to see through the fog-warped dock, but without stopping, Iain jumped from the carriage, crossed the gangway, a deck, and then entered a cabin, with doors shutting behind him seemingly of their own accord.

And then he set her unsteadily to her feet and pulled away, holding his hands over his face while he shoved more harsh breaths through his lips. And with them came words.

"Forgive me, *leannan*. I'm a fool and a wretch."

"Iain—"

"Nae! A wretch and then a fool! For what I've done! Doubly so for na' stopping—Hellfire! Get this ship underway!"

He yanked the door open to yell, sending waves of sound with it. Tira heard the noise of running feet, a grinding clatter, shouts and hollering from somewhere in the night, and she was almost afraid Iain meant to leave her if she didn't do something to stop him.

"Iain?"

She said it softly and got a stiff back and then a shut door. Iain turned toward her and appeared to hunch his shoulders slightly, as if expecting a blow. He wouldn't meet her eyes, either.

"Aye?"

"What . . . have you done?"

He pulled in a huge breath, looming so large he nearly touched the decking above his head, which was where he appeared to be looking. "I'm na' entirely certain I can tell you."

"But . . . can you do it again?"

His mouth opened. Closed. Opened again. Then he lowered his eyes to hers, and the moment they met, the lantern behind her flared, sending light onto all of him, while superimposing her shadow on the wall behind him. A blink later the light dimmed, returning her indistinct shadow to one caused by the faint golden glow basking on wooden walls.

"Yes. Like that. Just . . . like that." She was panting and the words revealed it. Oddly, it seemed to create the same exact reaction in him.

"*Leannan*—" he began.

"What does that mean?"

"What?"

"This *leannan*. You promised you'd tell me after our consummation—"

He swore in Gaelic. She understood it perfectly. Her eyes went wide. The light behind her flared again. Dimmed.

"You promised, Iain."

As a temptress, she was going to need work. Tira realized it as he paled and actually took a step back to the door at the low tone she used. His answer was garbled and difficult to understand and sprinkled with intermingled Gaelic and English words, coming in spurts with every ragged huff of air he used. It was visual and doing erratic things to every nerve ending in her body.

"I promised a lot of things, *leannan*. And I'm vexed. I've words that need saying. Truths you need to ken. You have the right to it."

"Now?"

"Lass . . . please. I ken you need civility and gentlemanly behavior. I've such little grasp of either, and nae control at the moment. I'm terrible afeared if we touch, I'll—"

"Kiss me, Iain."

"What?"

The high pitch of his voice surprised him, matching the width of his eyes as he noted where she'd moved and how she'd done it. If he looked closely enough, he'd note all the gooseflesh roving her skin, creating the most delicious shivers. She licked her lip and tasted blood and wondered when she'd bitten it.

"I said—"

He put a hand up, stopping her as much as the tremor that

scored him did. "Lass, please. Dinna' you hear me? I'm afeared of what might happen if I touch you again. . . ."

"Yes?"

Another step put her at where his hand was still out, defensively, the sensation as vivid as if it touched her. Tira stood, her entire being attuned to the vibrations emanating from just one open palm.

"There's nae going back! You doona' ken! I may na' be able to keep from taking . . . and I—Sweet mother of—"

The rest of his words disappeared into his intake of breath as the ship got underway, the sway rolling Tira right into contact with the hand meant to stay her, and that got her pulled into an embrace of trembling flesh-covered iron. Her feet left the floor and she barely felt it as Iain swung her into his arms, lowered his head, and gave her the kiss she'd asked for.

The lamp flared, sending brightness through her closed eyelids. It competed with the arc of lightning racing through her, spreading a hum of anticipation in its wake. Tira felt him moving across wood that pounded with each step, and then the cool crispness of sheeting met her back, her shoulders, her upper arms. The green silk filmed her skin as an afterthought, pulled away by one hand while the other held her head in place, her nose next to his, her lips matched to his, building roar of elevated sound all through her with every licking and sucking motion he made.

Tira undulated sinuously against the smooth material at her back and rasp of wool everywhere else, impatience and something else feeding her movements, something indefinable and raw, basic and elemental . . . and orchestrated with perfection by her new husband, Iain MacAvee.

Her fingers roved him, delving beneath buttons and around heavily woven leather belts and fastenings, pulling up on his shirt and yanking down on the plaid until she found flesh. The sensitive skin of each fingertip trilled along ridges of muscle, about the thick ropes of brawn in his belly, all over his chest, belly, shoulders . . . learning the shape, texture, and movement of them before she wrapped as far about him as she could, not even noting the wool getting yanked completely away, matching rock-hewn male to quivering female, skin to skin and heat to heat.

Thick, hard male slid along her belly, went between her thighs, teased along her core, came out again onto her belly, tendering heat and scorch and energy. Everything on her craved and demanded more and she didn't know how to request it. And then knew she didn't have to. The grunt accompanying each motion promised more as he moved his body to some primeval rhythm . . . sliding his maleness between her thighs, tormenting and teasing the wetness, back along her belly again, until Tira beat at his back with frustration and ache and absolute wantonness. A hand enveloped her hip, filled with her buttock, lifting her into position about him as he continued his massage, building passion that grew with every breath she pulled in and huffed back out.

Tira's legs wrapped about him, assisting her shoves upward, every fiber on her begging, pleading, sobbing with all-consuming fever. And then he shifted, lifting onto his free arm, putting chiseled male into view, his rod readied and at her apex, where everything that was quivering and suppliant about her strove for what he'd prepared her for. Gaelic words escorted the slide of his lips, licking down her chin and to her throat. Tira clung, lunging up at him in unrhythmic surges, begging him to fill the throbbing need, thirst, and want.

"*Leannan* . . ."

"Yes, Iain . . . yes. Now. Iain, please? Now—"

Something stabbed into her neck at the exact moment he plunged through her maiden wall, cursing her with stinging and fiery sensation in both places at once. Tira went stiff with pain and hurt. They echoed in the cry she made as it reached the planking above them, but when it filtered back down, it was filled with ecstasy and rapture and bliss. The next held more of the same. Or perhaps it sounded of the absolute wonder he created with every thrust of his body . . . complementing the absolute ecstasy emanating from her throat.

Again. Over. Deep. Full. Sucking and taking from her neck while giving and receiving at her woman-place. Tira's erotic cries filled the cabin, blending with the light that intensified and dimmed so vividly it was seen even through clenched eyelids.

"Ah . . . lass. Love. Tira. My *leannan* . . ."

Iain's whisper released his mouth from her flesh, and his hand pulled on her hair, forcing her chin upward to see what should be bare wood ceiling when she opened her eyes. It wasn't. Tira watched the perfect vision of clouds, red hued and dark at the edges, as they alternately brightened and then dimmed with every flare of light. Iain scraped a path to one ear, lapping at skin with the same rhythm he used to pleasure and possess her, each lunge getting fuller and heavier and harsher, in perfect sync with the increased thunder of his breathing.

"*Leannan . . .*"

He carried pleasure with his thrusts and ecstasy with his movements, and the sensations combined, warped, realigned. Still Iain plunged, pulled back out, plunged again. Over and over and over until the combination of wonders collided into such rapture, Tira's mouth opened in another burst of amazement and joy. She felt him lifting from her on both arms, gifting her more view of glistening male nakedness, rippled with muscle and taut with seeming agony. She couldn't keep from such splendor and ran her fingers about him as he arched upward, keeping his loins deep into hers. The skin she touched darkened, flushing as he sent the longest, most visceral groan into existence all about and over them. It reverberated in waves as he ran out of air and ended with soblike noise. The sound raised bumps along her skin and brought tears that flooded her eyes. Tira blinked rapidly, and when that didn't work, she shoved a hand across her eyes to keep her sight fixed on the beauty that was Iain as he held himself taut, trembling in place as his body pulsed deep within her.

"Oh . . . sweet."

He didn't finish the whisper but he didn't need to. If it was even a small measure of what he'd given her to feel, it was heaven, amazement, absolute divinity. The cabin darkened oddly, as if time passed and the lamp was low on fuel. The dark about her vision kept intruding, too. That just wasn't fair! She wanted this experience. She wanted to experience and see it and memorize it, so it would be forever hers . . . all of it. That's why she was wide-eyed and watching as he shook his head atop his shoulders before lowering his chin to look down at her, displaying what could only be blood on his lips and chin, and the sharp tips of canine fangs. And then everything went dark.

Chapter Ten

"That word . . . *leannan*. It means *sweet*. Or *sweetheart* . . . or just *heart*."

Iain forced his head to roll toward her, basked in what little light the lamp still projected. Her green eyes were darker, the lashes fuller and more lush, or something, while the dark red shade of her lips was spliced by the tips of sharp canines. She looked amazing, feline and erotic. She blinked, putting a shine to those eyes as she watched him from atop his right arm. Her head was cradled just above his bent elbow, numbing his arm all the way to his fingers. Iain licked dry, chapped lips and shuddered with chill. He'd rarely been as weak and fatigued, useless as a newly birthed bairn and twice as defenseless.

"Aye," he whispered.

"How do I know that?"

"I . . . gifted it . . . to you."

The words were spliced with weak pants of breath. Iain searched with his free hand for cover; the bed sheet, his *feile-breacan*, hell, even her silk gown would assist with muting some of this frailty! His fingers found nothing useful; even the muslin beneath them felt melded into position despite his tugging. And it was his fault. He'd had to open a slit on his wrist and share fluid with her. He had to! She was dying even as he'd done it, forcing his tainted lifeblood through her lips, draining him as it changed her. He'd never changed another human before. He hadn't known when to stop her, and then he hadn't the strength. He was in luck that she'd done it, apparently sated as she moved . . . rolling from him to rest atop his elbow. Where she'd stayed.

All of it happened what seemed hours ago, while he paced his heart and measured his breathing, and worked at rest. Using the time to will strength into his body to regenerate what little fluid she'd left him. So he wouldn't take any of it back.

"Gifted? How? And with what?"

She was getting annoyed with him. It sounded in her voice. What he wouldn't give for one drunken sailor! Iain huffed a breath of amusement, rolling his lips with it. He'd be forced to use the livestock in the hold long before they reached the coastline below MacAvee Hall. He'd already be there if he hadn't wasted time existing, reliving each and every bit of fulfillment he'd experienced with her. He still might visit the hold . . . if there were any hours left afore dawn and if he had the strength to reach it.

"Iain?"

"I'm listening," he replied.

"I didn't ask if you were listening. I asked for an explanation of this gift."

She lifted her head, giving him the sting of renewed feeling in the limb, although it was slow moving with every shallow thump of pulse left him. He needed rest, recuperation, blood . . . anything other than interrogation and truths. There was a decided trip of his heart as she went to her knees beside him to look down at him, every portion of her exuding sensuality and pleasure. She reeked of wanton abandonment and sexual satisfaction. Nothing seemed hidden despite the shielding of her hair. He'd known she was his mate, he just hadn't thought through what that meant. He licked his lips again, but it did nothing for the dryness.

"Iain, I don't understand. Help me."

"My sire . . . dinna' raise a fool," he replied.

"What does that have to do with anything?"

"Only a fool . . . tussles with . . . an armed woman."

"Armed?"

Puzzlement shaped her eyes into narrowed slits, the lashes shielding their beautiful green color.

"Aye." He licked his lips again and got the same dry feeling.

"I don't even have my clothes."

She crossed her arms before her, as if that worked better at concealment than the thick curtain of her hair. And she blushed. Color suffused her skin, sending Iain into such a vast chasm of need that he jerked with the task of reining it. It was too soon. She wasn't ready. He still hadn't told her—

"What is it, Iain? Iain?"

Soft whispers filtered over him, accompanied by the feel of her hands, roving his chest, shoulders, belly . . . her fingers sliding along flesh that craved the touch. Despite everything, Iain felt his groin stirring, taking the fluid he needed just because she was near.

"Tira." The name was ground through clenched teeth and sounded it.

"You're very handsome, Iain. Manly. I—"

She pulled her lower lip into her mouth and held it with her teeth, putting spikes on view. Iain watched them lengthen with trepidation, pulling in and tightening everything on his frame to endure whatever she deigned to do to him.

"Truly beautiful."

"Men . . . are na' beautiful, *leannan*."

"Oh, but you are. No wonder the women go crazed around you."

She'd changed to the Gaelic tongue, making the words more erotic and stimulating. His senses assimilated it while her fingers continued driving him mad.

"Or . . . perhaps it's how truly masculine you are. Large. Oh my. Hard. And I'm new to this."

His ears were abuzz with light-headedness, while everything male on him was getting primed and prepared and readied. She might be a novice, but he was already in severe trouble.

"Lass . . . you must . . . stop."

"It's my wedding night, Iain."

"I'm na' certain . . . I can perform . . . again."

"This part seems certain."

Iain groaned as she wrapped both hands about him, earning a full twinge into her palms and a groan of torment from his parched throat. He felt his own teeth lengthening as the beast within stretched, exhibiting its power and its thirst. He barely heard her next words.

"I mean . . . I don't truly know, but I think—"

"You ever hear of the Black Death?" Iain interrupted her, the words strangled and brutal sounding.

Her hands stopped. He waited one heartbeat before she answered, and since it was stuttered, it affected the next pulse beat, making it almost painful with the thud. He wasn't strong enough for this!

"Y-y-yes?"

"And . . . the death dealers that plagued the land? You ken them?"

She giggled. *Giggled?* And then she resumed her vicious stroking of his man-part, sending his heart rate into such stridency, it actually pained.

"Oh, Iain . . . you talk of death and ancient history? Now?"

"I dinna' believe, either. Once."

He answered the ceiling high above them, shadowed and indistinct with loss of light, while his body fought an onslaught of need that elongated and defined his teeth farther. Tira was new to this. She didn't know the power of her new existence. She didn't know what she was doing to him. But that didn't stop it, and it certainly didn't stop her.

"Nice . . . oh, Iain. Verra, verra nice."

He groaned. The slip of tongue she made into his own dialect toyed at his ear, sending tendrils about his senses. Enwrapping him. Binding him. He couldn't seem to move from enjoyment of her caress . . . and she did it all without use of even a cover. Lips grazed him, then a tongue, before a skim of burn lit through him as she sliced at an inner thigh, lapping at the flesh. Iain grabbed her arms and hauled her into view before she took everything he had left. His arms shook as he watched her lick at the blood on her lip. And then she blew a kiss through the air separating them. His tongue loosened and he told her.

"Lass . . . you need ken this! I'm one of them!"

"I need you, Iain. All . . . of you. In me. Now. Please, Iain . . . now."

Hellfire and damnation!

Iain could describe both as Tira slid her body along his, torturing him with her skin and the promise of her sheath wrapped about where he was pumping with little lunges his body made without any effort on his part.

His lips parted and he hissed, giving her a full look at his elongated spikes. He watched her glance there and back to his eyes, a flicker of fright deep within hers, interfering with the haze of sensuality wrapped all about her. But it was too late. He'd lost control. Again.

"Iain . . . I don't—"

"Trust me, lass, you will!"

He surged up at the same time he pulled her downward, latching onto her throat with the same motion he used to bring her down atop him, gaining hot wetness wrapped about where he most needed it. The beast within him flexed, roaring with the instant influx of lifeblood, and then he felt the prick of her teeth into the flesh beneath his ear.

Everything went absolutely wild. Primitive. Iain thrashed against her in seeming agony and she held to him. He rolled with her, pumping as the mattress shifted beneath them, and then toppled onto the floor, taking them with it. She met every one of his thrusts as he filled and refilled her, her loins matching him move for move, her legs wrapped so tightly about him it worked as a spring. Iain unlatched his teeth from her puncture, licking to seal the wound and felt her do the same. But nothing stopped the complete and total abandonment of where they were joined. Connected. Thumping into each other over and over until the tightness in his chest, back, and loins was impossible to contain. That's when glory erupted, ripping such complete and total ecstasy through him that he tossed his head back and yelled of it, ignoring how the deep throbbing tones of the beast burned his throat and tore through his chest.

The sound echoed through the cabin. Died. And then he looked down at this woman; Tira. His woman . . . his mate. Iain watched her view the blood coating him, assimilating and deciding it. Their blood . . . shared. Combined. His arms trembled slightly before they gave, collapsing him onto the mattress beside her, and then he felt her shudders. Like laughter . . . only . . .

She isn't sobbing, is she?

Iain rolled his head, using his forehead for the fulcrum, solidly terrified of what he'd see. Then he blinked her into focus. He was wrong. She wasn't crying. She was laughing, silently and with childish glee. She laughed? She knew what he was, and what he'd made her, and she laughed? For the first time since he'd met her, Iain relaxed completely and within moments he was unconscious.

A sunbeam brought him to awareness, singeing his shoulder as it speared the floor. The brightness stunned and then got action. Iain grabbed Tira to his chest, dragging her as he scuffled beneath the bed, inserted his forefinger into a knothole, and jerked up on the hidden door that led to his space. He swiveled to take the brunt of the landing. The drop wasn't far, four feet... exactly as he'd specified. Yet it felt farther. They hit with a thud atop his pallet, his ancient pallet, the one he'd had when he'd first turned. Although back then it had been plump with horse-hair and straw and not flat with age. Iain groaned with the loss of air. The door thumping shut hid it. The woman in his arms and atop him didn't do more than sigh, softly brushing his chest with air, and then she snuggled into the well he created at his side.

His arms tightened as did the band about his heart as he realized the full power of love. He'd failed his strongest vow—never to turn another without their full awareness of the deed *and* the consequences, yet nothing on him felt remotely guilty or anything other than aglow with rapture. Why... if he knew his maker's name and location, he'd even thank him. Iain lay back, looked over the seams of floor above his head, and shut his eyes for rest. With his woman's appetite, he was going to need all of it he could get.

Chapter Eleven

The smell of food woke her, wafting through to scent the air; the pungent aroma of roasted beef and creamed gravy mixed with the equally mouth-watering aroma of warmed, fresh bread . . . topped with a pat of butter. Tira lifted her head in appreciation and sniffed. It felt like weeks since she'd eaten, and her belly growled with emptiness while her mouth filled with moisture.

It was night dark, but that was odd unless she'd slept the day away. Tira stretched and moved a bit from the cool feel of what could only be Iain's skin. The sensation was a bit like sleeping beside polished alabaster marble. She shivered and pulled into a sit, sliding her buttocks along texture that resembled woven hemp or rough-finished wool. She spread her arms out, looking for covering. Useless. There wasn't a stitch of fabric anywhere. She was hungry and she was tired and she was chilled. And it was dark and foreboding. Cramped. Like a tomb. Tira grazed her hands along the pallet thing beneath her, reached bare plank floor, and within inches, her fingers met polished wooden wall. She ran her hands along the wall to a spot just above her head, where the delicious smell of a roast beef supper was getting overlaid by the sounds of someone eating it. And that angered her.

Tira narrowed her eyes and glared at the blackness, and from the exact spot came a glow. Feeble at first and then growing, it spread until the haziest bit of light carved out Iain's form for her and then her own. As well as the finite amount of room they shared. She blinked and the light disappeared.

"Iain?"

The name hadn't left her throat before she was seized, pulled into an embrace resembling iron, her mouth covered while Iain hissed a word at her ear. Tira's heart ceased beating with the fright, and then restarted with a thud that hurt. It was impossible for anyone to move as quickly as he had, or the darkness warped reality.

"Hush!"

She nodded slightly and the hand at her mouth eased. It took another moment before she could pull enough moisture into her mouth to swallow. And then breathe. It felt like Iain matched her, taking his own breath. His skin was growing warm, too. And then he was running a tongue along her shoulder, making her scrunch it with the tickle.

"What . . . are you doing?" She barely made a sound with the whisper. He returned it in kind.

"Keeping you occupied."

The touch of amusement feathered across her skin with the reply.

"Why?"

"Seems a pleasant way to spend an eve. With my bride. Whilst I await the sunset and our sup."

"But . . . that's not fair."

"Nae?"

"I'm hungry now."

His tongue lifted from her as she watched the compartment brighten again. This time a heady, golden glow infused it.

"You're doing that?"

"Aye."

"You truly can control . . . light?"

"I can illuminate in stages, but it takes from me."

"How?"

"That is just one of my powers, love. One."

Tira swallowed again, wondering at that vagary of nature as she nearly choked. Footsteps echoed across the floor above them and then the door shut. She felt the man about her relax. He eased the confine of his arms and legs as the light dimmed to a portion of before, making the planking about them indistinct and faint even when she squinted.

"Can I have just a small spot of tea? Maybe a scone? Or a bit of bread?"

"There will na' be any left."

"There won't?"

"Na' if Grant follows orders, as always."

"You order him to eat in your chamber?"

"And take the leavings when he finishes. Or pitch it all overboard. Must have been a verra good sup if he ate it, since he has his own to now partake."

"Your man eats your meal for you? And you allow it?"

"I canna' do it justice, *leannan*."

"That's ridiculous. Just look at the size of you. You eat. You have to."

"My size does na' change. Ever. This is what my Honor Guard works to avoid."

"Your size?"

"Rumor and speculation over such a thing. And how the years fail to dent any of it."

Tira shook her head to clear it. It didn't work. Everything felt muddled and fogged. "Where are we?" she asked.

"Safe."

"Where exactly is safe?"

"Beneath my cabin. In a chamber I had constructed and designed. In secret and with a fortune in bribe money."

"Why go to all that trouble?"

"So my Honor Guardsmen can partake of my meal and na' one soul is the wiser that it was na' me at that table."

"Maybe he didn't take it all. Maybe he left a slice of bread?"

"Bread? You want bread?"

"It smelled heavenly, didn't it? And I'm famished. I haven't had as much as a crust since sometime before our—uh . . . wedding and—". . . *the consummation that followed*. Her words dribbled off in recollection of how he'd shown her absolute heaven. And had it been twice? Last night was a darker blur than the space about them. It *had* been twice. She'd started the second one. Tira blushed. That made everything moist and warm in the enclosure where it had been chilled and inhospitable.

"You can smell it?"

"What?" Tira had to keep her thoughts on what he said and not what he made her feel. But how was she to do that when everything about him seemed created to heighten and enhance? No wonder women acted as they did around Iain MacAvee. She was in danger of it herself.

"Bread."

"Oh, yes . . . bread. Of course I smell it. You can't?"

"Na' unless I want to. All I smell is blood, *leannan*. That . . . and lust. Yours for me is particularly noticeable."

"Of all the odious, egotistical, arrogant—"

"Are you saying 'tis untrue?"

Tira turned her head and put her cheek against his chest and listened to the solid thump of his heart, oddly mimicking hers. Her tongue felt larger, thick, useless. She bit at it and felt the minute sting of a cut before shaking her head slightly.

"That's what I thought you'd be saying," he finally answered.

"I don't understand, Iain."

"I dinna' ask for this prowess, Tira. For a man of a score and five, though, 'twas a true gift. At first."

"At first?" She stiffened slightly.

"Anything done to excess becomes a bore. And then a bane. And then a burden. Trust me."

"To excess?" She choked on the word as one hand curled into a fist.

"Anything."

"You might not want to say another word, Iain." As a threat, it didn't do what she wanted. He simply sent a breath of possible amusement all over her exposed flesh.

"You canna' fight it, lass. Well . . . you can, but will na' change anything."

"And you'll be finding yourself locked out of my chamber quite often if you don't cease speaking, Iain Evan Duncan and-a-few-other-names MacAvee."

He pulled back. "I doona' ken you at all, and I'm na' fond of your track of thinking."

"Iain—"

"Hush. And listen. I've got words that need saying and deeds I canna' undo. And forgiveness that I dare na' even ask for."

"Forgiveness?"

He nodded. She felt it. And then he started talking again, the words low and clear through where her ear rested on his chest.

"The attraction of the lasses was always there. I dinna' ask for it. I dinna' want it in particular, but I dinna' fight it. What man would?"

"Iain—"

He ignored her low-toned outburst. " 'Tis said all MacAvee

lairds have this appeal. It came from birth. Passed on from sire to son. Even with the scars I suffered in battle. The lasses would na' leave me alone. 'Twas almost a curse."

"You expect me to believe that?"

"I could na' attend the slightest fest without an issue. There's a sonnet written about the fight that took place on May fest back in 1536. The laird's wife had a grand lust and was na' averse to showing it. And acting on it. That fight burnt down Glencairn's great hall. Took a century until I got the deeds and had it re-built."

"Did you say 1536?" Tira's voice accurately portrayed her disbelief even if he couldn't see her expression.

"Aye. I was na' even a score in age yet," Iain continued. "That was na' the first of my troubles, either."

"I don't want to hear any more. Really. You can cease regaling me with nonsense. I'll wait for my supper. I promise."

He ignored her again. "The worst incident was when I came to the attention of the wife of the Douglas of Loch Nyven. She was a right bonny one. Ripe. Inviting."

"Don't you understand English, Iain? I said I don't want to hear."

"I should have been forewarned. Na' of her husband. He was used to being a cuckold. I should have been told of bloody Stewart, King James the fifth!"

"The king?" The words were deadpan as disbelief had gone right over to complete doubt and skepticism. Tira closed her eyes. It was better than rolling them.

"How was I to ken he'd taken her for his mistress? Hell, he already had two of them at Edinburgh right beneath the queen's nose!"

"You truly expect me to believe this, don't you?"

"That's why I was at Solway Moss. I was ordered to be there. Fighting for the king. As punishment."

"Solway Moss?"

"Aye. November twenty-fourth it was. 1542. Cursed fogged day. See, your King Henry the eighth declared war but sent the Duke of Norfolk to fight his battles for him. It was another defeat for the Scots. One of many, curse them. Doona' you ken your own history?"

"I have to admit, Iain. One thing you do is spin a grand story."

"You doona' believe me."

"Of course not."

"I dinna' at first, either."

"At . . . first?"

"Aye. At first you fight it. You try and behave as normal. You eat as you used to. Will na' matter. Roasted meat. Bread. Even ale. Na' a bit of it will stay in your belly. Turns to poison if you try. You believe you can walk about like other men—in full sun . . . and you canna'. The sun's rays are worse than a burn from a fire pit."

"You're trying to tell me you're three hundred years old. Is that it?"

"You miscalculate. I am na' three hundred. I am two hundred ninety-eight. Unless you add in the score and five I was when that wretch turned me. That would make me a mite over three hundred."

"Iain, please—"

"Is it so verra hard to believe, *leannan?*"

"In a word, yes. Double yes. And then add a third. This is impossible to believe."

He gave another sigh. "You've heard of the Black Death?"

"You asked that last night, didn't you?"

He nodded. She felt it. "I was trying for a bit of honor. Restraint. I dinna' wish to turn you unless you agreed."

"T-t-turn me?"

"I love you, Tira. You believe that?"

The solid thump of his heart toyed at her ear, while the legs she perched atop had nothing cool about them anywhere. They still resembled iron, although it was flesh-wrapped metal now, while he moved a hand into hair that had to be a nest of snarls. Tira reached a hand to smooth it and collided with his. And that just got hers snatched.

"Y-y-yes."

"Your little stammer is verra endearing, love."

"What did you mean, turn me?"

"You'll recollect I love you, no matter what I tell you? Fair?"

It was difficult to concentrate with what had to be a tongue fixated on her wrist, lapping at the tissue there.

"Black . . . Death, Iain."

" 'Twas the start of the talk. Tales of death dealers started up,

creatures that walked the night, taking a man's lifeblood and tossing the flesh. You ever told these?"

"Everyone hears stories like that. To frighten . . . and entertain. I think plays are written about them. They're not called
death dealers. They're called—I can't remember the term . . ."

Her voice lowered, losing the words, but that was his fault as
he moved his ministration up her arm toward an elbow, wrapping
it about him as he went.

"We're called vampires, *leannan*."

"Vampires."

The word was softly whispered, engendering illicit sensual
overtones onto the term. She couldn't keep her mind function-
ing and that wasn't normal. Or sane. Or anything other than complete madness. His touch was at the core of her trouble, too. Just
like before.

"Aye, love. Vampires. Purveyors of death. Proprietors of the
night. Seeking only to satisfy their lusts while taking their pleasure. Is this the tales you've heard?"

She nodded. His voice created shivers that went over her entire frame before centering somewhere deep within her. Calling
to something primitive and earthy that stirred and came to life
in her very core. Something she'd never felt before. One thing
she believed about this story was his prowess with women. The
man's voice created pleasure, his touch generated energy, and his
frame and size guaranteed sexual satisfaction. She could well believe centuries of women swooned over him if the sensation
matched what he did to her. She only wished she had the forti-
tude to deny it.

"We doona' just take our pleasures, love. We give them. You
ken?"

"I . . . don't believe in . . . vampires, Iain."

"I dinna', either."

"You're crazed, Iain. Mad. Someone should've warned me. The
family curse is insanity, isn't it? This is why you chose an impoverished English girl to betroth."

"*Leannan* . . . look to me."

Look? Without light?

The glow was back, diffusing gold-washed light onto the walls.
Tira rolled her head along one of his chest mounds, reached a
shoulder, and tilted her head back before doing as he asked. Her

eyes went huge and her breath caught at the opened lips, sharp teeth, and the absolute power seeming to hum from him, filling the enclosure with energy.

"These are fangs, love. For drawing lifeblood. Go ahead. Touch. Feel."

"Iain . . . I—"

Do it!

The command went right through her consciousness without his voicing it. Tira trembled as she reached to run a finger along one long spiked tooth. She felt the oddest prick in her own bottom lip at the same time.

"Iain . . ."

"Now, touch your own."

Her heart was blocking her throat. That had to be the obstruction lodged there, impeding her breathing and her swallowing as she did what he ordered. Tira found two like spikes protruding from her upper teeth. They were sharp enough to cut her index finger, and she pulled it away to stare at the pin drop of dark blood.

"This . . . can't be." Her voice shuddered, matching the tremor overtaking her entire body.

"Tira, I—"

"This is . . . a nightmare. It is. It has to be! Please? No! This isn't real! It isn't! How could you do this to me? Oh, Iain . . . no!"

There was more, sobbed with a voice that broke along with her words. She lifted from him or got lifted. The space was black again, everything was. But Tira didn't see it. She clamped both hands over the horror that was her face . . . the horror he'd made her visualize and then feel. He didn't stop her. He didn't even touch her. But she knew he left. She didn't see it. She knew only one moment he was there, and the next, he'd vanished.

Chapter Twelve

Iain looked down at the moon-tipped waves with unseeing eyes and waited. He'd sated to such an overfull state his ears rang with the infusion of blood into his veins. He couldn't remember when he'd last taken so much, perhaps back when he'd first turned and found the taste ambrosia to the senses. He'd been insatiable then, too, but with a different result. Back then, he'd leave animals near death and shepherds begging for assist with their flock. Not now. Gluttony of this magnitude required precision and skill. All of which he'd practiced to such a fine art not one animal noted the pricks, nor would any consequence be visible in the morning.

And so he waited out here in the dark for his body to absorb the feeding. He'd done it for a reason. His bride was going to need sustenance, and she wasn't going to take it easily.

Iain pondered his situation in the soulless waves, growing high enough to wash the deck occasionally, wetting his boots and the bottom of his *feile-breacan*. He'd waited the last few years to go to her because he feared the demon within him. He lacked control of it—and the last thing he'd wanted was an eternity with a fledgling girl at his side. He'd wanted her full-grown, educated, and ready . . . and happy.

Iain sighed and reached for the railing. He was lying to himself. He wasn't waiting for his body to absorb the volume of fluid. He was out here because he was afraid. Him: Iain Duncan Evan James Alexander MacAvee, fourth Duke of MacAvee. Earl of Glencairn and Blannock, chieftain of Clans MacAvee, MacGruder, and two other clans. He admitted it. Freely. But only to himself. Iain was out here on a wave-washed deck, watching the black of an ocean until it disappeared, because he was afraid of facing one little woman.

If he possessed a gilded tongue, he'd have used it already, begging her forgiveness with words such as the English seemed to spout—at any time and for any reason. But he didn't have the gift. No MacAvee did. They were known for reticence. The past was filled with tales of victory and conquest and ruthlessness, all accomplished with few words and no emotion. That was another thing. A MacAvee didn't show emotion because it was said they failed to possess them. Made it easier to attack and deal with the responsibilities and spoils of victory. Taking a man's land and his castle and his clan required overseeing and controlling it. There wasn't a need of regret, emotion, or words. And in those, Iain did his ancestry proud.

He'd grown up with the tales and then he'd added to them. MacAvee lairds were all large men, handsome, fearless, descended from Highlanders that defeated more than one wave of Norse marauders. A MacAvee sought ostracism before dishonor, maiming before capture, and death before defeat. They acted with courage and valor. Honor. Pride. They were revered and feared by everyone, including their Honor Guard. It was part of the legend and one Iain added to with alacrity and a great sense of accomplishment and pleasure.

And now . . . it was all as dust in his mouth, tasteless, and endless. Joyless. Because of one woman.

The waves beneath him grew large. Not enough for worry, but enough to tell of the weather ahead. The moment they'd turned north, it changed. As if every portion of the ship and everything on it knew they left civilization and the stricture of massed groups of people behind and replaced it with untrammeled beauty and freedom. All you had to do was open your senses: Hike through a forest, run across a moor, ford a glen, climb along a dale . . . do any of these things, and you'd know beauty and freedom and happiness like no other. Scotland was filled with the grandness of men and women who'd lived and died for it. All you had to do was inhale it.

Iain pulled in a large breath and forced the experience into his consciousness; the moist feel of rain-laden air just waiting to release, the slight brine smell of seawater; the perfect blend of moonlit quiet and pending wave-borne fury. It was as it always had been, and would continue to be. And he was still out here, waiting and afraid. And alone. Iain exhaled slowly and twisted his hands into claws about the iron rail.

The view blurred into a mesh of ocean and cloud-laden sky. Iain shuddered and blinked and kept at it until everything went back into focus. Distinct and lonely. He sniffed, and then he watched in disbelief as the ocean blurred again. And then he pulled every muscle in his body into a mass of coiled anger, his back aching with the effort while braided iron marks got imprinted into his palms, until the weakness faded and then passed. And then got buried . . . as he should have been nearly three hundred years ago.

Iain frowned. And then he snarled. He was the MacAvee chieftain. He couldn't afford an exhibition of weakness. Ever. MacAvee lairds passed judgment, made war, granted favors, assumed full responsibility for their clans, and they never admitted regret. They were immune from human frailties, including something so close to weeping he'd kill the man who even hinted at it.

Iain looked to his right and left to make certain he'd had no observers. And that's when he saw her. This time he gripped the iron so hard, the ends loosened and it rotated one-quarter turn before he stopped. She was wearing the seafoam green gown, and there wasn't a mark on it, despite the damage he'd done. Her hair was unbound, sending a red-hued draping all about her as wind tossed the strands. She wasn't aware of her powers, yet, or she'd not be approaching, her steps doing little to alter the drape of her gown as it skimmed her legs. . . .

"Your Grace?"

At Grant's voice, Iain swiveled his head to the other side and glared at the man for daring to witness his Tira. Then he turned fully to face his second-in-command, blocking everything.

"You'd best have a verra good reason for being here, Grant. Damn good."

"Her Grace is asking for you."

Iain swung about to see nothing save open deck getting washed with wave water. He blinked twice and still found nothing. That's when he got the first glimpse of her power.

"Iain. Oh . . . Iain. Iain?"

Tira writhed on the bare mattress, trying to get as much of

her skin into contact with the ticking as possible. Her existence was becoming a nightmare. From the horror of that story he told her in that black cubicle beneath this bed to the sip of water she'd taken. All of it was horrid and getting worse. Her skin was too tight, the nightgown she'd donned impossibly restrictive and confining and creating sweat where it stifled her flesh. Tira tore at the material, hearing the rip of seams and clatter of buttons peppering the wooden floor as she worked at it.

She was thirsty, tired, hungry, with a massive appetite nothing assuaged. One sip of the water she'd ordered his men to bring her, and she'd spit it out in disgust, and then agony. Blisters erupted inside her mouth, closing off her throat and sending spikes of pain all through her until nothing assuaged the latest hurt.

"Iain . . ."

Tira yanked the shreds of fabric that had been her nightgown from her, shoving the jagged strips over the sides, seeking succor that only the bare mattress seemed to provide. Tira put her open mouth to the ticking and inhaled, sensing a cool sensation that she knew had no measure of reality to it, but she could have sworn her throat eased slightly, allowing breath. Each tormented breath seemed filled with the same name. Over and over, she'd called to him, and then finally he was there.

"I'm here, love."

The mattress dented with his weight, rolling her into the well of space created at his knee, and then she was clasping her arms about his neck and arching up into him, willing his essence into her as the only way from this newest torture.

"Iain . . ."

"What have you eaten?"

Tira shook her head.

"What have the fools given you?"

Light from dead candles flared into being at his words or the anger behind them, paining her eyes with the brilliance before it subsided into normalcy.

"They . . ."

"I'll have his head!"

Daylight wasn't as vivid as the spear of light accompanying his threat, and Tira lunged up from the mattress to cling to him, holding him even as he went to his feet and breathed with huge heavy movements.

"They wouldn't bring me anything! Oh . . . Iain . . . it pains."

"What, *leannan?* What?"

"Water."

"They gave you *water?*" He strode for the door, one arm holding her to him while the other reached for his sword.

Tira shook her head and started speaking, slurring the words around the obstruction of teeth and not even noting the blend of Gaelic and English. "They wouldn't bring me anything, Iain . . . and I begged for it. . . ."

"How did you get water, sweet?"

He'd stopped and was still glaring at the door, a pulse pounding in his neck right at her eye level, and Tira narrowed her eyes at it.

"For a bath."

"You got water to bathe in?"

She nodded, moving her cheek along his shoulder, although her attention was caught and held by the bluish tint of fluid right beneath his skin. . . .

"And you tried to drink it?"

Tira surged upward, opened her mouth, and sank her fangs right into his throat, earning a groan of reaction from the man holding her, as well as the sweet flooding through her mouth and down her throat, cooling the blisters that had been there. And then it got better. Tira trembled with the sensation of bliss, seeming to throb everywhere at once.

"Slowly, love. You must—oh, my sweet!"

The sword dropped, gifting him with another arm to hold and support her. Tira heard the sound of metal hitting plank floor, and the next moment she got lowered onto her mattress again, where the cool feel against her back collided with the warmth everywhere else. And then she felt a prick on her neck and slight suction before he lapped at the skin with a tongue motion that twined her innards into knots. Tira couldn't contain the sensation. She pulled her teeth free of his flesh, threw her head back onto mattress, and keened a cry into the air about them. And then she latched on to a shoulder, sinking her teeth deep and sucking pure rapture from him. Wool scratched at her skin and she pushed at it, shoving and pushing at his kilt thing until Iain shimmied it out of her way.

That was the catalyst. Tira moved and he let her, rolling so she was astride him, gripping one of his thighs between her knees as she ran her hands all over revealed skin. Her palms and fingers came alive with thousands of sparks of sensation. And then she used her lips. The man beneath her groaned and trembled as she slid her canines along his chest, slicing a thin cut the entire way. She reached his upper belly and teased the ropes of muscles with her tongue, toying and enjoying every movement they made before she shoved her spikes into him to take from there as well.

Iain lurched upward, lifting them completely from the mattress for a moment before falling back, sending flecks of down fill into the air from the landing. Crimson color added to the glow imbuing the chamber. Tira pulled free of his belly flesh and lapped at the holes, watching with narrowed eyes as the puncture wounds sealed slightly with every tongue swipe. The reddish haze he'd put into play gave her full view of hard male, readied and prepared, and aching for what she could give him. If she so deigned.

"Ah . . . Tira . . . love."

Iain ran his hands along her spine, his fingers losing contact with every bump, and she felt every one of them as vividly as if it were her fingers. It was another odd sensation and another new experience. And it was getting hotter and wilder and more erotic with every moment that passed. Never had she felt so alive, so urgent, and so violent.

"Don't you dare stop me, Iain."

"Stop you? Are you crazed?"

"Then lift your hands from me."

"Lass . . . please!"

"Now, Iain. Now!"

He answered her command with an indistinct curse, garbled from somewhere deep in his throat, but he did as she ordered and released her. Tira moved lower, suctioning her mouth to his side and tightening her knees about his leg, holding as he turned into a churning creature whose every thrash threatened to toss her. Tira breathed onto flesh slickened with moisture as she moved lower, her tongue grazing goose-bump covered skin. She pushed his rod out of her way, holding from it as if it had little value, and laughed at his snarl.

"I hate you, Iain MacAvee. I hate this."

"Lass . . . I—"

"I hate what you do. And I hate what you make me do."

"Then . . . why—"

"Shut up."

Tira opened her mouth to its fullest, felt her teeth elongating with the strangest feeling, and that gave her weapons to spear him in one side of his buttock. Deep. Intently. Fully. Iain's resultant yell filled the chamber, followed by the thunder of his heartbeat, and then the pounding of his hands at the edges of the mattress as he hammered full handfuls of it into the bed frame. Tira laughed at his antics, unlatching her teeth. That was just stupid, making it easy for him to move his grip from the mattress to her arms, biting into the flesh as he hauled her up into position, and then lowered her onto a shaft that was thick with need and want. And this time his bellow matched her moan.

"That's it, *leannan*. Right—"

"I hate you, Iain MacAvee. I hate you." Tira crooned the words with each move, matching her rocking motion with the cadence, making a chant of sorts.

"Fair enough."

"You . . . saying I . . . lie?"

Tira's voice caught with the beginnings of ecstasy and he knew it, for the next moment, he had her in a full kiss, catching the cry with lips that thrilled, teeth that cut, and a tongue that licked and caressed. And the moment he released her, she was pulling away and snarling at him again.

"I . . . hate you, Iain! Fully."

He grinned and it angered her into beating at him, but he caught her flailing blows with such swift hands she didn't see the move. And then he slapped them together in order to bring them to his mouth, slitting cuts open on her knuckles in order to lap at them.

"I hate you," she repeated when he moved his gaze from her conjoined hands and started her heart into such a painful beat he had to feel it.

"So?" The word was ragged and growled.

"Don't you ken, Iain? I hate you!"

"Prove it. You say you hate me?"

Tira narrowed her eyes and raised her upper lip, showcasing her spikes . . . nodded.

"We've . . . got all night. Prove it."

With that quip, he gripped her fully against him and rolled, changing her angered outburst to sounds of pure pleasure with a torrent of thrusts that melded them. Time and again he slammed into her, warping her into a siren of wanton desire and craving and need. Tira shoved her jaw along his, tangling for position, but the moment she reached a perfect spot on his throat, he did the same. His fangs sank deep into her throat first, changing the scream of anger into mews of delight that built and hovered and surrounded . . . and then received.

Chapter Thirteen

"Iain?"

Tira's whisper seemed loud. It might be due to the low gut of the candles, the minutes that ticked by without anything to measure them, or the long length of man reclining right beside her, contemplating something on the ceiling. It was probably the latter. She had it decided before he rolled to face her, putting masculine splendor on display with the move. Tira swallowed and waited for him to meet her gaze. But he didn't. He seemed fixated on an exposed bit of thread from the seaming of the mattress between them.

"Aye?" he finally prompted.

"I don't understand what's happening . . . a-a-and I need answers."

She watched him move his arm to trace circles about the thread that looked to have failed its sole purpose of holding top cover to bottom.

"Are you going to give them to me?"

"Do you still hate me?" He flicked a glance to her, imprinting a flurry of shiver with it, and then returned to his fixation on the thread.

"I . . . should."

Tira moved into a sit, pushing until she reached the headboard. It gave her stability in a world of cloudlike surface and defense in a realm of fantasy. The mattress shifted with her move, but Iain didn't seem to notice, or if he did, he covered it over with his continual attention to the loose thread now near her toes.

"Aye, *leannan* . . . you should. So begin. Ask your questions and I'll try and answer."

"Do your . . . men know?"

"The Honor Guard is special chosen. From all comers. They compete to keep the position when I allow it."

"Allow it?"

"Brawn is na' the only mark of an Honor Guard. They must have courage, great fighting skills, and loyalty to their chieftain."

"So . . . is that a 'yes, they know'?"

A smile might have touched his lip, lifting it slightly. It was hard to tell since he wasn't looking toward her and the light had dimmed.

"Grant kens all of it. The rest? Enough."

"Why Grant?"

" 'Twas his decision. Grant has nae wife and nae family. He gave up all to become my second-in-command."

"That's . . . rather harsh."

" 'Tis a position of great honor. Granted 'til death. His great-uncle had it afore him. Grant is emissary to the MacAvee laird, taking my place and issuing my edicts at all functions of the crown and the land. Especially those held in daylight hours."

"He's not a vampire?"

Iain shook his head. Lanky strands of dark hair accompanied the motion.

"None of them?"

"I've na' turned any . . . afore you." He tipped his head toward her, creating two lines in his forehead with the heart-stopping gaze. "And I fully wish I had na' done so."

"Why did you, then?"

Lashes shadowed his eyes before he returned his regard to the stupid thread. She had to wait four heartbeats before he answered. She heard and counted each one.

"I knew the moment you came into being, *leannan*. The exact moment. The entire earth seemed to tell me of it. My sentence of loneliness had an end. I'd have the mate I'd been promised. All I had to do was find you. 'Twas na' hard. You have an attraction that pulled at me. Even as a bairn."

"That's . . . not possible."

"Possibility does na' change this. Naught does. But I swear the truth. I'd been promised by every generation of Clan Fey that I'd be granted my soul mate. It was fated."

"There's no such thing as fate, Iain."

"Just as there's nae such thing as vampires?"

Tira didn't have an answer. There wasn't one. "It was you forcing the betrothal bargain. Wasn't it?"

"Force is wrongly inferred. My sword never left the scabbard. Na' once."

"There are other means of force."

He shrugged. "They had what I wanted. I had gold. Nae forcing was needed."

"Then . . . it was you."

"Of course. I've been the second and first dukes, and the earls of Glencairn and Blannock, as well. 'Tis nae hard thing to receive lands, titles, and castles when you're of use to kings. And I was of powerful use."

"Powerful?"

"I canna' be killed and I doona' lose. If the battle is enjoined on a dark, rain-filled day, I'm invincible. When MacAvee clan attends a battle, that side wins."

He shrugged, rippling muscle beneath the skin and drawing a hand she couldn't stay. The moment she touched him, he went taut, stiff, unmoving.

"You should na' touch me."

"Why?"

"Your nearness makes me craven and lustful and filled with need . . . to an impossible degree. I canna' fight it. I tried. And you already ken how that turned out."

"I wasn't going to ask about *that*." She lifted her hand.

"I was na' going to speak of it, either. But there it is. Everything about you is designed for pleasure. To a vast degree. . . . Beyond any other woman."

"Any other?"

He cleared his throat.

"How many others?"

"That is a dangerous sort of question, *leannan*."

"Dangerous?"

"Nae matter the answer, you might make good on your threat to lock me from your chamber."

"That's worse than hating you?"

"I could get fully fond of your brand of hatred, love. Fully."

It was softly said but carried weight like a boulder atop her belly. Tira went concave with it until the heaviness eased. He was right, and no amount of prevaricating changed it. She'd been the one seducing and attacking him . . . *despite her hate.* He'd called it craven lust to an impossible degree, and that was it exactly. That's when Tira narrowed her eyes as she realized he was using it to avoid answering.

"How many, Iain?"

He moved his hand from the mattress to hold it out as if studying his fingers held answers. And he'd better not be counting!

"I've had three hundred years, *leannan.* There were always lasses about. I was ever pursued by them. You've seen it. Women made certain sure I knew of their . . . interest."

"How many, Iain?" she repeated.

He blew a sigh that was very visual as it moved most of the muscle beneath all that naked skin. "I have na' lived this many years and learned naught. There is nae number to satisfy you. It would be best if you just simply continue hating me."

"That many, huh?"

It wasn't a question. She meant it that way. And then she got treated to the sight of him going to his haunches and lifting a leg, creating a rest position for his arms and then his chin. The way he'd done it put him in shadow, so the golden wash of candlelight lit her.

"That is na' what you want answers to, Tira. Be truthful."

"Change the lighting, Iain."

He smiled, revealing gleaming, pointed canines. "Why?"

"This isn't fair."

"Who says life is fair? Or death, for that matter?"

"I asked for answers and you avoid giving them. Now, change the light."

The candles immediately dimmed as if half of them had been snuffed.

"Now answer the question."

"You doona' want a number put to my prowess, lass. What you want is the why of it. The strength of it. And mayhap the reason 'tis so overpowering, you forget things as vast as hatred. This is what you wish to hear."

He lowered his voice and slanted toward her, cursing her with an absolute blizzard of shiver.

"Give me . . . a better answer, Iain . . . MacAvee."

His name dribbled into whiffs of sound, driven by goose-bump lifted skin from just the chance of his touch.

" 'Tis the same with me, Tira love. The exact same. I dinna' ask for it. I canna' control it. You ask of women? I canna' answer. I doona' note other women. I nae longer even see them. All I see and feel and yearn for is you. Trust me."

He moved again, scrambling her wits and tying her tongue and starting wetness and craving and sensual longing. She licked her upper lip, caught her tongue on a tooth, and narrowed her eyes at him, trying to mute the view of naked male on the bare mattress.

"Iain . . . this is cheating."

"I canna' help it, love. I've already spoken of it."

His shadow touched her, created by a stir of motion. Tira opened her mouth and said something so contradictory to everything he was creating, she was startled to hear her own voice.

"You are very close . . . to getting locked . . . out of my chambers."

Light burst, delineating her slide along the headboard until her elbow connected and stopped the fall. Each heavy breath he took punctuated a reaction to every hair and every pore on her body. And then he growled, deep and low, and menacing. All of him looked taut and angered, creating lines of striation about his chest and arms as he resumed his seat as if he'd never left it.

Tira watched as he just sat there, waiting, unmoving and statue-still, although the bumps and bunches of muscle defined beneath the skin displayed how much rein he employed to portray disinterest and nonchalance.

"Iain?"

"Ask your question." The answer came through clenched teeth. She didn't have to ask.

"This mattress—"

A snarled curse ruptured the air between them, accompanied by complete blackness. Tira's heart lurched into her throat, closing it off to a frightening degree. She had to swallow around it in order to speak.

"All I want to know is why."

"Why . . . what?"

She'd rather have every candle lit then have to squint in the dark and wonder if his anger matched the sound of it.

"Why is this mattress so important?"

" 'Tis your security. Granted from your first rest place after turning."

"Do I need it for survival?"

"I'm na' certain."

"Well, that's hardly fair."

"What?"

"I mean, in comparison to yours."

"Mine?"

"That piece of moth-ridden hemp I woke from. Tell me I'm wrong."

"That's my pallet . . . but far from moth eaten. I've taken great care with it."

"Well, I think it needs to be washed. Badly."

He was moving away. The barest shift in the bed was verification.

"I'm na' good with words."

Tira raised her brows. She barely kept the burst of laughter from erupting. "Now that's a surprise," she finally answered.

"I canna' sit here and attempt it."

"But I need to know certain things."

"If you've need of me, call."

His voice sounded choked. Flat. Tira concentrated on the dark and was rewarded with the smallest amount of glow before it dissipated.

"Are you running from me again? Iain!"

The words echoed back at her from the blackness. The cabin felt empty. Bereft. Lonely. He'd left. She didn't have to see it.

Was he running from her? What man wouldn't? It was impossible to stay near without taking every bit of rapture she gave him. It was equally impossible to act as if her proximity did nothing. Her nearness intoxicated him even as her words spoke on his guilt and treachery.

The drop was endless this time. Or he was ill. Or weak. Or something worse.

Iain landed on his side with a thud that pained, making more oddity in a world filling with it. This couldn't be happening. Trembling was overtaking him, giving him a new curse with worse ramifications. He was a Highland laird. Strong. Stout. Stoic. Masculine.

He pulled handfuls of pallet weave to his face and somehow kept the emotion where it belonged: hidden.

Chapter Fourteen

MacAvee Hall looked to be a massive structure, constructed of black-on-black stone atop more of the same. It straddled a cliff, looking over the village of Avee on the shore below it. Tira had observed it since the rain-filled evening turned to rain-filled night. It didn't require effort. All she had to do was focus. She'd watched as light after light speckled the castle, coming from so many windows the structure looked to encompass the entire rock face.

Grant came to her door to fetch her now-empty goblet. He didn't speak of it. She didn't, either. They knew what it had contained: the same liquid as the night before, and the one before that.

"His Grace's carriage has arrived from the hall."

Tira nodded.

"I'll be back to escort you."

The door shut and a key turned. Tira walked across to the armoire and pulled out a cloak to go over the skirt and blouse she'd donned without one bit of an assist. Iain was avoiding her. She never saw him. He might as well be invisible with his comings and goings. She knew the reason for that, too: his power. He was well versed in avoiding detection with the way he froze and stalled time. She'd witnessed it and been a part of it, which made it painfully obvious he'd shut her out of it now.

It appeared her sentence for questioning him involved solitude and reflection time—two full nights of it. And he'd locked her in. She didn't believe Grant's word it was for her safety. No, it wasn't. It was for Iain's. She hadn't labeled him a coward yet, but it was on the tip of her tongue more than once. Good thing she loved reading and he had a large store of books. And when that bored, she'd played with her enhanced senses, bringing the decks outside into focus. Almost like she was out there, watching the waves and the shoreline they followed. And sometimes she thought she was.

She was ready when the guardsman returned. The deck echoed beneath Grant's feet. Not hers. As if she'd suddenly become weightless. Tira didn't find it odd. She simply pulled the hood farther over her head and followed.

The ducal carriage was large, with no identifying marks. It stood out in its anonymity like a black ink splotch on a painting, until she factored in the four black stallions between the posts. A penetrating look showed Rory and Sean mounted on two more black stallions. They nodded and Tira returned the salutation from the top step. That's when she looked about and realized not only could she witness all sorts of behavior, but she could hear conversations and sounds in whichever direction she chose . . . to a near-cacophonic level.

If any noted her cry and the swift way she entered the carriage, they didn't say. Tira crawled along a bench to a far corner, shoved both hands to her ears, held her breath, and the next moment it all ceased.

Just like that.

Tira's heart pounded, her whole body trembled, and there wasn't anyone to even ask. *Damn Iain.* The least he could do was help her with this thing he'd done to her! When she saw him again, she was going to make certain he knew of it.

She could sense the dock outside but didn't dare put her attention to it again. She settled with observing it through the large window at her elbow, watching the ground mist wrap about every light post. A flick of motion caught her attention, and Tira moved her head in time to observe Iain at the gangway, the quay, and the carriage, rocking it with his entrance, all of it within a blink of time.

Tira opened her mouth to speak, but something about the droop of his lip and general melancholy of his frame stopped her. He seemed to be intent on the view outside as they left the houses behind and entered a well-groomed roadway lined with the black silhouette of trees. And then they started climbing.

She was tired of his avoidance, fretful over the continual silence, and anxious over her new home. She guessed that once they reached his hall, it might be next to impossible to find him.

Not unless she wanted to spend the rest of this eternity searching that monstrosity of a castle.

"Iain?"

He flicked a glance to the vicinity of her nose before returning to the view. The oddest impression of panic filtered from him
before it faded.

"You can look at me. I won't bite. At least . . . not yet."

Her voice was breathless, and at the end it dropped an octave, sending sexual-tipped meaning. She knew he flinched. She
heard the rustle of his muslin shirt against his skin. Upon licking her bottom lip, she could swear she *tasted* that same skin . . .
and the faintest hint of whiskey.

"Have you been drinking spirits?"

"I fed," he replied finally.

"They'd been drinking spirits?"

"Aye."

"Does . . . that intoxicate?"

"You should na' speak with me. Not . . . yet."

"Why not?"

"I'm . . . na' certain I've the strength for it."

"But you just said you fed."

"That is na' what I mean."

Tira sighed. "You avoid me for days and then you speak rid-
dles. You're the image of strength, Iain. And absolute male perfection. You probably always were."

He squelched a groan and shuddered with it, making more
erotic sounds of shirt fabric grazing brawn. Perhaps it was better
in the dark. That way there wasn't much interfering with the ex-
pansion of her new powers. Tira narrowed her eyes and focused
and brought him into view, his head lowered, lips open to allow
each pant of breath while his shoulders were so taut it pulled at
the shoulder seams. He should've worn a sleeveless shirt. It would
save on tailoring. He had his hands clenched about his knees,
looking to break bone, and that put every bit of strength he'd
just disclaimed on vivid display.

Tira tucked her bottom lip into her mouth and felt the prick
as her canines lengthened.

"You need to . . . cease this."

"Why?"

She rifled the reply with alacrity and power. That way she

didn't miss a bit of how he pulled in a huge breath that expanded the muslin to ripping point. She didn't need her enhanced hearing as his shoulder seam separated. And then he let the air out, sending words with it that tripped atop each other.

"Because I'm a man of action, na' words . . . and I'm full cursed, and I should've known better than to get into a carriage with you! There's little defense!"

"Defense?"

"Aye! Defense!"

"Against what?"

She released her lip and eased her feet free of the slippers. He sent a sidelong glance as if he heard it. It came with a flare of light spearing the interior, before it disappeared. And then she had to use her enhanced sight to see him again.

"You're not going to answer, are you?"

There was a shine atop the obsidian of his eyes before he looked away, blinking rapidly as he did so. The whoosh of volume through her chest startled her to a painful degree.

"You want an answer, *leannan*, I'll give you one."

"I'm listening."

"You hate me."

"Do I?"

"You've every right. I've shown little in honor and naught in self-control, and I— What did you just say?"

He'd poised in midmove, half turned toward her, with his head lowered and those two creases splicing his brow. Tira's heart stalled at the picture he presented. Stunning. Perfect. Manly. Tira ran her tongue over her teeth, manipulating around the two spikes as she reached them. He reacted, seeming to fill his side of the carriage with blackness as if he somehow grew in stature. And then he went back to his usual size, the fading brightness behind showing how he'd done it.

"Your road . . . is very well groomed," she told him.

"Wh—at?"

He split the word in two and that was just endearing and sweet and creating tension and longing atop more of the same.

"I suppose everything you own is well groomed. You've had years to see to it."

"Tira—"

The low groan attached to her name sent a vibration of sound with it. Tira pulled pins from her hair, releasing it into a mass she finger-combed into a veil. She could see his response as both hands grabbed wads of plaid material from his kilt hem and tore.

"Most coaches have a sway to them as they travel uneven cobblestone or mud-pitted road. But not yours. Oh no. Your drive is perfectly groomed. Smooth. Even when traveling in the rain at night. There's not a hint of the smallest rut."

"You want a rough ride?"

"I want an excuse, Iain! That's what I want!"

"An . . . excuse?"

"An excuse for falling against you! Something to blame when I soothe this ache within me. Something I can curse for longing to match my skin to yours! I want to run my hands all over you, and sink these fangs into you. I need it so badly!"

The blouse had too many buttons. She was reduced to yanking at the placket, separating it as buttons got plucked and dropped, making little spattering noises on the carriage floor.

" 'Tis the vampire speaking."

"So?"

"I have vowed I will na' use it—"

"Shut up and help me!"

She had the blouse opened, ignoring how the satin chemise stuck to her skin, displaying and lifting her breasts. She tried to shed the skirt, but the waistband was an issue. Tira circled it twice, her fingers shaking as she looked for the fastening, before gripping the fabric and tugging and gaining absolutely nothing. *Damn dependable serviceable tweed!*

"I will na' . . . take you this way! I will na'!"

"Who said anything about you?"

She leaned into the gap between them with a snarl, making certain he saw the length of her teeth.

"Tira . . . please!"

She didn't feel the leap, and yet it was her body atop him, slamming his back into the carriage with the same move that sank her teeth into him. And then she was erupting with bliss so large no black carriage on a black night could contain it. His fangs slid along her neck, and she ignored them, sucking and absorbing life fluid while yanking and pulling material apart in order to match breast to chest and belly to belly.

"Tira . . . please! Na' like this. Please? Oh . . . *sweet!*"

Tira had him in her hands, stiff and readied, while the skirt hid her motion to latch on to him, sheathing him at the exact moment he punctured her neck, and then she was flying. Soaring. The entire experience blended into an ecstasy of full-out paradise with Iain at the center. Tira shoved her body at him, over and over, rocking with a discord of rhythm, and that got his hands gripping her buttocks in order to hold her in place for a roll beneath him. The move unlatched his fangs and gave him freedom to slide them along her skin, searching for and finding a breast tip. Tira went wild at the first hint of suckling attention. She couldn't stand it! She swung at him and connected with solid-muscled back flesh, turning her blows into caresses.

There wasn't space to contain such rapture! Tira arched up and into his mouth, glorying in the sensation, hauling in a deep breath while another full-fledged bloom of ecstasy overtook and consumed her. And then she was falling, exhaling with the drop, and hearing the words he was whispering.

"Ah, lass. Forgive me."

"Don't stop, Iain. Please. Don't you dare stop."

"Stop?"

The word was grunted, intensifying the pummeling he was doing, taking her into realms of existence she'd never before imagined. And then he did stop, poised in place by the weave of his body in flexed perpetuity of motion, shuddering and pulsing deep within while she held on and reveled in it. This time she was determined he wouldn't leave her, or escape, or do anything other than hold her.

She clung to Iain but he moved anyway, placing her with great care on her own bench, going to his knees in the carriage well to do so. And then, before Tira's surprised eyes, he lowered his face into the bench and shook.

Chapter Fifteen

Tira had her hand hovering over Iain's shoulder when the clatter of horse hooves on wood stopped her. The coach rolled beneath a gateway, darkening the interior—not enough she couldn't penetrate it, but enough to show arrival. The sound of a portcullis rising came next, and within a blink they drew to a stop. Iain regarded her from his seat, fully attired and immaculately groomed, proving he'd stalled time again.

"I wish you'd cease that." Tira dropped her hand. It should be chilled in the carriage with just a skirt for modesty. Tira flicked a glance down at herself. She had the shredded remains of her chemise and blouse still dangling off her shoulders. But it wasn't chilled. And it wasn't warm. It felt vacant.

"What?"

"You . . . alter time. Change . . . perception."

"So?" It was soft-spoken.

"I thought it magical until you shut me out."

He sighed heavily but didn't answer.

"I mean . . . I want to be with you when you do it. I want to be part of it again. To share in it."

"Cover yourself."

She pulled the cloak from where it was crumpled beneath her, wrapped it about her, put the hood over her head, and held both ends together at her chin for good measure. "Is that better?"

"You canna' have it both ways, *leannan*. I thought it possible, but I was wrong."

"Both ways?"

"You want me because of the vampirism. It stirs the blood,

mixes up the senses, overrides objections. There's nae stopping it. We just proved it."

Her skin tingled as he listed exactly what happened and what was starting up again. It was easy to hear the effect in her reply. "Does it matter why?"

"Aye. And to a degree I'd na' thought possible."

"I . . . want you, Iain." Her heart rate had elevated, her nerve endings started twitching, and her canines lengthened.

His face went grim. Dark. Then Grant opened the door to receive a hissed snarl from her, showing full teeth. Fear touched his face for the barest moment before it was gone. He nodded at Iain and got a nod in reply.

"Everything is prepared, Your Grace."

"What's been prepared, Iain?" She hadn't much control over her voice or it wouldn't rise with what sounded like worry. Then she admitted it. She was worried. Where was he taking her? Would he be with her? Would he lock her in again? And for how long?

"Come, Tira." Iain stood outside the carriage, the sway of the coach the only indicator he'd moved. "My household is up and dressed to welcome us."

"All of them?"

He nodded.

"At this hour?"

"MacAvee lairds keep odd hours. The households adapt."

And here she was still suffering waves of illicit yearning and desire, her hair unbound, clothing in disarray, and covered over with a wrinkled cloak. Tira concentrated and felt her teeth retracting. "You could've warned me," she whispered.

"Would it have mattered?"

No. The need and desire were too strong. Too vivid. Too massive. And she'd been the instigator. Again.

"Come. They've been told of your illness."

Tira stopped at the door in a stoop, one hand on the railing while the other held her cloak together. "My . . . illness?"

"You suffered massively from seasickness. The entire voyage. You were too ill to venture from your cabin."

"I was locked in, Iain. I couldn't leave it."

"Semantics."

"Why are you acting like this?"

"Like what?"

"Cold. Distant."

"Because anything else is beyond me! Can you na' just come down? Please?"

The hand held toward her trembled, warming her heart, strengthening her legs, and making it feel like she flew to his side. Tira lifted her chin and turned to face a virtual sea of faces and welcoming smiles. An elderly man stepped forward, clad in a MacAvee plaid kilt, black jacket, frothy white lace-fronted shirt, while he held a large feather-topped tam in one hand.

"Greetings, Your Grace! Even without introduction, I ken you as MacAvee laird. At first glance! You're the image of your grandsire. I was but a wee lad, but I swear . . . the verra image. Welcome to the Hall. We've kept it readied and prepared for your arrival at any time, to orders."

"Thornton . . . is na' it?"

The man bowed, displaying a bald spot ringed with silver hair. "Aye. Gerard Thornton. Steward and comptroller of MacAvee Hall. This is your new wife?"

"Her Grace, the Duchess of MacAvee."

Sean announced it with a voice that seemed incongruous on such a thin frame. Tira curtsied, holding the cloak like the most perfect ball gown.

"Come in. Please. Follow me. We've prepared . . ."

There was more. Tira heard a portion as the man led them, speaking his words to the air in front of him. But then it didn't matter as her eyes widened on the breath-taking sight of MacAvee's great hall. The two-story carved entrance doors opened to a raised entry that dropped down into such an enormous chamber; the size was impossible to gauge, despite the volume of torches they'd lit. Tira had to use her new power, enhancing her eyesight to bring everything into perfect focus.

A hammer-beam ceiling spanned the entire chamber, its surface covered with colorful paintings in the Jacobite style. There were no less than four fireplaces carved into both walls, with stone sides and thick wooden mantels. Black rock walls peeked from between tapestries and banners, framing sizable paintings that could only have come from the paintbrushes of Renaissance masters.

Each step echoed through the chamber, blending into a beat of thumping noise, dragging her pulse into it. They passed through an archway at the far end into what might be a hall, although the width couldn't be easily spanned with a glance. This space had dark wooden walls rising only two stories, framed wherever she looked with more tapestries, more torches in sconces, and more paintings, although these mainly featured Iain in several different poses and costumes. Tira noted more than one portrait of a woman as well. And everywhere was the glint of silver, gold, or crystal. It appeared the castle hadn't been changed or modified in the years Iain refrained from visiting it. Or perhaps Iain liked medieval period. He didn't offer it and she didn't ask. It felt nearly too sacrosanct even to whisper in such magnificence.

Thornton hadn't the same issue. He turned and addressed Iain and then her. "I'll show you the chieftain chamber now. If you'll follow me?"

Another set of doors was opened at the end of the hall, leading to a four-man-wide spiral stair, or maybe it was wide enough to accommodate three men on horseback, such as a Seton chieftain had built at Fyvie Castle. She'd heard of it but never seen such a thing and wondered why such trivial things occurred to her now.

The landing at the top was another rock-walled edifice, with but one ending. There was a smaller set of doors, surmising a small room. That was proven a misnomer upon opening them. Tira felt the same slack-jawed response to even more spacious, torchlit luxury. MacAvee's chamber had one wall devoted entirely to a window. If it wasn't a rain-filled night, the view would be extraordinary: ocean as far as the eye could see, topped by sky just as broad and all-encompassing. Tira followed the steward and Iain into the center of the room and then pirouetted in a slow circle.

It already felt big and incredibly desolate. Tira tightened her hands on the cloak's opening. Large and lonely . . . and that window couldn't be safe. There wasn't a drape attached to either side of it that she could see. There were various shapes of furniture along the other walls, two fireplaces, as many groupings of chairs, as if conversations took place in the chieftain's chambers, and on a raised platform to one side was a structure she immediately knew was a bed, with three wooden sides enclosing it.

"Thornton? Her Grace and I thank you. Grant? See to things."

Iain spoke for her. Tira didn't move. She kept her eyes on the raised bed while projecting with every fiber of her new powers. *Don't leave me! Iain . . . please!* She heard the doors thumping together before they thudded into place. Then she heard the distinct sound of a key turning in a lock.

He'd locked her in. Emptiness settled around her, making everything even more chilled and vacant and lonely. Tira moved slowly toward the window, her hands out like a sightless person. If this was her future, she'd rather face pure sunlight and have it ended and done with. But then her fingers touched cold black stone. She splayed her hand open and found nothing but solid rock.

"I had it walled in over a century ago."

Tira whirled to see Iain standing near the door, directly beneath a candlelit chandelier, highlighting his beauty, arms folded, showing their size, legs apart, showing his readiness for confrontation. He'd untied his hair, as well.

"You didn't leave?"

"I doona' concede defeat that easily."

Black eyes locked with hers as he just stood there, unmoving.

"We . . . have to talk, Iain."

He stopped breathing for a moment, looked over her head and way up the wall before returning to her gaze. "Can we na' do something I have a fair chance of success at?"

"I can't even heft a sword."

One side of his lip lifted. "I have other skills."

"As I'm very much aware."

This time he grinned. Then he sobered. "You wish to talk?"

She nodded.

He gestured her to one of the groupings of furniture about a fireplace. A fire sparked to life in the grate before she settled into an overly large, stuffed wing chair. Tira studied the beginning flames for a bit before looking up at where he stood, an arm reclining on the mantel.

"How do you do that?" she asked.

" 'Tis part my power. Yours appears to be an ability to see through solid rock walls."

"It's an incredible view," she replied.

"Still is. If you wish, I'll take you there."

"Where?"

"Either tower. Or along the battlements. The view does na'

discriminate. Every guardsman has noted it as well as every guest."

"You take in guests?"

"MacAvee does na' turn down wayward travelers."

"What of the women?"

She could tell he stiffened. "What women?"

"You can start with the ones in the paintings."

"Oh. Paid ones. Mostly."

"Not wives?"

"The first duke took a wife."

"You mean *you* took a wife when pretending to be the first duke."

"There's nae pretence, love. I was the first duke. As such, a union was forced. I dinna' marry of my own free will. Na' until you."

His voice cracked slightly. Tira narrowed her eyes. "Forced? You?"

" 'Twas the best way to end the MacGruder clan feud and gain Castle Blannock."

"You're *married?*"

"You see? The more I speak the angrier you become."

"Iain—"

"I'm widowed. She passed on. A decade ago. An auld woman of ninety-two."

"No children?"

"She locked me from her chamber. I dinna' fight it. We had little in common. She golfed. Rode to hounds. Hunted. Fished. She excelled at every Scot pursuit."

"Sounds divine."

"Did I fail to mention a face like a horse and frame to match? There was nae way to get drunk enough to tup her."

"Why don't you move closer?"

He straightened. She could hear the rustle of his clothing. "That would be unwise."

"Why?"

"I canna' keep a strict enough leash on it . . . and I am still a gentleman born."

"It?"

"I need you, Tira. Vastly. To a consuming level. 'Tis ever-increasing and ever-present. If I'm near you, I lose control . . . and do things that make you hate me."

His voice dropped as did his gaze. The man was mistaken. She didn't hate him at all. What she felt startled and shocked her, sending a surge of emotion with each beat of her heart that blended with the rivulet of shivers coursing her skin. And he had a great gift with words, especially when they snagged in the middle.

"You must excuse me now. I've . . . things to see to yet."

"Things?"

"Grant is bringing my pallet and your mattress."

"Oh. Good. I'd hate to think I have to tote it."

Tira pushed the hood off her head. She probably looked a sight. It had been impossible to tell on his yacht since he didn't keep any mirrors. She looked about as it occurred to her. There hadn't been any in the lower rooms, either.

"Why are there no mirrors, Iain?"

"I had them destroyed."

"Why?"

He cleared his throat. "A vampire has nae reflection. Such a thing could cause rumor and speculation."

"You fear those?"

"There's only one thing I fear."

His voice was nonexistent. If she hadn't used her enhanced hearing, she'd have missed it.

"And that is . . . ?"

He flinched. She saw it and heard it. As well as the rapid beat of his heart. And the next moment he was at the chamber door, twisting the key and showing he'd used his power again.

"Iain! Don't you dare leave! You hear?"

Chapter Sixteen

Could he hear?

His body was thrumming with the sound of her voice, the feel of her presence, and the view of her perfection. She didn't need a mirror. There wasn't a woman to match her. And the damn key wasn't turning. He couldn't see clearly enough. His hands weren't working properly, either. Then she added to his torment with the feel of her body pressed against his back, her arms looped about his belly, holding him.

He'd been wrong on all fronts. This was hell.

"Iain?"

"Let go, Tira."

"Why?"

"I need . . . a bit of time."

She giggled. "*You* need time? You?"

He nodded.

"Why?"

To get these accursed woman tears banished back where they come from! He shook his head and concentrated on the chieftain chamber door, looking over the entwined vines, thistles, and thorn-bushes they'd carved into it. Yet, the more he worked at staunching the emotion, the worse it all got.

"Lass . . . you need to . . . let me go."

"What if I say no?"

Iain pulled in a shuddering breath. "You ken I canna' control it and what happens . . . and yet you torment me apurpose? To what end, lass? Well? You wish me begging?"

"Would you?"

Iain pulled her arms apart, spun, and glared down at her before blinking a tear trail into existence. He didn't even care. But when he moved from her, he got more anguish as the step took him to his knees.

"Iain?"

"All right, lass! All right. You win! I'm filled with fear. I fear this existence without you. I'll say it. I'll shout it, if you like! I love you and I fear you'll never forgive me . . . and then I'll be damned to a worse existence than afore. There. I've said it! You've got me on my knees begging. What more can you wish of me?"

The last was sobbed and he detested that the most. And then she was on her knees facing him. He didn't look to verify it. He could feel and sense her, and it stirred the very beast he was straining to keep caged.

"Iain?"

He shook his head, glared at the spot of floor between them, tightened every muscle in his body. He was *not* giving in to the power this time. No matter what the prevarication. He wasn't.

"I'm not a morning person, anyway."

"What?"

He blinked. Grimaced. Watched another tear drop onto the wood. He was still looking as the wood soaked it up.

"And—and that pallet of yours could use a bit of padding . . . like a mattress."

Puzzlement wove through the other emotion, helping to calm and pacify it. Iain dared a glance at her and then jerked away as if scorched. She was too beautiful! Too beloved! A russet cloud of hair enveloped her, lit with torchlight he'd just sent to a blinding level. Her green eyes glistened with secret messages. Her lips were open just slightly, allowing fang tips to peek out. . . . The beast flexed and he held to it, curling forward into a hunched ball for the effort.

"A-a-and . . . I have my own demons to satisfy. My own passions. Cravings. Lusts."

The roar consumed him, ripped from his throat to encompass the entire room. Iain fought with everything at his command but felt the grip slipping as his canines lengthened and prepared.

"Are you going to make me say it?"

"Lass, you have to move away from me. Now! You hear? Away!" The words came through teeth clenched so tight, his spikes jabbed his chin. The effort scorched every muscle into fire.

"Where?"

"Any . . . where!"

"What if I say no?"

Iain swore, lunged for her and had her beneath him, smashed between the unforgiving wood and his frame. Her clothes were missing as well. The knowledge barely made it through his senses since she held his face in her hands and was covering him with kisses and saying the sweetest words. Iain used the entire scope of his power to stall time, encasing them in a bubble of it so he could experience and store every bit of it. Forever.

"I love you, Iain MacAvee. I love you! I can't imagine this world without you, either. It's desolate and bereft . . . and I'd rather die! You hear me, Iain? I love you!"

"You love me?"

"Yes! And yes. And another yes! Desperately!"

"You're sure? 'Tis na' just the vampire speaking?"

"Oh, Iain. I think I fell for you the moment you claimed me at the ball. I just didn't know it."

"You truly love me?" Joy was radiating through him, tempering the beast, and then she added more sweet words.

"I love you! I just didn't know what it was. Forever, Iain. I love you . . . and thank goodness you didn't make me say it!"

He pushed up from her to slide his lips along her jaw to her neck. That's when his breath caught in surprise at the way her hands delved beneath his kilt and shoved it open, gripping and guiding and making certain he got captured in her woman-place—exactly as she wanted.

She may have sent a cry from the throat he was lapping at before he sank his fangs in, but he didn't hear it. He was experiencing such joy it slammed to the top of his head and near took it off. The strength of it ever-increasing, louder and larger, and so powerful it was impossible to experience anything else. That's why he didn't hear Grant pounding at the door, or his obedience to her words to guard the items until required, easily heard through solid wood. Everything was exactly as it should be.

THE GUARDIAN

Michele Sinclair

To E&H, you have been and will forever be the loves of my life.
Prepare for each day as if a million were to follow,
but live each moment as if it could be your last.

Prologue

Northern Japan—1365

Dorian examined the unique long, slender blade that fit singularly in his palm, creating a seamless extension of his arm. "Do you have any others?" he asked as he expertly swung the sword at a phantom attacker. Pivoting on his left heel, he deftly ripped a swathe through the neatly manicured bushes. He grimaced at the unintentional destruction and forced his eyes to raise and receive the warranted glare from his brother. "My apologies."

"Akihiko will not be pleased," Aeolus murmured, eyeing the damage to the once beautiful shrubbery before answering his brother's question. "Masamune was a genius. It was he who thought of combining soft and hard steel for use in swords. You are in luck that I made sure he taught his technique to others before his death. So if the katana entertains you, keep it. I shall also offer its mate. Somewhat smaller, but just as deadly."

"I find it surprising you would so easily give up such a prize," Dorian commented. "What is wrong with it?" he asked, speaking from past brotherly experience.

Aeolus chuckled and waved his finger, pointing at the sword. "Look at the *saya*," he said, gesturing toward the handle.

Dorian shifted his grip to examine the handguard portion of the sword. The intricately carved design was a true work of art in which the lambda was prominently featured. The upside-down V-like symbol had played a role in both of the empires he had built, making it clear that the sword had been constructed for only one owner—him.

Dorian nodded, accepting the offer. Only a slight glimmer in his smoky gray eyes revealed his appreciation. He knew Aeolus understood that he was amused by little these days. Such feelings came and went with the decades. His brother was currently finding pleasure by building a dynasty in the East, an area of the world most of their kind refrained from inhabiting. Their considerable size and dark Greek features stood out, making it impossible to blend into the crowd—but discretion had never been Aeolus's style.

"I'm impressed," Dorian said, once again speaking about his unexpected gift. "You must be inspiring these humans for them to create such beauty."

"And they are skilled fighters, able to defeat men twice their size," Aeolus added, hinting that his own height was not quite the intimidator it had been elsewhere.

"Perhaps," Dorian sighed in mock agreement. He was in no mind to argue, but he doubted Aeolus's growing army could ever match Scotland's Highlanders in strength or skill. Then again, the chances of the two cultures ever battling were incredibly slim.

"Why don't you return to your beloved mountains and form something of those barbarians who live there?"

Dorian sighed and watched the sparkle of afternoon sunlight play on the waves from the safety of the shaded garden. "I already guided men to better lives—twice."

"The Peloponnesian League and then Rome. Both times you prematurely left and both empires gave in to war and eventually crumbled so that now only a few of us can remember their glory," his brother asserted, commencing one of their more common debates. "I'll never understand why you abandoned them."

The comment startled Dorian, for the discussion typically took a turn of encouragement, with Aeolus attempting to persuade him to end his wandering ways, plant roots, and establish another empire. "I would argue that I did not let it crumble. Mortals cannot grasp the value of anything beyond their own lifetime, and dealing with them is tedious and wearisome. I only walked away when staying became pointless."

Aeolus stroked his long braided ponytail styled in the way of *bushi*. "Humans are bound to destroy anything great built, either by them or us."

Careful to remain under the heavy shade the garden's foliage provided, Dorian stepped forward and waved his arm at Aeolus's men training in the distance with precision and stamina rarely seen in humans. "Hopefully not this?"

Aeolus sighed and nodded with knowledge of someone who had seen the future and knew what it held. "No, not anytime soon, but you and I both know that we will live to see it end. Meanwhile, it entertains me."

Dorian stared quietly at the training fields, listening to the short staccato of the words the men barked with each movement. "I envy humans sometimes."

"You wish to train in the sunlight?" Aeolus teased.

Dorian shook his head. The harsh rays didn't immediately kill his kind, but they burned, making the warmth of the sun one of the few things humans enjoyed that he could not. But after nearly two millennia, the desire for sunlight no longer pulled at Dorian's soul. "It is their mortality I covet. Living such short lives changes their view of the world."

"It limits them, you mean."

"Aye," Dorian agreed. "And such ignorance is something to be desired."

Aeolus shook his head. "Think, brother, you have been here in Japan, what? Five short years? To us, an extended vacation, but to a human that is a significant portion of their brief life. If you are to envy a mortal being, then envy a *spawn*. They at least live long enough to taste a sample of what life could be like."

Dorian arched a single brow. Aeolus had a point, but a spawn's lifetime was just long enough to make them crave true immortality. As a result, they were consumed with extending their already long lives. In the end, they possessed the same flaw as humans. Greed, something immortals understood to be unnecessary—and unfulfilling.

Aeolus and Dorian followed the green canopied path back to the house, pausing to look out at the calm bay where fishing vessels were returning with the afternoon's catch. "You are welcome to continue to stay as long as you like, but your increasing boredom will not be alleviated here. You should find Ionas. He tends to keep your mind occupied . . . for at least a while."

Dorian grimaced but kept his eyes focused on the bay. Aeolus was right. He was bored. For the past couple of centuries he had passed the time fighting, mostly covertly, and often as a Scot, just to antagonize his nephew. Ionas had initiated the Viking raids in an effort to prove a point—civility was not a requirement to conquer a people. Dorian believed otherwise. Either grow and prosper or be vanquished to the next brutal bunch of nomads overtly seeking power. All people secretly wished for a better life—no matter who they were or where they resided. Ionas held fast that it was power not prosperity that drove men. An old circular argument that had no end.

"I'm not Ionas's keeper."

"Who is? Who could be for any of us, at that point?"

It had been nearly two hundred years since Ionas went away to lick his wounds after losing their last quarrel. Communication concerning that part of the world rarely came to the distant islands Aeolus had chosen for his current home, but Dorian had no doubt his nephew was hatching up a new way to spoil the majestic lands Dorian had grown to love. To his kind, revenge was not something rushed or personal, but an art that required time to both plan and execute, a simple concept mortals could not grasp.

Unfortunately, to learn of his nephew's newest brutal scheme meant interacting with humans, something Dorian now avoided whenever possible. Humans were ingenious, but tedious. Their short lifespan affected everything about them—their thoughts, ambitions, desires, accomplishments, and most especially their relationships. And yet, dawdling, when it came to Ionas, was nearly a guarantee of spending even more time mingling with mortals to clean up the mess. Two hundred years was not a lot of time, but it was enough to recover and plan bigger and yet less obvious forms of revenge.

Dorian twirled the long sword effortlessly in his palm, letting the sleek edges catch the light as he debated the idea of returning to Scotland. Never had Dorian held any blade of its like, and though he knew it was a petty emotion well beneath him, he secretly enjoyed the idea of irritating his nephew Ionas by possessing it. "I think it's time to check on Kilnhurst," he finally said after some time.

"And perhaps find another thorn to stick in Ionas's side?" Aeolus asked, echoing Dorian's thoughts. "He wasn't pleased with the last one."

"Nay. Just stop whatever he is planning."

"Same thing," Aeolus argued.

"Come with me. Last time you had fun, if I recall."

"I was in between children then."

"So?" Dorian remarked. Like him, Aeolus disliked coupling with spawns, which left one feeling more empty than satisfied. But his brother had no issue mating with a human, something he did regularly and not just with one. At first, Dorian believed Aeolus's seemingly constant desire for more children was driven by the hope of eventually producing another immortal. But the mysterious inherited element that made their immediate family nosferatu was too diluted in their offspring to grant the burden of perpetual life. Their children could not digest blood. As a result, they ate meat and lived like all other humans—briefly. After nearly two millennia of watching Aeolus continue with his cavorting ways, Dorian decided that his brother's affinity for human female flesh and the resulting mortal offspring was sincere and most likely would never change.

Aeolus shrugged, acknowledging Dorian's simple but telling comment. "Still, this time our nephew is all yours. I intend to spend the next several decades seeing what these Eastern men can achieve. They are good, quick, and surprisingly clever."

Dorian laughed out loud, hearing the spark of genuine interest in his eldest brother's voice. "Well, 'ruler of the winds,' can you spare me a ship?"

Aeolus returned the chuckle. "An ancient title I have not heard for some time. I'm feeling generous. I'll give you two ships and let you keep one. Just return both crews, and send back news of Ionas and whatever else might be of interest. When do you want to leave?"

"Soon," Dorian lied.

"I know you, dear brother. Your voice says indifference, but Scotland holds your heart like this place holds mine. You may pretend otherwise, but now that you have decided to return, I know you are quite eager to depart."

Dorian continued to stare out at the bay, which was now crowded with anchored fishing boats due to impending nightfall. Yes, he loved Scotland. Living among the massive peaks made him feel vulnerable, ignorant—mortal. It had been one of the few places where his unusual height and size did not look out of place.

But Aeolus was wrong about his desire to return. Then again, his brother was unaware of the real reason Dorian had left his beloved home.

Chapter One

Badenoch, Scotland—1365

Moirae Deincourt rounded the last turn of the keep's steps and stopped at the door before exiting. She extended her hand out the opening and sighed as cool droplets hit her skin. At least the afternoon rain had slowed to a sprinkle. She surveyed the path across the small bailey toward the noisy party held in the great hall. Glenneyrie was not an extensive castle. There were several larger in the area, most notably the vacant Kilnhurst only an hour's hard ride away, but Glenneyrie's smaller size suited her needs.

The two-story keep was made of stone and completely enclosed, allowing entry and exit through an attached tower that also formed part of the gatehouse. The other inner buildings, including the great hall, had been built of wood. Aside from the keep, the only other structure made of stone was the small but functional curtain wall surrounding the castle, making it neither a sought-after prize nor an insecure shelter. Ideal for Moirae, who required a home that provided some degree of comfort and security, but one that also didn't draw attention.

Unfortunately, Glenneyrie's occupants and visitors could not be categorized similarly.

Moirae took a deep breath and hobbled toward the party. Several men stood in her way, but not a one looked directly at her or moved to allow her easy passage. Moirae paid no attention to their rudeness. Being ignored was far better than the alternative—the subject of deliberate ridicule. With the flawless skin of youth, long honey-kissed hair, and a tall thin frame, she was just shy of beautiful, needing only a few more womanly curves to transform her into a stunning vision. But it was not her immature bosom that kept men away. It was her less-than-perfect leg.

Some called the night she turned seventeen a tragedy, others called it a miracle. Caught in a burning barn, she should have died along with her beloved grandmother and mother. The fact she had defied death and learned to walk with only a limp after being crushed by a beam was indeed a miracle. But her family's death had been no accident. Moirae's memory of that horrid night had not faded with time. Just the opposite. Their death had become the sole motivator of her life.

Moirae held her breath as she maneuvered through the mixture of rotund, brawny, and bony male bodies, all needing a bath. The doors to the great hall, like usual, were open, beckoning those to enter and make merry with their laird and fellow clansmen. She stepped inside and instinctively rubbed her aching thigh, stiff from a week of inactivity—something she intended to rectify before dawn.

Faking a smile, Moirae waved at the overweight man who fancied himself a Highland laird. Raised as a Lowlander, the man was no more a Highland warrior than she, but he had inherited the title, and until he was unseated, the man would frivolously spend his clan's wealth on a stream of festivities. Until such time, she would stay and pretend to be his cousin.

He acknowledged her presence with a bare movement of his chin and slight flutter of his fat fingers. She didn't miss his look of relief as she headed away from him to the other side of the room. The debauched man was spooked by her, but she came with a sizeable purse, and in return, he gave her a private room and—with the exception of requiring her to make token appearances at his parties—he left her alone. The arrangement had served them both well, and she hoped it would for a few more years before someone became fed up with his ineptness and seized control, forcing her to find other arrangements. And whenever that day arrived, she would just disappear. No one would search for her. Upon her grandmother's wrongful death, she had become truly alone—a fact Moirae had only just recently begun to accept.

She had arrived later than usual to the party, and the hall's small gathering room had already become quite full, making it difficult to sit down at the bench she normally occupied. Typically, she liked to come early and leave the same way, but tonight, she sought information that came with the later crowd—more specifically, the clan's most effusive and notorious three gossips.

"Lady Moirae!" they all exclaimed simultaneously in mock surprise. The largest and most vocal of the women, Esa, continued with a lopsided grin. "You missed our last two celebrations."

Moirae swallowed the sarcastic desire to ask which babe had learned not to soil himself. Recently, the celebrations, as Esa generously called them, had been so numerous and prompted for such ludicrous reasons, Moirae wouldn't have been surprised to learn that it was the laird's achievement of finally seducing his chambermaids they were celebrating. Instead, she returned Esa's smile, knowing that if any of the clansmen ever changed their minds and decided to pay Moirae attention, the warm female welcome she just received would be her last. But as long as she was no threat, her presence would be neither overtly welcomed nor shunned.

"Perhaps you overslept, my lady?" asked Saundra with a touch of malice, hinting at Moirae's strange sleeping habits.

Moirae shrugged off the rhetorical question. Fact was the evening suited her more than the day. As a result, she spent her nights awake and her days asleep, which made her seem odd to others. But again Moirae didn't care. It enabled her to avoid people and engage in more reclusive activities. "Enion is dead," Moirae offered, wondering if they would even care.

"The old hunter?" Esa half asked.

"Aye," Moirae replied, not correcting the gossipmonger. To Esa, Enion had been an archer, the lowest of all fighting men and, therefore, nothing more than a peasant. But to Moirae, he had been one the best bowmen of Badenoch, a skill he had done his best to teach her. The man had been her only true friend, serving as the father she had lost as a child and re-instilling her with a purpose for living. The least she could do was be with him during his final days.

"My son told me he had died. Nothing catching, I understand," Esa lightly pressed, not really wanting or expecting an answer.

"Just old age," Moirae replied, and then quickly fabricated, "I heard there was another attack."

Being at Enion's side for the past week, Moirae had not heard about any incidents, let alone violent ones, but knew from experience that it was best to guide the old woman away from launching into wearisome stories about her son as quickly as possible.

Esa bit down on a piece of deer meat, not even bothering to wipe the juice dribbling down her chin. With her mouth still full, she answered Moirae's question. "Aye! Have you not heard? *Twice* this week."

Moirae grimaced. Badenoch was almost entirely wild mountainous country. Its myriad skyscraping hills, glens, and lochs brought together the borders of many clans, not just a few. Consequently, skirmishes were common as the forests held some of the best deer hunting in the Highlands. The temptation to trespass and engage in petty thievery of animals and tools while hunting was too great to resist.

Bedina, whose love of gossip rivaled Esa's, could sit quietly no longer. "Aye, *and* the demons are back."

Moirae mentally dismissed the comment, for she was one of the rare few that had actually seen a demon. When the menlike creatures did reveal themselves, they rarely left anyone alive. "How do you know it was a demon?"

"Shamus said that it looked like a man but with incredible strength and had sharp teeth that dripped with blood," Esa added.

The description caught Moirae's attention, for if the report was true, her real enemy had finally arrived. No longer was clan infighting plaguing Badenoch's inhabitants—but something far more menacing.

Word had arrived more than a year ago about a string of bizarre attacks in England that were slowly making their way into the Lowlands. Pillaging had been replaced by men on a destructive search for something, and all too often they killed just for pleasure. Yet just what they were looking for remained a mystery.

At first, Moirae had no interest in the outrageous rumors and had planned to leave Badenoch if and when the danger arrived, but then details that described the fearsome invaders reached Glenneyrie. The creatures raiding the houses and villagers were unlike any men anyone had ever seen—except Moirae. They were the ones who attacked her and her family the night her leg was crushed. Learning of their existence and impending arrival had changed everything.

Soon afterward, she had met Enion, began her training, and started to prepare for the day the demons would arrive. After spending nearly six months building the necessary musculature and perfecting her aim, Moirae had decided to test her abilities under the stress of real combat. As a result, the mysterious Guardian of Badenoch had come to life, defending the weak against those who harassed them.

But if the old farmer who had been ambushed during her absence knew what the demons looked like, that meant he had lived through an attack . . . but that was impossible. "Esa, how did Shamus get away?"

Esa and Bedina scoffed concurrently. "How else? The *Guardian*. He saved Shamus and then his kin."

Moirae was struck dumb. Had she heard right?

"Shamus's mother, Biddy, actually *saw* him," Esa continued with a wide, toothy grin just before taking another bite.

Bedina licked her lips, loving that she had Moirae's rapt attention. "Biddy said the Guardian was the finest man she had ever seen."

"Huge—" added Esa.

"Aye, huge, with black hair and matching eyes and riding a new horse as dark and large as the Guardian himself."

"Biddy called the horse a nightmare," Esa interjected, remarking on the story Shamus's mother spoke of just last night.

Perturbed at Esa for interrupting, Bedina frowned at her friend and stated pointedly, "Biddy also said the Guardian used a long thin sword made of moonlight that could send the demons flying."

Moirae sat in shock, barely registering what the two women were jabbering. With each new description, Moirae's jaw became more rigid and the outrage in her emerald eyes grew. Moonlight? A sword? *A new horse!* All things she had been forced to avoid because of what she was—a woman.

"Shamus said he looked like a Highlander but didn't sound like one from around here," Esa continued to prattle, smacking her lips.

"Oh, his voice!" Bedina sighed longingly as if she had been

the one to hear it. "You should hear Biddy describe it! Deep, like a hero's song."

Moirae groaned, throwing her face into her hands. *A deep voice!* Whoever had the impudence to take over the role she had so carefully created was executing it in a way she had only dreamed of doing.

Placing her palms on the table, Moirae rose to her feet. The thief may have more flair than her, but she was not about to surrender the role of Guardian without a fight. It was her idea. She had earned that title after a significant amount of pain and anguish, and most importantly, the role was critical to her plans. So she was not about to share—let alone relinquish—the one thing in her life that gave her pure satisfaction.

The invaders had gone for Shamus and his family, which meant they were near Loch Ericht, where several dozen farmers made their living. If rumors continued to be correct, the demons would be in the area for weeks, possibly months, randomly attacking households before finally moving on. Plenty of time for her to find them and seek her revenge.

First, however, she had to end someone's misplaced ambitions. With tonight's party, many would be traveling at night and the possibility of an attack would be high. The fraudulent Guardian was no doubt riding nearby, hoping to play hero.

Well, let him, thought Moirae. Tonight it would be his turn for a surprise. For whoever the fool was, he had yet to meet Moirae Deincourt—the true Guardian of Badenoch.

Moirae entered the narrow passageway leading to her bedchambers and waved her hand at the servant assigned to her before entering. The girl scampered off, knowing by now that such a signal meant to leave and not return until called. The maid probably suspected much of Moirae's activities, but she had the good sense to keep quiet. Comfortable duties and undemanding masters were rare to find, and Moirae was possibly the least difficult of any noblewoman the girl was ever likely to serve. Gossip could be incredibly alluring, but coveted positions in the castle were of even greater value.

Hearing the maid's retreating footsteps, Moirae crossed the room and pulled out a key from around her neck to unlock the large chest at the end of the bed. Following the click, she opened the lid and pulled out the items it contained. Stripping off her gown, Moirae quickly donned the male garments of a simple linen shirt, bruchen, hose, and a dark quilted jacket. The black gambeson was designed to protect a knight's skin from his armor, but the thick garment itself provided more than enough protection. It enabled her to preserve her two strongest advantages—speed and dexterity.

After slipping on worn boots and pulling her hair back into a single, loose braid, she grabbed a dark cape and secured the black hood in lieu of any headgear. Kicking aside the rushes, she lifted two loose floor planks to reveal the machicolation. The gap between the supporting corbels had originally been intended for defense by allowing stones to be dropped on enemies, but Moirae had found other uses for the opening. Grabbing a knotted rope from the chest, she secured it to the leg of the bed and then dropped it through the hole before scurrying down.

From there it was easy to sneak out of the keep and make her way to Enion's stable. Someday she would have to find another option for her horse, but Enion had lived somewhat apart from the clan, and his cottage needed numerous repairs. For now, no one was eager to assume residence there.

Moirae saddled the gentle mare, which though dark brown, would never be mistaken for black or be considered large enough to be called a "nightmare." But she was quick and seemed to understand that Moirae's right leg could not grip like a normal rider's, and so never turned sharp in that direction. The animal also knew Badenoch as well as herself.

Feeling the cool air whip against her face, Moirae felt a sense of peace envelop her. Some longed for the warmer months, and while she didn't relish winter weather, the chill of night was far more preferable than the summer sun.

Tugging the reins gently to the left, Moirae rode north until the sights and sounds of the castle faded. Then she stopped, closed her eyes, and let her senses talk to her. The rain had finally completely stopped and the clouds were beginning to break apart, allowing the light from the moon to shine down—both a blessing and a curse. Sometimes Moirae had to wait, but tonight she did not have to linger for very long before she became instantly alert.

A raid was happening and it was close by.

* * *

Dorian shifted his gaze to assess each of the attackers as he rode straight into the heart of the ambush. Two humans and one spawn—Metrick, who most likely had gotten a whiff of Dorian's arrival and was already disappearing into the Alder forest. One could change his appearance throughout the years but not his scent, and both knew of the other from years past.

Metrick had been one of Ionas's men during their last encounter. Being only two removed from an immortal, Metrick's expected lifespan was somewhere around two hundred and fifty years, and he now reeked of the one thing a spawn most feared—imminent death. A feeling Dorian could not fathom but often envied. Death itself had no allure, but it represented mortality, which gave man the inner drive to accomplish something . . . the desire to create in order to leave behind a legacy.

With Metrick's sudden disappearance, only two human attackers remained—both imposing physically and possessing mercenary hearts. It was very unlikely either of them knew the truth behind their being hired to terrorize and raid. So far, not a human Dorian had encountered had heard of his nephew, let alone knew what Ionas sought.

Urging his horse over the stone wall, Dorian grabbed the largest man by the head and tossed him aside. He then dismounted and headed for the one dragging a woman who appeared to be in her mid to late fifties out of her home. Reaching forward, Dorian gripped the assailant's beefy shoulder, and with one hand, flung him close to where his associate lay. The crack heard from his head hitting the trunk of the tree made it known he was dead.

Damn. If he intended to eat tonight, it would have to be soon while the blood was warm. Not that he couldn't ingest it cold, but drinking stale blood was the equivalent of eating rotten food. One avoided the idea.

"You!" Dorian barked at the haggard-looking farmer standing immobile in the doorway. He then pointed at the hunched female form on the ground and the two small blond heads cautiously poking out from behind their father. "Get your mother and children inside, *and stay there.*" The emphasis was enough to produce action from the stunned, aged Highlander, who scrambled to do as he was told.

The moment the door closed, Dorian went to his horse and

214 / Michele Sinclair

removed his sword. He then moved to stand beside the two limp bodies. He inhaled the scent of blood and then kicked the backside of the man pretending to be dead, flipping him over. Like the others, Ionas had hired them to search for something.

The attacker's blue eyes flew open wide as Dorian kneeled down. "What were you told to look for?"

Visible fear rippled through the man's frame. "I don't know."

Dorian spun the long sword in his palm and sliced the air, stopping just before the blade penetrated the man's throat. "I won't ask again."

"An . . . an . . . old wo-wo-woman," the man finally managed to get out. "One w-w-with scars on her neck. Sh-sh-e has something the white-h-h-haired one wants. He—he's sending men everywhere to hunt for h-h-her."

Dorian grimaced. The *white-haired one* meant Patras—his nephew's lead henchman for the past few centuries. The albino spawn was intelligent and ruthless, and Dorian would have thought him to be dead by now. Why was Patras spending his final years helping Ionas look for an old woman with scars on her neck? Once bitten, humans either died or changed. Only in rare circumstances would they live, and then only if a blood eater punctured the skin but did not feed. Disease was one of the few things that would stop a feeding once begun.

So, Ionas was interested in a human female who survived not only an offensive-tasting ailment, but being bitten. Why?

Sensing there was no more information to be retrieved, Dorian pressed the blade into the man's neck without further thought. Whoever the mercenary was, he would not be missed and his disappearance would cause no stir. Standing, Dorian lifted the nape of the now lifeless form and bent his head to feed, but the scent of someone nearby halted him before he punctured the warm flesh.

The onlooker was a female, and she was young. She smelled human sweet . . . and yet different. She was watching him from behind the untended hedge opposite to where he rode in. He inhaled her fragrance again, and smiled. She was wearing a man's chausses and a wool gambeson . . . and the girl bathed too often to be a pauper. Whoever the lass was, she wasn't there by accident.

Curiosity momentarily fluttered through him, but the interest the girl generated was not enough to seek her out. He was not hungry enough to deal with the retribution of killing her, a necessary consequence if he decided to let her see him feed. Disappointed, Dorian released his hold and let the body fall to the ground with a thump. He had fed last night, and if need be, he could go several more days without nourishment, but he had been looking forward to a quick drink.

After taking one last whiff of the woman's tempting scent, Dorian went to his horse and, in a single, graceful leap, jumped on the animal's back. Urging it into a gallop, he headed straight for the hedge. With a single kick to the flanks, the destrier went soaring over the woman's head. As Dorian flew by, he caught another whiff and looked down.

Brilliant jade eyes flashed at him in the partial moonlight as wisps of light brown hair flew around her incredibly striking face. For a brief second, the temptation to seek her out seized his instincts. The young woman's gaze had not been filled with horror, but with seething anger. He knew as he headed over the fields that the look would haunt him.

What was she doing out alone? Why did she despise him for saving an old man and his family? Was it that he had killed the two men attacking them? But mostly he asked himself, why did he care?

It had been many centuries since a human woman had caught his attention beyond that of fulfilling simple physical need. And though he would admit to being mildly intrigued, it was not nearly enough to compel him to be foolish. So, whoever the sweet-smelling maiden was, she would have to remain a mystery.

Moirae almost had not stopped in time as she rode in with bow and arrow prepped to stop the attack. At the last moment, she realized her competition had already arrived and was more than able to handle the once three, now two men. Hanging her bow on the saddle, she quietly dismounted and crept into the prickly hedge. There she spied the dark, lean figure fulfilling her role as Guardian in a way she had only dreamed of doing.

Regrettably, her rival was good. Worse, he possessed a grace using a weapon she had never before witnessed from any man. He was also much more agile than she would have guessed, given his size and muscular frame. His features remained obscure in the shadows, but his hair was indeed dark and styled shorter than the average Highlander's. Only when his horse had flown over her head had she been able to glimpse the color of his eyes. They were not dark as she had been told, but gray, like a perpetual fog that lured innocents in, causing them to be forever lost.

Every instinct screamed, *Avoid the fog!* Instead, Moirae got on her horse to follow him, obeying the other inner voice reminding her of who he was and just what he had stolen from her.

Unfortunately, the thief's mount was larger and faster, making catching up to him an impossibility, despite her superior knowledge of the mountains and lochs. But it did not matter. Moirae slowed her mount down and stared into the distant shadows. She knew where the imposter was going. Kilnhurst. A place everyone knew to avoid. It may be unoccupied, but it was not undefended.

The man was heading to his death.

Chapter Two

Dorian raced through the open gatehouse, slowing as he approached the stables. His horse, now knowing the nightly ritual, entered his stall after his master slipped off its back.

Frustration filled Dorian. Three fruitless nights had gone by. With no attacks to stop, he had no sources of information. Who Ionas was looking for and why the woman was important remained a mystery. Dorian could feel the tiny interest he once held about his nephew's plans begin to ebb.

He rounded the stable door and was about to yank it close when he spied a brown mare eating hay in one of the stalls. Cursing, he took a deep breath and confirmed the young female who witnessed the attack that happened earlier that week was nearby. He shut the door softly and let his gaze sweep the courtyard until he saw a dark figure leaning against the inner wall of the gatehouse. Discarding men's clothes for those fitting a noble, the woman was wearing a dark bliaut and a black hooded mantle to shield her from the icy air. No longer was she hiding in the shadows, but standing outside in plain sight, waiting for him, unafraid of being inside Kilnhurst Castle—infamous for the disappearance of all who dared to venture near its walls.

Ionas had built the stronghold decades prior when he pushed Edward I to erect stone forts to better withstand attacks. Kilnhurst was large, nothing like the estates Dorian had inhabited when he lived in Crete a millennium prior, but he had taken great satisfaction at capturing the castle from his nephew. And though Kilnhurst was far from lavish, it was ideally located in the heart of the Highlands and built to survive Scotland's brutal northern weather over many years. It also conveyed an uncomfortable sen-

218 / *Michele Sinclair*

sation that made humans want to avoid it. Something the young woman clearly was oblivious to or too dim-witted to realize.

Not in the mood to tangle with an obstinate and senseless human female, Dorian was about to turn and enter the castle through a back door. But before he looked away, she reached up and pulled down her hood, revealing rich brown hair, neither dark nor light, intricately braided and piled into an elaborate knot. Rebellious strands that had won the fight to come loose curled into ringlets, highlighting the pale skin of her unusually long nape.

The woman shifted and looked in his direction, causing the moonlight to catch her face. Only slightly narrow, the oval shape accentuated her cheekbones and emphasized the fullness of her lips. But it was not her angelic features that had caused him to hesitate. It was her eyes. The dark green orbs did not shine with innocence and youth as her scent indicated but belonged to an adult woman— who was still every bit as angry as she had been three nights ago.

Moirae fought restlessness, wondering when her nemesis would return. She had mentally rehearsed a hundred times how she was going to handle his arrival. She would patiently wait as he bellowed about her presence, and then she would make it clear that he was unneeded and, more importantly, unwanted, as the Guardian. But the longer she was forced to wait, the more unlikely she was going to remain the calm herald she had planned.

Moirae closed her eyes and took a deep breath.

The scents around Kilnhurst were unlike anywhere else. There was an absence of fear, sorrow, anger, and despair—all the negative emotions that accompanied the hard lives of those who lived in a castle. In its place was something dark and vacant and strangely welcoming. She suspected the castle's designer had hoped to evoke another feeling, but to her, the effect was enticing, not repellent.

Until three nights ago, she had never ventured close to Kilnhurst. Rumors had circulated for years about those who dared to breach its walls supposedly disappearing, never to be heard from again. And yet, she had watched this squatter come and go without concern.

Built to be a fortress, six equal, three-story towers formed the shape of a hexagon and were connected by a double curtain wall. Within, there were none of the usual internal structures. No great hall, kitchens, buttery, silversmith, or other buildings one expected to see. Only a well, the stables, and the gatehouse were recognizable. Besides the formidable walls, the castle's main defense was a mote. A sizeable one that fully surrounded Kilnhurst, preventing any entry unless the gatehouse bridge was let down— as it was tonight.

For two nights, Moirae had sat in the forest, waiting for an event and the chance to confront the dark avenger who thought to steal her role as Guardian. But no attacks came. Frustrated, she had decided to ride to Kilnhurst and hope for a chance to intercept the want-to-be hero and persuade him to leave the area. Seeing the drawbridge down, she had darted inside, uncaring of the rumors, and waited for the opposition.

Patience, however, had left her hours ago. Dawn would soon arrive and Moirae was debating if she should leave when a small branch snapped to her right. She immediately froze. No one ever snuck up on her. It was impossible. She inhaled. Nothing. And yet every one of her other senses screamed that someone was beside her.

She spun around to see a large figure not quite ten feet away. Though silhouetted by the moonlight, she could still discern enough features to confirm he was the same man she had witnessed fighting the other night. He was tall enough to be a Highlander and radiated a primitive masculine vitality like those men born in the north, but he did not belong to these majestic mountains any more than she did.

He lacked the overall brawn Highlanders possessed, and yet, Moirae suspected he could take care of himself and any enemy that happened along. His face was formed by severe angles and planes, creating high cheekbones and a rock-hard jaw. His nose was unusually straight, and his mouth was broad and firm. With the exception of his dark hair, which looked seductively ruffled, there was no softness about him anywhere. No wonder she hadn't sensed him. She doubted this man surrendered to any kind of strong emotion.

He walked toward her with a poised, almost erotic grace that assaulted her senses. If he were anyone else . . . and if she were free of her past, she might have been interested enough in him to make a play for his attentions. But her life had another purpose, and a man—especially this one—was not to play a part in it.

"I wasn't aware you had returned," she stated simply.

Dorian was impressed. She exuded calm composure in both stance and voice. He would almost think she was bored if not for the jutting out of her chin. "That's because I didn't want you to know."

Her eyes instantly flashed with anger and he inhaled. Only true, full-blood nosferatu could sense animals, even inflict their emotional will on them. And yet what stood in front of him was an enigma. It wasn't that he couldn't smell her. He could. She was definitely a human, and despite her underdeveloped bosom, he knew without a doubt that she was a mature woman in her mid-twenties. And yet, only his eyes could discern the obvious frustration that exuded from her every pore. Perhaps he was hungrier than he had thought.

"Find no one to save tonight?"

Her caustic question surprised Dorian. Usually women, especially young human ones, were uneasy in his presence. A few pretended to be enamored, but he could not recall in his entire life one that was sincerely defiant. And though he could not be certain without being able to smell her scent, one thing was unmistakable . . . no fear reflected in her green depths. His curiosity took hold. "And just who might you be?"

"Someone you should listen to."

The man grinned, and the unexpected response shook Moirae's core. He had not looked like the kind of man who would even know how to smile. It relaxed his eyes, and their smoky color went from cool and distancing to hypnotic, causing her to shiver with apprehension. Then it suddenly occurred to her that was exactly what he wanted.

Swallowing, Moirae regained her composure and reminded herself that she was there for a reason and just because the thief turned out to be attractive changed nothing. Moirae forced her eyes to look into his. He was still just smiling, but she could see that he was more than slightly amused. He was laughing at her. He thought her a silly, little girl and was toying with her for amusement. That was a mistake.

Smile while you can, for you won't be very soon, she silently promised. She flicked an imaginary speck of dirt from her gown and then stared at him directly in the eye. "You are an interloper, stranger. You are unwanted, and most of all you are a fool."

Moirae added the insult at the last moment. The man may

think he was fighting regular thugs like those of the other night, but there were far scarier things in the area. Things only a fool would intentionally seek out.

The realization that she was just such a person hit her at the same time she perceived the change in his expression. The menacing scowl he suddenly wore should have caused her to quiver with fear, but all Moirae could feel was elation. She suspected it was a rare occasion that someone could cause emotion to rise from this man of stone. Good, maybe if she made him mad enough, he would want to leave and never return.

Dorian stilled as he assimilated the intentional slight. Then a cold anger flared to life. The time for playing with humans was over. He pivoted and stepped into the stables, returning less than a minute later, handing the woman the reins to her horse. Ignoring him, she refused to take them, and instead, she arched a single brow most aggravatingly as she reached up to unhook her cloak and remove it. The cheeky woman was actually refusing to leave!

With her mantle off, he could see that while her slender frame made her appear petite, she was far from small. Rather than frail as he first perceived, her unusual height reminded him of what it felt like to be a man and not a giant among men. A flicker of sexual desire coursed through him, immediately followed by a flash of self-directed anger.

He had learned long ago how to control his physical urges and let them surface only when he was guaranteed of no entanglements. It wasn't that he refused to mate with humans. Just the opposite. He preferred to be with them, as their passions were uncontrolled and less manufactured. But he had learned the hard way that humans and his kind were incompatible, for immortals and mortals could not coexist for any length of time. Human lives were too short and it affected everything about them—their thoughts, ambitions, desires, accomplishments—but most especially their interactions with others.

Dorian was just about to pick the audacious woman up, physically place her on her horse, and force her to leave, when she threw her coat over the saddle's pommel and took the reins from his still extended hand. Then, in one smooth movement, she leapt onto her horse and looked down. For the first time, she smiled, and he knew it was because of his openly shocked expression. Very few men had ever possessed the strength and agility she had just demonstrated. In his experience, only nosferatu or their spawns had such abilities, both of which she was decidedly not.

"Heed my counsel," she warned. "Leave Badenoch and this castle. Both harbor great danger."

"For you maybe, but I know Kilnhurst's owner. And I am fairly certain that you do not."

Moirae swallowed as frustration began to take over. "Badenoch holds danger for those who ride at night. Halt your acts of heroism. Your help is neither welcomed nor wanted by those who live here. Another protects these lands. Stop or be at risk of being in the path of their arrows."

Dorian glanced at the bow and arrow hanging on the hindquarters of her horse. Was she actually inferring to herself?

Moirae swung her horse around, but before she could leave, Dorian stepped in front of the gate's opening, preventing her exit. Her beautiful eyes widened in surprise. "Just who are you to think you can order me about?" he demanded.

A wintry smile overtook her expression. "My name is Moirae. Moirae Deincourt. I, and I alone, am the Guardian of Badenoch." Then, with a swift kick, she skillfully guided her horse around his frame and disappeared into the night.

Dorian stood transfixed in a state of shock. Moirae. The name was not Scottish, Gaelic, or even English. It was old. Very old. And he had not heard it in a long time. Turning, he went to the gatehouse and raised the drawbridge, ensuring the woman could not again appear when least expected.

Moirae. "Why did she have to be a Moirae?" he asked himself aloud before turning to the obscure door that led inside. Moirae was the name of the fabled Goddess of Destiny, and while, he knew there was no entity that controlled the thread of every person's life from birth to death, the few times he had ever encountered a Moirae, his life had changed in ways he never could predict.

Maybe she was right. Maybe he should leave. Now. Tonight . . . and yet, even as Dorian thought the words, he knew he was going nowhere.

At least, not yet.

Chapter Three

Moirae realized too late that tonight's attack was not like the others. The family was not the intended victim—*she* was the target. And whoever was after her was not taking any chances. The most men she had ever encountered during a raid was four, but tonight, at least a dozen, maybe more, surrounded her. And they were closing in fast.

As quickly as she could, Moirae restrung her bow and shot arrows into the flesh of as many assailants as she could see, but severely outnumbered, she knew it was only time before one reached her. She had taken down at least six or seven when a large hand clutched her shoulder from behind and knocked her off her horse and onto the ground. A second man lunged at her with a sword. Reacting on instinct, she sat up and reached for the never-before-used blade dangling off her saddle and pulled it forward with lightning speed just in time to deflect a mortal blow. Unfortunately, she had not been fast enough to avoid the strike altogether, and pain shot through her side as jagged metal slashed through her clothing and into her skin.

Moirae dropped the heavy sword Enion had insisted she take with her despite her lack of skill. Until now, she had always fought at a distance with a bow and arrow. It enabled her to keep her mysterious identity and prevented her from advertising her weakness with the blade. The man pulled back and started to swing his sword in the air, flamboyantly preparing for another attempt.

Moirae wondered if death might finally be upon her. Relief mixed with a strong desire to live flooded her senses as she stared into the eyes of the brute who was going to issue the final blow. Then instinct took hold again and, without warning, the attacker's face changed from glee to shock as the dagger she yanked off his dead friend's belt plunged into his chest. Then the world went dark from the impact of her head hitting the ground as he fell upon her.

Dorian let go a stream of Greek curses. He had been aware of the attack, but because he had sensed no spawns, only humans, he had held back—too far back. He knew the woman was there, but she had claimed to be the Guardian of these lands and demanded to be left alone. Fool.

His fury with Moirae was genuine, but he was equally furious with himself for believing that because of her speed and skill of getting onto a horse she could actually defend herself.

He had yet to determine the purpose of Ionas's raids, but Dorian was relatively sure they were based on a personal quest versus something larger and involving revenge. Whoever his nephew was looking for most likely wasn't in the vicinity, and Ionas would soon be sending his henchman farther north, if he hadn't already. Dorian was dithering on leaving just as she "asked" when at the last moment he decided to see for himself how a sprite of a girl performed as the Guardian of Badenoch.

To prevent her or her attackers from knowing of his presence, he had kept at a distance. At first, he had been impressed at the speed and accuracy of her shots, but then everything changed. The numbers of assailants suddenly grew and became too much for her to handle alone with only a bow and arrow. Within seconds they had her surrounded. Dorian instinctively readied his katana and spurred his horse into a full gallop.

He peered through the distance, seeing Moirae on top of her horse. He yelled out, but it was too late. One of the attackers came up from behind and knocked her down to the ground, lifting his sword high before swiftly plunging it down. The smell of her blood filled the air. A second later Dorian was upon them. With inhuman strength plus a millennia of training and expertise in combat, he ended the fight, killing the remaining half dozen men within minutes.

Yanking one body up by his hair, Dorian bit down into the neck and drank the warm, life-giving beverage. He threw the corpse away and studied the large mass that hid Moirae's body. He could still smell her sweetness. Human women with her spirit were rare, and Dorian regretted that he had not been able to save her.

Repugnance filled him at the absurd idea. Aeolus was right. He was bored. He must be for it was incredulous that a single woman's death could mean anything to him. Why should it? It changed nothing in the larger scheme of things. Thousands of mortals died every day, and yet they still bred, rebuilt their numbers, and continued with their greed. It had taken several centuries for him to comprehend that even an immortal could not change the nature of man. Humans were who they were—limited by their own mortality.

Still, Moirae had intrigued him.

He reached down and started to pull off the one who had dealt the death wound when he heard her groan.

"Moirae?" he whispered, easily tossing aside the massive body that had her pinned to the ground. Her shirt and mantle were soaked in blood, but he could hear her breathing. She was still alive.

On impulse, he lifted her into his arms and jumped back into his saddle. Holding her close, he rode as fast as he could back to Kilnhurst, unthinking of what he was doing and why. The attraction he felt for her wasn't fading. If anything, it was growing.

It had been too long since he had encountered anyone interesting, and even longer since he had been with a beautiful woman. Having both in his arms pounding his legs across the countryside was lunacy. But the idea of letting her die had suddenly become unacceptable, leaving him with two choices. Take her to safety and find her help or make her his spawn. And he was not about to do that.

True nosferatu were limited to those direct descendants of Hellen, but with each generation, the blood disease that made them immortal became weaker. No nosferatu had been born in over fifteen centuries. A bite from one, however, could change a human into a spawn with enhanced abilities. And while spawns lived for time spans much longer than that of a human, they were not immortal. Spawns could create spawns, but with each siring, the regenerative element became more diluted, significantly hampering their offspring's abilities and lifetime. Not a single spawn was truly immortal.

Dorian glanced down at Moirae's limp body, and the flawless white skin of her long neck caught his eye. He had no desire to fall back into impulsive feeding habits that too often created unforeseen results with impacts that lasted far too long. Still, she was tempting.

Upon the clattering sound of his mount's hooves hitting the rockier soil, Moirae's eyes popped open to reveal haunting green orbs. The blood on her leine proved she was injured, but the fire in her eyes suggested that she was not quite in the mortal danger he had believed. Quite the opposite. Moirae Deincourt was very much alive and very angry.

Moirae's senses told her where she was before she even opened her eyes. Elation that she was not dead had been almost instantly replaced by the realization of just who had saved her. She was mortified. The man probably had witnessed her humiliating failure and had taken pity on her. Well, she needed no one's compassion, and certainly not his. She opened her eyes and flashed him her most withering look.

He blinked. Good.

In an effort to sit up, she pushed against his chest, but that turned out to be a mistake. He was not wearing a cape, only an unusually dark, smooth, shimmering shirt. The loosely strung garment allowed her fingers to touch his flesh, from which she immediately recoiled. He was rock hard and cool to the touch, as if he had been outside just a little too long. But more than that, the sensation of feeling his skin excited her, a feeling no man had ever induced.

"Let me down," she weakly commanded, annoyed that her voice betrayed what he was doing to her.

When her flaccid demand resulted in no response and no release, it bolstered her indignation and she tried again. "Let me down *now*."

"You're hurt."

Her annoyance was growing with each second, and the dismissal in his voice was more than she could take. "I assure you than I am not hurt," she replied and began to squirm in ingenious ways that should have assured her freedom. But the damn man seemed to predict her every move.

She had thought he would tire of fighting her, but it seemed to be a game of wills, and she refused to be the first to surrender, so the struggle continued right until they reached the winding path that indicated Kilnhurst was in sight. He raised a hand to some unknown lookout, and immediately the drawbridge lowered just in time for their arrival. The portcullis raised and they went through, stopping just inside the bailey. He lowered her to her feet before throwing his own leg over the animal's back and landing on the ground with a thump.

A figure suddenly appeared from nowhere and just as quickly disappeared with the horse. So her opposition wasn't staying alone in the castle. Well, of course he wasn't. And he did say that he was not trespassing.

Moirae was so lost in thought and questions, she had not realized her savior was about to disappear into the gatehouse, when he turned around and asked, "Are you coming, Lady Destiny? Or would you prefer to again profess your skills as the Guardian out here in the night air?"

Moirae gritted her teeth, clenching her lips together even tighter. Self-humiliation was one thing—being openly mocked was another. Squaring her chin, she cocked a brow at him, and then moved as gracefully as her bad leg would allow through the opening. Only then did she grasp just where she was. *Inside* Kilnhurst.

The wooden gatehouse entrance looked like a simple tower door, but it opened into something quite unexpected. She had assumed she would see a typical storage area or perhaps a stairway opening that led to the castle's curtain wall. What she saw was nothing of the kind. She was indeed in a room, and opposite of her was an ornate archway that led to a hallway on its other side. Understanding suddenly flooded her. Kilnhurst's double curtain walls were not just protective barriers but formed a huge quasi-building that went around the complex. The idea was unique and Moirae was positive no one else had conceived of such an idea. Such a structure would have aroused envy and eventual duplication.

Moirae could feel the dark figure smiling with pride as he sauntered past her, indicating for her to follow. It was the first time she had been able to sense any emotion from him. And while part of her was relieved to know she could sense him at least some of the time, her focus was on assessing the man who had turned her life upside down.

He was a noble, or had been raised like one, for there was nothing subservient about him. His stride was long and smooth so that he appeared to glide—not walk. Far from feminine, the controlled movement gave him an aura of power most men only dreamed of possessing. Moirae found herself growing jealous as she did her best to disguise her ungraceful limp, which was near impossible at the pace he was moving.

Deliberately slowing, she let him disappear ahead and continued to pass through one archway, and then another, following the bend of the dimly lit hallway that conformed to the circular structure of the curtain wall. Sporadically, she would see doors. Most were closed, but a few were open, enabling her to glimpse the dark interior. Most appeared unused, and if the rooms had windows, they were not visible. The resulting darkness created a comforting atmosphere she had grown to prefer.

Turning one last time, Moirae saw Dorian standing in front of large double doors, waiting for her to catch up. Upon seeing her, he opened them and stood aside, allowing her to pass. As she moved by him, she inhaled, getting a whiff of two large dogs hidden farther down the hall. Both were alert to their presence and ready to attack if signaled, but just what their master wanted, she had no clue. Once again she could not discern any emotion from Dorian. Only her sense of sight and touch told her that he was there. It was as if he had the ability to turn on and off his feelings. She was tempted to ask how but had no idea how to phrase the question without revealing too much about herself.

With a puzzled brow, she entered the room, which, unlike the others she had spied, was glowing with candles that cast shadows everywhere. Moirae got the impression she was being invited into his lair. The leather furniture was large and padded and she knew no one local had made such items. There was an elaborate desk in one corner with both recognizable and foreign items on its surface. But the most remarkable object was on a narrow table centered on the far wall. Propped in a wooden frame was the unusual, deadly sword she had witnessed him use that first night. Beside it was an empty holder, hinting that he possessed more than one of the rare weapons.

"You have nice taste, Laird," she said, turning around to face him.

The title caused a slight smile to crack his deadpan expression. For a brief instance, Moirae could once again sense him. She had surprised him and he had enjoyed the feeling. "I am no laird. I just own a castle," he corrected her.

Moirae shrugged her chin, glad to learn that he did not just know Kilnhurst's owner—the castle actually belonged to him. It was also heartening to hear him admit the truth about his lack of title. She had known he was not a laird, but in her experience, most men would have let such incorrect assumptions continue for as long as they could benefit from it. "I wonder what clan you purchased it from."

"Does it matter?"

"Aye," she answered, gazing at him intently before continuing. "But I have a feeling that asking questions about how you came to live in this place would be waste of time." She licked her lips. "The previous owner had nice taste."

"My nephew still does. He prefers to live well."

"And you?"

"Sometimes."

"But not all of the time?" she asked, truly interested.

"No."

Moirae nodded with sincere understanding. "The comforts of life all too often entail unwanted complexities and responsibilities. To balance the two can be a challenge."

Dorian attempted to suppress his shock at her comment. It simply was not a statement he had expected a human to say, let alone truly believe, especially one so young. Forcing his limbs to move, he came up behind her and reached out to touch her shoulders. "Let me take your cloak."

Without argument, she unhooked the clasp and released the blood-soaked garment. Once again, she was wearing men's breeches and a leine with a gambeson. The woolen armor had been slashed down the side and was still wet with her blood. "Take that off," he ordered. "I need to examine your wound."

Moirae, still looking around the room, froze, forgetting just how she had come to be there. "I don't have one," she said truthfully.

"Your clothes say otherwise," Dorian countered, forcing her to stand still as he lifted the heavy material to reveal the flesh beneath.

He inspected the area as well as he could without making her strip, but he could find not a scratch. Like her neck, her skin was flawless. Relief filled him and yet the fact made no sense. Dorian took a deep breath but could detect only her humanity and burgeoning womanhood. And yet her blood, as well as the man's she had stabbed, were unmistakable on her clothes. Could the rip be a result from a previous injury? Instinct said there was another explanation, but without her being a spawn, he could not fathom what it was.

Moirae swallowed and stepped back, unnerved by his closeness. "Kilnhurst is most unusual. Whoever designed it considered both defense and upkeep. Time can be destructive to castles, especially unused ones."

Dorian felt his jaw grow hard. Was she toying with him? Had Aeolus found her and instructed her on things to say to gain his attention? It was possible, but he would swear her statement had been unrehearsed. And yet mortals thought about time in segments related to their own lifetime, not those that encompassed their descendants'. Whoever she was, Moirae was living up to her name.

Dorian threw her mantle over a chair and went to light the fire, realizing that she most likely found the room to be rather cold. After getting the flames to catch hold, he asked, "Are you hungry?"

Moirae shook her head and watched him remove a large curved sword from his belt and place it with its smaller mate. Though different lengths, each had an ivory handle carved with strange markings. Both were mesmerizing, compelling her to reach out and touch them. Unable to resist, she walked up to the first, but before her finger could feel the cool surface, Dorian grabbed her wrist from behind, halting her.

Realizing what she had just been about to do, she apologized. "I've just . . . well, I've never seen a sword like it before."

Dorian let her go and stepped back. "And you probably never will again."

Moirae exhaled and turned around abruptly, bumping into him. Damn. She had thought he had moved farther away. Normally, her sense of smell told her just how many people were in the room and where they were standing in relation to her. Unfortunately, the man in front of her was the one person with whom she truly needed the ability.

Dorian lifted his finger to move back a wayward piece of her hair and stroked her cheek. Moirae really was beautiful. Her delicately carved cheekbones held just a hint of rose in the dim reflection cast by the shadowy light. With a small nose and a soft pert mouth composed of a lower lip slightly fuller than the upper, her face was ·the model of feminine delicacy. And yet one only had to glance into her expressive eyes to know such fragility was a lie. The woman had strength, of will and spirit—a captivating and, therefore, dangerous combination.

His fingers trailed down her cheek to her neck, and he could feel the beat of her heart racing. He was not alone in his reaction to their close proximity. He may not be able to sense her emotions, but he could smell her response. Desire pumped through her pores.

Tilting her head up toward him, she looked directly into his gray eyes, peering at him intently. Slowly and seductively, Dorian let his gaze slide downward and witnessed the resulting shiver that went through her. The woman was a virgin. He had had many in his past, and some were pleasing, but most were so timid they failed to inspire. He suspected Moirae Deincourt would prove to be just as surprising in bed as she was out of it, but the possibility of a small, brief thrill was not enough to make him want to play with fire. And that was what Moirae was. Someone to be avoided.

Dorian stepped back and waved for her to sit down on one of the four padded chairs that were placed in a semicircle around the hearth.

Moirae went to the closest chair, irked by his cool, aloof manner mostly because she had been anything but composed. It was time to refocus. "I want you to stop being the Guardian," she said directly.

Dorian's scoff was soft but still painful. "An unwise request. Tonight was proof enough that you are unable to fulfill the role. Maybe it is you who should stop, lest next time I'm not nearby."

Sudden anger lit her eyes. "I don't fear death. And for nearly a year now, my bow has been more than enough."

"Miraculously. I cannot believe anyone can shoot with your grip."

"And yet I hit my targets," she uttered through clenched teeth.

He laughed. "That you do."

The acknowledgment should have made her feel better, but his laughter pricked her pride. "Then why should I change?" she challenged.

"Because no one should aspire to do things incorrectly. None of the men who ever followed me into battle would have done so if I fought ridiculously, even if I was somehow successful."

"It is not loyalty I crave—"

Moirae halted in midsentence and Dorian wondered what she had been about to admit. Just what did a woman like Moirae crave?

Before he could press her, she decided to put him on the defensive. "Besides you do not fool me. You profess to lead others, and yet it is clear, there is no one that follows you. You command the loyalty of what? Your two hounds and husband and wife staff?"

His eyes narrowed. Moirae had only glimpsed one male servant, and he was positive that she had seen nothing of his dogs. She obviously knew much more than he realized. Time for playing was over. "It is time you left, Lady Destiny."

She looked at him with mute defiance. If possible, her expression was even more stubborn than his own. "Not until you agree to leave Badenoch."

"And if I refuse?"

"There is a danger of pushing me too far, my lord," she warned.

Her emerald eyes were wide, brilliant, and slightly mocking. She was utterly intoxicating, standing right up to him, defying him, twisting her lips, making them all the more tempting. Dorian felt every muscle in his body tighten with hot, intense, primitive need.

He reached out to catch her chin between his thumb and forefinger. He turned her head so she was forced to meet his eyes. "Not laird. Not lord. Just Dorian," he murmured.

He had intended to tell her to go home, but when Moirae sucked in a quivering breath, Dorian could hold back his curiosity no longer. Moving his hand to the back of her head, he took her mouth, kissing her with an inviting passion that caused her to shiver in his arms, but she did not pull away. Instead, her arms stole around his neck and her lips parted, inviting him to deepen the kiss.

That encouragement was all he needed, and Dorian plunged inside, tasting, teasing, kissing her mouth hungrily. Tentatively at first, then with growing urgency, she matched the intensity of his kisses, creating a hot tide of passion to rise rapidly between them.

When he paused to let go, she opened her eyes and met his. Her luminous dark green and gold pools blazed with desire, and he was hard with wanting her. He could still taste her on his tongue, hot and wet and woman sweet. It took all his concentration to control the most elemental of his male urges and not take her in his arms again and end things with more than just a kiss. He truly could not remember the last time wanting a woman, any woman, as much as he desired her. It was almost enough to shatter his long-held ideas of immortals mixing with mortals.

Almost.

The kiss had been meant to establish she was a young inexperienced woman with nothing to tempt him. Unfortunately, it had proven quite the opposite. He was tempted, but she was dangerous. There was something different about her, and while it was undeniably appealing, she was also undeniably human. And he was not.

Leaning toward her, Dorian cradled her face in his strong hands and gently brushed his lips softly against hers. He then stepped back and pulled a cord, a clear sign that he was ending whatever had erupted between them. Moirae was not unsure that she wasn't glad for the interruption. She had just been burgeoning into womanhood when her world had been turned upside down. Men, relationships, love . . . these were no longer options for her. Her life had a different purpose.

"Thank you for the kiss," she whispered, and then willed her voice to strengthen. "But it changes nothing. Leave Badenoch."

Dorian smiled. He liked her tenacity. She was new to desire and yet she refused to let it rule her. He wondered what it would be like with her if she ever genuinely let go. "I'll leave when I am ready, my lady. And not before."

Just then, a short dark-haired man appeared in the doorway. "Did you retrieve the lady's horse?" Dorian asked. Upon the man's nod, Moirae felt the large fingers of Dorian's hand upon her back.

Sweeping up her cloak off the chair as he escorted her out the study door, Moirae went without argument, but not without a promise. "You will be seeing me again . . . Dorian. And on my terms."

Somehow, Dorian didn't doubt it. He was fairly certain Moirae had not a clue how she intended to make her vow a reality, but he was just as positive that she would come up with a plan.

And he was looking forward to discovering just what it might be.

Chapter Four

Moirae drummed her fingers on the very armchair she had been sitting on seven nights ago, just before she had been summarily escorted to the stables and to her horse. It had taken a week for Moirae to devise a scheme that would, in the end, suit her true needs. It was only last night that she realized her initial desire for Dorian to leave had been not only narrow-minded and improvident, but damn near foolish.

Rising, she went over to study the long sleek blade that was so unlike any weapon she had ever before seen. She fingered the empty frame that held its mate, reminding herself that an opportunity had presented itself and a wise person would seize the chance, despite the risks.

Enion had been the only one willing to train her on any type of weapon, and unfortunately, his expertise had been limited to that of archery—not the sword. The near deadly trap she had stumbled into the other night was proof that such skill limitations could not only be lethal for her, but for those she sought to protect. She needed to learn how to fight. But seeking that type of training from a Highlander was not only highly inadvisable as a woman with a bad leg, it would breed personal questions that she had to avoid—not attract.

But Dorian was a swordsman who also held secrets he wanted kept private. He also had a most unusual sword.

Moirae reached out and clasped the ivory-engraved handle, but before she could pick up the weapon, the study door opened. She knew without turning around that she was in serious and imminent danger.

Unfortunately, this time Dorian was not nearby to save her.

* * *

Dorian returned to Kilnhurst disgruntled. There had been no new attacks beyond normal clan rivalries since the night he had saved—or *thought* he had saved—Moirae. And yet the spawns tormenting the humans had not left the area. Whoever it was they were after, Ionas obviously did not want Dorian to find them first.

To break the stalemate, Dorian decided to covertly search the area himself for anyone matching the flimsy description of an old woman with two puncturelike scars on her neck. Because of its water access, Badenoch brought together the borders of many clans, and an abundance of clansmen. Finding a particular woman without divulging his presence not only made things more difficult, but significantly delayed his departure. Not enough years had passed to allow him to ease back into local Highland life. A few more decades. Maybe then he could return.

Dorian sauntered down the hall toward the study, glad he had satiated his hunger for blood earlier that night. A rare smile crept into his expression as he inhaled Moirae's sweet unusual fragrance. He had found her horse hidden on the outskirts of Kilnhurst tied to a tree. The idea that she thought she could surprise him, pleased him. He had thought their kiss had scared her off, and he was markedly happy it had not. Nor had it changed her into a timid girl, suddenly shy after being introduced to the power of sexual desires.

Female laughter echoed down the hall and his smile vanished. Puzzled, Dorian hastened his pace only to come to an abrupt stop at the door. He had been mentally rehearsing a feisty encounter, with her impatiently waiting for his return so that she could once again demand his immediate departure. He even imagined the less likely, but still possible idea, of her eagerly waiting for him in hopes that he would introduce her to passions she had not yet fathomed. What he had not prepared himself for was the sight of Moirae on the floor *playing* with his two massive and supposedly deadly dogs.

He had carefully selected animals bred to be huge and ferocious, intentionally cultivating their naturally volatile traits so that only he could constrain them. And yet both giant hounds were acting as if they were friendly, sweet puppies, licking her and yipping as the three of them played keep-away with a large stick she must have pulled from the woodpile.

236 / *Michele Sinclair*

"Hello." She giggled, detangling herself from his hounds and rising.

He arched an eyebrow, hoping that it hid his shock, and unhooked his cape to throw it over one of the chairs before cradling the katana in its holder.

"Dyavolsko. Erebes. Come," he ordered and both dogs sauntered up to him in obedience. They sniffed and wagged their tails a couple of times before turning right around to lay down at Moirae's feet. He could not read her, but he could read them. Both dogs loved her. And until now, neither had ever given their affection to anyone but him.

Forcing his jaw to relax, Dorian glanced at the bread and drink on the table and said, "I assume Holland offered you food and drink." Moirae smiled mischievously and Dorian knew that she had charmed his manservant and no doubt his wife the same way she had the dogs.

With intentional flair, she sat down in the padded settee behind her. "He did. As you can see, I have already indulged myself while I waited for you."

"Your presence was not expected, Lady Deincourt."

"Really?" she asked with mock astonishment. "Based on my parting comment, I would have thought you to be surprised it took me so long to return."

The truth of her statement rankled him. "Kilnhurst is not a place for visitors."

Moirae sighed, unperturbed, and leaned back. "Then you should have made it much more difficult to breach your defenses." Then, she made the same gesture he used to get in the castle when he carried her back to Kilnhurst thinking her injured.

Dorian narrowed his eyes. She was teasing him and enjoying it. And in a strange way, so was he. "Are you here to beg me once again to end my activities as the Guardian?"

Moirae smiled and shook her head. "Not at all. You obviously have your own reasons to steal my role." Dorian could feel the corners of his mouth twitch at the blunt accusation. But her tone held no malice.

"Being the Guardian of Badenoch must serve some mysterious purpose for you," she continued. "For no one of intelligence spends their nights doing something that provides nothing in return. My guess is that you are looking for whatever the attackers are. You are just going about it in a less destructive, and much less noticeable manner."

Dorian reclamped his jaw. Again, Moirae Deincourt was proving to possess an understanding of the world—and him—that was astonishingly accurate and uncomfortably unexpected. Plus, he still could not fathom her own desire to continue playing the hero when the level of danger associated with the role had significantly risen in recent weeks. Was it adrenaline? Some humans were addicted to danger, but Dorian was certain simple excitement was not Moirae's motivation. She was right that he desired the role of Guardian for personal reasons, but so did she. And those reasons had driven her to once again come to Kilnhurst and confront him. That, and the sexual desire he could smell coursing through her being.

It had been a long time since Dorian had met someone who had interested him enough to make him want to seek out physical relations. For the past several centuries, he had restricted his mating to female spawns just to eliminate the possibility of emotional attachment often associated with humans. But too often, spawns gained a sadistic quality fairly soon after conversion that came from the sudden misperception of invincibility. After enough flat encounters, Dorian had concluded that bad sex was not necessarily better than no sex. And based on the kiss he and Moirae had shared, he suspected that the act would be far more enjoyable than in recent memory.

The idea of taking her right then was tempting. Very tempting. But her name . . . Moirae. To fool with one's destiny was dangerous. That, and she was human.

"Then just why are you here?" he finally asked.

Moirae uncrossed her legs and stood up to look him directly in the eye. "I want you to teach me how to fight using a sword. More specifically, one of those," she said, pointing at the long elegant blades.

Dorian stood frozen for a second. Of all the requests he had expected her to make, that one had not occurred to him. "No. Absolutely not," he blurted out without thought.

"Why? Is it because I am a woman?" she challenged, rejecting the finality in his voice.

No, because you are tempting me, he answered privately. "Because of other reasons," he countered aloud.

"Such as?" she asked, taking a step closer to him, clearly not intimidated by the difference in their sizes.

"Your limp for one."

A tremor touched her soft, pink lips, and he wanted so badly to kiss her he stopped thinking of anything else. With lightning speed, Moirae spun around, and in a single smooth movement, she seized one of the swords and sliced it through the air with incredible speed. Instinctively, Dorian twisted on his left foot and arched his back to avoid her attack. By the shocked look in her eye, he knew that while Moirae had exceptional agility, she lacked the control attained through training and practice. Her intent had not been to harm him, but to prove she had potential.

After the blade passed over him, Dorian pivoted to grasp the remaining katana. Yanking it free of its frame, he clashed the blade against hers, believing the force of the impact would easily disarm her. Her size and gender belied her strength, reminding him once again that Moirae Deincourt was significantly more than she appeared. Deciding to use skill, not strength, he rotated the tip of the katana for distraction, before flicking her sword upward, forcing Moirae to release her grip and give him control over both weapons.

"How did you do that?" she exclaimed with a twinge of envy.

His gray eyes fastened on her green ones, and Dorian could feel himself being drawn deeper and deeper into a place he desired to explore. Grimacing, he cut the connection and deftly twirled the instruments in his palms before placing them back safely where they belonged. "It was a simple maneuver anyone with even limited knowledge of a sword could perform."

"If anyone could do it, then teach me," she responded sharply, abandoning all pretense.

Her sincerity amused him. "Why?"

"My aim is lethal at a distance, but to be the Guardian, I need to be able to better protect myself in a fight. I cannot ask anyone else to train me without questions."

Dorian frowned. "That's not what I meant. Why do you need to be the Guardian? Why unnecessarily put yourself in danger?"

Moirae crossed her arms and overtly studied him. She considered telling him a partial truth—that she wanted to protect people—but suspected half answers would not persuade him to her cause. "Because I seek the man who killed my family, and when I meet him, I intend to kill him, and a well-placed arrow may or may not be the weapon I need to achieve that goal."

"Just whom do you seek?" Dorian asked, his voice drifting into a hushed whisper.

"Does it matter?"

He blinked. She was right. It really mattered not why she wanted to be taught, whom she wanted to avenge, or even why she sought revenge. He wasn't going to teach her. "My answer is still no," Dorian repeated, but the resolve his voice had previously evoked was missing.

"Then I will let it be known who the Guardian is, spread the word about Kilnhurst's new tenant, and I may even let it slip about these lovely unique weapons of yours. People may not believe me, but many will come to this place just to prove me wrong, making it much harder for you to achieve your goals."

Dorian almost laughed aloud. So that was her strategy. He knew Moirae had come with one. She had been acting too confident since his arrival. But if he agreed to her demand now, she would believe she had won. Then again, training Moirae had several distinct advantages. Distraction was one, and discovery of just whom she was after was another. But mostly, it gave him the perfect opportunity to seduce her . . . and he hoped it would not be easy.

"I've changed my mind. I will teach you, but only on my terms."

"Agreed."

"We meet only at night." Again, Moirae bobbed her head.

Dorian caught the relief in her expression and he wondered if the reason she had agreed to come when it was dark was a fear of being caught. If so, by whom? Deciding that he could answer those particular questions another time, he continued. "You follow my instructions without argument." Her eyes narrowed, and before she could refuse, he stated his final condition. "And last, you must promise to end any attempts to be the Guardian until I say you are ready."

Alarm flashed in her eyes, but immediately she suppressed it. He had expected some resistance on that point, but with pursed lips, Moirae gave a single nod.

Dorian crossed the distance between them, wondering if she would step away. When she didn't, he had to shift his stance as he felt himself begin to harden. Moirae had the power to inspire his lust, and he no longer was pretending that he didn't intend to discover if she could satisfy it as well.

"And one more thing—" he whispered, his voice deep and husky with desire. He reached up and lightly fingered a loose tendril of hair on her cheek. Moirae swallowed and he could feel her heartbeat quicken, but her eyes never left his. She was daring him to continue, so he did, tracing his index finger down her throat, over her shoulder, then along her partially exposed bust line. "Know this, Lady Destiny, I agreed to train you because I intend to seduce you."

Moirae gazed into his turbulent, storm-colored eyes. Every nerve ending in her body was responding to the unspoken message in the dark look, and only through sheer will was she able to force herself to glance down. With her right hand, she plucked his finger from her chest and then flicked it away as if she were removing an insect from her personage. "Seduction implies a willingness on my part, does it not?"

Dorian quirked a single eyebrow questioningly. "Indeed it does."

She was doing an excellent job of appearing to be unmoved by the unmistakable sexual tension between them, but he could smell her body's response. She absolutely wanted him just as much as he desired her.

Stepping back, Moirae flashed him a brilliant smile and reached down to gather her things lying on the settee. Donning her mantle, she said, "Excellent. Then you shall have a long wait, for I have no intention of being seduced. By you or any other man."

Then she was gone. And it was several seconds before Dorian realized he was still grinning. Intrigued no longer sufficed what he felt for her. Fascination filled his every pore, and he felt more alive than he had in centuries.

He was embarking on a simple game of pursuit. But for the first time in a very long while, he was eager to play.

Moirae shifted uncomfortably, checked her stance to ensure her feet were shoulder width apart, and then looked out over the battlements to the target below. Lifting the bow, she nocked the arrow, and then curled her fingers around the bowstring so that all her joints were aligned and began to pull.

"Thumb," came the soft reminder from behind.

Moirae fought the instinct to ram her elbow into his rib cage. "I know!" she grumbled and tucked her wayward thumb into her palm.

"You must use a consistent hand position."

Moirae squeezed her eyes shut. Relearning a skill she had thought she had mastered was not the type of lesson she had been seeking. But Dorian had been insistent. And after that first humiliating night of training, she had no choice but to agree to his terms and improve her archery abilities before training on the sword. Her only source of solace was that her skill really was improving, and thankfully rapidly. She now could shoot long distances, even when the target was moving—neither of which she could have hoped to do beforehand.

"My grip was exceptionally reliable until you forced me to change it," she muttered as she struggled to draw the arrow back.

He lightly placed his hand on her shoulder. "Do not allow your shoulder to rotate up or it will shorten the draw length—"

"—and, therefore, the distance and power of my shot," Moirae gritted out, mimicking him as she released her grip.

Dorian watched the arrow slice through the night sky, piercing a distant small rabbit that had been munching on some food it had found. He grimaced. Moirae had hit the target and she shouldn't have. He had given her his bow, which was strung significantly tighter than the average aerial weapon, enabling the force of his bolts to travel much faster and much farther. A bow's draw length depended on the strength of the archer, and few men could exert the force she had just demonstrated. Somehow the taut strings of his bow must have slackened.

Taking his weapon from her, he returned her own. "Practice," he ordered, examining the strings on his longbow. They seemed unyielding, but they were obviously not firm enough.

"For how long?" Moirae asked.

"Until you no longer have to think about shooting it correctly," Dorian answered, ignoring her exaggerated sigh meant for him. But he knew that if Moirae were really as riled as she pretended, she wouldn't be there night after night, following his counsel.

Dorian went to his bedchambers and took apart the bow and began to reconstruct the weapon. He was not a skilled artillator but he had learned the art of stringing a longbow years ago. He examined the glue-soaked hemp and decided it still seemed strong, then slowly began twisting the fiber one way and then back again until the weapon was restrung. He plucked it and the inflexible string barely moved under the semi-light pressure. Satisfied, Dorian sat back and decided to check on Moirae's status.

Upon exiting his chambers, he realized that restringing the bow had taken him much longer than he had realized. Sunrise was imminent, and yet he could still smell her presence. Believing her to still be practicing, he headed down the hallway toward the tower staircase and almost missed seeing her asleep on the settee in his study.

He retrieved a blanket from his room and gently placed it over her, studying her as she slept. Moirae had been coming to his home for nearly a week and he had not once touched her. Surprisingly, the effort to keep from doing so had been quite difficult. Moirae was a remarkable beauty for one so young, but it was not just her appearance that appealed to him. Her irreverent wit coupled with unexpected remarks about life kept him curious. Too many times had he needed to fight the urge to kiss her, and seeing her asleep on his couch the feeling was even stronger.

Pivoting, Dorian headed to his room to go to bed. He knew, however, that sleep would not find him quickly, and by the time he did awake, she would be gone . . . or at least he hoped she would be.

Moirae kicked off her slippers, leaned back against the settee's padded cushions, and contemplated her not-so-perfect plan. It was unusual to find so many comfortable furnishings in a single castle. The cost and upkeep of such items made it prohibitive. And yet Dorian—who lived alone, with the exception of his two servants, a husband and wife who rarely came into view— had nearly three times the furniture as the typical Highland laird of a sizeable clan. This she had confirmed earlier that evening when she had sneaked off to explore the castle when Dorian had vanished once again to play her role as the Guardian. She had hoped to discover a hint about the man, who he was and from where he came, but unfortunately, she found only more questions.

For the past two weeks, she had come to Kilnhurst soon after sunset to receive instruction. After a few hours, Dorian would leave the grounds to go out on patrol while she continued training until exhaustion took over. Then, she would retire to the study, intending to stay conscious until his return, only to fall asleep before he did so. She would awaken to find a blanket draped over her or a pillow under her head, proving he had been there. But tonight, she had stopped practicing soon after his departure.

Though she had initially resisted training on a weapon she thought she could already effectively use, Moirae knew her skills as an archer had dramatically improved in the past fortnight. She could always hit a target reliably at a distance, but now she could aim and draw faster and, most importantly, do so even if the target was small, in the shadows, or moving. But while the improvement would no doubt be an advantage to achieving her goals, mastering archery was not the reason she was there *or* the reason she had agreed to temporarily stop playing the role of the Guardian.

Learning the sword was her goal.

Moirae drew a deep breath and released it in a long sigh as she flipped onto her side. Once again, she pondered the question that had been plaguing her for nearly a week. Both she and Dorian had been up front in what they hoped to achieve during these training sessions. She wanted to become skilled in close combat; he sought to seduce her. And yet, not once had Dorian tried to kiss her. He even avoided touching her, doing so only when absolutely necessarily, and even then, briefly. Moirae hated to admit it, but she was disappointed.

Though positive she could fend off an advance, she had been looking forward to getting the chance to do so. The kiss they had shared was far from the first kiss she had ever had . . . but in an odd way, it was. Never had an embrace affected her or plagued her thoughts like the single kiss she and Dorian had shared. In mere moments, desire had spiraled out of control, sending tendrils of fire into every nerve of her body.

During their lessons, she caught herself wanting to lean back into him until his lips were touching the skin of her throat. She imagined her mouth kissing his rough-hewn cheek and how it would feel to nestle her head on his shoulder. What she really wanted, she thought wryly, was to feel Dorian's arms around her and rediscover the smoldering passion that had lain dormant within her.

And if a first kiss could cause such stirrings and create lasting memories, Moirae suspected Dorian could make her feel much more. The idea was both very appealing and carried low risk. A kiss, even a very passionate one, was something from which she could easily walk away. Physical pleasure only. For no matter what transpired between them, she was not going to become emotionally entangled.

Dorian would never understand her need to be the Guardian. No man would.

She accepted long ago that her life was to be one lived in solitude. But that kiss . . . until then she had not realized her life also was one without passion.

Dorian crossed the threshold of the study and eyed the sleeping figure on the settee just as he did every night. Her right palm faced upward, allowing her relaxed fingers to curl and expose the red, inflamed calluses that were forming. The woman was an enigma. Humans just did not endure pain voluntarily. So why was she?

If he were to ask her while conscious, Dorian knew her answer would be—*to become the Guardian.* But just why Moirae felt it necessary to protect the local lands remained a mystery—one that had stalled his plans for seduction.

When he had made her that promise, he had planned to conduct the lessons with indifference, with absolutely no hint of interest in her physically. Knowing the idea he had planted and the way she had responded in his arms, Dorian had expected her to become anxious and possibly even try to tempt him. What he had not expected was to enjoy her stubbornness, feisty personality, and most of all, her sheer company. Moirae saw the world as no human did. As a result, he was not tiring of her as quickly as he would have expected. And several millennia of experience had proven that after the seduction, whatever thrill he was experiencing now would quickly turn to boredom. And he wasn't ready to end things with Moirae.

He had met, been with, and enjoyed many women over the years, of all types and personalities. As a result, he could go nowhere, meet no one, that he could not understand and, therefore, predict rather quickly . . . until Moirae. She, he could not read. Her unusual perspective was like a drug beckoning him. A trait he suspected repelled the males of her kind. Humans feared anyone unique. But for someone who had lived for centuries, meeting someone atypical had great appeal.

Moirae alleviated his boredom. She gave him something to look forward to and helped speed the monotony of time, but her charm had become something more than sheer stimulation. None of those reasons explained his desire to see her smile and be the reason behind it, to hear her laugh, and most of all, to touch her skin. Something, he had forced himself to avoid.

Her pale skin was the tone of Greek Parian marble, giving her delicate features a refined beauty. Slender and tall, she appeared to the casual observer a gentle creature, but one only had to glimpse into her green eyes to see the fires of passion flash within. And though she tried to hide her feelings, he knew she desired him. Her longing mixed with his own, Dorian knew that when he did succumb to his need to touch her, it would not be the slow seduction he had promised, but an explosion that would either consume them or leave them panting for more. And based on what he had learned earlier that night, they would soon know which.

Once Moirae heard the attacks had resumed, she would be eager to place herself in danger once again. For her to survive, she would have to know how to fight not just from afar, but up close.

Tomorrow evening her lessons would begin in earnest. No longer would he be instructing dispassionately at a distance. Combat was physical and close. Whether Moirae was ready or not, she was going to learn not just how to wield a blade, but what it was like to be truly and uncontrollably seduced.

Chapter Five

Moirae slipped off her mount and wrapped the reins loosely around one of the stable posts. She never saw Holland in the vicinity of the stables, yet whenever she was ready to leave, her horse had been brushed and fed. The couple that supported Dorian was quiet, unobtrusive, and eerily intuitive, but where they came from and why they were there was a mystery. And like many other puzzles connected to Kilnhurst, Moirae suspected this one would remain unsolved when she and Dorian parted ways.

Squaring her shoulders, she took a deep breath and headed toward the tower entrance. Moirae wished she could march indomitably down the hall and into the study to make her demands. The reminder that she couldn't made her pause for a brief moment and reconsider her plan. The broken bones in her right leg had mended in such a way that quick movements were impossible. As a result, the most difficult part of learning to wield a sword would not be figuring out how and when to defend or attack, but compensating for the lack of quick footwork. But just as she found a way to walk, ride, and even climb steps, Moirae vowed she would grasp the basics on how to wield a blade.

Shoving open the doors, Moirae stepped through the study entrance with more grandeur than she had intended, but it did get Dorian's attention. She watched his piercing gray eyes sweep over her, taking her in from head to toe in one swift, heated glance, and she suddenly doubted her choice of attire.

Instead of the normal floor-length gown she had been wearing, she had dressed in a boy's chemise and tunic that only reached her knees, exposing her hosed legs. She had chosen the outfit with only ease of mobility in mind, and yet the desire of Dorian's gaze was unmistakable. It scorched through her, igniting sensations and latent passions she thought had died years ago. Then, just as suddenly, Dorian's smoldering eyes went blank as he released his stare, as if he, too, had felt the searing heat.

He arched a single dark brow and leaned back in the chair, crossing his arms. "I assume by your choice of clothes that you aim to end your lessons with the bow and begin them with the sword."

Moirae cocked her head slightly in acknowledgment. She had intentionally worn gowns since her training had started. A kirtle did not interfere with aiming and releasing an arrow and she knew they were flattering on her. Despite her wish that she were completely indifferent to his promise to seduce her, deep down Moirae wanted Dorian to at least try. But tonight was the first time he had shown any interest in her. And the fact that she was dressed as a boy—well, rankled.

At first, she had believed his indifference to be a ruse in order to compel her to make the overtures he had so candidly promised. Not a common ploy, but one she recognized. As a result, she had done the opposite, purposefully not doing or saying a single thing to make him think she thought of him beyond that of a mentor. But she had. More than that, she had been keen to discover just what other methods he would employ to get her to succumb to his charm. But Dorian failed to try even one. She had concluded that either he had lied in an attempt to rattle her nerves or that after being around her, simply had changed his mind. For if he truly had meant to seduce her, by now he should have tried *something*.

While Moirae had little experience taking advantage of someone flirting with her, she easily recognized it when it happened . . . and Dorian had definitely *not* been flirting the past few weeks. He acted more like an older brother . . . or cousin . . . or a friend of a cousin that had been warned not to say or do anything untoward. She was considering ways to test his resolve and see if he was as truly disinterested as he seemed when word arrived that the attacks had resumed last night. That changed everything. Old priorities ranked once again of the highest importance.

"I would like you to start training me on the sword. Tonight," Moirae said pointedly, half hoping he would argue, for she was ready to challenge any objection.

"Turn around," Dorian instructed.

Moirae furrowed her brow, but after a few seconds, she did as directed. Through the open study door, she could see across the hall. Not more than five minutes ago, the double doors had been closed as they had always been. Now open, she could see partially inside. More than likely, it had been originally designed to be a receiving room, but based on the variety of weapons in view, the somewhat narrow space had been converted to an interior training area.

Dorian had already decided to begin teaching her the sword.

"Why the grimace?" Dorian asked, still sitting. "Does this not comply with your request?"

Moirae bit her bottom lip in an attempt to hide her emotions. She hadn't planned to *request* anything. She had been ready—maybe even eager—to demand he begin training her on the sword. But what really riled her was his aggravating ability to anticipate her intentions, almost as if he were a mind reader.

Dorian rose to his feet and walked over to the two unusual swords. He lifted the first one out of its frame and unsheathed it from its scabbard, studying its beauty. Moirae waited for him to remove the second sword, but he left it alone and breezed by her into the hall, pausing only after he reached the training room door. "If you are ready, let's begin. There is much you have to learn."

Moirae twisted her lips and nodded, a secret smile forming inside her. Dorian believed himself to be in control and that he could dictate the conditions of her lessons as he had the bow. However, his arrogance revealed something very interesting. Moirae wasn't the only one who wanted her to have the lessons; he did as well.

Why, Moirae could not fathom, but it did not matter. That knowledge gave her leverage—albeit very small—but enough for her to get back what she desired most in the world. The role of the Guardian.

Moirae watched as Dorian spun the long thin katana in his palm. Her stomach fluttered, and she drew an unsteady breath, inhaling his scent of self-satisfaction. His rich black hair hung loose, barely touching his shoulder. She clenched her hands together tightly, resisting the impulse to reach out and feel the silky tresses run through her fingers.

His attire was like that of every other evening, minus the

cloak. He wore a simple leine, open at the throat, revealing the wide chiseled planes of his chest. His dark belted plaid belonged to no Scottish clan she knew of, but yet the wool tartan still looked appropriate on his figure, emphasizing the force of his thighs and the slimness of his hips. He may not have been born a Highlander, but he looked like one. Unfortunately, a very good-looking one.

"Walk toward me," Dorian ordered.

Moirae's green eyes narrowed in reflexive defiance, but she didn't argue. She took a regular step with her left foot and then a quick one with her right, minimizing the weight and the time the leg had to support her. It wasn't exactly a shuffle, but being in men's clothing, her fettered walk could not be disguised. Over the years, she had learned to keep her body erect, skillfully using her gown to misdirect attention and hide her awkward movements.

"Your leg—" Dorian began.

"It was crushed when I was seventeen by a falling beam."

Dorian sent her an exasperated look and finished his original question. "Your leg, does it hurt when you move?"

"No," Moirae answered truthfully.

"Then why don't you put weight on it and walk normally?" Dorian knelt down and began to knead the muscles in her right leg.

Moirae swallowed and tried to fight the tears of humiliation that were forming. His touch was not erotic, but indifferent, as he fingered the fragmented bones. By the time she had been found and freed from the broken beam that had fallen on her, her leg had already begun to mend, but not correctly. How could she explain that the thigh bones one takes for granted now felt wrong, and that each time she took a step, her body screamed not in pain, but with warning that her leg would not hold.

Dorian stood and his smoky gray eyes drove into her. "The bones are misaligned, but they are connected and should provide ample support. So, our first lesson will be how to walk."

Moirae's jaw slackened in dismay. "You do not understand—"

"Some think strength and the ability to block an attack is the secret to sword fighting, but victory lies with proper physical balance—which starts with your feet. One *must* be fluid and grace-ful—"

"I will never be either."

"Then you shall not learn how to fight, by me or by anyone."

"Then I shall teach myself," Moirae declared, thrusting her chin into the air.

Dorian, sensing Moirae was not issuing a threat but a promise, sighed with frustration. The woman was going to put herself in danger, and unless she could defend herself, she would soon be dead. And why he cared, he could not comprehend. "It is by choice, not fate, that you limp. Your leg has the strength; it is your will that is weak."

Moirae fumed. After weeks of training, withstanding fatigue, soreness, and the agony of repeated abuse to her hands, he had the audacity to claim her to be weak? "I believe you know me to be otherwise," she hissed through gritted teeth.

"Aye, at least until a few minutes ago, when I learned that you would rather hobble than walk. For you could walk, if you chose to."

Moirae inhaled, her fury still swirled within, but the man actually believed what he said. Could he be correct? "Prove it," she said, knowing he could not.

Dorian waved his arm. "Walk across the room."

Moirae did as commanded, but before she could take a step with her right foot, Dorian kneeled in front her and twisted her ankle so that the foot jutted out at a disturbing angle, and not forward. He put it down and motioned for her to put her weight on it and take another step. She looked down and the sight of one foot properly facing the direction she was headed and the other like it had been broken off and poorly reattached was revolting. Instinctively, she turned her right foot back forward. Her hip, now out of alignment, forced Moirae to hop and as quickly as possible shift her weight back to her left foot.

Dorian twisted her ankle again to the unsightly angle. "This time do it my way."

"I cannot walk in two directions at the same time!" she almost yelled, showing him her meaning by repeatedly bending her right foot from heel to toe. Each step she took would alter her body's direction.

Dorian quirked a brow, seeing her point. "Then don't. Instead of walking from your heel, roll your balance from one side of your foot to the other so that it is in the direction you want to go."

Moirae tightened her grip on her crossed arms as memories crashed into her so vibrant it was like they happened just moments ago. "Did you think I never tried this?" she questioned, remembering people's laughter. A pretty woman who hobbled was pitied, but no woman was pretty enough to escape scorn when she fell down, which is what happened each time Moirae had attempted to walk the way Dorian was instructing. To prove her point, she took a step on the side of her foot and it promptly slid out from underneath her. Moirae threw out her hands to soften the fall, but there was no need. Dorian had caught her and immediately stood her upright once again.

"Stop being afraid," he grumbled and reached down to adjust her ankle once more.

Moirae was tempted to strangle him. "How you construe fear from what—" She stopped in midsentence as Dorian began marching in an exaggerated slow fashion around the room. "You won't make me feel better by appearing more ridiculous than I."

"When a person walks, they shift their weight completely to the foot that is on the ground," he said, ignoring her comments and surly attitude, demonstrating in slow motion what he meant.

Moirae had to bite her bottom lip to keep from laughing. It was hard to reconcile this tall, lumbering version of him with the one who was always poised and in control. Then Dorian suddenly changed his gait so that it imitated hers. He rotated his foot out and took a step forward, but he didn't commit to the effort and kept the majority of his weight on his left foot. It was exactly what just happened when she had tried the same thing. He was trying to move forward with his left foot and since the right was not positioned for him to shift his weight, Dorian stumbled, something Moirae doubted she would ever see again. Then he repeated the maneuver, this time fully committing to his right leg, and while it did look awkward and far from elegant, he kept his balance.

He stopped and stared at her, defying her to challenge his point. Squaring her jaw, Moirae stepped forward with her right leg as if she fully entrusted it to support her . . . and it did. Without thought, she tried it again and again. Each time she was able to maintain her balance and move substantially quicker, looking no doubt extremely odd, but far less clumsy. It would take practice, but given enough time and a gown to hide the odd way her leg was turned, people might actually think her graceful. A term she thought would never be applied to her.

Standing tall and wearing his arrogant smirk once again, Dorian said, "For your second lesson, you shall learn how to dance."

Moirae came to an abrupt halt and stared at him, unable to prevent her jaw from slackening until her mouth was completely wide open in shock.

Dorian watched from the battlements as Moirae rode into the bailey at a full gallop, slowing just before she reached the stables. In one effortless move, she slipped off her mount and then escorted the animal inside. Less than a minute later she reappeared, and directly underneath the light of a scone, she removed her hooded mantle, hooking it over her arm. Immediately he felt his throat tighten.

Instead of the hose and short kirtle that revealed her shapely legs and played havoc with his desires, she had donned a dark blue corset. The fitted fur-lined winter gown laced in front and hid much of the floor-length kirtle beneath, but it did not hide the elegant train, or the long fitted sleeves that reached her knuckles. But what held him spellbound was her hair. For the first time, her tawny locks were not captured in a snood or hidden within braids, but long and flowing. His blood roared in his ears as it raced like liquid fire through his body. God, why had he ever agreed to this?

Just before Dorian moved to go down the stairway and meet her in the study, Moirae turned and looked up so that her gaze was fixed upon him. He was standing in the shadows and out of sight, but nevertheless, she knew he was there. Once again, he was reminded that there was much more to Moirae Deincourt than appeared.

The woman had uncommon reflexes, made only faster since she had learned to properly compensate for her bad leg. Her lithe, feminine frame belied her true strength, for the broadsword he gave her to practice with should have been almost too heavy for her to lift, let alone wield like she did. But it was not just Moirae's physical abilities that mystified him, but her mind.

She had picked up the basics of swordplay within the first week, and often times he found himself having to resort to more and more complex attack sequences that should have had her flustered and frustrated. Instead, she would summarily decipher them and then attempt to execute them herself. Soon, there would be nothing left he could teach her beyond that of practice so that combat became a natural response and not a conscious one. He had completed one of the two things he had sought to do. Moirae would now most likely live if attacked, something that would undoubtedly happen if she returned to her role as the Guardian.

Releasing him from her stare, Moirae turned and glided across the bailey with regal certainty, her gown masking the unusual gait. Moirae's beauty was now complete. She exuded all the qualities men coveted. She was delicate but strong, enjoyed a vivacious spirit that was tempered with self-control, and possessed a mixture of youthful features and shrewd green eyes that sparkled with a lifetime's experience. Moirae Deincourt was a mystery beckoning him, and he no longer had the will to prolong his agony.

Tonight he would end the anticipation. He would claim her and then prepare to leave Scotland. Ionas be damned. He had been here nearly two months, and for the past handful of weeks he had been focused on Moirae, not his nephew's plots against some old woman. And in truth, it no longer mattered. Tomorrow, he would seek distance between him and Kilnhurst and he would not return until after Moirae's death and her bones had become dust in the ground.

Dorian pivoted and hurried toward his study, wondering how he was going to refuse when Moirae begged him not to leave her.

Chapter Six

Dorian stepped behind his desk just in time before Moirae sashayed into the study. "You're late," he said, with feigned boredom.

Moirae tilted her head and a secretive smile softened her lips. "I know and I apologize. My cousin believes in enjoying his role as laird with numerous celebrations. I think he believes it engenders those of his clan to like him when, in truth, they have no more affinity for him than I."

"Then why do you stay with him?"

Moirae shrugged her shoulders. "Like everyone else, I take advantage of his hospitality. The only price I must pay is to make an appearance at his parties. I avoided the past two festivities, but he refuses to excuse me from another. So I shall be late every Saturday night forthwith," she finished with a sigh, tossing her cloak over one of the chairs.

Dorian studied Moirae. Her expression and demeanor had changed. Focused determination had been replaced with gaiety and a touch of whimsy. "Have you been drinking?" he asked as the possible reason just occurred to him.

She nodded and bestowed upon him a radiant smile. "I have. And dancing. For the first time I actually joined that pompous group. You should have seen the shocked, jealous looks of the gossips. I doubt I will be asked to sit with them again."

"I see. I'm surprised you made it here at all," Dorian muttered under his breath, as unfamiliar and possessive emotions swirled within his veins.

"Me, too! I thought I would never be released to leave. I was dancing so much that my snood fell off. But don't worry, I brought it so my hair won't interfere with practice," she said, dangling the jeweled net that was in her palm.

Dorian stared at the waves of her chestnut locks daring his fingertips to touch its silky strands. *Later,* he promised himself. "I'm less worried about your hair than your dress."

Moirae's eyes opened wide and then sparkled with laughter. A fission of anger ripped through Dorian. Until now, he had never seen her this lighthearted. He had always known she would be irresistible with a buoyant spirit, but *he* had planned to be the reason behind the sheer happiness beaming from her face.

"I'll just take this off." She giggled and started unbuttoning the dark blue corset to reveal the off-the-shoulder parti-colored kirtle beneath.

The dress was made of two patterns of brocade. One half was of sky blue patterned with small fleur-de-lis and the other was of rich navy velvet. The sleeves were long and tight fitting, each matching their half of the dress. The expensive, modern ensemble was breathtaking on her and further proof that she was not a mere cousin to a laird from a small, unimportant clan.

To fight in a dress was foolish, but Dorian needed the activity to calm the desire raging through him. Otherwise it would not be a seduction but an uninspired taking of the flesh he would be performing. "Maybe it is well you wore a gown," he stated coolly. "You might not always be suitably dressed when you meet your foe."

Moirae's eyes sprang open with surprise, but she did not argue and followed him across the hall to the training room. She unsheathed the broadsword from its scabbard and turned toward him, her soft and jovial features now hard and resolute.

Not waiting until he was ready, she bounded forwarded aiming down to make him think she was going to strike in one area while attacking another. Dorian quickly righted his katana and deflected the tip before it could glance his shoulder. "Eager, are you?"

Moirae shook her head, oblivious to her long mane flying about her. "I am merely at a disadvantage in this garment and intend to use all means available to distract you."

Dorian circled the tip of her defending blade, but no longer did it disorient her or make her loosen her grip. "Remember, an enemy will use more than just his weaponry skills to gain an edge."

"I'm ready," she replied and Dorian decided it was time to remind her just who was the master.

He lunged, striking his katana across the weak inside line of her blade and drove his sword straight downward in an attempt to snap her wrist and disarm her. But her grip held, once again proving that her true strength remained unknown to him. Then, with implausible speed, she took her blade and landed it along his own. The threatening pressure was so unexpected and the force of the impact was so significant, it almost worked.

Determined not to underestimate her inhuman strength again, he extended his arm to its full length, using his height and size to prevent her from returning the thrust. Then he moved the tip of his blade around her bell guard in a tight circle, trapping her blade before swinging it away.

"Damn," Moirae cursed in English.

Before she could retake her weapon, he grabbed her chin between his thumb and forefinger, forcing her to look at him. The joyful fire that had been shining in her eyes was now an inferno. "The Highlands are not your home and whoever your 'cousin' is, he is not your family."

"I am no more a Highlander than you are," Moirae spat back, wrenching free to retake her sword. This time she stood still, eyeing him, letting him take the initiative.

That evening she had come to Kilnhurst happier than she had been since childhood. She had renewed hope and confidence in herself as a woman. The men at the party had flocked to her, and the women, who had once pitied her, could only look on with envy. There had not been a man present she couldn't have conquered, but Moirae had not wanted any of them. Ignorant and self-serving, they thought about nothing except their next meal and their perpetually aroused loins. She wanted someone who made her heart race and her body ache with need.

Tonight, there was to be no training, no fighting, no swords. Just Dorian and his promise. Only he had failed to understand what she was offering.

Only a fool could have mistaken what she wanted with her dress and her hair. She had pasted on her most enticing smile, which she knew from experience could warm even the coldest of hearts, and yet Dorian had been unaffected. He was not a man. He was something cold, hard, and without passion or physical desires.

Unwilling to wait any longer for him to make a move, Moirae lunged. "You may look like the giants that live in these mountains, even talk like them, but you are certainly not one of them," she huffed. "The only Gaelic thing about you is your name— *Doireann*, which you mispronounce, making me doubt it is even your real name."

Dorian stepped back from shock. The accidental accuracy of Moirae's comment struck Dorian off guard. He studied the dissipating rise and fall of her chest, trying to decide what he should or should not reveal about himself. Since he first came to these mountains, no one had ever guessed he was not a Highlander. His physique, fighting skills, and ability to speak flawless Gaelic were too much evidence otherwise. But he had not fooled Moirae any more than she had him.

Moving quickly to the right, he swung his blade in an arc until it connected with hers underneath, but again she held on. "You are correct. My birth name is actually Dorus," he answered, twisting around to try the same move but in the other direction. "I later changed it to Dorian, thinking it more fitting to whom I am now."

Moirae reacted quickly to his change in strategy and aimed her broadsword upward, deflecting the force of his katana's impact. "If one lived long enough, I could see the desire to change their name," she mused through gritted teeth, "but you are not yet of an age to be tired of anything. Losing interest in a place or a type of food or even another person is commonplace enough, but it takes years to become bored of one's name."

Dorian blinked. He knew Moirae was not as young as she looked, but he'd seen enough women to know she could be no more than a handful of years past the age of twenty. And yet her understanding of people was far greater than that of a spawn who had lived an extended life.

Moirae spun around, and the frustration that once had filled her was being slowly replaced with another emotion—the enjoyment of an honest challenge. "Where are you really from?"

"Greece," Dorian answered truthfully, relieved to see by her expression that she had never heard of his home. "It is a mountainous land that at its end breaks into islands, which spread out into three seas." Spinning on his left foot, he swung his tip toward her weak side. She had not been prepared for the unorthodox move, but her reflexes enabled her to avert his attack. "And where are you from, Lady Destiny?"

"I'm unsure," Moirae answered, matching his movements so that they were slowly going around in a circle, waiting for the other to make their move. "My mother and grandmother moved around a lot when I was young."

"And your father?"

"Died when I was an infant. Supposedly the sea took him," Moirae said acerbically, moving just in time to avoid his downward thrust.

"You sound doubtful."

Moirae regretted letting him hear her sarcasm. How could she explain that she did not know who she was. That one night, her life, both past and future, changed in an instant as her grandmother whispered her last words.

Moirae changed the topic to one she hoped would be just as unsettling. "Have you ever been in love?"

Dorian stood upright in surprise. Taking advantage of the mistake, Moirae lunged with more deftness and speed than he thought possible given the heavy garment she was wearing. He darted to the left, barely missing the point of her sword, which was not nearly as sharp as the katana, but dangerous nonetheless. It would take several dedicated years before Moirae would have the skill set to match his own, even at her accelerated learning rate, but the woman was clever, and her size falsely represented her strength. He would have to pay more attention.

He gave a quick bob with his chin, acknowledging the cunning maneuver, and then resumed a defensive position. "Many times, my lady. Have you?"

Moirae smiled enigmatically. "Once."

"You are too young to have ever been truly in love," Dorian replied, rejecting the idea that her heart already belonged to someone.

"I will admit that my youth played heavily into my feelings," Moirae admitted.

"Then what happened? Why are you not married?"

Moirae glided left, and coming off a high arc, she attempted to push his blade aside. "We saw life differently."

Ahhhh, Dorian thought to himself, *the fool had not understood her.* But then, who besides someone like him, could? "This man, it sounds as if he didn't love you in return."

Moirae's jaw snapped shut. The truth stung. She pretended to disengage his halfhearted thrust and swung around to attack the opening he had left by stepping in close in an effort to remove the advantage his height gave him. Instead, he surprised her by looping his arm around her waist to bring her even closer.

"You give your heart too easily, I think," he murmured with barely checked passion.

Moirae's eyes sprang upward to meet the superheated gleam of his gaze, and a slow, powerful wave of lust washed over her. Feeling powerless, she tried to pull free. "That is where you are wrong."

Dorian held tight. "I think you have given it to me."

Her green eyes clawed him like talons. "My heart is my own."

His left hand plunged into her hair, keeping her head near his. "I don't believe you," he whispered.

Moirae swallowed hard, lifted her chin, and boldly held on to his gaze. "I assure you that my heart is safe. I may desire you physically, but that is all."

Dorian clasped both swords in his right hand, and bringing them out from between them, he released the handles. The resulting clatter filled the room, but he ignored it. "And I desire you, Moirae. More than I have desired a woman in a long, long time. But understand this, if I have you, make no claims upon me and weep no tears, for we will share nothing more. Promise me."

He heard her make a small hungry sound deep in her throat, and she pressed her body against his. "Promise me," he repeated with barely controlled restraint.

"I promise," she whispered, and upon hearing the words, Dorian swooped down and hungrily captured her mouth, his tongue delving deep inside, fervently tangling with hers.

He drew his thumb across her bottom lip, and as her mouth parted under the gentle pressure, he retraced the path of his thumb with his tongue. His hands moved of their own accord, lightly over her shoulders, following the smooth curve of her back, stroking, caressing. The innocent playful tip of her tongue brought him back, and Dorian realized the passion growing between them was truly new to her. Tonight, he would guide her into a world few ever experienced, for the art of making love required exquisite restraint and consummate finesse. And in return she would take him to a hallowed realm where there were no words, only ecstasy and pure pleasure. A realm he had almost forgotten existed.

Pulling her tightly to him, he pressed his hips firmly against hers. She let go a soft moan as he let his need for her be known. "Kiss me," he demanded hoarsely.

Immediately Moirae obliged, teasing his mouth with her lips, awakening every dormant nerve in his body. He groaned, lost in the innocent beauty of her touch, forgetting his promise to make tonight about her. His Lady Destiny had arrived. Their meeting, their inevitable mating, had been fated. Nothing could touch them, neither her past nor his future, only the awareness of the present that enclosed them.

Moirae closed her eyes as his lips kissed her lightly, feathering over the arch of her neck to the soft spot behind her ear. She craved to savor the moment, to draw it out. How long had it been since someone had kissed her like this? Too long. Perhaps never. For she would remember this burning deep inside, this overwhelming desire to lay with a man and have him know her intimately. It was tempting to throw him on the floor, strip off her gown, and have her way with him there and then. But her strength had deserted her.

As if he could read her mind, Dorian swung her up into his heavily muscled arms. She couldn't stop herself from stroking his chest through the thin material of his shirt as he carried her down the hall and into his bedchambers.

Placing her back on her feet, he turned and closed the door. A small fire had been lit, causing shadows to sprinkle the walls of the cavernous room. It was the first time she had been in his private chambers, and the dark setting reflected his preference for fine furniture and decorations that obviously came from another land. Tapestries had been hung high, depicting both familiar and foreign landscapes and people.

Moirae turned to ask about one when she was suddenly lifted

off her feet. Seconds later, she was crushed into soft bedding as Dorian settled on top of her. Her mind, ready to argue, calmed as his mouth reclaimed her lips, numbing her thoughts to all but him once again.

Then his kisses moved from her lips and down her neck as the fingers of his free hand unfastened the tie at the back of her gown. He slowly slid the garment down her shoulders, letting his lips follow, leaving a trail of fiery hot kisses along her collarbone at the edge of her chemise, which he soon discarded.

Dorian sat up to look at her as the firelight cast a warm glow over her skin. He was awestruck by her beauty. He had lived nearly two millennia and yet, in all those years, never had any woman so captivated him mentally or physically. He could pretend that her pull was due to prolonged abstinence, but it would be a lie. He was in desire's full grip, and the need to possess Moirae, have her cry out his name, was unlike any he had ever known.

Dorian stood and quickly threw off the remainder of his clothing, enjoying how her emerald eyes caressed his body, her desire becoming evident when she glanced at his straining manhood. He lowered himself slowly on top of her, until he covered her body with his own. His eyes never left hers as he leaned toward her, cradled her face in his strong hands, and gently brushed his lips against her mouth.

Moirae felt her body once again begin to burn with need. She wanted to be touched, kissed, everywhere, when Dorian's mouth made its way from her lips down her throat to the valley between her breasts. She gasped as he took one nipple into his mouth and licked his tongue over the sensitive flesh, teasing it until she cried out with want of him.

When she arched upward, Dorian shuddered in response. He had planned to move slowly, but her impassioned cry caused all thoughts of restraint to vanish and he began to suckle. Using his thumb, he coaxed her other nipple into responding. When it was hard and straining, he shifted and took it into his mouth, relishing how Moirae writhed beneath him. Her response was uninhibited, full of honest passion that stemmed from being alive. Sexual tension seized his insides. His hand lowered, parting her thighs, until he could lace his fingers through the soft thatch of hair between her legs.

The unexpected stimulus was almost too much, and Moirae twisted and moaned while her hands clung to his shoulders. She arched her hips upward, begging for more. "Dorian, please," she whispered.

He complied with her demand, closing his fingers around her heated flesh, letting a single finger trail along the rim of her wet core before sliding into the liquid warmth. Blood pounded in her veins and she began to shake as his fingers lightly brushed her knowingly, probing her with exquisite care. He seemed to know exactly where to touch her, lightly, slowly, deeply, finding all her secret, hidden places and making them come alive with need.

He dove deeper, and Moirae felt herself reaching another peak. "Oh, God," she wept, lifting herself against his hand, convulsing as her body took over. Dorian smiled victoriously. The satisfaction he was drawing from her own pleasure was addictive. She was so incredibly hot and wet, and it was because of him. She belonged only to him.

Unable to wait any longer, he settled himself between her thighs, lifted her hips, and drove forward, filling her completely with one long, powerful stroke. Instinctively, she met his thrust. He began to move, slowly at first, and then with growing need and force, they began to move in a deliberate rhythm.

When he felt her body begin to peak and go into hard, tight convulsions, his arms clenched around her and he came into her with deep fierce thrusts that carried her right over the edge. Then, simultaneously, his own passion raged beyond his control. An obliterating need unlike anything he had ever experience enveloped him. Every muscle in his body tightened almost to the point of pain. The sounds he emitted were unintelligible, but every sense, every thought was tangled in the web of pleasure she had spun over him. And then it began. The release welled up from the base of his spine, gathering under Moirae's innocent cries until, with a great shudder, he came, so violently he was left acutely shocked . . . gasping like a man coming up from near drowning.

Delirious from pleasure, Moirae wrapped her arms around Dorian as he buried his face in her hair and let go a savage cry as his body shuddered uncontrollably.

They remained that way for some time, neither able to move

or speak. Their souls had connected, and for a brief moment in time, they had become one. Neither was ready to end the illusion.

After a while, Dorian lifted his head and looked down at her with dark, passion-filled eyes. "Thank you," he whispered in her ear, just before planting a kiss on her nape.

Moirae closed her eyes and reminded herself of her promise, not to just him, but herself. She had a destiny to fulfill and it was time she renewed her efforts along that predetermined path. She had to let him go, which would now be even harder. She had lied when she had claimed her heart was her own. As he had correctly guessed, she had given it away weeks ago. Dorian was its keeper now, and wherever he went, he would unknowingly take her love with him.

Forcing her mouth to curve into a smile, she said, "You are unlike anyone I shall ever meet again." Then she quickly planted a kiss on his lips before rolling out from underneath him.

Dorian turned over to his side and watched her dress. She was doing exactly as promised, making no claims and weeping no tears. And it bothered him greatly.

The ease of her movements would almost lead him to believe that what they had just shared had been merely pleasant and not the rare thing it was. Only her haunting expression before she had risen confirmed she felt the same as he did. Her smile had not reached her eyes. Instead, a profound sadness had reflected in the dark green pools, conveying how she was giving up something she desperately wanted but knew she could not have.

And she was right—she couldn't, Dorian reminded himself.

Humans and his kind could not sustain a relationship for any length of time. To be together, he would have to change her, and the idea of Moirae becoming a spawn, losing what made her compelling and desirable, was not an option. Still, the idea of never touching her again was also unfathomable. Maybe he didn't have to leave so soon.

Flinging his legs over the side of the bed, Dorian puckered his brow. "I think you should continue your lessons, for at least a little while longer."

Moirae momentarily paused before slipping her second shoe

on her foot. "I'm not ready to give you up, either," she replied, answering his unspoken question.

Hearing her honest response, he reached out and grasped her hand. With a convincing tug, he lay back down, pulling her on top of his naked form. "Tonight?"

Moirae almost giggled upon hearing the hopeful excitement in his voice. She knew by agreeing she was just postponing the inevitable and increasing whatever pain her heart would experience when they finally did part, but at that moment, she didn't care. Some people were fortunate enough to find several great loves throughout their life. Moirae knew that she was not one of those lucky few. Dorian was hers, though she would never tell him. And whatever they shared, the memories would have to last a very long time.

"I'll be here."

Dorian let go a rare brilliant grin and spun her around so he could jump up and get dressed. As he finished belting his plaid, he glanced at her. "Spar with me one last time before you go?" he half asked, half pleaded.

"Now?" Moirae asked incredulously.

"Aye, now."

Wide-eyed, she nodded her head and followed him down the hall back to his study where the smaller katana waited for someone to wield it. Removing it from the frame, Dorian turned and gently placed the precious item in her trembling palms. Then, he gave her back a gentle nudge toward the training room.

Offering her the katana would alone ensure of her return that evening. Whenever they did finally part, he would give it to her as a gift. In a few decades, he would seek out where she passed away and reclaim the unusual sword, but until then, it would remind her of him and that gave him some peace.

Inside the training room, he picked up his own sword from where he previously dropped it on the floor and examined the blade. Such a treasure should not have been treated so shamefully, but he knew he would repeat his recklessness if similar circumstances presented themselves again.

Moirae unsheathed the smaller sword and slowly maneuvered it in the air. "It's beautiful," she murmured aloud.

"Once you are skilled in its use, it will be yours."

Moirae stood frozen in shock. Almost a full minute went by

before she recovered enough to thank him. "I'm not sure why I'm being offered such a gift, but I am not foolish enough to refuse."

"The katana is lighter, stronger, and much sharper than the broadsword," Dorian began. "As such, it enables one to react with deadly force to sudden attacks, using cutting motions—not blocking ones. For upright targets, swing downward and diagonally while rotating your body."

Moirae then imitated the simple move against an imaginary foe several times. After some minor adjustments, Dorian nodded in satisfaction and then showed her how to defend herself against a frontal attack.

"Now, using the same angle, slice upward. The injury is the same but much different to defend." Dorian normally wouldn't have even considered showing her such attacks and defense moves, but Moirae was unusual. She had the necessary strength and the speed. "But if you truly want to inflict maximum injury to an opponent, ensuring immediate death, move the blade in a straight downward cut."

Moirae nodded, seeing how it would cause the most musculature damage.

"Knowing how to attack an opponent is necessary to ending an assault, but the ability to adequately defend oneself is primary to surviving one." Dorian nodded for her to sheathe her sword and kneel as if she was sitting by a fire. "It is important that you learn how to draw a sword from any position, including when you are sitting."

Slowly, Dorian demonstrated the technique of shifting from a sitting position to avoid an attack while at the same time drawing the katana and positioning it to defend himself. Moirae repeated the series of actions against a phantom opponent several times, gaining confidence and speed. Deciding to test her, Dorian raised his katana and brought it down diagonally. Immediately, Moirae leaned right and eluded the blade while drawing her own. Swinging it around her body, she was just a fraction of a second too slow to halt his second attack, and the skin on her arm was sliced open.

Moirae's eyes sprang open wide as she dropped her sword and grabbed her arm. She could feel the blood ooze between her fingers. Her brain was registering the pain, but it was her survival instinct that dominated her thoughts. She had to get out of there now. The wound was deep and it would take time to heal, maybe a few hours, but the scab that was even now forming underneath her fingertips would prove she was not like everyone else. Dorian would demand answers she had no way of providing.

Seeing him step forward, she threw her arms around him and kissed him deeply, succeeding in distracting him. Then teasing his nose with her own, she said, "I must go. It must be morning by now. I will see you this evening." Then after a final quick kiss, she fled down the hall and into the bailey.

Dorian stood dumbfounded. He truly believed he had severely injured her, but he must have just missed, startling them both. For there was no way she could have disguised the pain he believed he had inflicted.

Sighing, he leaned down to pick up her katana, pausing midway as he saw the drops of red blood clinging to his sword. He *had* cut her. Obviously not bad, but enough to cause her to bleed. The sweet scent of her blood overtook his senses and he did not resist the desire to wipe his finger down the smooth metal surface and then lick the blood.

The flavor was not sweet as its scent promised, but rancid and he immediately wished he could spit the little he had consumed out. Never had blood tasted so vile. Not even a decayed corpse produced such nastiness. The blood was definitely human, but it was different and most probably the source of what made her so strong, fast, and different.

Reacting on instinct, Dorian raced out of the tower and into the bailey in order to catch her, but he was too late. Walking to the middle of the courtyard, he stood in front of the gatehouse opening and watched as she rode into the distance. Her long hair caught the sunlight one last time before she disappeared into the forest. Dorian sighed with relief. At least it was daytime and she would be safe from Ionas. He turned to go inside as understanding suddenly slammed into him. He lifted his hand and stared at it.

Moirae was not just different with her sense of smell, enhanced reflexes, and unusual strength. She was an anomaly. By just tasting her blood he, for the first time in nearly two millennia, could feel the warm rays of the sun on his skin without the painful sensation of being burned.

He knew what Moirae was protecting. The same person his

cousin was looking for—her supposedly dead mother, perhaps even grandmother. Ionas must have figured out sometime after his attack who had given him his new abilities . . . and that the effects were temporary. Moirae's nape was flawless. Because he never fed on her, Ionas wasn't aware that she too possessed what he was looking for. For why else would his cousin be searching so relentlessly for an old woman? That question started a flood of others to race through Dorian's mind.

Was Moirae's blood an evolution of the disease that afflicted him? How many generations had it been passed down? If it gave him the ability to enjoy the daylight, what other coveted gifts could the blood give a nosferatu? And most importantly, just how much did she know about her unusual abilities? Dorian doubted she was aware of the effects her blood had on his kind, but she obviously knew she was different, for it explained Moirae's driving need to be the Guardian. She wasn't just protecting Badenoch, but her family. And she should, for if Ionas ever discovered such secrets flowed in her veins, Moirae would be in danger.

An overwhelming need to find and protect her washed over Dorian. He fought the urge to get his horse and chase after her. Things were already complicated—and the emotional ties he could feel begin to wind around his heart would only further confuse matters.

Before Moirae returned that evening, he needed a plan that prevented Ionas from finding his prey or discovering that she had offspring. Such power in the hands of only one of their kind would incite a war that would change the balance of power.

Moirae and her family would either need to disappear or they would have to die.

How many times did he need to learn the most basic of truths? Love between mortals and immortals could not be.

Chapter Seven

Dorian stepped out onto the battlements and stared out into the thick fog, wishing his eyesight could penetrate the murky depths. Moirae was late. Too late for him to believe that something had just delayed her arrival. Either she had chosen to stay away or something had prevented her from coming.

While it was indeed possible that Moirae had decided it would be best to end their relationship as per their original agreement, Dorian found it difficult to believe she would do so without facing him. Her personality required her to confront challenges, not avoid them. But it also compelled her to seek out that which she felt entitled to—and he knew Moirae wanted the katana he had promised her. So either something at the castle had thwarted her from coming that evening . . . or she was in trouble.

Movement on the outskirts of the forest caught his attention. He took a deep breath and furrowed his brow. The haze was too thick for him to see who it was, but he recognized the faint, almost indiscernible scent. What was Metrick doing there? There was only one way to find out.

Dorian urged his black horse into a full gallop before he exited the gatehouse. If he could detect Metrick, then it was certain that Ionas's spawn was aware of him. And based on the dissipating odor, the henchman was not there to confront Dorian but to watch and let his superiors know if he left.

After weeks of playing the Guardian and racing through the woods at night, Dorian was intimately familiar with the terrain—more so than Metrick. Within minutes, he was upon the hasty henchman, and with a single slice of the katana, the spawn's side was ripped open, causing him to fall to the ground. Not waiting to slow down his mount, Dorian expertly spun off his still racing horse and landed on the ground.

Feeling the katana's tip on his throat, the spawn knew he was facing imminent death.

"Why did Ionas send you to watch me?" Dorian asked impatiently.

Metrick smiled and the blood filling his mouth outlined his teeth. Death, the one thing he had feared most, was upon him, and he was grateful. But he would not die without issuing one final blow. "You're too late, Dorian. Patras has her."

"Patras?" Dorian echoed. "Just what does he want with Moirae?"

"I told him," Metrick sputtered. "You . . . standing unharmed, unburned in the sunlight. . . ."

Dorian flicked the katana's tip, and it divided the spawn's head from its body, ending the halted speech. Dorian needed to hear no more. Metrick had been hidden in the forest and he had seen them that morning and informed Patras, who no doubt had notified Ionas before leaving to abduct Moirae. She was still alive, of that Dorian was positive. But she would be tortured before too long. As soon as Ionas and Patras realized that she had inherited the unique blood they coveted, they would want to find all in her family and would use any means to get her to talk.

Dorian broke the water's surface and inhaled. Relief flooded through him when he detected Moirae's sweet, alluring scent. There was only a handful of places Patras would have taken Moirae, and none of them were close to the other. But the Wolf's Lair, located on the northern edge of the hills of Am Monadh Ruadh, was the closest and most fortified. Situated in the middle of a remote loch, the fortress Loch nan Doirb had been gifted to Robert II by his second wife. His merciless son, Alexander, tended to rampage the area and had no problem offering use of his father's stronghold to someone like Patras, who fueled both his ambition and his cruel streak.

Bringing Moirae to Loch nan Doirb gave Dorian a distinct advantage, but it also presented a major problem. The loch allowed him to temporarily mask his scent and approach undetected by means of water, but once there, the place was nearly impossible to breach. Four towers were connected by a curtain wall approximately six feet thick and nearly twenty feet high. With the exception of an impressive iron gate, the east wall had no discernable defense and was the primary entrance from the shore. Consequently, it would be well manned with spawns. On the south wall, there was a second gateway, but because it provided no access to the inner court, the chances of him being discovered before getting to Moirae were high, leaving only one option. The western wall behind the chapel. All attempts to climb it had been futile . . . but never had it been tried by a nosferatu.

Carefully, Dorian rose out of the water, and though not without effort, he managed to scale the curtain wall. He moved quickly, for once dry, his scent would be strong enough to alert Patras and his men that he was near. Reaching the top of the chapel, he inhaled once again to assess the situation. Two things stood out. His nephew had not yet arrived, and the numbers of spawn were far less than Dorian would have guessed, but those he recognized were old and heavily experienced in combat.

Creeping near the rooftop's edge, Dorian glanced around the inner bailey. Every scone was lit, and anything that could be used to hide a person, such as carts and barrels, had been removed. There was nothing left to conceal a sneak approach. Patras, who had always been strategically gifted, had grown even wiser since their last encounter.

Dorian was debating when and where he should drop down when Patras exited in the keep. It had been several decades since Dorian had seen the lead henchman. His brilliant white hair had grown long, but otherwise he looked the same. His body still possessed the hard-edge strength that enabled him to command a sizeable force of volatile spawns.

Patras extended one long arm and pointed to the largest of the men heading toward him. "Bring me the girl!"

Dorian did not recognize the bulky spawn, but it was obvious that the once Highlander was not the type who was easily intimidated. Nevertheless, he immediately turned and strode toward the kitchens. But before he could take more than a handful of steps, Patras stopped him. "Why is she in there?!"

The angry bellow could be heard throughout the stronghold, catching everyone's attention. Undeterred, the spawn straightened his shoulders and pivoted to once again face Patras. "She refused to tell us the location of the others. So I ordered her to be bled."

Patras marched right up to the man and demanded, "And just who gave you permission to issue such commands?"

"You did. You said to make her talk and you also promised that she was to be shared."

"Dead, she is only good to us once. . . ."

Dorian could not hear the rest of Patras's response, but it was clear he was furious. It was just as apparent that the Highlander Patras was dealing with had enormous sway among the other spawns and was not someone who could easily be eliminated without repercussions. Otherwise, the man would have been afraid not defiant, and most likely already dead.

Still composed, the spawn said calmly but loud enough for all to hear, "Just so you understand that when this is done, *we*"— he paused to point at all who were watching the interaction— "will no longer live according to your or anyone else's will. She is for *all* of us. You are not the only one who is opposed to dying." With those final words, the spawn turned and disappeared into the kitchens.

So that was why Patras was so interested in Moirae, Dorian thought to himself. It also explained why he had not spied or sensed his nephew once since his arrival. Ionas had no idea Patras had finally found who he had been looking for or that his henchman had discovered just why she was so important. Obviously Patras believed Moirae's blood could do much more than just protect him from sunlight. Was it possible that it could also extend a spawn's life?

If that was true and word spread about her or her family's existence, it would not be simply a fierce battle among nosferatu— it would be the beginning of a major war that would affect all life. No longer would spawns be aligned with their masters. They would be masters themselves. Painful, destructive, and costly lessons that had taken a handful of nosferatu a millennia to learn after repeated attempts would have to be discovered by thousands of spawns. The human race would not survive such a future.

A cry from below caught Dorian's attention. Moirae was being hauled outside. She was still wearing the same gown from when he last saw her, causing him to grimace. That meant she had been abducted on the way home. He had been a fool to think his teachings could keep her safe.

Her arm was bandaged and he could see blood stains through the strips of cloth, but by the force the spawns needed to control her struggles, the bleeding must have only just commenced, making her blood loss minimal.

Patras walked up to her and lovingly stroked her cheek. "Where's Metrick?" he asked to no spawn in particular.

"He has not yet returned."

Hearing the answer, Patras looked up and surveyed the curtain walls. Dorian knew he could not be seen where he was, but if he moved, his position would be revealed. But time was not on his side. He was drying, and soon the moss covering him from the lake water would no longer mask his presence. Whatever he was going to do, he would have to do it soon.

"Double the men guarding both gates."

Moirae grinned with false confidence. "You are monsters, but there is one who can defeat you."

Patras returned the smirk. "And you think Dorian is coming to *save* you?"

The color drained from Moirae's face as she realized that her captor not only knew of Dorian, but was unafraid of him.

"Of course, Dorian is coming," Patras mocked, "but not for the reasons you would like to believe."

"I think he will come to kill you and your fellow monsters, or do you believe you can convince him to become friends?" Moirae spat out.

Dorian smiled, hearing her response. The woman was terrified, but she refused to give in to her fears.

Patras, however, laughed aloud. "Kill us monsters?"

"Yes." The answer lacked complete belief, but it was not vacant of hope.

"Silly human girl." Patras sniggered. "Don't you know by now that he *is* one of us monsters? And with the exception of perhaps one other of his kind, your would-be savior is the most unmoved by mortals and their plights."

Dorian listened to what Patras was telling Moirae, knowing that upon hearing the truth, she would believe it, but he forced his mind to focus on what was happening. Patras's orders to increase gate security had caused the inner bailey to be evacuated, leaving only Patras and the two guards holding Moirae.

Shifting his attention to one of her guards, Patras asked, "Is the blood that was drained still in the kitchen?" Upon getting an affirmative nod, Patras continued. "Bring her to my bedchambers. I will be there shortly." Then he turned to enter the kitchens.

Dorian scampered lightly to the other side of the chapel rooftop. It was not adjacent to the keep, but it was close enough. He waited until the two guards were in view and then dropped down onto them. He was able to instantly knock out one and then kill the other, but not before the spawn could issue a shout to alert the castle that Dorian was inside.

Freed, Moirae stared at Dorian. No warmth was in her eyes, only wariness, and he knew she was replaying Patras's last words and realizing they were true. He threw her the smaller katana, and she snatched it out of the air, unable to reconcile that the monster Patras had described would arm her with such a weapon.

"Explanations later, Lady Destiny," whispered Dorian. "We need to get through that gate."

A sparkle leapt back into Moirae's eyes just as the first wave came to kill them. Reacting on instinct and what training she had received, Moirae sliced with deft movements and strength the spawns had not been expecting. But the second group, seeing how easily the first had been defeated, came in more cautiously and dismissed the concept they were fighting a human woman, but something far more powerful and deadly. But it did them no good.

Dorian felt renewed hope. They were going to have to fight their way to freedom, but Moirae was performing in combat as he wished more humans would after hours of training and skills development. She had no fear. She was accurate, unemotional, and surprisingly creative. For the first time in his life, he felt like he had found a woman that could be more than a companion, but an equal. Someone whom he knew he would never tire of, someone who could instill daily meaning into his life . . . someone he could respect and love. It was absurd. She was a human, the one thing he had sworn to avoid, but it was too late. He did love her. Fully. Completely.

He also knew that even if they survived . . . it changed nothing.

They broke free and dashed to the gate only for a final small group of spawns to jump down and block their way. The large Highlander was among them. Dorian immediately lunged for him, fearing that Moirae, despite her inhuman strength, would not be able to tackle the giant. After several minutes of fighting, he finally struck him down. But just as the katana slammed down into the large frame, ending the spawn's life, Moirae cried out. This time in sheer fear.

Dorian swung back around to see Patras biting down into her neck, drinking. Seeing Dorian, the old spawn released his grip and let her limp form fall to the ground. "I'm like you now, Dorian. A nosferatu. An immortal. We are brothers. You can try to harm me, but I will now heal. You cannot kill me."

Patras slid out a blade from his belt and smiled broadly. It was not a smile of arrogance, but one of absolute confidence. After four hundred years, he was the best of Ionas's men at wielding a blade. But he had lived those years as a spawn, protecting his body, never learning how to defend the one thing that would end an immortal's life.

With lightning speed, Dorian leapt into the air and spun around, swinging the katana with precision. Before his feet touched the ground again, Patras's brief experience with immortality had ended.

Human, spawn, or immortal. One needed their head.

Chapter Eight

Moirae stirred to the unusual sensation of being gently rocked. She opened her eyes and quickly surveyed her surroundings. Close quarters, wood floors and walls, distinct odor of fish and salt, and on a far table were two katanas, sheathed and in their holder. She was on a ship and Dorian was with her. Swinging her legs over the side of the bed, she realized she was naked and immediately searched the room for her clothes.

In her youth, she would have been embarrassed to awaken in such a state, but based on her last memories, Moirae was more thankful to be alive. But how Dorian had saved her, and why he did so considering what he was, remained a mystery. She needed to find him, but not just yet. First, she needed to consider all that she had learned and just what that meant to her and her future—if anything.

It was not Dorian, but a creature like him, that had killed her family and, twice now, tried to kill her. Was he truly different? It was obvious now that the reason he had coveted her role as the Guardian was so that he could disguise his bloody activities. Like the others, Dorian fed on people and he was not remorseful about doing so. But he chose to feed on criminals whom she, too, would have killed, if given the opportunity. In addition, he could have fed on her many times, and yet he elected not to. Why?

Dorian was indeed unlike the monsters she had sought to find and kill. He had saved people—including her—by putting himself in danger. But Moirae had always known that he did so for an ulterior motive, not from altruistic urges. He had known from nearly the beginning that she was unusual—stronger, faster—but it wasn't until she was captured did he learn just how special her blood was. And yet, here she was. Still alive and relatively whole.

Whatever Dorian was, he possessed a soul, and even more importantly, he owned her heart. Nothing had changed that. He was still the man who understood her, challenged her, fascinated her, and made her feel alive in a way no normal man ever could. And she suspected the reason she was still alive was because he felt similarly about her. No other reason explained her continued existence when her death would be so much easier.

The door opened and Moirae's head snapped to the large figure entering. It was Dorian and he was carrying her clothes, which had been cleaned. He briefly hesitated at seeing her naked form before handing them to her. Then without explanation, he went and sat down in the small compartment's only chair.

Moirae watched silently as he adjusted the seat several times, pretending to find a more comfortable spot to sit and extend his legs. She knew he was waiting for her to ask questions, and she had many. Most of which were personal, but she decided to start with the easiest, or the one whose answer she thought she already knew and therefore would be the least surprising. That would give her a guide as to how Dorian would answer the ones that were much more important—where was she going, what he intended to do when they got there, and how did he feel about her?

Shaking the chemise free from its folds, she dropped the soft, clean garment over her head. Feeling somewhat more on an equal footing, she picked up the kirtle and asked pointedly, "What are you exactly? Do you admit to being what that white-haired one said?"

Dorian crossed his legs and intertwined his fingers across his stomach. He had known the question was coming. Moirae was not one to pretend or wish a problem away. In a way, he admired her for that trait. To confront an issue, even if it could possibly mean harm, was in essence, pure bravery. And that was a quality so rarely found in humans. As a result, he felt compelled to answer her question honestly and completely, when typically he would have ignored it.

"Yes and no. Like I told you before, I was born in Greece and I have lived for a very long time. My grandfather was a human man, but after surviving a large flood, he discovered his blood had changed, giving him unusual abilities that were inherited by his offspring, of which I am one. This 'blood disease' gives us extended life, as well as an increase in strength and sense of smell, among other things. It also makes us crave blood, to the point we will die without it."

Moirae listened intently as she finished donning her kirtle. She waited to see if he had just paused, but when he didn't continue, she pushed. "And just how are you different from the brute with the white hair?"

Dorian raised a single brow but otherwise did not move as he assessed Moirae's strange response to what he had already revealed. No shock registered on her expression or her mannerisms. Just as surprising was the lack of repulsion. It was if he were telling her an interesting story of his childhood, not that he was a monster who could and did kill her kind. He wondered at what point she would have a negative reaction.

He was positive, however, that one was coming.

"Nosferatu or *nosophoros*," he began, "as we are called in our native tongue, are actually very few in number. We suspect the disease that changed our blood weakened with each generation, but it is also possible that whatever caused our change disappeared before we discovered its origins. Because the disease only begins to manifest during later stages of physical development and full change can take several years to complete, we did not realize our children were mortal and had not inherited our abilities for many years."

The word hit Moirae like a hammer to the chest. She should have known Dorian would have children . . . several children, and that knowledge was disconcerting.

"So you don't die . . . ever?" she asked, skepticism finally creeping into her voice. "The others I saw feared death, something you are claiming to elude. Why aren't they chasing you and your blood?"

"Patras was a spawn. When nosferatu feed on humans, they die. But a millennia ago, one of my brothers discovered by accident that if he did not kill a mortal upon feeding, a small number would survive the experience. They gained many nosferatu abilities, including the extension of their life, sometimes up to several hundred years. Greed rules most spawns' actions. And the one thing they covet the most is unending life."

278 / *Michele Sinclair*

"And that is why the white-haired one wanted me."

"Yes. He thought you could give them immortality."

Moirae sank back onto the mattress and licked her lips, taking in all that Dorian had just told her. Part of her screamed to ask about where she was going, why she was going there, and a dozen other questions, but mostly she needed to know that with everything that happened, did it change things between them? Because for her, it had significantly.

She had been consumed with finding and killing whatever had murdered her mother and grandmother. Now that she had, her purpose had vanished. In its place was not a void but something far scarier. A new overriding need that was even more powerful. She loved Dorian. He completed her. Learning what he was did not make them incompatible but possibly made him the only man in the world perfect for her.

Moirae knew he felt something for her. Nothing else explained his actions. But would he admit to being in love?

"And what about me?" she finally asked.

Dorian rose to his feet and went to stand to look out the room's one small window. "You are on my boat. I'm taking you somewhere safe."

"I'm talking about you and me."

"There is no you and me. You promised you understood that," he stated coldly, still looking out at the horizon.

Moirae moved to go stand by him. She rested her hand on his arm and felt a small flinch beneath her fingertips. It confirmed that he was not as dispassionate as he wanted her to believe. "Why?"

Dorian turned to look at her straight in the eye so that she would know he was being earnest, and that there was no compromise in his decision. "I will not stay and watch you grow old and die. I've done it before and I won't do it again. I can't do it . . . especially not with you." He turned to look back out the window. "So I'm taking you to safety and will go back for your family. Once I'm assured that you are secure, you will never see me again."

Moirae nodded her head in understanding. Dorian loved her. He could not say it, and she, more than anyone else, truly understood why. She now knew who he was. It was time for him to discover her secrets.

Resting her head on his forearm, she joined his gaze out to the rolling waters. In the distance, she could see the hazy outlines of mountains, but they were not the mammoth hills she had grown to love. "I have no family for you to save."

Dorian held his breath. He had been afraid that was a possibility, though he had hoped otherwise. Having no family made it a lot easier to keep her safe and her uniqueness unknown, but it would also mean that when he left, she would be alone with no one she knew or trusted.

"Were their deaths recent?" The question was a selfish one, but he needed to know if it had happened while he had forced himself to be the Guardian.

"No." She raised her head and tugged his arm to make him look at her. "My grandmother was beautiful."

"I'm not surprised," Dorian whispered.

Before he could return his gaze to the window, she continued. "No, not just beautiful, but stunning. No one ever believed she was my grandmother. In truth, neither did I until years after she had passed away."

"I am sure your mother told you otherwise."

"She did, but not convincingly. I think my mother was jealous of my grandmother, and in a way me, since I am so much like her."

Dorian cocked his head and studied Moirae for a second. She was trying to make a point, but he could not grasp what it could be. "Why are you telling me this?"

A large smile came over Moirae's face. "How old do you think I am?"

A puzzled expression overtook Dorian's brow. "I am not sure. But I suspect you look younger than you are."

Moirae chuckled. "I should hope so. I will be four and sixty before the end of this year."

Dorian's attention was immediately captured, and he stared at her to see if she was in earnest. Instinctively, he inhaled. "But you are human," he mumbled.

"If you mean I don't drink blood, you are correct. But I also don't age. I haven't since the night my mother and grandmother were killed. I was seventeen."

"Were you bitten?"

Moirae shrugged but nodded. "Yes, the one who attacked us

fed on my mother and then tried to feed on me, but immediately stopped. I don't think he liked how I tasted," she said quietly, remembering the event not with horror but curiosity. "My grandmother said that she knew I was different as an infant when a dog accidentally bit me and I healed within hours. My sense of smell grew throughout childhood, and my strength came later, but whatever I am, it is not because of that night. It is the reason I survived."

Dorian was quiet for several minutes as complete comprehension took over. How could he have been such a fool not to realize it before? The night he first brought her back to Kilnhurst—she *had* been injured. Just like when he had thought to have seriously cut her arm. Both times she had healed. It was why she did not taste anything like the young, sweet thing she smelled. It also explained her unusual view of the world and those around her. It was not a mortal's view, but an immortal's one.

And yet, despite her being human, there were too many similarities between their capabilities. There had to be a connection. "You've mentioned your grandmother, but who is your father? Could he be the reason why you are different?"

"Perhaps," Moirae answered, stepping away. "I never knew him."

"You said he died at sea."

"I said that is what I was told."

"I got the feeling then, as I do now, that you do not believe that."

"What I don't believe is that he was married to my mother. She would never talk about him, describe him, or tell me stories about him."

"Then you know nothing that could tell you who he was."

"Very little. My grandmother would bring me aside and tell me what a wonderful man he was and that of all the sorrows in her life, that I did not know him was her greatest."

"We have to find out who your father was."

"*We* do?"

"Well, you want me to come with you, don't you?"

Moirae crossed her arms and tried unsuccessfully to look dismissive. "I thought you had to drop me off, save me, and never see me again," she said with more than a hint of sarcasm.

"Well, that was before . . . I mean, now that I know you are,